A Man's Hungry Heart is the sequel to master storyteller Jim Carson's powerful trilogy that takes place in the river town of Memphis, Tennessee overlooking the mighty Mississippi.

After the début novel, *A Chasing After The Wind*, Mack Shannon continues his quest for power and recognition by gambling all that he owns and can borrow to design and construct, a development consisting of the Trinity Towers: three, 33 story corporate towers, a world class shopping mall, and The Astor Hotel and Casino.

This is the largest private endeavor in the history of Tennessee. Mack spends every waking hour fighting to insure its success, but two of his childhood nemesis, Crazy Ray and Dago, return and continue their revenge to destroy his empire.

Mack, a patron of the arts, has offered his palatial home to celebrate the 125th birthday of The Beethoven Club. Among the guests is Chancellor McKenzie O'Connor, a woman who can finally match him in wit and ambition, and when introduced: *Mack turned at the call of his name and was so stunned by her natural beauty and magnetism that his heart skipped a beat. He was close, so close he could smell her minted breath. He stared for the longest time into her green eyes and for the first time he understood what the songwriter meant when he wrote, "When Irish eyes are smiling, they steal your heart away."*

Fantasy is not reality. Reality, of which he is unaware, is that she has signed a warrant for his arrest.

Now, at the top of his game, he has narrowed his objectives to what is most important in his life: his legacy and his 10-year old daughter, Irish Shannon. Will Mack complete his life long dream of power and fame? Or will he have to risk more than just his fortune to save his young daughter?"

Praise for Jim Carson's
A CHASING AFTER THE WIND

A Sense-Sational Novel. "I read fiction with the expectation that the author will take me to a different place, not just tell me about a different place. If he doesn't, I don't bother to read anything else that he writes. In "A Chasing After the Wind," Jim Carson meets my expectation. I could feel the heat against my face in the burning house. I could smell the fear and the burnt gunpowder with my face in the grass at the park. I could feel the cobblestones bump under my tires at the Memphis riverfront and smell the Mississippi River. His protagonist, Mack, and I drank a cold Guinness at the local pub. We told lies and laughed. I look forward to all the other places Jim will take me and to meeting many more interesting characters. This is an author I will come back to as often as he writes because he meets my expectation."

—Robert, MD, December 16, 2014

Jim Carson has done some real fine work. A rare flare for descriptive expression and an astute observation of humanity, bold, colorful, primitive, yet far from naive. Jim's a seasoned, saging son of the South.

—Pejuta, January 14, 2015

From the very beginning, the book grabs the reader's attention and continues to hold it throughout each chapter! It is a feel good book, in that the character progresses from an uneducated boy to a worldly man, with all that it entails. Great read!!!

—Ruth K. Dec. 2014

The real deal. As a frequent action reader of many great authors to include the late Tom Clancy, I found "A Chasing After the Wind" to be fresh and exciting. As an active duty Solider, my deployments are frequent with multiple long plane rides, this book is entertaining and will be added to a must re-read on my next trip. I believe the passion and knowledge throughout the book made it come alive. I would highly recommend this to my community of peers and look forward to the next book by Jim Carson.

—*Captain D. Parnell, January 8, 2015*

An awesome read! Looking forward to many more novels by Jim!

—*Sara Morris 11.29.14*

A MAN'S HUNGRY HEART

A NOVEL BY

JIM CARSON

ISBN 978-0-692-37835-9

A MAN'S HUNGRY HEART

A BABY DRAGON PRESS, Inc.
www.jamesacarson.com

Edited by Jonathan W. Thurston
Cover design by the Damonza.com team
Printed in the United States of America
10 9 8 7 6 5 4 3 2 1

For my daughter

McKenzie Carson

"You are my sunshine."

CHAPTER 1

H E PUSHED OPEN the old screen door, stepped down into the backyard, and followed a worn path through the uncut grass. He stooped under a laden clothesline with a 2 x 4 holding the wire up in the middle to keep the clothes from dragging on the ground. As he walked through the second clothesline, he felt the dampness of a woman's slip brush his face.

Standing in the rear of the backyard, he wiggled his toes, enjoying the wetness from the morning dew. With both arms extended horizontally and his head held back, he scanned the skies and slowly rotated his body until he felt the southwest wind on his naked back. He smiled and jumped straight up, about four feet, and floated down, landing on the balls of his feet. On his second jump he bent his knees and pushed off hard with his toes, holding his arms close to his sides. He felt real power in this leap as he stretched his neck to get all the height he could steal. He watched as he passed the rooftop of his neighbor's storage shed, going higher than he had ever been with his second leap, and faster. He was above the rooftops in seconds, going higher and higher.

Looking down he noticed that the clotheslines made a perfect V, with a rainbow of colors. A gust of wind pushed him forward as he held out his arms to steady himself. Then, he began to fly, soaring—riding the air currents as they lifted him higher and higher.

The lush green carpet of trees that covered the city had deep surgical cuts where the Interstate crisscrossed and encircled the city. He was over I-240 now and recognized the Walnut Grove Road overpass. Cars and trucks whizzed under and across, like thousands of ants rushing in all directions. Now is the time to go for it. He tucked his chin, pulled his arms in close to his side, and using his hands for rudders, he dove for the overpass.

"No guts . . . no glory."

Like a missile, he roared down the Interstate, bucking the opposing traffic, and blasted under the overpass. He did two slow rolls on his climb-out and, when he peaked, he turned over on his back and floated through the air. That's when he heard a familiar sound and rolled over, reducing his speed. What was it? The wind rushed by too fast. He slowed his speed some more and flew lower, listening anxiously . . . was it a scream for help? Was it someone yelling? He started coughing, and his eyes burned from the exhaust fumes of the bumper-to-bumper traffic. He started a big wide circle away from the Interstate and slowed his speed even more. He cupped his ear with his hand to block the wind and noise, straining to hear the cry.

Oh no, not now. The cry was calling *him.* He didn't like this; he didn't want to stop flying, but there was no stopping now. It was like a whirlpool, sucking him down into a dark hole. The sound was loud, determined, pulling him into the vacuum. He lost his speed, stalled, and was tumbling fast and out of control. The only thing left to do was to dive, gather speed, then hopefully with enough power, he could pull out of the dive. He tilted his head downward and let his arms and hands fall to his side, building speed fast, way too fast.

Kill the throttle! Full flaps!

He was much closer to the ground than he thought, the vortex dragging him downward. He couldn't lift his head, nor move his arms or any part of his body to check his speed. He was wrapped in a death dive, spinning like a bullet.

"Left rudder, left rudder!" he shouted. "Pull up! PULL UP!"

*

Mack Shannon bolted upright in his bed, his heart racing. Was the burglar alarm going off? He tried to focus on the blurred numbers on the digital clock. He fell back, his head sinking deep into his pillow. Relax, he told himself. With his eyes staring at the ceiling, he lay very still and listened . . . not a sound, only his deep breathing. This was the first time he had ever crashed. He closed his eyes and concentrated; sometimes if he tried hard enough, he could go back to his flying dreams . . . but not this morning. Her cry came roaring into the bedroom like a cyclone, echoing off the walls of the long hallway and then bouncing off the tall ceiling in his bedroom.

"Daaaaddy! Come-get-me-out-of–this-bed!"

He rolled over on his side and pushed himself upright with his feet dangling off the side of the bed. He checked the time again; it was 5:26—well, time to get up anyway. He grabbed his remote control and slid off the bed, punching in a code to turn off the alarm system on the second floor. Standing in front of the mirrored doors to his closet, he turned sideways and patted his flat stomach, then watched himself pull on a pair of sweat pants. He stepped up the one step out of his bedroom into the hallway and heard her shout again.

"Daaaaddy!"

Mack rocked, side-to-side, down the hall with loud, stomping steps, beating his chest and giving out a loud Tarzan yell, the call of the apes, "Ahhh-Eh-Ahhhhhhh!"

She responded with the same, "Ahhh-Eh-Ahhhhhhh!"

He continued stomping down the hallway to her bedroom door and delivered three loud knocks on the door.

"Come in," she giggled.

He stepped down into her bedroom and stomped in, rocking from side to side, grunting gorilla sounds, "Ugh, Ugh, Ugh," until he reached her bed. She had her old baby blankie, white soft cotton and fluffy, with embroidered green shamrocks, pulled over her head. He bent over her, making loud sniffing noises and gorilla sounds until his nose touched her head. He sniffed loudly. She jumped up screaming as loud as she could to scare him, and they both jumped up and down in the bed. She thrashed him with her blankie He grabbed her in a bear hug, blankie and all, and rolled out of the bed to the floor, rolling over and over, both of them making gorilla sounds. Wrapped in her blankie and breathing hard, he could hardly hear her over the laughter when she squealed, "Daddy, Daddy, I got to tee tee!"

CHAPTER 2

THE 60-YEAR-OLD RESTORED Porsche 356 Cabriolet balked at slowing to 55 mph while crossing the Mississippi River Bridge from Arkansas to Memphis on I-40 East. McKenzie downshifted to slow her speed and pumped her brakes while tailgating the pickup truck in front of her—impatiently waiting for an opening. The concrete median on the left and a semi-truck on her right had her boxed in. The pickup was covered with mud and had a large diesel-fuel tank mounted in the bed with a crane-like nozzle sprouting out of the top. She stared at the painted Magnolia flower embossed over the State of Mississippi license plate and covered her mouth and nose as a flume of black diesel smoke belched from the truck's exhaust pipe.

Why do these rednecks have to farm in Arkansas, Mississippi, and Tennessee? And when they do come to the big city, they always have to drive in the left lane, jamming up traffic.

"Come on Grandpa, move it." Her phone rang as she edged the car forward, closer to his bumper. Searching through her briefcase, she found her phone, stuck in the earpiece, and flipped it open.

"O'Connor."

"You out of court?" Abby Jones asked.

"I'm crossing the river now."

"The room is packed; you know they start on time, *exactly* twelve noon?"

"If this old fart in front of me will move over I can make it." The top was down on her car, and she had to shout over the noise of the wind. "What time is it now?"

"You've got ten minutes. Don't forget your appointment with the mayor at two o'clock."

"Did his office say what he wanted?"

"I pumped his secretary, 'Mister Cum La'de' you know, the one with all the degrees, but he wouldn't tell me a thing. Only that one of his aides would pick you up a little before two. Which is higher, summa cum laude or magna?"

"I don't need his bodyguards to pick me up; for Christ's sake, it's only two blocks."

"I thought about that, and the meeting may not be in his office. Guess what," Abby whispered. "Your two o'clock just walked in the door."

"Summa."

"What?"

"Summa cum laude is the highest." McKenzie pulled her earpiece out while moving closer to the truck's bumper, blowing her horn.

Looking in his rearview mirror and shaken by the closeness of her car, the pickup slowly increased its speed and pulled over to the right in front of the truck to let her pass. The Porsche was still in 3rd gear when she saw the opening and slammed the gas pedal to the floor, launching the two-seater forward with a roar and almost touching the corner of the truck's bumper. She looked up as she passed the pickup, and the red-faced farmer hung halfway out the window, pumping his left fist with the middle finger extended, screaming, "Up yours, lady!"

At 75 mph, she shifted to fourth, took her hand off the gearshift, and waved to the pickup. McKenzie O'Connor was not going to be late for this meeting.

*

The church bells at old St. Mary's in downtown Memphis heralded noon as her car tires screeched turning into the parking lot of the Peabody Hotel. She braked hard when she saw the cars backed up, bumper to bumper, in all three lanes of the rear entrance, waiting for valet parking. Young men scurried back and forth parking cars. She threw the gearshift up to first and pulled to the right, between two signs into the hotel's exit lanes. Watching for exiting traffic, she drove directly to the porte-cochere and parked at the concrete median, separating the incoming and outgoing cars, facing the wrong way.

McKenzie grabbed her suede briefcase as she opened her car door, but stopped when she looked up and saw the huge black man blocking the car door from opening. He was dressed in a rich, milk chocolate tunic, large gold epaulets on each shoulder, and a top hat that made him look taller than his six feet six inches. Smiling up at him, she removed the plaid tam she was wearing and threw it on the passenger seat. Her thick, red hair fell over her shoulders.

"You're late," he said in a deep voice, extending his hand to help her up and out of the car.

"Am I that late? You think they've started? Is it in the Continental Ballroom? Is that on the mezzanine?"

"You're *welcome,* Your Grace!"

"Oh, I'm sorry. *Thank you,* Reggie!"

"Now, to answer your questions . . . *Yes'm,* you're late. *Yes'm,* they have started. No *ma'am,* they had to move it to the Memphis Ballroom—the Continental only holds five hundred—and *yes'm,* it's on the mezzanine," he said, in a sing song cadence. "Abby sent word that you were running late. Just hold on while I take care of the car, and I'll walk you upstairs and sneak you in the back, behind the stage," he whispered, taking her by the elbow and leading her to the entrance.

Catching a parking attendant out of his peripheral vision, he moved with surprising agility and grabbed him by his upper arm and led him over to the Porsche.

"Can you drive this car, stick shift?" Reggie Brown asked.

The young man lowered his sunglasses and looked up at Reggie. He poked both thumbs into his chest and, rocking from side to side and bobbing up and down in rap tempo, sung out,

"Mr. *Brown,* don't you *frown*

When I shift up or *down*

There is no *sound*

'Cause I'm the best in-*town.*

So, Reg'*gee,* give me the *key*

This ride and *me* is like honey and a *bee.*"

"Park the car, *Ice-T*, under the roof in the VIP lane and bring the keys back to me. I'll be back in a minute," he said, shaking his head and walking back to McKenzie.

The tires let out a terrible squeal, and McKenzie and Reggie turned just in time to see the parking attendant driving off in her Porsche with her green tam cocked to one side on his head.

Following Reggie up the back stairs to the Memphis Ballroom, she watched him limp up each step and remembered how insulted he was when she told him she could arrange the "doorman's job" for him at the Peabody.

He hadn't been out of the hospital long and stood in her office on crutches. This was his fourth operation, a complete knee replacement, and football was over for him. They had told him he would never play football again after his third knee surgery, but this fourth one was the end: four operations and four divorces. Was there a parallel?

She remembered listening patiently to how the "All-Pro Reggie Brown" was *not* a charity case, and it would be "a cold day in hell when he dressed up in a monkey suit and embarrassed himself in front of all of his friends by kissing 'Whitey's' ass for tips."

Just thinking about it again made her mad. She recalled her response that day to his ungratefulness: "Sit down, shut up, and listen for one time in your life." The secretary raced to close McKenzie's door. "You came to me for help and advice, didn't you?" she asked.

He leaned forward in his chair to say something, and she cut him off quickly.

"You're too damn good to wear a uniform, right? Well, what the hell do you think you have been wearing for the majority of your life? Everyone wears a uniform . . . judges, priests, firemen, policemen, postmen, nurses, doctors, soldiers . . .."

"But, the football uniform is not a monkey . . ." he tried to finish, but she cut him off again.

"Oh really, what is it Reggie, some machismo battle armor?" She charged on. "No, you're right Reggie, it's not a monkey suit. It's a Cro-Magnon suit for intellectuals, right?"

"Now wait a minute . . ." Reggie stood up.

"No, *you* wait a minute! I don't want you to say another word until I finish what I have to say. Do you understand? First and foremost, I am your lawyer—four divorces, that does qualify me, doesn't it?" She looked up at him towering over her and could see the anger boiling within his huge frame. His breathing was heavy, and every muscle in his face was taut, his huge nostrils flaring, and his rage close to exploding. She had gone too far.

"Sit down, Reggie." She lowered her voice, *"Please."* Swiveling her chair around, she opened the double-doors to her credenza. Taking her time, she opened her bottom drawer and lifted out an off-white, ceramic-looking jug with two glasses. She poured three fingers of Scotch in each glass and walked around her desk. Handing Reggie a glass, she sat down in the chair next to him.

"Reggie, when did your mother die?"

"My . . . she passed last year."

"I'm sorry. I know you two were close."

"Yeah, real close; my biggest fan."

"And your father?"

"He's a drunk, shows up every month or two when his drinking money runs out." Reggie emptied his glass of Scotch in one gulp.

"Reggie, this Summons the deputy sheriff served you with says you are over ten thousand dollars in arrears for child support."

"Can you believe that?"

"Yes, I can. Can you believe Judge Ford will throw you in jail if you don't pay your child support?"

"She better not. I got her elected, you know?"

"Then you remember her campaign promise, that she would fill the city and county jail with men who didn't pay their child support, and she has."

This didn't seem to bother Reggie in the least, so McKenzie changed the subject.

"How old are you now, Reggie?"

"Well . . . the truth?"

She nodded her head.

"I'm thirty-eight. But the NFL has me down as thirty-five," he chuckled.

Noticing he had calmed down considerably, she stood up, set her glass of Scotch on the corner of her desk, checked her watch for the time, then walked back behind her desk and sat down. She checked her appointment book, then raised her head and stared at Reggie for some time before she started.

"Reggie, I want to talk to you for a few more minutes, then I have to be in court at 9 this morning."

"Sure."

"I don't want you to think of me as your lawyer or your friend right now. Think of me as an advisor to whom you are paying $300 an hour for her services." She had his attention.

"I'm going to talk to you the way my daddy talks to me now and then. He'd say, 'Honey, we are going to talk man to man, and if you can't handle it, then you need to go back to culinary or cosmetology where you belong.'" She didn't smile.

"Football," she paused to let this word sink in, "is over for you. You will never play another pro game as long as you live. The NFL and the Players Union are through with you. Football is strictly a capitalistic product; you don't produce, you're history. You should have quit after your second operation, but you elected to play on because you said you didn't know anything else to do. You should have prepared for this day, but you didn't. You didn't save a penny of all the money you made, nor did you invest . . ."

"My agent invested," Reggie cried out.

"In what, FRIED CHICKEN?" she screamed, rising out of her chair. "*Church's Fried Chicken, Popeye's Fried Chicken,* and that damn *Pit Bar-B-Que Restaurant* you dropped over $150,000 in. I told you not to . . ." She stopped and sat down, shaking her head.

"You're not too smart, Reggie. Memphis is the barbecue capital of the world. There is a barbecue restaurant on every corner in this town. You wouldn't take my advice, remember? Finestein was an Einstein you said, a brain, a moneyman. I said he was a con man. Now who was right? Where is that agent now? Better yet, where is your money?" She leaned back in her chair, stared at Reggie, and waited.

Reggie just stared at the floor. He wanted to say something, but what could he say?

McKenzie checked her time again, then stared at Reggie until he looked at her. She started talking in a serious, professional tone, barely audible.

"I have to be at a hearing in fifteen minutes. Before I leave I want to finish what I started, without interruptions." She paused to make sure he understood the last part.

She leaned forward on her desk.

"Reggie, you're an old man. Forty-six years old, not thirty-eight. You have a body full of broken bones and smashed blood vessels. You're black, unemployed, untrained, broke, and on crutches. You owe the IRS God only knows how much in back taxes, interest, and penalties. You are more than ten thousand dollars in arrears in child support, and Judge Ford is going to lock you in jail and throw away the key for non-payment. You have thrown away more money than the average man's lifetime earnings on sycophants, drunks, whores, four wives, bookies, dogs, horses, and casinos. You wear thousand-dollar suits, a diamond Rolex, and drive a new Mercedes. You come into my office without an appointment and dump all of this on my desk. You expect me to drop whatever I'm doing, without any suggestion of compensation, and perform a miracle. Then you have the audacity to insult me when I offer you a job where you can make fifty thousand dollars plus a year." McKenzie pushed her chair back and stood up.

"Let me leave you with this," she said. "You can limp over to the projects mid-morning in your designer sweat suit or *uniform*, as you will, and your Air Nikes. You can buy all your bros their morning beer or wine and sit in the sun telling them your battle stories. Because, Mr. Brown, as a friend or client, *you* . . . I don't need." She picked up her briefcase, walked across the room, checked her hair in a wall mirror, and was out the office before Reggie could say a word.

Reggie sat bent over, his elbows on his knees and his head in his hands. He didn't know how long he had been that way when he heard a knock on the door and looked up to see McKenzie's paralegal standing in the doorway.

"Are you all right, Mr. Brown?"

Reggie stood up, picked up his crutches, and limped over to McKenzie's desk. He picked up her untouched glass of Scotch and held it up as if talking to it.

"You know, there's only one person who ever got away with talking to me like that, and he was my college football coach. The only difference is he didn't serve up such fine Scotch whiskey with his ass chewings." He downed the Scotch, set the empty glass back on her desk, smacked his lips, and said, "Make me an appointment to see her tomorrow, Abby. And tell her to find me a tailor for my monkey suit." He hobbled past her and down the hall to the reception room.

Abby had a puzzled look on her face as she watched Reggie open the door to leave the building, then she remembered. "Mr. Brown," she called out.

Reggie stopped.

She came running up. "I almost forgot. On her way out, Ms. O'Connor asked me to make sure to give you this before you leave."

Reggie took the document, hobbled outside, and, leaning against his car, opened the envelope and pulled out the paper. It appeared to be a folded poster of some kind. Reggie unfolded it, and staring at him was one of those Uncle Sam's, "I WANT YOU" posters with Judge Ford's face instead of Uncle Sam's. It was her campaign poster of last year, and she was pointing a finger at him. At the bottom of the poster, in large red letters was, "YOU PLAY! YOU PAY!" Reggie crumbled the poster up in his large hands and threw it like a football out into the street. He tossed his crutches into the back seat and climbed into his red Mercedes convertible. Popping the lid of the center console, he unwrapped a thirty-dollar Cuban cigar, snipped the end off with his gold Davidoff cutter, and fired it up. His cell phone rang,

"Yo! Brother Andre, was'up . . . it's a little early for that, ain't it? Oh yeaaah, tell me more. Ah huh, yeah, I know, it's *all* good Brother, but she ain't fat is she . . . for real? I don't mind one with a bootie, but that last one, Bro; it would hang over a number two washtub. You got that right. Why man, I remember you setting an empty Bud on that thing when it wobbled by." He took a couple of big puffs from his cigar.

"Hold it, hold it, man," he started coughing. "You're killing me, man. What's that . . . you know it's cool, Bro. What about a bottle of Remy, Napoleon . . . got that right, the breakfast of champions. On my way, *An'dre* . . . ten minutes."

With his music blaring, he backed out of the parking lot and spotted the crumbled poster he had thrown out in the street. Stomping on the accelerator, the 600 horsepower engine rocketed the car forward, and Reggie, taking careful aim, squashed the balled-up poster.

"*Women,*" he shouted, throwing his head back and laughing as he roared down the street, leaving behind a pungent cloud from his smuggled seven-inch, Cohiba Esplendido.

CHAPTER 3

THE BEDROOM WAS dark except for a ray of morning light breaking through the east window. The soft voice of the young woman kneeling beside her bed broke the quietness.

"Our Father, who art in heaven, hallowed be thy Name. Thy Kingdom come . . ." Lea Perez stopped praying and raised her head.

Why does my mind wander when I'm praying? What I'm saying is so memorized. I feel hypocritical.

"O Lord, punish this sinner who has plenty to say when she needs something." She dropped her face into her hands. *It was easier being a Catholic; I just said my rosary every morning and night without thinking and went to confession when I thought I needed to.*

Leaning back on her heels and pressing her hands together, she said, "I'm sorry God. I promise I will try harder. The preacher at the river church said that praying is no more than just having a conversation, so I will start with 'Thank you.' Thank you for watching over me and bringing me to this country, to this house, Señor Shannon, and for little Irish; I love her very much. Thank you for protecting my Papa in Cuba. And the last thing I need to talk to you about is . . . well, sex. I know you gave all of us a sex drive for the purpose of reproducing, but could you dial mine down a little? I'm burning up sometimes. Or maybe just send me a husband—no, I take that back. No husband, not now." She stood up with her head bowed. "I ask all these things in the name of your son, our Savior, Jesus Christ." She made the sign of the cross, stopped, thought about it, turned, and hurried out the door of the guesthouse.

Lea felt for each step as she placed her foot on the stone pavers. There were louvered, recessed lights in each riser, but the morning dew sometimes left the stone steps slippery. She walked along the curved pathway that cut through the dense woods to the main house. A canopy of tall trees blocked any light from the sky, but mushroom-shaped landscape lights guided her along the walk.

She stopped. *Were those footsteps?* "It's my imagination again," she said, "Too many late night monster movies."

She heard a limb crack and turned quickly. *Was that a shadow?* She stood perfectly still. *It's just squirrels chasing each other, Lea.* She saw a baseball-sized rock next to one of the landscape lights and picked it up just in case.

Her walk quickened as she heard some running through the woods parallel to her. Then a loud, blood-curdling scream made her stop, her heart racing, her arm back ready to hurl the rock. She whispered in Spanish, "Hail Mary, Mother of God . . ."

She looked up just in time to see two huge raccoons breaking through the shrubbery, screaming and racing across the walkway, one after the other, with a huge dog chasing them.

She kneeled on the damp stone walkway, laughing and berating herself for being such a scaredy-cat, "Stupid, stupid, stupid," she said.

She heard heavy breathing and looked up at a large head sticking out of the bushes with two piercing black eyes and a long red tongue, his breath warm.

She sat, spread her legs and patted the stone with the palm of her hands, talking to him in Spanish, "Bear . . . come here, you black devil." Bear was named after his great-grandfather from Shamrock Farms. From the championship paper showing his bloodline, and all the photos Lea had seen, they looked identical.

The large woolly dog, a Bouvier des Flandres, with pointed ears and a thick Fu-Manchu mustache, walked out of the dense shrubbery and over to Lea.

"What are you doing home? You scared me to death! I thought you were still at tracking school. Is that what you were doing, tracking those raccoons?"

He nudged her, pushing her onto her back with his large muzzle, and licked the sweat from her face. She didn't try to move away; instead she hugged his thick neck and told him how much she had missed him. Bear was a birthday present to Irish from her father, and for the first year the puppy slept with Irish every night until he got so big he took up most of the bed. Lea and Irish had played hide and seek with Bear since he was a puppy, and he never failed to find them, no matter where they would hide or how far away. Lea had raised them both and secretly felt they were hers.

Bear followed Lea to the main house, and, when she reached the top steps, he turned and ran back to the woods. She lifted a small brass plate next to the kitchen door and punched in a number to the keyless entry system. She listened as the door unlocked automatically. Inside the kitchen, she walked across to the pantry and punched in another code to turn off the alarm system.

*

Mack was in the gym on the second floor running on the treadmill set at an eight-minute mile. He watched the three televisions mounted on the wall tuned to FNN, FNC, and NBC. He looked up as a laser of red lights bounced across the room, signaling a breach of the alarm system. With his remote, he switched the TVs over to the house monitoring system and pulled his earphones down around his neck while looking over at his daughter, Irish. The first thing he heard was Beethoven's "Moonlight Sonata," not something Irish would normally be listening to, but something she had been practicing on the piano for hours each day for the past week.

Two weeks earlier, playing the same song, she had placed second in a piano competition at the University of Memphis School of Music for ages 8-12. Irish didn't like losing and reacted in an unacceptable childish manner by refusing to play the piano again.

Mack, a patron of the arts, had suggested to a friend that he was considering an important gift to The Beethoven Club for their upcoming 100th-birthday celebration. Of course, for this to happen, there was one prerequisite. The friend was to propose, delicately, that if Mack found an invitation in his mailbox to Irish Shannon, inviting her to perform in their outdoor garden to celebrate the club's birthday next week, this would certainly influence his generosity. Before the week was over, an elaborate invitation appeared, hand-delivered to Miss Irish Shannon. Immediately—without any sugges-tions—she started practicing nonstop.

Irish appeared not to be listening to her music as she jumped up and down on a small, round trampoline, counting in Spanish with each jump, "Noventa y dos, noventa y tres, noventa y cuatro . . .." She caught her father's eye as he motioned her to the TV monitor, and they watched Lea entering the kitchen from the outside.

"Vámonos." Mack formed the word with his mouth while looking at Irish and nodding his head toward the TV monitor. Irish avoided him and continued to jump and count, testing her father.

Mack looked at the numbers on the treadmill, saw his five miles were almost up, and hit the stop button, jumping off as it slowed to a halt. Three quick steps, and he snatched her from the trampoline and ran across the gym and through the doorway, hollering, "Fire! Fire! Fire!"

"Noooo Daddy, no," she laughed. "You're sweating on me!"

"Fire! Fire! Fire!" he continued to yell, as he turned down a long hallway. He moved her to his back, piggyback style, as he stopped at a pair of bi-fold doors and pushed the release to open them. Inside was a fireman's brass pole bolted to the ceiling and running through a hole to the bottom floor. Mack kicked the spring-loaded latch, opening the door that covered the hole, pre-venting anyone from falling through. Now you could see down the hole to the first floor.

"Gerrrronimoooo!" they both screamed, and Irish held on to her father's neck as they eased down the pole and landed on a four-inch rubber cushion around the bottom.

Two steel doors led from the room they had dropped into, and both doors had panic-bar openers. The door to the outside was painted a bright red, and the other was to a hall that led to the kitchen. Mack hit the panic hardware on the door to the hall, and it opened automatically.

"Find Otis for me, then go see Lea in the kitchen while I go for a quick swim. I'll meet you on the tennis court after that."

Contrary to current research on multitasking, Mack believed in giving Irish as much as she could handle. He started her out that way, and so far she'd handled it well. Regardless, it was their lifestyle. He patted Irish on her bottom and directed her down the hall to the kitchen, "And don't forget, no English. Solamente habla español, por favor, and take your vitamins."

CHAPTER 4

WALKING UP THE steps inside the Peabody with Reggie, McKenzie could hear the members and guests of the Rotary club singing the end of "God Bless America."

"Remember, Mr. Anderton sits to the right so you will sit to the left of the podium." Reggie whispered to her before opening the rear door to the stage and guiding her inside.

McKenzie took a step inside as Reggie gave her a thumbs up, turned, and eased the door shut.

"And now," she heard someone say, "to introduce our guests, the President of the Memphis Rotary Club, Mr. Bob Anderton."

McKenzie stood behind a curtain separating the stage from the back wall. She took her shoes off, walked down the narrow walkway, and opened a door to a janitor's closet with brooms, mops, and a metal folding chair. There was supposed to be a dressing room back here somewhere, but she didn't have time to look for it now. She stepped into the closet, lifted up her dress, and pulled down her panty hose as she listened to the speaker.

"It is an honor and my pleasure to welcome you today to the largest attendance of guests and members in the history of any Memphis Rotary Club luncheon. As President, I would like to take the credit for this historic turnout, but we all know it is because of our guest speaker that we are here today."

McKenzie smiled. There was one thing she liked better than making a speech and that was making one to a full house. If only they wouldn't eat while she was speaking. She could hear the rattling of dishes all the way back here. She had asked Reggie to talk to the manager and see if the waiters could wait until *after* her speech to bus the dishes.

Bob Anderton continued, "There is not enough time to introduce all our important visitors today, but the press would roast me in barbecue sauce if I failed to introduce the following people:

"The Honorable Mayor of our great city, Dr. William Washington.

"The Attorney General of the State of Tennessee, Mr. Haywood Fox.

"The Publisher of the South's finest newspaper . . ."

McKenzie continued to listen as she opened her brief case and pulled out a frizzy blond wig, a pair of lacey red stockings, and a pair of knee-high patent leather, bright red boots. She sat on the metal chair gathering one side of the red stockings up and easing her toe into the end. She hoped that Bob Anderton remembered that she was not coming on stage before he introduced her.

"One of the most enjoyable parts of being the President of The Memphis Rotary Club is that I have the opportunity to meet with our Guest Speakers prior to the luncheon. I get to know them a little or, in some cases, renew old friendships. The second enjoyable part is that I get to introduce them to you and tell you something about them."

McKenzie started to panic. *I'm not ready!*

"Today I will surrender my second part to a higher authority. Someone who knows more about our speaker that I will ever know." Anderton turned and looked behind him at a long- legged and ruddy-looking man.

Thomas O'Brien was known to have given up wine, women, and song . . . but not his whiskey. His elbows rested on his knees as he squinted while shuffling through a couple of white index cards. He was tall, with slumped shoulders, and had the beginning of a potbelly, which gave him the mistaken appearance of clumsiness. He could have played forward on any college basketball team, or defensive linebacker, but instead he played number one on Notre Dame's tennis team and was their champion heavyweight boxer for three years. His black suit was rumpled and fit his demeanor, while his white round collar stood out as the only badge of clerical recognition.

Anderton continued, "One of Memphis' own, the Bishop of the

Roman Catholic Diocese of Memphis, the Most Reverend, Dr. Carroll Thomas O'Brien."

There was loud applause as he moved to the podium in long strides, nodding his head in thanks. He placed the index cards on the podium and reached for his bifocals.

McKenzie exhaled a sigh of relief, made the sign of the cross, and whispered, "Holy Mary mother of God—thank you," as she rushed to pull on her red boots.

"The reason I asked Bob here to let me do the introduction is that the guest speaker and I have a lot in common." He slipped on his bifocals. "We are both Catholics, we are both Irish, both of our last names start with the letter O, we both have red hair, and . . . we both love good Scotch whiskey."

After a short pause for laughter, O'Brien started again.

"I was at a dinner last night and during the cocktail hour, we were all standing around when this young fellow asked me if I was from Ireland. I said, 'Yes, I was born in Dublin.' He then asked me if I knew that other than the African-Americans, the Irish have the largest ancestry group in Memphis and Shelby County. I said, 'Yes, I was aware of that.' He then asked me if the Scotch-Irish were included in that group. I said, 'Yes.' The young fellow then looked at me with a puzzled look on his face and asked, 'What exactly is Scotch-Irish?' I said, 'Son, that's a group of Irishmen who love good Scotch.'"

McKenzie had to stop putting on her hot glow lipstick as the noise of the crowd made her smile. "Wake them up, Uncle Tommy—prime the pump."

She sat her compact mirror on the chair seat as she picked up the blond wig and started stuffing her red hair under it.

As the laughter died down, Bishop O'Brien took his glasses off and looked out over the crowd, smiling.

"I knew our guest speaker's grandfather. I know her father and I was with her mother at Saint Joseph Hospital when she was born. I christened her, married her, and I guess that's why I'm introducing her." He turned to see if she was in sight, shrugged his shoulders, and said, "And as long as I have known her, she has always been late . . . which reminds me of a story a friend told me that happened back in Ireland.

"It seems this farmer named Muldoon lived alone out in the country-side with his pet dog that he loved and doted on. After many long years of companionship, the dog finally died, so Muldoon went to the parish priest: 'Father, my dear old dog is dead. Could you be saying a mass for the creature?' Father Patrick replied, 'I'm so very sorry to hear about your dog's death. But unfortunately we cannot have services for an animal in the church. However, there's a new denomination down the road. No tell-ing what they believe, and maybe they'll do something for the animal.' Muldoon said, 'I'll go right down and see them. Do you think $500 is enough to donate for the services?'"

"Father Patrick said, 'Mr. Muldoon, why didn't you tell me the dog was Catholic!'"

O'Brien looked over his shoulder to the rear of the stage, waited for the laughter to end, and announced, "May the good Lord take a liking to all of you . . . but not too soon." He looked to the rear of the stage once more. "The Honorable Chancellor McKenzie O'Connor." He waited a few seconds and walked back to his seat.

On the stage was a long speaker's table covered with a white tablecloth, and a tabletop lectern in the center. On the floor, along the front of the table, were pots of blooming hydrangea. An American flag was at one end of the table, and the Tennessee State flag at the other.

McKenzie walked out from behind the back stage curtain along the wall to the end of the speaker's table. She was dressed in an outfit she had worn in college, when she and some friends in her sorority put on a skit about a prostitute who became a famous burlesque queen. Ten years ago that skit caused quite a stir with the faculty. *What good did it do to work out and not be able to show the results?* she often thought.

There was never any doubt who played the lead in the college skit. She was dressed in pink, skintight hot pants, with red lace panty hose, and red high heel boots. A black sequined tube top, now one size too small, pushed her breasts precariously upward. With a black sequined shoulder bag, the hot glow lipstick, heavy eye shadow, and the frizzy blond wig, there was little doubt of her occupation.

Everyone in the ballroom stopped talking. The waiters and bus boys stood motionless. There was no rattling of dishes. As she turned and walked across the front of the stage, a wave of silence covered the remaining audience as all heads followed her walk; many wondered if this woman had stumbled into the wrong room. The only sound was the high heels of the red boots tapping on the wood floor as she sashayed in and around the potted plants, dragging her shoulder bag in one hand and a cigarette in the other.

When she got to the opposite end of the table, next to the American Flag, she made a slow turn and stopped. Facing the audience, she took an exaggerated draw from her cigarette and, with the other hand, swung her shoulder bag in a circle, winding it around her hand. Slowly exhaling her cigarette smoke and continuing to chew her gum, she turned and walked off stage to the back curtain.

Most of the people turned and stared at each other. Some looked embarrassed, some shocked, and some were smiling—was this some big mistake?

With a Ph.D. in Biblical and Theological Studies from Wheaton College and a Trustee and often guest Minister of Central Baptist Church, Isaac Z. Brenner, CEO and President of Shamrock International, was thought of as a religious man. He was tall, lean, and impeccably dressed, sitting at a table close to the stage with five other men.

Sitting to his right was the CEO of the Planters National Bank and, on his left, was the President of Walls and Associates, one of the largest CPA firms in the Mid-South. They both looked at Isaac for a reaction as McKenzie strutted off stage.

Isaac's expression never changed. He had cultivated this poker face from his childhood friend and employer, Mack Shannon. Yet, if you looked closely, there was a hint of a smile in the corner of his mouth. *IF this was the Chancellor, I'm sure only a few ever imagined a body like that could exist under her robe.*

The audience had very little time to discuss who or what had just happened. McKenzie had performed her quick-change act and was back on stage.

She walked directly to the podium from the back stage curtain. Her walk was deliberate, yet not masculine, with both arms swinging and taking long steps. Her red hair was combed back on the top, and the sides were pulled back and tied with an emerald green ribbon, leaving her long hair to flow freely and bounce as she walked. There was never any doubt where she was going or what she was going to do when she got there. She carried no notes.

She stood at the microphone, sweeping the audience with her eyes. When she had everyone's attention, she looked back to the center and asked demandingly, "What I want to know is, honestly, how many of you would have hired me if I had walked into your office looking for employment dressed like that? Would you have even interviewed me? I don't think so."

No greetings to the guest and members. No "thank you for asking me to speak to you today," just straightforward, hard-hitting questions. That was her style—brassy, bold, and direct—some thought too direct.

Pointing out to the audience, she said, "Guess what? You *better* interview me. And you better have a good reason why you don't hire me. Furthermore, the reason cannot be that I am not qualified." She picked up the portable microphone and clipped it on her dress as she walked around to the front of the podium.

"The truth is, nowadays, in most cases, only applicants who are *not* qualified will be considered. I ask you; is that *stupid* or not?" She took two steps forward and looked down at the mayor's table.

"During my short lifetime, our mayor could not eat in the same restaurant with me. Judge Ford could not use the same ladies' room, and worst of all, their children had to endure this humiliation." She moved down the line of the first row of tables. "When my grandfather came to this country, his son, my father, had to endure this prejudiced humiliation." She moved to the next table looking down at them, "Louis Gomez, CEO of one of the largest construction companies in the mid-south and an MIT graduate, is on the board of Fed-Ex, International Paper, St. Jude, and I don't know how many others. His family had to endure this same humiliation. And lastly, women . . . well, I won't even try to get into the thousands of cases of discrimination against women."

She turned and walked back to the podium. "Many of you may think what I'm about to tell you is pure fiction, but I can assure you it is not. These are documented facts: In *The Memphis Appeal* newspaper, dated June 5th, the U. S. Forest Service advertised for women, asking for, 'Only applicants who do *not* meet standards will be considered.'"

"On the front page of *The Wall Street Journal*, July 16, an article read,

'The Department of Energy has ordered that 65 percent of its top executives must be women or minorities.'

"James Babcock wrote an article in the July issue of *TIME* magazine, that the Pentagon could not promote white males without *special* permission. This is true in most States, not only promotions, but also hiring in general. In most counties and cities, including here in Memphis and Shelby County, the Divisions of Fire, Police, Schools, Parks, Housing, Sanitation, and General Services have been forced by the government to follow these same guidelines.

"The largest lawsuit I heard this year was a reverse discrimination case that ended in the Supreme Court, and they won. There is a savage cry out there, people; I hear it in my courtroom every day, and you had better listen. 'The Angry White Male' is raging. The pendulum has swung way too far off center. Every day in my courtroom I am faced with a middle-aged white male whose world has broken to pieces. He has lost his business or job and can't find another one, his wife is divorcing him and taking the children, his house is being foreclosed on, the bank is repossessing his car, and he is being forced into bankruptcy. His next step is alcohol, drugs, or a heart attack, and with no insurance, his last straw is suicide, and he might take *you* with him. You want to feel 'Atlas shrug'? You want a dystopian society? Easy—just stop the white male from producing!"

McKenzie waited for this to sink in.

"Whose fault is this? Some say equal rights, some say civil rights, and a lot of people, certain news media, say the flaming liberal judges. The truth is it's the white male's fault. They were the majority in the Senate, the Congress, and the Supreme Court that passed the laws to make the changes." She moved over to her left and picked up a glass of water from her place setting, took a drink, and dabbed her mouth with a napkin.

"Enough is enough. Where is our common sense? I think the pendulum has swung too far to the left. What do you think? As a Chancery Court Judge, I have done all that I can do." McKenzie stopped and smiled. "I have a wonderful friend who happens to be my hairdresser. In her salon there is a sign hanging on the wall that reads, 'I am a beautician, not a magician.' Well . . . I'm a judge, not a politician. I don't make the laws I enforce them." She paused a moment to check her time. "So, *you* out there who make the laws, start changing the laws, and *I* will start enforcing those laws."

McKenzie O'Connor had finished her speech and the packed room was applauding, some even standing. That is, all the white middle age males, which McKenzie knew to be ninety percent of the Memphis Rotary Club.

Isaac Brenner was not applauding. Being a black male, he was not quite sure her speech wasn't discriminating. He read in the morning paper that she was a Democrat and some referred to her as a liberal chancellor. One thing was for sure, hidden somewhere under the Chancellor's robe was not only a beautiful body, but he would wager a large set of balls too . . . probably steel.

CHAPTER 5

THE BLACK MERCEDES moved in and out of the night traffic along I-240. Isaac Brenner, with a drink in his hand, leaned back against the soft leather seat, somewhat relaxed. He turned to Mack Shannon, "Are you getting hungry?"

"Why, you hungry?"

"I'm starved."

"Where you want to eat?"

"That's the hardest part. What do you have a taste for?"

"I'm tired of making decisions; you pick. I don't care."

"Okay, French or Italian?" Isaac asked.

"How about Arthur's?"

"You sure?"

"Why not? We can take care of one more piece of business before the day's over."

Isaac smiled, "Look outside. The day is over!" He pressed the speaker-phone to the front seat.

"Not for us, it's not . . .." Mack stared out of the dark tinted window, swirling the ice in his empty glass. "What's the tally on the fat man, anyway?"

Isaac spoke into the speaker to the driver. "Otis, the boss would like to eat at Arthur's, out in Germantown."

Isaac reached inside his coat pocket and punched in some numbers on his phone. "Let's see, close to a quarter-mil by now, I imagine. To be exact, $248,986.26 including interest."

Mack stared at Isaac a few minutes, smiled, and shook his head. "I haven't forgotten that you advised me not to do business with Arthur . . . I'll pay for dinner."

*

When Otis pulled into the driveway of Arthur's, there were other cars waiting for valet parking. He swerved around the cars without hesitation and stopped at the entrance of the restaurant, double-parking.

Isaac opened the car door, and Mack moved across the seat and followed him up the steps into the restaurant. A dozen people stood around with drinks waiting to be seated. The manager saw Isaac, came over immediately, and announced a little too loudly, "Good Evening, Mr. Brenner. We have your table ready. Right this way, sir."

"Thank you, Charles."

Charles led them through the crowded restaurant to a private table in a corner. He stepped back to let Mack pass.

"It's very good to have you with us again, Mr. Shannon. Is this table alright, sir?"

"This is fine, thank you, Charles. Could you remove the two extra chairs, please?"

"Yes sir." He motioned for a waiter as he pulled two chairs away from the table. Another waiter removed two of the place settings, and Charles whispered for him to bring two double Macallans on the rocks and a basket of hot garlic bread. He removed the reserved sign from the table.

"If you are having dinner, can I recommend a dish that was made special for tonight?"

"Please do," Isaac said.

"The chef has made a wonderful Beef Wellington. The beef is from Mr. Dobbs' farm. As you know they are all grass fed, very tender, and, of course, hormone free."

"When was the pâté made?" Mack asked.

"Yesterday, sir. There was a request made for Beef Wellington yesterday for a party of six tonight. The Chef made a couple of extra ones for our special guest." He nodded with a smile and lit the candle on the table.

Isaac looked over at Mack. No response.

"That will be fine. We want the hearts of palm and artichoke salad with olive oil, sprinkled with blue cheese, and a bottle of Bordeaux, nothing real expensive, but a good vintage say '06 or '07. But first we . . ."

Charles interrupted Isaac, "Two double Macallans on the rocks, 15 year old?" He turned, taking the drinks from the waiter standing behind him.

Mack nodded his approval. Charles smiled and walked to the side of Isaac's chair. Isaac discreetly laid a folded fifty dollar bill on the table and asked, "Is Arthur here?"

"Yes sir. He's in the kitchen. Can I get him for you?"

Mack shook his head, and Isaac said, "No, maybe later. Oh, and Charles, would you take care of Otis as well, please?"

"According to our new young waitress, Claresa, he's in the kitchen now." They all smiled. "I'll check on your salads," Charles said as he put the hot garlic bread on the table and backed away.

"Charles, one more thing, how about some of that liquid gold Mussini Balsamic Arthur hides back there, to soak my garlic bread in?"

"Yes sir. Do you want the bottle or by the ounce?"

"How many ounces in the bottle?"

"2.4, sir."

Isaac looked over at Mack and said, "You're buying, right?"

Mack smiled. "The bottle is fine, Charles." Mack looked over at Isaac, "Didn't you eat today at the Rotary Luncheon?"

"No, I was too mesmerized by the speaker, a Chancellor O'Connor. Do you know her?"

"No. What about her?"

"She's an extremely attractive Irish woman, and smart too."

"Is O'Connor her married name?"

"No. Her husband's name is Randolph Winchester, old Memphis money. He's an anesthesiologist, runs a big pain clinic out here in Germantown, mega bucks, according to Adam Steen, over at Planters National. No children. I hear she does what she wants, mostly without him. He works all the time."

"I know the feeling. His name is *Randolph*. How many people you know with that name?"

"Randolph Scott, the cowboy."

"He was queer."

"No? Don't tell me that. He's one of my favorite old-time cowboys."

"Yeah, afraid so. Old Randy never rode off into the sunset alone, not without, Cary Grant."

Ahhh, Cary Grant, too? You're killing me," Isaac said.

"Sorry." Mack shrugged his shoulders. "Pass me the bread."

"Are you changing your stripes?"

"Why?"

"I thought you always like to do business before pleasure. You going to talk to Arthur *after* we eat?"

"Did you want me to talk to him first and *then* let him prepare our food?"

"You're right. I wasn't thinking."

They both looked up as a waiter approached the table with their salads on a tray. He first served Mack, then leaned over and whispered in Isaac's ear while placing his salad in front of him, and walked off.

"How many in this restaurant do you have on the payroll?"

"It helps," said Isaac. He leaned over to Mack, "Our bird is about to fly the coop. Arthur knows we're here and is leaving by the kitchen door. We can cut him off in the parking lot if we leave now."

"You enjoy your salad. I'll be back before you finish." Mack stood up and walked directly to the kitchen. The kitchen was working like a beehive, and no one was paying him the least bit of attention. He looked around, saw the exit door, and was in the parking lot before anyone noticed.

The driver-side door was open on the white Cadillac, and Arthur's 300-pound butt was hanging outside. He was leaning over to the back seat, positioning Styrofoam cartons of food from the restaurant. His white toy poodle was barking and jumping back and forth from the front seat to the back.

Mack eased the car door against the back of Arthur's legs and leaned hard on the door. Arthur tried to turn, but the door had his legs pinned.

"I have no money," he shouted. "Take my car."

Mack let the pressure off the door. Arthur turned, saw Mack, and fell into the driver seat.

"*Shit!* You scared me to death. Those niggers been holding up restaurants out here once a week." His huge stomach was heaving up and down against the steering wheel, as he gasped for air.

"What *niggers* you talking about? Isaac's inside, you talking about him?"

"No, I didn't mean . . . you know what I mean," Arthur said.

Mack walked around and sat in the front passenger seat. The poodle jumped in the back seat, growling and showing his teeth.

"Mack, it's good to see you. I wasn't feeling too well—my blood pressure you know—I was going home for a short rest. Let's go inside, and I'll fix you a special dinner on the house. You with friends or just Isaac?"

"Isaac *is* my friend. We'll talk here, and make sure you keep that dog in the back seat."

"It's okay, really, she won't bite." Arthur turned to the back seat and, with a whisper, said, "Now Baby, you hush that barking and be daddy's good little girl." The dog continued to growl and bark.

"Mack, if it's about the money I owe you."

"It's more than that." Mack's voice was low and unemotional. "Our business is over. I'm calling your note. You have one week to come up with a half million in cash. That's $250,000 for the balance of the loan . . ."

"Mack. Wait . . ."

"Don't interrupt me. As I said, $250,000 for the balance of my loan and another $250,000 for my 25% ownership."

"Mack! You know I don't have that kind of money. Let's work a deal."

"Isaac will have all the paperwork for you Monday. There is no negotiating—no lawyers, no letter writing, and no continuances. Listen closely, if I . . ."

"You can't threaten me like that."

"This is not a threat, fat man, it's a fact. You've been riding on my money for over two years, and I'm tired of dealing with your lying ass. *Listen to me.* If you do not have my money in one week, I will take one of my bulldozers and push this restaurant into the middle of Germantown Road."

Mack opened the door and stepped out of the car. The poodle jumped in the front seat right behind him, barking and snapping. Mack dropped his hand in front of the dog, and the poodle bit down hard. Mack grabbed the dog with his other hand, quick as a cobra strike, and like a twig, snapped the bone that held the foot to the leg. The poodle let out a loud yelp and went limp in Mack's hand. His hand was dripping with blood as he held the dog up and dropped him in the front seat.

Arthur was screaming, "Baaaaby, my Baaaaby!"

"One week, Arthur." Mack turned and walked back into the restaurant . . . he was starving.

CHAPTER 6

THE RESTORATION OF the downtown courthouse was a first-class job. All things considered, the original designers and craftsmen of 1910 would not be disappointed. The courtroom of Chancellor McKenzie O'Connor was on the top floor in the southwest corner. The tall windows looked out over the Mississippi River, and the room was a show-case for heart-sawn mahogany: the walls, doors, window frames, and all the furnishings were mahogany. The white, vaulted ceiling and polished brass hardware were the only contrast to the reddish-brown mahogany.

Friday morning the courtroom was almost empty, except for a few lawyers, the bailiff, a court reporter, the Chancellor, and her clerk, Abby Jones.

"Any other announcements or orders?" Chancellor O'Connor said.

The doors of the courtroom opened, and McKenzie saw a lawyer rush in with another man lagging behind. The one in front was struggling with two stuffed and worn-out briefcases under one arm, one on top of the other, and his other arm was wrapped around a stack of legal folders. His suit was wrinkled and looked as if it had been slept in. He was short, and there was a garland of tight, wiry, black hair wrapped around his head with a shiny bald plate in the middle. A black wire hung from his left ear and ran down to the breast pocket of his coat. Sidney Goldman looked a lot older than he was.

The other man stood three steps behind, as if Goldman might be contagious. He was tall, young, and slender with a full head of hair. He looked as if he had just stepped out of *GQ* magazine. His ultra-slim Gucci briefcase hung lightly at his side, garnishing his attire. McKenzie wasn't sure if he was a lawyer or a client.

"Good morning, Your Honor." The folders fell from Goldman's arm onto the table as he dropped the briefcases on the floor.

McKenzie thought he looked a little taller now. "How can I help you, Mr. Goldman?"

"Sorry we're late. I was making announcements in Part Two and it was backed up. Your Honor, this is Arthur Fox, doing business as Arthur's versus Mack Shannon. Global Construction, Inc., and Shamrock International. I represent the Plaintiff in this case, Mr. Arthur Fox, individually and doing business as Arthur's, a restaurant. Mr. Bickford represents the Defendant . . ."

"Hold on Mr. Goldman, what's the docket number, and do we have the jacket?"

"Sorry, Your Honor," shuffling through his folders he found what he was looking for. "Case number 05-9469-3, Your Honor."

"Mr. Goldman, is that wire coming out of your ear going to a cell phone? You know I don't allow phones in my court room."

Goldman unplugged the cord from his phone, "Yes ma'am. It's off now."

Abby Jones started looking through the folders on her table. "I have the jacket, Your Honor." The bailiff walked over, took the file from Abby, and handed it up to the Chancellor.

"Your Honor, if it pleases the court, Mr. Bickford and I are a little confused about the procedure in moving forward with this case, and we're hoping you might give us some guidance. This is the case where . . ."

"Excuse me, Your Honor, Mr. Goldman speaks for himself. I am not confused, nor do I seek guidance in this case. I am ready and prepared to . . ."

"Mr. Bickford, that is your name . . . only one lawyer speaks at a time in my court room, and I always have the common courtesy to let him finish uninterrupted. In regard to being confused—at one time or another—*all* of us around here are confused. When you have argued as many cases before me as Mr. Goldman has, you will learn that."

"I stand corrected, Your Honor, and I apologize to the court and to Mr. Goldman. Admittedly, I have not had the pleasure of meeting you or presenting myself before the court. My name is S. Charles Bickford the Third. I am with the law firm of Bickford, Overton, Guthrie, and . . ."

"Mr. Bickford, please *sit* down. Continue, Mr. Goldman."

"Thank you, Your Honor. This is the case that started over here in Chancery. After hearing the charges, Chancellor Hackett suggested that my client, Mr. Arthur Fox, might have grounds for criminal charges, specifically extortion. I took it over to the prosecutor's office, and they agreed with Chancellor Hackett. But when we took it before Judge Riley in criminal, he threw it out. He was very clear when he told the prosecutor and me, 'Keep the civil cases across the street.' The civil charges were still pending in Chancery when I got a call from Chancellor Hackett's office that he will have to recuse himself from hearing this case. He has a conflict with Shamrock. Then the clerk's office set the case for Chancellor Stephens, but she's on maternity leave and won't be back 'til sometime next year."

"What about the sitting Chancellor?" O'Connor asked.

"Retired Chancellor Jimmy Morgan is sitting this month. Each morning he makes the announcement that if anyone doesn't want him to hear their case and wants to wait for Chancellor Stephens to return, he will honor their request. Mr. Bickford's office requested to wait for Chancellor Stephens."

"Your Honor, I object. Mr. Goldman is making it sound . . ."

"Mr. Bickford, please be patient. I promise you will have your turn. Move on Mr. Goldman."

"In summary, Your Honor, I have two requests. We have service on Shamrock International and Global Construction, Inc., but we have been unable to serve Mack Shannon. Everyone whom we have talked to refused to give us any information on him. He is obviously hiding out and avoiding service. We have deposed Mr. Isaac Brenner, the CEO and President of Shamrock, but he swears Mr. Shannon is out of town and doesn't know when he will return. I would like for Mr. Bickford to accept service for his client. Secondly, Your Honor, am I on the right track? Will you hear this case?"

"Let's hear from Mr. Bickford."

Bickford took his time. He had his stage now and had waited for this for a long time. He rose and walked to the opposite end of the table from Goldman.

"Your Honor, I have been standing here patiently listening to the most one-sided prevarications I have ever heard. Our law firm, Bickford, Overton, Guthrie, and Crump, has represented Shamrock International and Global Construction for over 15 years. I can assure this court that no one is *hiding* or avoiding being served. We emphatically deny all charges filed. If Your

Honor will allow me the time, I have prepared a brief statement in regards to answering each charge, one by one." He opened his briefcase and laid out a legal pad and one folder.

A cell phone chimed the tune of "Rocky Top." Chancellor O'Connor looked around the courtroom for the guilty party. Goldman dug deep into one of his briefcases, then the other one, finding the off button on the third course of the University of Tennessee's fight song.

"I thought you cut that phone off, Mr. Goldman?"

"Sorry, Your Honor, this is my other phone. I thought it was off."

"How many *other* phones do you have?"

"Only the two, Your Honor."

"Will the two attorneys approach the bench please?" Chancellor O'Connor put her hand over the top of the small microphone, moving it to one side, and motioned the attorneys to come forward. The clerk stood and looked at the Chancellor. O'Connor shook her head.

"This is off the record." She leaned forward as they huddled in front of her.

"I want to make sure there are no other announcements this morning, and then I would like to see you both in my chambers." The two attorneys gathered up their briefcases and folders.

"If there is no other business before this court." O'Connor stood up, and the bailiff announced adjournment. O'Connor stepped down and opened a door located directly behind her into her chambers. Abby Jones grabbed an armful of folders and left the courtroom.

Walking into O'Connor's chambers, Abby dropped one of the folders on McKenzie's desk. "Here's the file on that case. Do you want to see the attorneys now?"

"In a minute, I have to tinkle." McKenzie took off her judicial robe and walked to her private bathroom. She wore a solid white tennis outfit: sleeveless shirt, tight fitting shorts, and tennis shoes, all with Nike's Swoosh emblem imprinted on them.

"It's 10:45 now. Is your game still at 12 noon?" Abby asked.

McKenzie walked out of the bathroom, putting her hair up in a pony-tail. "Yes, and make sure my butt leaves here no later than 11:15, okay?" She stopped at her desk and opened the file.

"This shouldn't take long," she said, while perusing the contents. "Looks like Global Construction hired one of its construction workers for a little overtime work. Another Irishman, drinking and fighting—will we ever live down that reputation—went for a little night ride on the company bulldozer." Head bent over, she continued examining the pages. "Thank God the dumbass didn't hurt anyone. No property damages, that's good. Ask them to come in, Abby."

"You remember that night don't you?" Abby said.

"What night?"

"It was a Saturday night, the same date. I checked the folder." She pointed to the folder on McKenzie's desk. "Arthur's was packed, and it was you, me, Rudy, and Jerry. We were all standing by that big window in the bar having a drink and waiting for a table. You thought it was an earthquake—the bar glasses on the shelves were rattling, and the floor was moving. Remember, you grabbed my arm and said, 'Let's get away from the window.' That's when we saw that huge yellow machine, with the monstrous tracks, come rolling off its trailer onto the parking lot."

Abby was infectious, her black eyes flashing and so animated when telling her story, describing everything with her hands. McKenzie smiled as she listened, then stood up from behind her desk and pointed and laughed as she picked up the story.

" . . . and everyone in the bar ran to the window and saw Arthur—in his attack mode—his neck stretched forward like a goose waddling across the parking lot, waving a piece of paper."

Abby laughed as she continued the story, " . . . and you had everyone in the bar falling on the floor when you asked, 'Is it the bulldozer or Arthur that's causing the tremor?'" The two were booming now, high-fiving each other.

There was a knock at the door. They both froze in their tracks, as if they were two school kids caught at something they shouldn't be doing.

"Come in," McKenzie said.

The door opened, and Goldman stuck his head in. He looked first at them holding hands and then at the Chancellor in her tennis outfit. A cautious smile broke out on his face.

"Come on in, Sid, and bring S. Charles with you." Both Abby and McKenzie stifled a giggle.

Sidney Goldman and S. Charles Bickford walked into Chancellor O'Connor's chambers, and Abby went to her office.

"Have a seat, gentlemen. I have to leave in thirty minutes, so let's get right to work. First things first, Mr. Bickford, I believe you stated that you and your firm represent . . . let's see, Shamrock International, Global Construction, Inc., and Mack Shannon individually, is that correct?" She continued without waiting for his answer, "and is Mr. Mack Shannon an officer of one of those corporations?"

Bickford paused, uncertain. "No, Your Honor, I don't think he is."

"What is his relationship to the corporation? Is he an employee of the corporation, sub-contractor, or what?"

Bickford hurriedly opened his briefcase, searching inside.

"I know you represent Shamrock, Mr. Bickford, but are you also representing Mack Shannon?"

There was no answer. Bickford buried his head deeper into his briefcase, avoiding eye contact, stalling, while fumbling with some papers.

McKenzie stood and walked around to the front of her desk between the men. "How long have you been out of law school, Mr. Bickford?"

"About a year. I passed the bar back in November."

"And what law school was that?"

"Vanderbilt."

"Good school. That's a lovely briefcase, Mr. Bickford. Is it new?"

"Yes, well sort of, a passing-the-bar present from my fiancée, Emily Overton." Bickford held out the opened briefcase like a serving tray for McKenzie to inspect. "It's a Gucci."

"May I?" McKenzie closed his briefcase, and took it by the handle and let it drop by her side. "Light, very light, and expensive, I bet?"

"Around two thousand dollars."

Damn, that's four of my retainers, Goldman thought.

McKenzie handed the briefcase back to Bickford. "Do you know Mack Shannon, Mr. Bickford?"

"No, Your Honor, I have never met him. This is my father's case, and I came to court this morning to ask for a continuance until my father returns from out of town."

Sidney Goldman started to object to any mention of a continuance but decided to wait. All was going well, so far.

"Where is your father, Mr. Bickford? I know he is out of town, but where?"

"He's in Montana, Your Honor."

"Is he on a case up there?"

"No, Your Honor, he's on a fly-fishing trip with Harvey Overton."

"Are you talking about Judge Overton with the Supreme Court?"

"Yes."

"Oh, I see. And you want me to continue the case until his return from their fishing trip, is that correct?"

"Yes."

"And earlier, when you said that you were 'ready and prepared to answer each charge one by one,' you were bluffing, right, winging it? Mr. Bickford, your $2,000 briefcase is empty, except for that legal pad and the one folder. Is that all it takes for you to be ready and prepared?"

"Well, Your Honor . . ."

"Answer my question, Mr. Bickford!"

Now, Goldman thought, *this is the time.* "Your Honor, I wouldn't object to a continuance if Mr. Bickford would accept service on Mack Shannon. Obviously, Mr. Shannon works for Global Construction, Inc., which is a subsidiary of Shamrock International. I have affidavits and eyewitnesses that saw the man driving the truck and the bulldozer the night of the extortion and could identify Mr. Shannon if we could get him into court. Both pieces of equipment had the company initials, GCI, printed on them."

This was all news to Bickford. But if all he had to do was to accept service for a construction worker to get out of this mess, he would jump at the chance.

"Your Honor, I will accept service on Mack Shannon for a continuance."

Goldman was ready; he walked over and handed the subpoena to Bickford.

"What is the subpoena for, to take his deposition?" McKenzie said.

"Yes, Your Honor," Goldman said.

Looking down at her calendar, McKenzie asked Bickford. "When does your father return from his fishing trip?"

"In two weeks."

"I will hear this case one week from today. Be prepared, Mr. Bickford, good day."

Bickford started to protest but rushed out the door, gripping his brief-case snug against his leg.

Goldman sat smiling, "You playing at The Racquet Club?"

"Yes. What's happened to you? I haven't seen you at the club in ages. Have you quit officiating?"

"I have no time; not enough hours in a day." He loaded up his folders and brief cases.

"Come on and walk with me downstairs." McKenzie picked up one of Goldman's brief cases and, with her other hand, slung her sports-bag over her shoulder. "You look beat. Are you okay?"

"That's because I am beat. When you work hundred-hour weeks, with no days off, you're supposed to look tired."

Walking out the door, she saw Abby was on the phone and motioned for her to call her when she got off.

"Why so many hours?" McKenzie asked, walking down the corridor.

"Simple . . . don't forget you asked. You remember our first year out of law school; we were all so full of idealistic, set-the-world-on-fire dreams. I started out my first year of law making $25,000, and Joyce made around $12,000. We lived in a mid-town apartment and were very happy. I dou-bled my pay the next year and again the following year and the year after. Soon we were making pretty good money combined. We bought a house in Germantown, a second car, and had a kid. Then we a bought a bigger house, had another kid, and then another, and hired a full-time maid. I had the sex change, you know, a vasectomy. She quit working and fifteen years later she and the three kids tell me they cannot live on less than $12,000 a month."

"You've got to be kidding, $12,000 a *month*?" McKenzie stopped on the steps going downstairs. "That's almost hundred-fifty grand a year."

"Bingo! That $12,000 is after taxes, and that's not counting my overhead at the office, or insurance, or any money for me. My body has aged ten years in the last two. I have lost twenty-five pounds in the last year, and Joyce has gained fifty. I don't see my kids, and I don't want to see my wife."

McKenzie held the swinging doors open for Goldman as they walked outside and down the steps. They stopped on the sidewalk, across the street from two construction workers sitting on the tailgate of their pickup truck eating lunch. Seeing McKenzie in her tennis outfit, they gave her a wolf whistle; she turned and gave them her middle finger. Turning back to Goldman she asked, "Have you talked to a professional about this, Sid?"

"Yeah, you." They both laughed.

"Hell, how many domestic cases do you hear, one a day? Anyway, the shrink would have to make an appointment with *me,* and then I couldn't pay him. Hey, that sounds like practicing law, doesn't it?"

"Sid, you are one of the smartest lawyers I know. You graduated in the top five in our class. Why not go with one of the big law firms so you can get some help and be more selective in what you take on? I can ask around if you'd like."

"Thanks, that sounds great, and I have thought about it, but I have always been my own man, that is, until I got married. I'm just not a company man; besides, it's not the work, it's my home life—I hate it."

"I'm so sorry, but I have to run. Call me for lunch next week, will you, promise?"

"I didn't mean to unload on you."

McKenzie handed him his briefcase, paused a second, then gave him a big hug.

"Thanks, I needed that," he said blushing. "Listen; be careful with this Shannon fellow. My client is scared to death of him and told me that Shannon was the power broker. I'm talking *big power,* and they say he's not shy about using it. Judge Riley's whole demeanor changed when he heard the name Mack Shannon and was adamant about sending this case back to Chancellor Hackett and then, all of a sudden, Hackett recused himself?" Goldman shrugged. "As I said, be very careful; you have a great career ahead of you."

McKenzie watched Goldman laboring back up the steps into the courthouse. *Strange . . . Goldman was politically connected, sat on numerous boards, and very savvy. Why would he warn me twice about a drunken construction worker?* She turned and walked to her car, and the two construction workers whistled at her again. McKenzie did a deep curtsy before getting into her car, smiling. They threw her kisses as she roared off in her red Porsche.

CHAPTER 7

I N THE YEAR of 1890, high on the bluff overlooking the Mississippi River, the Memphis Brewery rolled out its first barrel of GOLDCREST beer. Ninety-three percent of the ingredients of a great beer is *pure* water. Memphis, with its subterranean treasure of over 100 trillion gallons of the sweetest tasting water in the world, made for an ideal marriage to the 250,000 barrels of beer the Memphis Brewery produced each year.

The high level of craftsmanship that went into the building of the Romanesque arches and vaulted ceilings caused the creation of a monument that still stands as a landmark, its bright red bricks visible for miles up and down the river.

A black limo eased over the cobblestones and down the long drive to the brewery entrance. A guard stepped out of the gatehouse and tipped his cap as they passed. The only signage was a carved shamrock of green marble embedded in each gate column.

Otis slowed the limo as he entered a tunnel lined with glossy white-glazed tiles, which led to the brick courtyard. Crossing the courtyard, he stopped at a concrete loading ramp next to a triple-seated golf cart. An attractive female security guard opened the doors of the limo and directed the guests to the cart. While weaving the golf cart around large cypress columns throughout the warehouse, she explained the history of the building. Old photos lined the walls, showing drivers loading their wagons with kegs of beer for their morning deliveries. She stopped in front of an old wooden elevator gate, lifted the gate, and opened the door.

"This will take you to the top floor. Don't worry; it's a new elevator and completely safe. Enjoy your lunch." The cylindrical elevator moved laterally through the dark shaft, like a Disneyland ride. A strip of miniature lights embedded at the base of the floor gave off the only light. After a short distance, the glass elevator swung out into a 5-story atrium where the huge beer vats used to be. Suspended in mid-air by a 3-inch steel cable with a swivel at the end, the elevator turned as it ascended. During construction, some of the workers referred to it as "the coke bottle on a string," but it was much more than that. The refurbishing of this historic landmark was a labor of love for Mack Shannon. It was his flagship, the home office, and he spared no expense in the latest design to promote Shamrock International. As the coke bottle rotated upward, the guests were presented, through a long curtained wall of glass, a panoramic view of the Mississippi River and the two bridges crossing over into Arkansas.

The guests were still in a state of awe over their ride when the elevator door opened to a long marbled hallway on the 5th floor.

"Good afternoon, gentlemen, and welcome to Shamrock International." A tall, middle-aged female, with black eyes and dark hair pulled back into a tight French braid, greeted each guest with a firm handshake. "I'm Anna Brown, and if you will follow me, the other guests are here, and lunch is ready to be served. I hope all of you are hungry because we have a wonderful lunch prepared."

Walking down the hallway, the men could not help staring at the long legs and the heart-shaped bottom. This was a full-bodied woman, not some thin, half-starved model type.

Two women ushered the guests to their seats as they entered the conference room with Anna. Name cards were at each place setting on the long oval table. Anna walked to the end of the table, and a female attendant was quick to pull out the chair next to Mack Shannon. Isaac Brenner, seated on the other side of Mack, stood and addressed the guests.

"Welcome to Shamrock International. We are delighted that you have taken the time from your busy schedules to accept our invitation for lunch."

Isaac's fashionable attire and deep resonant voice commanded everyone's attention. "In the shamrock-shaped box beside each napkin is a small token of our appreciation for your being here today. Standing behind the table are employees of Shamrock who are working on this special project that will be presented today, so please feel free to let them be of service to you. What we share with you today will be unique and groundbreaking, and for the time being we ask that you join Shamrock in keeping everything you hear and see confidential. To save time, we have printed a program outlining our presentation." The attendants handed each guest a program. "If you open the program to the first page you will notice a diagram of the seating arrangements at this table. We may all be partners in this adventure, and this will help introduce you to each other. We have not attached any financial documents for confidential reasons. Dr. Brown is available to you or your CFOs. The name and a short biography of each guest are numbered and match the numbers on the seating chart, with one exception." Isaac walked behind Mack's and Anna's chairs and stopped behind an Asian couple. "Their names were not left off the program by mistake. We were all disappointed when we received a call last week notifying us that they could not be here for the luncheon. Then, at the last minute, an opening in their schedule allowed our two guests, who traveled all night, to be with us today.

"As some of you know, I'm not a big fan of flying, but after this morning's visit to the airport to pick up our guest who flew in nonstop from Brazil, I might reconsider. I watched Mr. Sama land his new G650 Gulfstream, and then he was gracious enough to give me a tour of the tailored, custom-designed cabin. Now that's the way to travel: a private bedroom, two luxurious sleeping divans, two galleys, a shower, and exercise equipment. Go to sleep in São Paulo and wake up in Memphis. After the tour, I was introduced to his daughter, Ms. Lily Sama, who immediately made me forget all the beauty of the G650.

"It is my pleasure to introduce and welcome to our city Mr. Takumi Sama. Seated to his left is his daughter, Ms. Lily Sama, Chairman and CEO of the largest bank in São Paulo, Brazil, The Bank of Japan. Lily is one of Mr. Sama's five successful daughters." Isaac walked back to his seat as the light applause died down.

Takumi Sama and his daughter sat with their heads bowed and somewhat embarrassed by the attention. Sama was short, stocky, and bald. After months of radiation treatment for prostate cancer, he was now in complete remission but without his hair. To him this was of little concern, as the experience of this near tragedy was a wake-up call that deeply changed his life. The loss of a few strands of hair was more than a fair tradeoff for such an illuminating experience. No more a slave to the clock and calendar, he had abdicated the daily control of his companies to his five daughters. Where Takumi's complexion was a dark copper color, due to the Brazilian sun and his Japanese ancestry, this was not the case with his daughter Lily. Her skin mirrored white porcelain. Her dark brown hair and round green eyes were inherited from her Brazilian mother. Although there were no outwardly features to distinguish her as being Asian, her mannerisms and dress, her very presence, exuded an air of Asia. She wore a black, sleeveless, raw silk dress with a mandarin collar. She was the same height as her father and loved to wear high heels, but never did when she was with him for fear of appearing taller.

Isaac nodded to start serving the lunch. "This will be a working lunch for us, so please do not wait to start eating. Now, I would like to ask Anna Brown, our Chief Financial Officer, to give us an outline of today's program. Anna?"

"Many hours have been spent on the presentation you'll see here today. Again, I promise you that when you leave here today you will take with you a vision that will dazzle your mind and elevate the prominence of our great city of Memphis to heights never reached in our history. Not only will this spotlight our city, but the whole state of Tennessee and the eight other states that touch our borders. Please enjoy your food, and if you have any questions after the presentation, I will be available." She smiled, making eye contact with each guest.

"Our program today will consist of three parts. The first part is taking place now, our lunch and introductions of our guest. The second part, and hopefully the most exciting, will be our 12-minute film presentation. Lastly, it is such a beautiful day; we have arranged to have our coffee and dessert on the rooftop where there is plenty of room to meet, talk, and get to know one another. And now I would like to introduce, as they say in the navy, our Fleet Commander. He not only commands our flagship, Shamrock International, but all of our ships at sea, as we like to refer to our subsidiary companies: Chairman of the Board, Mack Shannon."

Mack stood and helped Anna with her chair. "Dr. Brown's father is a retired Admiral in the U. S. Navy," he turned and looked at Isaac, "and Dr. Brenner is a former Captain in the Marines, so I have to make sure I am ship-shape when I am around these two." Mack noticed all the guests had been served and were eating.

"Shamrock is our headquarters, the heart of all of our operations, and it pumps 24/7, from São Paulo to Tokyo, to Mexico City to London and back through this building. As I speak to you now, that information is flowing throughout this building like blood flowing through your body. There is little I can add that is not on the film you are about to see, so enjoy your lunch, and we will start the presentation as soon as you finish." Mack was not eating because butterflies were flying around inside his rib cage—first time in a long time. This was the delivery room, and from conception to birth, this was his baby. The cost for today's presentation had exceeded his budget of two million dollars—a big loss if this promotion was not successful. But in Mack's mind, small potatoes when you were promoting the most costly development in the history of the South and what now had extended way past its original design and estimated construction costs to a final figure of one billion dollars.

After lunch, the attendants cleared the table, closed the blinds, and dimmed the lights. A projection screen hummed as it descended from the ceiling to the floor. The screen covered one full wall, was curved at each corner, and covered half a wall on each side of the room. The OrbitVision screen was like a pair of wraparound sunglasses.

The room was in total darkness except for a minute green dot, blinking at the bottom of the dark screen. All eyes watched the dot as it grew with every beat of what sounded like a heartbeat. The green dot grew larger as the heartbeat grew faster. The Bose surround-sound speakers amplified the rapid beat, and the green dot exploded out of black soil like a volcanic eruption and ballooned into three leaves of a large shamrock. Everyone watched the shamrock as the leaves grew longer and rotated to a thumping sound that increased as each leaf transformed into a rotor blade on top of a jet helicopter. The Sikorsky Executive lifted off the rooftop of the proposed Trinity Town Towers. The three 33-story buildings, wrapped in green reflective glass, were situated on King's Island in the middle of the Mississippi River, across from downtown Memphis. As the helicopter ascended, the guests could see the green rooftop of each tower, which was in the shape of a cloverleaf. At 1,000 feet the three towers closed in around each other, forming a large shamrock in the sky.

*

On the rooftop of Shamrock International, the guests and employees mingled over coffee and dessert.

"What do you think?" Isaac asked Anna.

"We all worked hard, and I think it showed. What did the boss think?"

"I haven't had a chance to talk to him," nodding his head toward Mack. "He's been in deep conversation. Negotiating one of the loan packages, I would imagine."

Anna looked across the rooftop and saw that Mack and Lily Sama where huddled in the far corner, "And . . . possibly other things?"

"You said that, not me. Uh-oh, watch out, approaching from your starboard," Isaac whispered. "What's his name, the skinny guy from Planter's Bank?"

"Just who I was looking for," the banker said.

"Mr. Hunter. Did you enjoy your lunch?" Anna said, looking at Isaac's nod of appreciation for announcing the banker's name.

"That's strange," Hunter said, "I would have thought you'd ask me if I enjoyed the presentation?"

"Ah, you're too smart, Mr. Hunter. That was my second question." *Something about this nerd that doesn't pass the smell test: the brown shoes with the tight-fitting blue suit, the thick bottle glasses, and that beaver-like smile of his all make me ill.*

"Well, I don't eat very much. I'm a vegetarian, you know, and not the one you should ask about food."

Sorry about that, Hunter. I never trust a man who doesn't eat meat. "Next time, if you call ahead, we will make special arrangements for you."

"Mr. Hunter," Isaac said, "What did you think of our presentation?"

"Elaborate . . . very elaborate. Expensive too, I imagine?"

None of your business, Nosey. Why is he ogling me while talking to Isaac?

"Do you see Planter's National having any interest in the permanent financing?" Isaac said.

"That would totally be up to Mr. Woodlawn. I will write a report to him on my meeting today. I was going to talk to Mr. Shannon, but I see one of my competitors, Ms. Tokyo Rose there, whatever her name is, from the Bank of Tokyo, beat me to him. Have you all completed the Volkswagen project in San . . . something? I can't think of the name of the city, somewhere in Brazil."

Again, none of your business, you redneck racist.

Isaac spoke up before Anna, "Mr. Woodlawn called Mr. Shannon yesterday from the hospital. They are meeting first of the week. Regardless, Mr. Hunter, you are talking to the lady who has all your answers." He removed his vibrating phone from his pocket and started walking off. "Please excuse me; I need to take this call. Give my best to Mr. Woodlawn."

Thanks a lot, Isaac. "Is Mr. Woodlawn still in the hospital, Mr. Hunter? I hope it's nothing serious." Hunter watched Isaac walking across the rooftop, mingling into the crowd. *This jackass doesn't want to do business with a woman.*

"Hemorrhoids," Hunter said, with his back to her. Turning back to Anna, "You are familiar with hemorrhoids, *Doctor* Brown?"

Yes, I'm talking to one. "Mr. Hunter, were there some questions you had about finance?"

"Not at this time. I do need a list of all the participants, equity partners, and the amount of their contributions, all loans with foreign lenders, a copy of your latest P&L, and your Pro Forma."

"We have a financial package put together for all qualified investors, Mr. Hunter. I will have that couriered over to the bank tomorrow."

"Tomorrow is Saturday, Ms. Brown, the bank is closed." He turned to walk away.

"Mr. Hunter," Anna stopped him, "in case you get to talk to Mr. Shannon, there are a couple of items that might be important to remember—it's the Bank of Japan, not *Tokyo*, and that is the bank's Chairman, the same one who financed Shamrock's construction of the 2,000,000 square foot Volkswagen plant, in the third largest city in the world, *São Paulo*." *Keep smiling Anna; hold your cool.*

"Ah, of course, I have all that written down somewhere. I'll be looking for your courier Monday, *Doctor*."

Don't hold your breath. Anna followed the swaggering banker across the rooftop when her eyes were pulled away; she felt someone staring at her and stopped to scan the crowd.

Leaning back against the parapet wall, with his back to the sun and his foot resting on a wooden bench, Takumi Sama had been caught studying his quarry. Sipping his coffee, he smiled and bowed his head to Anna as if to say, "Touché, you got me."

He watched her walking across the rooftop with long strides, directly toward him. A westerly wind pressed her sundress against her, outlining the contours of her voluptuous body. *Anna Brown*, he thought . . . and rebuked himself for not paying closer attention to her in the past. A flash fantasy, and he saw her nude. Whatever her age, she had made sure there were no wrinkles, no fat, and no gray hair, no matter the cost.

"Mr. Sama, you look to be enjoying yourself?" Anna said, walking up to him.

"My friends call me Sam." He knew that if Isaac Brenner was Mack Shannon's good right arm, Anna Brown was his good left arm.

"Sam Sama?" Anna said a little too fast.

They both laughed. Anna noticed his straight white teeth against his bronze skin. She thought of Yul Brenner and laughed again.

"Like samurai?" Anna asked, laughing and slicing through the air with an imaginary sword.

"Exactly."

"Oh, Mr. Sama, I'm so sorry. I shouldn't take such liberty; I've embarrassed myself. That glass of champagne on an empty stomach, I guess."

"Didn't you eat?" He moved his foot and wiped the bench with his hand. "Here, please sit and join me."

She sat, feeling better now that she wasn't hovering over him. "No, I was too nervous to eat."

"Dr. Brown, I like your . . . freedom of ceremony."

"You do?"

"It is refreshing. One of the many things I like about the South, the informality and the intimacy."

"My friends call me Anna," she extended her hand.

Sam took her hand and continued to stare into her eyes.

"What's the matter?" she smiled at him.

"I was just thinking, what could I possibly say to this beautiful woman that someone hasn't said before?"

"How about, 'Would you like another glass of Clicquot?' That would be original. I think I'm having a meltdown. I have been so uptight dealing with all this for months."

Sam helped her up from the bench and turned her toward the river. "Look, the sun is shining, there is a warm breeze, and the great Mississippi River is at our feet. How about a walk along the river?"

"Better yet, can you pilot a boat?"

"What size?"

"You can take your pick." Anna waved one of the servers over. "Christy, could you call Otis and tell him I will need one of the limos in about 10 minutes, with two cold bottles of Clicquot. Oh, and call my office and tell them I'm on my way down with a 5-minute stop. And Christy, thank you. You did a great job today."

Taking hold of Sam's arm, Anna whispered, "Christy will bring you down to meet me. I have one short stop at my office, and I will be right down." Squeezing his arm, she turned and rushed off with her cell phone to her ear. She needed to get out of her high heels and into some flat shoes and, her baby-size bladder was about to explode.

Sam turned and leaned with both hands on the parapet wall, watching the river. *Careful, old man; don't light a fire you can't extinguish.*

Mack looked across the rooftop and saw Sam looking out at the river. "Your father looks a little lonely over there. You want to join him?"

"I would rather stay here with you. He'll want to talk about the VW plant," Lily said.

"That's okay; I might want to talk about Trinity. Don't you think we have been a wee bit conspicuous standing here the whole time?"

"Do you feel conspicuous?"

Mack shrugged his shoulders.

"The only reason you might feel a wee bit conspicuous is because we have been talking about your penthouse up there instead of the financing of your Tower project, right?"

"Could be," Mack said. "Come on. Let's go talk to Mr. Sam."

Approaching her father, Lily thought about his cancer, "You okay, Papa?"

"Fine, I'm doing great. What a beautiful view. That's Arkansas over there, right Mack?"

"Yes, at this part of the Mississippi, the middle of the river splits Tennessee and Arkansas, and from here you can see all three states. Just north of the Hernando de Soto Bridge," Mack pointed up river to the bridge, "we can see Tower One (T-1) of the Trinity Town Towers on King's Island where the Mississippi turns back west. I wished I knew half as much about Brazil as you do about the USA."

"Ah, mi amigo, you are very educated about Brazil. Few Americans know as much as you do."

Mack thought: *That may be true. It's shameful how most Americans know very little about other countries.* "What did you think of the presentation, Takumi?" When Mack was in Brazil, he always called Sama *Takumi*. But Sama had asked Mack to call him Sam while in the States; Sam was easier for Americans to say and remember.

Sam rubbed his bald head. "Mack, your building here is five stories?"

In meetings over the past year with Sam, Mack had picked up on this tick of pausing, rubbing his head, and then asking a question instead of answering one, a sign Mack knew meant to stay alert. "Yes, five stories. That's not counting the penthouse that I added during the renovation."

"And the Trinity Town Towers are thirty-three stories with a footprint of about 33,000 square feet each floor? That's almost seven times the height of this building; a beautiful view I can imagine and a lot of square feet to lease?"

"We can go to the top of T-1 if you want. I'm not trying to compete with the Asian super-structures, but Trinity will be a landmark, a definite statement. My goal is to have T-1 leased out and the casino up and running before we finish construction of T-2 and start on T-3," Mack said.

"This is a big gamble for you?"

"No, I don't think of it that way. I have lease commitments on 70% of T-1 as we speak. I have contracts on the two top floors of all three Towers and a 15-year lease of the casino. True, one million square feet is a lot of rental space compared to my office building here, but compared to the high-rise buildings like the Petronas or the one in Yokohama or Taipei, they are twice the size of the Towers. Besides, when we talk about a million square feet, we're talking about all three buildings, which include the hotel and condominiums, the lobby and atrium, the shopping mall, and the casino. Remove these pre-leased entities, and you come up with a lot less square footage to rent."

"It will be a beautiful development, Mack, and a great location."

"Thank you. It's going to be the *Crown Jewel* of the South. A landmark of distinction planted right in the middle of the mighty Mississippi River . . .

as Anna said, 'A vision that will dazzle your mind and elevate the prominence of our great city.'"

Sam saw Christy walking across the rooftop. "Can we meet and go over some details tomorrow, say around lunch, and then maybe visit the construction site? And Lily, could you check with Dr. Brown about getting some copies of the financial package, including their estimated and actual project cost, a pro forma, and their IFRS, if they have one?" Sam looked over at Mack, who nodded his head, signifying he had one. "We'll FedEx a package to some of our investment partners and see who's interested in a billion dollar project."

Sam thought of a recent Sino-American relations meeting in Tokyo where the guest speaker, a banker from China . . . *what was his name?* Hanchen, that's it, Lu Hanchen. His speech was about advocating the Sino-American ties. He remembered writing down an axiom Hanchen had quoted that he liked, about how both sides should "cherish and protect the fruits of a good situation, as they were not easily achieved." Hanchen had told everyone he had a meeting in Washington, DC, next month with Treasury Secretary Gettlefinger. *I'd better call JB and let him know; maybe he can open a few doors.*

"Did you inform Mack about Herr Mueller's phone call?" Sam said.

Lily stood a little behind Mack and put her index finger to the middle of her lips and shook her head.

Mack turned and looked at Lily, then at Sam. "Is there something wrong at the plant?"

Sam stared at Lily.

"No, nothing is wrong," Lily said, and looked at her father. "We have been busy with more important discussions. I was hoping to go over the changes with Mack later."

"Mr. Sama . . ."

"Excuse me," Sam said. *Saved by the bell.* "Are you ready, Christy?" Christy had been standing behind them.

"Whenever you are, sir," Christy said.

"What is it American children say to their parents? Don't wait up." With a wily smile on his face, Sam took Christy's arm, and they walked to the elevator.

"Well, I guess he wasn't *too* lonely, huh?" Lily said to Mack.

CHAPTER 8

LILY SAMA WAS stretched out on the bed with a sheet pulled over her nude body, basking in her afterglow. The windows were open in Mack's penthouse, and a single candle flickered as a breeze off the river drifted across the room.

"What was that all about with Karl Mueller and the VW plant?" Mack asked, walking to the bed with a bottle of wine.

"Ohhh, do we have to talk business now?" She held out her glass for a refill. "Did you see me motioning to Papa?"

"Duh . . . yeah." Mack filled her glass and sat in the oversized chair at the foot of the bed.

"Okay." She plopped a pillow against the headboard and leaned back, pulling the sheet up around her. "I was saving this for a surprise, and I had asked Papa to let me tell you. But now is as good a time as any." She toasted Mack with her glass and took a large sip of wine.

Mack waited.

"Well, aren't you the least bit curious?" Lily asked.

"I think I started this conversation with 'What's this all about?'"

"You're no fun; you're always so serious. Anyway, Herr Karl Mueller wants you to build him an addition to the new plant. Knock out a couple of walls next to the body welding shop and add 150,000 square feet for a new water-borne paint department."

"Why didn't *he* call me about this?"

"He will; you're not supposed to know about this yet. Please, I told you this in confidence. He came to me for the loan."

"How much?"

"Mack, you've got to promise me. I could get into a lot of trouble with our banking laws, not to mention Karl and my board of directors."

"I promise. I've always protected our relationship."

"Twenty-five million, that's everything, our fees, interest, closing costs, construction, and FF&E," Lily said.

"How much for the FF&E?"

"Around eight million."

"Paint shop—there's very little furniture and few fixtures, mainly overhead lighting. Equipment will be a big cost. So, after the Bank of Japan takes their cut, and the FF&E, that leaves about $15,000,000 for construction?" *A 150,000 sq. ft. addition—figuring the sq. ft. cost of the main plant—maybe 12 million: yeah, I can live with that.*

"Can I see the cost breakdown?" Mack asked.

"You're pushing."

"I'm worth it."

"I'm not so sure about that."

"Oooh, touché. That hurt." Mack grabbed his chest.

"I'm sorry. But as I've heard you say so often, business is business."

"Can we switch gears for a minute? What about my final draw? Did Karl say anything about that? We turned in our final Application for Payment over three months ago, and we are about finished with the punch list," Mack asked.

Lily crawled to the foot of the bed and handed Mack her glass of wine. "Quid pro quo?"

"Whatever your heart desires."

Lily got up with the sheet wrapped around her and, with tiny steps, walked to the open closet where her clothes were hanging. She picked up her briefcase, pulled out an envelope, and walked back to the bed. Sitting cross-legged at the end of the bed, she tapped the envelope on her knee, smiling at Mack.

"There is a check for $1,500,000 in this envelope made out to you and signed by me and Karl. This is the most I have ever paid, directly or indirectly, for a lover," she said. "But in all seriousness, you are the best lover I've ever had." She handed the envelope to Mack.

Mack took the envelope and sailed it across the room as he climbed over the foot of the bed.

"And just how many lovers have you had?" Mack said, looking down on her.

"Just you," she giggled.

"Ahhh, you lie with remarkable ease."

"Okay, you weren't my first, but you did open the door for me. I've had a string of bad lovers, and now you've set the bar so high no one could come close to you."

"Thank you. You never told me that."

"You didn't ask."

"I shouldn't have to."

"True, but you do make a girl, what is your saying . . . a *wee bit* cautious."

"Who was your *first* lover?" Mack asked.

"That would be really stretching it to call him a lover." She plopped a pillow against the headboard and leaned back.

"I was in college . . . Wellesley, an all-girls school. Oh, I forgot, you know that. Well, one Friday I rode into Boston with some classmates, and they stopped at Cambridge and picked up one girl's brother at Harvard. It was freezing cold. He had a bottle of vodka, and by the time we got to Boston, we were all pretty much wasted. I woke up the next morning in a hotel with this kid passed out beside me. I had a terrible hangover and felt embarrassed and ashamed. I snuck out, stepping over bodies sleeping on the floor. I remembered very little. I got a cab and, on the drive back, I thought: 'Well, no longer a virgin.' It was not how I envisioned I would lose my flower. I never saw or heard from the boy again and can't even remember his name." Lily took a large gulp of wine.

"Sounds like a tough experience." Mack moved in beside her and hugged her tightly. They lay together that way for a while, and suddenly Lily pulled away from Mack, the sheet falling and exposing her breast in the candlelight.

"Okay, now it's *your* turn."

Mack propped himself against the headboard, wrapping his arm back around Lily. She rested her head on his chest.

"I will, but first, are you going to help me with the Towers' loan?"

"Oh, that's the way it is, huh?"

"Quid pro quo. No, you know better. Have I ever refused you anything? It's just that every day the interest on those bridge loans are eating at my profit, and the lenders are breathing down my neck."

Lily raised her head and nibbled on his neck. "Don't you worry; I wouldn't let anything happen to that neck of yours. Now tell me who was your *first* and who taught you to be such a good lover?"

"Her name was Ruby. She was a hooker, and I was 16 or 17. The very first thing she taught me about being with a woman was to go slow with everything. She would say over and over, 'When making love to a woman it should be in slow motion. No matter what the woman says or does, *you* stay in *slow motion*.' She said to think of the fable 'The Tortoise and the Hare.'"

"A hooker, really, and she used the word '*fable*?'"

"Yes, she was a hooker; who better for a teacher? No, she didn't use the word fable. Does it matter? Do you want to hear the story or not?"

"Okay, I'm sorry. Go on, please. I promise I'll be quiet . . . this is too good."

"The second thing she taught me was to start between the ears; you must make love to her mind first, not her body." Mack reached down and tapped Lily playfully on the head with his knuckles and then lifted her head up to his and said in a deep, exaggerated voice, "This is the golden key to unlocking the treasure chest of the psyche." He bulged his eyes, "A crucial step in releasing the full power of the five senses." Still holding her head, he leaned over and kissed her mouth.

Lily moved down from Mack's chest and rolled over, sprawling face down on the mattress with her head resting on her crossed arms.

"Do you want me to stop?" Mack asked

"Nooo, please don't. I love this. Tell me more." She wiggled, nestling into the down pillow top.

Mack stretched out beside her, resting on his elbow, and whispered, "One of the senses is touch." Mack moved her dark hair away from the curve of her neck, brushed his lips across the top of her shoulders, and then up the back of her neck and ear. His fingertips outlined the contours of her body.

"Another is the sense of taste." Mack rolled over and let his tongue and lips explore, traveling down the middle of Lily's back and glazing over the dark fuzz of hair in the hollow of her spine, breathing hot with excitement. He rolled her over and rested his head on her belly.

Lily reached down and ran her fingers through his hair, moaning, trying to pull him up.

"Not yet. Remember, slow motion," he whispered, and moved up covering her complete body with his—both hearts pounding against each other. "Miss Ruby also said that women loved to be talked to and told how beautiful they are. But if you are not a talker, then make an effort to commit to memory something beautiful, a poem or verse. Would you like to hear some words I borrowed from Walter Benton?"

"Yes . . . no! I want you now!"

Mack resisted, holding fast and whispering: "If I was Pygmalion or God I would make you exactly as you are . . . in all dimensions. I would change nothing, add or take away. The same full red flower would model for your mouth . . ." Mack covered Lily's mouth with a light kiss and moved his lips to her ear, "and from the same seashore would I bring the small translucent earshapes of your ears. O the lovely throat that I could duplicate! The tender arms!" With his tongue, he moved from Lily's ear down her neck, arm, and the inside of her elbow.

"I would shape your breast the shape of the hungry little faces they are now . . . and tip them with the same quick mouths." Skillfully, he caressed one of her breasts in his mouth, then the other. "I could not make your eyes deeper than they are . . . nor softer to look into . . . nor could I turn your hips, your thighs, your belly in a sweeter curve: nor indent the hollows of your loins more tenderly—or store more honey there or fire."

Lily mumbled inaudible words as Mack, like an artist, painted her with his lips and tongue.

"Maaack, *now!* Meu *Deus!*"

CHAPTER 9

WITH THE SHIFT to daylight saving time, it was in an early morning low light that Mack eased the penthouse door shut and stepped out onto the rooftop of Shamrock International. He wore lime green stick-on reflective tape on his shorts, t-shirt, and running shoes, walked to the elevator. For some reason Memphis drivers—all at the same time—seemed to be trying out for one of the NASCAR series; not a safe place to run.

Inside, as the elevator descended, he propped the heel of his shoe on the handrail and tried to touch his nose to his knee; that would be the extent of his stretching.

Outside the gates, Mack jogged north on Riverside Drive. A warm breeze from the southwest pushed at his back as he coasted downhill in long strides before cutting through Tom Lee Park to the jogging trail. It was still a little dark along the river's edge, and he kept a watchful eye where the river had washed out large bites of the bluff. One wrong step and you could pop up in New Orleans a week later. He checked his time at the first mile marker, a slow nine minutes, then cut back up onto Riverside Drive, avoiding the cobblestones. Running cleared the cobwebs and allowed Mack to focus on his immediate problems of operating a business. He learned a long time ago that a large part of his job was putting out small fires before they became major conflagrations. But sometimes it was hard to stay focused on problem-solving while running, especially along this part of the river where the boats and barges were anchored—childhood memories kept flooding his mind.

He turned right and charged up the hill on Adams Avenue, past City Hall, and turned left on Front Street. He was really sweating now. Overhead was the Tram that crossed over Wolf River to Mud Island Park: *Congratulations, Memphis leaders. Is that the best name you could come up with . . . some tourist thought it was a park for racing Monster Trucks?*

On Mack's right was the Cannon Center, another construction project wrought with multi-million dollar over-runs. He continued his run north, passing the abandoned Pyramid Arena, a $100 million dollar fiasco paid for by the taxpayers of Shelby County and the City of Memphis. He turned west at the Auction Bridge that crossed over the Wolf River into Harbor Town. The sun was now up and hot on the back of his legs. He slowed at the top of the bridge and studied the Pyramid. A great idea, but what a boondoggle: How many failures does it take for a government to learn to stay out of private business? How long has it been sitting there empty, ten years now? The media word is that they leased it to some non-denominational megachurch for 20 years.

Trinity Town would be different, a successful development, privately funded, totally independent of government control, that would lure businesses from all over the world. The key to success wasn't that complicated: presale and prelease every square foot while under construction. When he finished this project, there would only be a few places that could come close to his creation, maybe Brasilia, the utopian city by Niemeyer—*yeah! Well . . . a wee bit smaller than Brasilia.*

He turned north on Island Road, his breathing even and relaxed now, and could hear the heavy equipment: the big scrapers, power shovels and draglines, bulldozers and loaders filling dump trucks as they cleared and moved thousands of yards of dirt and material on the Trinity Town construction site. This was the favorite part of his run, alongside the Mississippi River, not above it but almost on the same level and less than 1,500 feet across to King's Island. He could see Tower One soaring 33 stories above the treetops. At the end of Island Road, the construction was almost finished with the four-lane highway connecting the cloverleaf interchange to the new Superhighway I-69 and I-40. The park-like median strip of the east-and- west divided highway connected the "BTN" (Bridge to Nowhere) that spanned the river and ended into a double-tiered round-about in Trinity Town.

Mack was a little over halfway on his run when he reached the highway and turned east on the old Mud Island Road, over to 2nd Street, and headed back to Shamrock. This stretch along north 2nd Street spawned many childhood memories: there was Pear, and then Plum Ave, and up ahead was where 7th Street dead-ended into 2nd Street, with the old Waterworks building on his right, and across the street his favorite playground as a kid, the Anderson-Tully yard.

He remembered how every Saturday all the 7th street neighborhood kids would choose sides—good guys against the bad guys—and the bad guys had a five minute lead to ride their bikes, with their Red Ryder BB guns across the handle bars, to the "log yard" at Anderson-Tully to hide. Not every boy had a bike, so your buddy rode on the handlebars, carrying the guns, or sat on the cross bar. Most bikes were built from the junkyard and had no fenders or brakes.

A crane had placed the huge hardwood logs on top of each other—helter skelter—sometimes reaching three to four stories high, with crawl spaces inside, creating long tunnels that were vertical and horizontal. When you were shot, you had to shout, "*I'm shot,*" then sit under the big walnut tree until the game was over and choose sides all over again. We all wore thick coats or cardboard in our shirts.

Mack felt the small scar at his temple where Norman Wilson, waiting behind a telephone pole for revenge, shot him close-up, knocking him to the ground. Mack's best friend was Norman's older brother, Ed. Earlier that morning, Mack had snuck up through one of the tunnels behind Norman as he sat on the end of a log. Not wanting to shoot his best friend's brother at that close range, he worked the barrel of his BB gun through a small hole and touched Norman in the back and shouted, "You're dead."

Norman, always a little jumpy, screamed, "Shit!" Recovering quickly, he yelled, "No I'm not, you didn't shoot me." Norman's foot slipped as he tried to get away and fell forward across a log, his ass in mid-air as Mack pulled the trigger, shooting him mistakenly in the balls. Norman cried and hollered he was bleeding and that his balls were shot off. Everyone declared time-out, came running, and picked him up and carried him down from the log-pile to the yard. Norman rolled from side to side, holding his crotch, moaning, "Oh my balls. Ooooh my balls, they're bleeding." His brother Ed was there, and an older boy named Buster helped Ed unbuckle Norman's pants and pull them down. Norman's younger brother, Ervin, came running up and looked down at his brother, "He ain't bleeding. He pissed his pants." They all roared, laughing. Norman stood up, and pulled down his wet jockey shorts, and looked at his balls. One was bright red and swollen to the size of an orange. Norman started crying again and said, "Look at that," pointing at his balls. Ed slapped him on the back of his head, "Ahh shut up. Quit pissing and moaning. Act like you got some *real* balls."

"Yeahhh, all he needs now is a pecker to match that big ball," his little brother Ervin said.

"Come on, let's get back to the game," Ed said. They all headed back to the log-pile, laughing, as Norman stood in the middle of the yard, his head bent almost to the ground, inspecting his balls.

Mack chuckled at himself—*those were good days.* They were all gone now. This end of Second Street was deserted, full of potholes and over-grown grass—buildings closed and all boarded up. He turned into Anderson-Tully and jogged around the yard. Not one log in the yard and no sawmill, just a faded rough-sawn cypress building. He'd forgotten they had moved the sawmill operation down to their Vicksburg location years ago. A 117-year-old company bit the dust . . . well, that's not true. He remembered reading they had sold the company for around a half-billion dollars, so biting the dust wouldn't be correct.

He jogged back out to 2nd Street and picked up speed as he headed south. He turned right on Washington, then up the steps to City Hall, and back south on Main Street, which was only for pedestrians and the trolleys. Running between the trolley tracks reminded him of when he and his buddies used to chase the trolleys and hopped a ride on the back for a couple of blocks until some adult hollered at them to get off.

Mack wiped the sweat from his forehead with his sleeve and checked his time again; he was right on pace for his eight-mile run. This would give him plenty of time to shower and dress for his seven o'clock meeting this morning. He turned on Beale Street and coasted downhill to Riverside, then picked up his speed, charging the last hill on Riverside Drive and feeling the muscle of his heart pumping, faster and faster. Endorphins flooded his blood stream as he opened up full speed. He turned into the driveway leading to Shamrock and slowed to a jog as he stopped the timer on his watch—a little under an hour. He walked now, taking deep breaths, as his mind drifted back to Lily and their time together last night: her smell, her clean smooth body and sweet taste. His heartbeat was back to normal, and suddenly he noticed he was getting an erection as he approached the guard standing outside the gate. He shoved his hand in the pocket of his running shorts and hurried through the gate, smiling and waving to the guard with his free hand. Once inside the building he reflected on why he loved running so much and remembered the article he had read recently in a runner's magazine: "Endorphins . . . not only regulate pain and hunger, but are also involved in the release of sex hormones." *What more could you ask for?* Mack thought: *Run, run, run as fast as you can; you can't catch me. I'm the Gingerbread Ma*n.

*

It was early in the morning when Isaac and Anna stood in Mack's outer office, drinking coffee and talking to Maureen O'Brien, Mack's Personal Administrator. Her corporate title was Secretary/Treasurer, and she wheeled all the power she needed. With Isaac and Anna, she had just become the fourth member of Shamrock's Golden Parachute Club. Maureen, once a nun and administrator over religious matters of the Catholic Archdiocese of Dublin, was involved in a scandal with the married Chairman of the School of Religions and Theology at Trinity College. She abdicated her position with the archdiocese and her vows of poverty, chastity, and obedience. Her brother, Carroll Thomas O'Brien, Bishop of the Catholic Diocese of Memphis, suggested she interviewed for the position at Shamrock International. When asked, the Diocese referred to Sister Maureen, esoterically, as a "fallen angel."

Mack entered his office with a steaming cup of coffee and waved everyone in as he pointed his cup to the ship galley. "Fresh pot if anyone wants a refill. God, I feel great this morning."

No one else exuded any enthusiasm about this 7 a.m. meeting. This was not something unusual for Mack; he preached and practiced the old axioms of Ben Franklin: "The early bird catches the worm."

They all sat down at the round conference table, and Mack looked over at Isaac. "Has everyone been notified of your 9 o'clock meeting this morning?"

"I haven't had time this morning to check but will as soon as we are through here. Sally has a list, and I think she faxed a copy to Maureen," Isaac said.

Maureen placed the faxed copy in front of Mack.

"If Maureen will make a copy for each of us, let's make sure we didn't forget anyone."

"I have extra copies." Maureen handed copies to everyone. Looking at Isaac, Maureen said, "Earlier this morning Sally said she would be down with the list of all who had been notified."

Mack smiled. "If you see someone whom we left off the list then give them a call as soon as we finish here." Mack looked at his watch, "We should be out of here no later than eight. Isaac, do you need me at your meeting?"

"I don't think so. I gave Maureen a list of topics for discussion, and I know some of the department heads will have their own lists as well."

Maureen placed the list in front of Mack. He noticed all the division heads of Global Construction were listed in alphabetical order, with the department head's name, telephone number, and email address to the side. On the next line was a list of topics. He perused the list, stopping and spot-checking some of the divisions: Architectural & Engineering, Chief Estimator, Concrete, Mechanical, and Electrical.

Mack looked up from the list, and Anna asked, "Do you want outsiders, maybe legal, or just our people?"

Isaac spoke up, "I called and left two messages at Charlie Bickford's office and on his cell phone. I finally called him at home last night, and his wife told me he was out of the country for two weeks. She told me his son, Junior, has taken over most of Charlie's caseloads. We may need to start looking for another firm. I can't get anyone to return my calls."

"Okay. Maureen, call their office this morning and tell them to have someone here for the nine o'clock meeting or we will retain another law firm," Mack said. "Any other questions about Isaac's meeting before we move on?"

"What about financing? Any of the bankers or investors?" Anna asked.

"That's one of the items on my list, but no, we won't need them for this meeting. We'll have a separate meeting to deal with that. Maureen, on second thought, don't call Bickford's office . . . get a list together for Isaac and me of other law firms. This may be a good time to change firms."

Mack got up, walked to the bar, and filled his coffee cup. "Anna, did Sam mention anything yesterday about the VW plant?" Mack was careful to say *yesterday* and not *last night.*

Regardless, Anna paused too long, looked embarrassed, and answered a little too defensively, "Why, is something wrong?"

Mack walked over, filled her cup with coffee, and said, "Did he mention anything?"

"Oh, I'm sorry. No, he didn't mention the plant."

"Well, I have good news," Mack said as he set the coffee pot back on the bar. "Karl Mueller wants us to build an addition to the new welding shop; a water-borne paint department, about 150,000 square feet."

"I haven't heard a word about this," Isaac said.

"It's strictly confidential, and let's keep it that way, okay? Mueller's supposed to call you or me today, so act surprised."

"I am surprised," Isaac smiled.

"What about our last draw? I haven't heard a thing," Anna asked.

Maureen handed an envelope to Anna. "A million and a half dollars, including the change orders and retainage."

Mack added, "We're not finished, but we billed them the total amount, and they paid it."

"We must have some inside pull?" Isaac said.

"We did a very good job down there; everything ran smoothly without any major problems," Mack said. "Maureen, work me up a thank you letter for all the people involved. Isaac, we made good money on that job, so how about a nice bonus for our key people, especially Sonny Newman. Speaking of Sonny, I want to bring him back to Memphis and put him in charge of the Towers."

"You know he has no experience with high-rises."

"Hell, who does?" Mack said. "Sonny took a copy of the plans of T-1 when he was here last and should be familiar with the job by now; he'll do fine with one of us there every day."

"Who do you want to run the job down there for the new addition?" Isaac asked.

"What about the superintendent, the Brazilian fellow, Roberto. Couldn't he handle it?"

"Maybe, let me talk to him. A lot will depend on how much we sub out."

Subs were always a consideration with Mack. *Sure, more money in your pockets if we do the work ourselves, but more liability too.*

With Trinity Town he subbed as much as he could, focusing on making his money in the management of the construction and the real estate. Hell, he owned the island. But the island would be tied up as collateral on the loan for a long time. There are always a couple of points from the financing, the selling, leasing, concessions—you have to work the deals.

There was a knock at the door, and, before Maureen could move, the door opened and Sally Martin, Isaac's secretary, stepped into the room with a smile on her face.

"Good morning, you all, sorry I'm late, but Maureen can fill me in." She handed Isaac some papers and then walked to Maureen and whispered something to her. Sally was always dressed in a dark suit with lots of white lace, bright scarves, and gold jewelry. She was in her early sixties, but personality and looks placed her at a young 50.

Maureen leaned over to Mack and whispered, "A delivery man is in the outer office with a large package with instructions to deliver to you only."

Mack looked at Sally, "Who's it from?"

"No name, just *Fresh Market* printed on the package, and a small envelope attached."

"Well, tell him to bring it in."

Sally opened the door and motioned the man in. He rolled the tilted dolly into Mack's office and deposited it where Maureen was pointing. The package was cylindrical, wrapped in brown butcher paper, about five feet tall. Maureen held out her hand for the receipt to be signed.

"Are you Mr. Shannon?" the man asked Maureen with a grin on his face. Maureen didn't smile but stared at the man with her hand still in the air. He handed her the receipt. She signed it, looked at him and then the door.

"Would you like me to unwrap the package?" he asked.

Sally hurried over to the man and led him to the office door, dragging his dolly.

"Do you want me to unwrap it now?" Maureen asked.

"Why not? I'm sure all of you are as curious as I am."

Maureen removed an envelope marked personal and laid it down in front of Mack. She then walked in a circle, peeling the paper until branches ballooned out, forming a canopy over the container, like an opening umbrella. Each limb was loaded with fruit, some yellow and some green, each the size of a Ping-Pong ball. There was a tag with wire twisted around the trunk, inside a red clay pot. Maureen gave the tag to Mack—he read the tag somewhat puzzled.

THIS IS AN AUTHENTIC, FIVE-YEAR-OLD, KEY LIME TREE THAT HAS BEEN DWARFED WITH TLC. HAND GROWN, GRAFTED, AND WATERED IN THE SOIL ON THE TROPICAL ISLAND OF KEY WEST, FLORIDA. THEY MAKE EXCELLENT CONTAINER PLANTS FOR THE PATIO OR INDOORS, AND THEY ARE NOT ONLY DECORATIVE BUT ALSO GREAT FOR COOKING, BAKING, AND MIXED DRINKS. PICK WHEN DARK GREEN FOR A STRONGER TASTE AND GOLDEN YELLOW FOR A MILDER TASTE.
(Shipped from the Conch Republic)

Mack walked back over to the table and stood looking down at the envelope. He removed a lavender card from the inside and immediately the scent of Lily was all around him. He read the slanted script of Lily's writing:

"For 'twas not into my ear you whispered but into my heart.
'Twas not my lips you kissed, but my soul."
God bless MISS RUBY!

Mack picked up the lavender card and moved it across his nose, inhaling, smiled, and looked up. Everyone in the room was smiling with him.

CHAPTER 10

MCKENZIE HEARD THE hum of her cell phone vibrating. She pulled out the center drawer of her desk, and looked down at the display window of her phone and read, "United States Government."

"Excuse me," she said to the two lawyers seated across from her desk and opened the phone, "Hello."

"O'Connor, are you alone?"

"No sir, but I could be in a minute."

"Call me back immediately on my private line." The phone went dead.

McKenzie pressed a button on her desk phone, and a red light flashed on the phone of Abby's desk. McKenzie stood up as Abby walked into her chambers.

"I'm sorry, gentlemen, I have to take this call. Could you please wait in the outer office? Thank you."

Abby shut the door behind the two attorneys and raised her eyebrows at McKenzie. "What's up?"

"Senator Parnell just called and wants me to call him back, *immediately.*"

"Something wrong?"

"He didn't say."

"Do you want me to leave?"

"No, stay, I might need you." McKenzie dialed the private number of James Burton Parnell, Senate Majority Leader from Tennessee.

"Good morning, JB. Why so solemn? You don't love me anymore?"

There was dead silence on the other end.

"JB! Has something happened? Is anything wrong . . . Margo? The kids?"

"No."

"You scared me. What is it then?"

"You're on your cell phone?"

"Yes." A long pause, "You always make me *work* to get anything out of you. Is it something I've done?"

"Yes."

"Okay. Business or personal?"

No answer.

"Business?"

"Yes."

"Ah ha, I'm closing in. Well, let's see, I assume it's in *my* courtroom, sooo . . . I haven't ruled on anything lately that the higher courts would be interested in . . . must be something I'm working on now, right?"

"Yes."

"You taught me well, JB. Have I screwed up?"

"Almost."

"Okay. Let's see, there's the FedEx case, and then International Paper, but we just settled that one. I know, the Congressman's divorce—domestic is always big trouble. What an ass he is. Oops, he's a friend of yours, right? Is this the case?

"No."

"Aw, come on JB, give me a hint."

"Shamrock."

"Shamrock?" She picked up a legal pad, waved it at Abby, and mouthed the word *Shamrock*. "I don't think I have a case styled *Shamrock*." Abby nodded her head as she hurried through a stack of folders.

"Hold on just a minute, JB, let me look through these folders on my desk." Abby found the folder marked Arthur's vs. Shamrock, et al, opened it, and placed it in front of McKenzie. She remembered the case now— Arthur's Restaurant and the bulldozer. She didn't like the smell of this at all.

"Is it the plaintiff, the defendant, or the lawyers?" McKenzie asked.

"Shannon."

"Mack Shannon, the drunk Irishman? You got to be kidding me? He has this much clout to get you to call me? Damn JB, I was there that night at Arthur's Restaurant. This . . . this drunk construction worker drove this huge piece of equipment, a bulldozer or something, across the parking lot and scared the hell out of me and everyone else in the restaurant. He broke all kinds of laws: public drunkenness, reckless endangerment, assault, and in all probability, extortion."

"Get it dismissed," Parnell said.

"I will not!" McKenzie fired back.

"*What* did you say?"

McKenzie's mouth was frozen shut. *Oh my God, what have I done? Don't let that mouth of yours overload your brain. THINK! Get out of this quick.*

Abby waved and mimicked to McKenzie to cover the phone with her hand.

"Hello, hold one minute, please." McKenzie held her hand over the phone.

What did Goldman tell you . . . "Be careful with this Shannon fellow. My client is scared to death of him, said that Shannon was the power broker. I'm talking big power, and when needed, they say he's not shy about using it."

Abby put her lips against McKenzie's ear and whispered, "Tell him you were talking to Randolph, who's all in a twit waiting for you to go to lunch."

"JB? You still there? I'm sorry someone came into my office."

"*Who?*" Parnell said.

"Randolph. I'm late for lunch, and he was trying to be bossy and told me to get off that phone. I told him, 'I will not.' Sorry about that. Where were we now?"

There was a long pause as McKenzie held her breath.

"Is Randolph still in your office?"

"No, he's in Abby's office. He just stuck his head in the door to give me a hard time. He doesn't know who I'm talking to."

In a measured voice, Parnell said, "We were talking about Shannon—Mack Shannon, a very *close* friend of mine—and I asked you to take care of this . . . misunderstanding. Is that going to be a problem?"

"Of course not, JB. Consider it done. I'll see you at the judicial conference?"

"I will call you when I get in town."

"Goodbye, JB, and tell Margo hello for me."

The line went dead.

"He hung up on me."

"Was he mad?"

"I don't know, but thanks for the rescue."

"What made you say . . ."

"I DON'T KNOW! Stupidity I guess. My big Irish mouth; I can't stand it when someone *orders* me to do something."

"Well, with this one, you're going to have to, without questions."

"You got that right. But how does this Shannon get off having JB call me?"

"What did JB say about Shannon?"

"'A very *close* friend of mine' is what he said. I mean, he drives a bulldozer, how can he have that kind of pull? I wonder if he's doing this as a favor for someone else?"

"Who cares? Let it go Sweetie; don't get involved personally. You've got your marching orders, and all we got to do is what you told JB . . . consider-it-done."

McKenzie thought about the Petition for Contempt of Court Goldman had filed when Shannon refused to show up for his deposition. She didn't even think about what Goldman had previously told her. Then—on top of that—she signed an Order for Attachment Pro Corpus. The Sheriff went out a couple of times to pick up Shannon and was told he was not there. This really made her mad so she had S. Charles Bickford brought before her, and he stated he was told that Mack Shannon was out of town and they didn't know when he would be back. He said he sent a letter to Mr. Goldman stating that fact. Of course Sidney failed to mention that fact when asking for the Order.

"You ready for me to call the two lawyers back in?" Abby asked.

"No, but go ahead." Abby headed for the door.

"Hold it. They can wait; I'm doing them the favor. Sit down." McKenzie stared at the opened folder.

Abby didn't sit down. She had been with McKenzie now for six years, and they knew each other like sisters. She had both her hands on McKenzie's desk and leaned over, "What's wrong? Honey, you've got to turn it loose; let this case go."

"Goldman told me to be extremely careful with this Mack Shannon, but I didn't listen. He told me that Shannon was a power broker, big power . . . and he rides around on a bulldozer?"

"See, more the reason to let it go. I know you. You're just like Shannon on that bulldozer: straight ahead, full charge, don't back down. Sometimes—now listen to me—sometimes we have to walk around trouble, and this is one of those times. We don't want any questions to come up when it's time for you to be appointed, okay . . . okay?"

"Okay, but how do I get it dismissed?"

Abby picked up a legal pad and sat down in a chair across from McKenzie. "Let's break this down. I'll write and you talk." McKenzie just stared.

Abby continued. "We know, for example, and Shannon knows that he is guilty of something. Money-wise, how guilty is he? We need a figure for Shannon, so you can assess a fine. If he's as strong as everyone says, that shouldn't be a problem. Next, will he agree . . .?"

"Wait! It can be a settlement agreement." McKenzie scanned the documents in the folder. "What damages does Arthur have? He wasn't injured physically, and Shannon didn't destroy any property. Well, he did break the dog's leg."

"Didn't the dog bite Shannon?"

"Yeah."

"Okay, even-Steven. There's justifiable homicide, is there a justifiable . . . what, assault?"

"Okay, counselor. Goldman told me that Arthur was scared to death of Shannon; let's play with that. You getting all this down?"

Without looking up and still writing, Abby said, "Just keep talking, we're getting there."

"Okay, if Arthur is afraid of Shannon, then Shannon needs to huff and puff on Arthur. How? A threat—Arthur knows that Shannon means business and doesn't make idle threats. Shannon's lawyer, what's his name, Sir Charles, stated Arthur is guilty of trying to rip off Global Construction—what was the amount—around a quarter of a million? Okay, this is good.

This is going to work out perfect." McKenzie stood up from her desk and started pacing the room.

"Shannon needs to file a counter-claim for breach of contract, a set-off. I'm sure there are two or three articles in Global's construction contract that Shannon's attorney can hang his hat on."

"Keep talking," Abby said.

"Now, the problem is, ethically, I can't broker this settlement. What we need is a mediator."

"How about a Special Master?"

"Yes, that would work, but who?"

"Well, can we figure Shannon is Catholic?"

"Most likely; with that name, he's got to be Irish. I mean, for God's sake, the Shannon River runs right through Ireland, doesn't it? But what's that got to do with a Special Master?"

"I was thinking of Father O'Brien. You've used him before."

"Oh my God . . . that's it! Arthur goes to my church. I saw him taking communion one Sunday; he's Catholic. This is perfect." McKenzie hurried over to Abby's chair and gave her a big hug and a kiss on the cheek. "You're so smart."

"Do you think he will do this?"

"He will for me. I might have to buy him a case of Macallan. I'll have him hold the hearing at St. Mary's; give it a little more virtuous and commanding presence than in someone's conference room. Get him on the phone for me, and let's put this baby to bed."

"What about the attorneys outside?"

"Oh shoot! See if you can get the Bishop on the phone and have them come on in."

McKenzie stood up and looked at her watch as the two attorneys walked into her chambers. "Gentlemen, it's 11:20; I'm sorry, but something has come up, and I'm going to need till about noon to finish. I'm not going to lunch, and you're welcome to continue waiting or do you want to reschedule?"

Both lawyers agreed they would come back at noon. As the two attorneys walked out, Abby stuck her head in and said, "Bishop O'Brien is on the phone. I'm going to lunch. Do you want me to bring you back something?"

McKenzie shook her head and picked up the phone. "Good morning, Your Excellency, thank you for taking my call."

"Cut the blarney, O'Connor, I know you want something. It's the only time you call me," O'Brien said.

"I called you last week and invited you to lunch?"

"Yes you did—at 1:45."

"Okay, I'm sorry, you know me too well. I do need a big favor, Uncle Tommy."

"What favor could an old Catholic priest possibly do for a young, brilliant federal judge?"

"Now, who's dishing out the blarney? You know you're not an old man, and I'm not a federal judge—yet."

"You'll get my vote."

"Thank you, but you know it's by appointment and not by election."

"I assume everything on the Democratic side is wrapped up . . . both our senators working hard, especially our Majority Leader?"

"Yes, I hope so. JB just called, and that's why I'm calling you. I have a sensitive situation that's going to require someone with your diplomacy and negotiating skills, yet a heavy hand if needed."

"I'm listening," O'Brien said.

"First, this is strictly confidential . . . I'm sorry, Uncle Tommy, I know I don't have to tell you it's confidential; it's just a habit with me. Anyway, this case came into my court involving Arthur Constantine—Arthur's Restaurant—you do know him, right? He's a member of St. Mary's?"

"I know Arthur."

"Well, he's the Plaintiff and owes a considerable amount of money to this construction company—the Defendant in the case—that built his restaurant. Arthur couldn't or wouldn't pay the construction company when they finished, so they worked out an agreement for Arthur to pay off the debt in monthly payments. Well, after a couple of payments, Arthur defaults on the note and hasn't paid anything in over a year. I guess the construction company got fed up with him, and they sent out this guy with a bulldozer—on a Saturday night when the restaurant was full—to destroy the building. I just happened to be there that night and saw the whole thing."

"Where do I come in?"

"I need a mediator. But I want you to have more power—just in case they won't settle—that way they can't just walk away. If you would accept a Special Master appointment, as you did for me before, then they would know that whatever you wrote in your report would be—more or less—final."

"Ah, then you make me the villain?"

"No, no. It would never go that far. You are to settle it; hence, the heavy hand. And, the court will order the Plaintiff and the Defendant to pay the Special Master's fee . . . let's say $400 an hour for your time and services. That could be a nice donation to St. Jerome's Orphanage, right? Plus, you would be doing God's work at the same time by *counseling* two of your flock; it's a win-win situation."

"You've thought of every . . ."

"*Wait!* I'm not finished. Drum rolls please . . . the coup de grâce. How about if I personally throw in—to sweeten the kitty—a case of your choice of the best single malt? What do you say?"

"Ah, the devil is in you girl."

"Naw, I have a selfish reason; I get to help you drink it."

"Now that's the best offer I've had in years. But what's JB's interest in this?"

"I almost forgot. JB's a friend of the Defendants, Global Construction and Shamrock. He told me, no, ordered me to get it *dismissed*. Uncle Tommy, I can't just dismiss it. I could get in big trouble. But if I could get you to settle it . . ."

"Shamrock, did you say?"

"Yes. I issued an arrest warrant for a Mack Shannon. My deputy told me there was no Mack Shannon at this Shamrock location, and they wouldn't let the deputies through their gates; they almost had a riot. Then I get this call from JB, and he tells me this Shannon is, and I quote, 'a very close friend of mine.' That's the drunken construction worker who was driving that big yellow bulldozer. Fortunately, there were no damages, Arthur gave him a cashier's check, and he drove the bulldozer back onto the trailer and left."

"Did you say you issued an arrest warrant for Mack Shannon?"

"Yes."

"Are you telling me you've never met Mack Shannon; you don't know who he is?"

"Holy Mother! Please! Please don't tell me he's a friend of yours too?"

"Listen to me, McKenzie, you are in way over your . . . wait a minute. Hold on, I'll be right back." O'Brien walked across his office, picked up an open envelope, and pulled out the card inside. He stood thinking, tapping the card against his opened hand. Finally he walked back to his desk and picked up the phone.

"I need a favor."

"You name it."

"This coming Sunday the Beethoven Club is celebrating their 125-year Anniversary, and I don't want to go by myself with all those women. Do you know where the Beethoven Club is?"

"In Midtown, isn't it?"

"Yes. Can you pick me up, say around 4:00 p.m.? The celebrating starts at 4:30."

"Wait a minute, what about this Mack Shannon problem?"

"What did you tell JB?"

"I told him to consider it done."

"I rest my case, Your Honor."

McKenzie sat with the phone to her ear, listening to a dial tone. *He hung up on me . . . this is becoming a habit.*

CHAPTER 11

BISHOP THOMAS O'BRIEN sat on a redwood bench in his enclosed flower garden, waiting for McKenzie to pick him up. The day was beautiful. The temperature was in the mid-seventies, sunny with no humidity and a light breeze—a perfect day outdoors for the celebration of the Beethoven Club's birthday. The sun's rays streaked through the drooping limbs of the oak trees that towered over the brick walls. The azaleas were no longer in bloom, but the red crepe myrtles bloomed all over the garden, and the Italian jardinières were full of blooming red and yellow hibiscus. O'Brien watched a hummingbird flit from one red flower to another. He had brought a book to read but was feeling somewhat reflective today. He often sat here in his garden, breathing in the tranquility until one of many occurrences would develop. Answers would come to some of his problems or he'd have a conversation with God or his right brain would take over, and no telling where he would go. He enjoyed this meditation or daydreaming or whatever you wanted to call it. Today, he revisited an old question he hadn't thought about in years; what would it have been like if he were married and had kids?

In the early stages of his priesthood, it never crossed his mind; he was always busy and never questioned or doubted his vows. But now he felt as if he were out to pasture. He felt old and lonely at times. It would be nice to have a companion, someone to share his intimate thoughts with, a touch, or a smell of perfume. *Why should I feel guilty? As the women in his confessionary used to say about their husbands, "A wee bit of affection, Father, is that asking too much?"* His answer was always the same—"No, my dear, it is not. It is a minimum of what you would give your dog. I will have a talk with him."

He wasn't complaining . . . or maybe he was, but he was also thankful. He was in good health for his age. He wasn't taking any medicine except a baby aspirin each day. No cancer, no bypasses, and no hip or knee replacements. Sure he was stiff, his knees popped, his hips ached when he stood up, his hair was falling out, he had to get new glasses every year, and he couldn't piss a straight stream if his life depended on it. He was better off than most after 40 years as a cleric. It was too late now; he would soon be Bishop Emeritus. Regardless, he had made a contract. God had lived up to His end, and O'Brien was going to live up to his.

He heard the door from the house open and watched his housekeeper shuffle toward him. McKenzie followed, darting left and right, trying to move around her without success.

"Dispenseme, Padre," Maria said.

McKenzie, with one long step slipped around Maria, and, as O'Brien stood she kissed him on the cheek, "Your garden is just lovely."

"Thank you. Maria's husband is responsible for all this. You should see the raspberries and blueberries I got this year, big as your thumb."

Maria stared at McKenzie as if she had just committed a mortal sin by kissing the Bishop anywhere other than his hand.

"Gracias Maria," O'Brien said. They watched as Maria, with small steps, ambled back to the house, stopped, and stared back at them before going inside.

"I don't think she likes me," McKenzie said.

"No, it's not you; it's me. She is very protective, and I don't know what I would do without her. She keeps the house immaculate and sews, irons, and makes the best home-made tamales. Look at my stomach." He laughed as he took her arm and said, "Are we ready to go?"

"I hope I look alright. I didn't know what to wear."

"You look beautiful, as usual. You could wear a croaker sack and look great."

"A croaker sack," McKenzie shook her head and laughed as they walked out of the garden gate to her car.

"Ah, the red Porsche."

"It goes perfectly with your sporty outfit today," McKenzie said. O'Brien was dressed in khaki pants, white oxford shirt, a blue blazer, and loafers.

"Oh, don't say anything. Maria stayed up last night pressing my cassock and fascia and is mad at me because I'm not wearing any of my vestments, except my pectoral cross."

"Do you mind the top being down? It's such a beautiful day."

"Not at all, it's easier for me to get these old legs in and out. By the way, I forgot to tell you there has been a little change in the plans. It appears the invitation list for the celebration has outgrown the garden at the Beethoven Club, so they moved it to the home of one of their members."

"Okay with me. How do I get there?" She pulled her hair back and stuck it in her tam.

"It's not too far. Just go Belvedere to north Parkway, and then take a right on a little divided road called Humming Bird Lane across from Overton Park."

McKenzie almost missed her turn off North Parkway. Magnolia trees on each side of the street marker blocked her view. Humming Bird Lane was like its namesake, small, with hardly room for a car to pass. There were no sidewalks, red bricks paved the street and antique lampposts lined both sides of the lane. An entrance sign read, "No Thru Traffic—Speed Limit 15 MPH." All the houses were on large lots, 3 to 5 acres, with a setback from the road of about the length of a football field. They were of mixed architectural styles, mostly Colonial and Tudor Revival with a few Georgian and Italian Renaissance.

"Nice homes. I didn't know this little nook existed," McKenzie said.

"I think it was planned that way. It has seen a revival in the last five years. Everyone was moving out east for a while, and then the tide changed. Now this area, East Mid-Town I call it, is a hot location. Some are paying a half-a-million and tearing down the house and rebuilding; there's been a waiting list in here for years."

"Don't let me pass the house. Am I getting close?"

"We need to go to the end of this road . . . Watch it!" O'Brien shouted.

McKenzie, coming around a slight curve way too fast, slammed on her brakes and wheeled to the left, just missing a stopped car in front of her and a tree in the median strip. In front, as far as she could see, cars were bumper to bumper.

"That was close," O'Brien said. "Looks like they're backed up at the gate. Let's don't wait; go around the cars—but please drive slowly—we'll go in at the delivery gate."

Dropping down into first gear, McKenzie eased past the line of cars. Some blew their horns, but McKenzie stared straight ahead, waving as she passed.

"Just before you get to the main gate up here, there is a drive off to the left. Turn there," O'Brien said.

McKenzie saw the ornamental iron gates up ahead next to a gatehouse. A tall brick serpentine wall ran off each gate column, disappearing into a thick jungle of trees and shrubs. She turned left down the drive, failing to notice the large green emblem of a Shamrock over the top of the gatehouse. McKenzie looked over at O'Brien when she saw the sign *Private Drive Do Not Enter* and he nodded his head to keep driving. She noticed the brick wall weaving in and out of the woods but not the guard behind the tinted windows who was reading the morning paper and reacted too slow to stop them.

"What is this place? Who lives here?"

"This is all a virgin forest, around 170 acres. The state owned it for a long time and gave it to the city with an understanding they would develop it as a park. It sat dormant for years, overgrown with kudzu and unkempt. Each new Mayor would commission an architect . . ."

"Uh oh, we're in trouble," McKenzie said. About 100 yards in front of her was a man standing in the middle of the road with his arm extended and his palm up. The other hand was on his hip resting on an automatic pistol. Behind him, parked in the middle of the road, was a camouflage-painted ATV.

"Who *are* these people?" McKenzie asked.

"Well, we are trespassing; just tell them we're guests."

McKenzie gave O'Brien a look that said, "You're the one who said to keep driving."

"They probably called from the gate. I forgot about the video cameras."

McKenzie rolled to a slow stop. The guard stood like a huge oak tree, blocking the road and towering over the small sports car. He was dressed in a black t-shirt stretched over a hard body, with camouflage pants tucked into black laced-up boots. His arms bulged from the sleeves and were covered in colorful tattoos. A black baseball cap had white letters, MPD, and silver captain bars pinned above the bill of the cap.

"Did you all miss seeing the sign at the entrance of this *private drive,* the one that's printed in large red letters DO NOT ENTER?"

"No we did not. Who are you, and what do you want?" McKenzie said.

"Ma'am, I'm the one who asks questions here. You are *trespassing* on *posted* private property. Now, you either back this little toy back down the drive to the main gate, or I will have a wrecker load it up and haul it off."

"Let me tell you something . . ." McKenzie jerked the tam from her head, and her hair flew over her shoulders as she opened her door to get out.

"Ma'am, do *not* get out of this car." He moved closer, blocking the door with his leg.

O'Brien intervened. "Captain, please, I am a frequent guest here, and sometimes I come through the delivery gate when visiting. I'm sorry I haven't met you before, but my name is O'Brien with the Catholic Diocese." O'Brien reached his hand out over the top of McKenzie's head. The Captain hesitated, then saw the large cross hanging from O'Brien's neck, recognized his name, leaned over McKenzie's head, and shook his hand.

"Captain, this lady here is my guest, Chancellor O'Connor of Shelby County Chancery Court, and if you will use your radio and call Director Maddox—I'm sure he is a guest here today—he will verify what I've just told you."

"Do you know Director Maddox, I mean, personally?" the Captain asked.

"Yes, I do."

"I'm married to his daughter. I mean I'm his son-in-law, Kevin O'Shea." O'Shea reached back over the top of McKenzie and shook O'Brien's hand again, vigorously.

"You're not Commissioner O'Shea's boy, are you?" O'Brien asked.

"No sir, he didn't have any boys, all girls. He was my uncle, my dad's older brother, but I was named after him because of my hair." With a wide smile, he took his cap off, and curly red hair covered his head. They both laughed.

"Okay. What is this, old home week? Are you going to let us go or not?" McKenzie said, looking up at O'Shea.

"Of course, Your Honor, anything you want. If you ever get in any trouble, here's my card, not that *you* would ever get into any trouble, I can tell. But just in case, you just call me, and I will take care of it for you, okay?" With a big smile he leaned over, almost touching her, and picked up her tam from the floor behind her seat and twirled it on his finger in front of her. "Nice. You won't forget me now, right?"

She looked at his card, *Captain Kevin O'Shea, Memphis Police Department.* "Rest assured, O'Shea," snatching her tam from his finger, "I never forget a *bully.*"

O'Shea laughed and said, "Follow me, O'Connor."

Just when McKenzie started to move, a siren started going off. Everyone looked up and down the road and saw a pink go-cart coming around a curve at a high rate of speed. A Marine Corps pennant, attached to a fiberglass pole, flapped in the wind. Close behind the go-cart was a four-wheel drive ATV that appeared to be chasing the go-cart. The go-cart skidded to a stop about five feet from O'Shea's ATV.

Irish unbuckled her seat belt, grabbed the roll bar, and pulled herself up out of the go-cart, and stood on the seat. "Yo, Captain Kevin, you all are blocking my road." Bear, the huge black Bouvier, was on his haunches seated next to Irish. Bear stood up on all fours and watched as O'Shea hurried over to Irish's go-cart. Bowing like a humble servant, he said, "So sorry, Your Heinous . . . I mean Your Highness. I will shoot every one of these dogs—no, no, Bear, I didn't mean you, big boy. How dare they impede the Princess's private drive!" Bear moved in front of Irish and stared at O'Shea, his big black eyes hidden by the furry, hooded eyebrows. O'Shea backed away from Bear and whispered to Irish, "Why are you not wearing your helmet? I told you about that."

"Uncle Tom, Uncle Tom!" Irish yelled seeing him walk up. She ran and jumped into his arms; Bear bolted from the go-cart and moved right next to her.

Uncle Tom? What is this? McKenzie thought.

"Aren't you performing today?" O'Brien asked.

"I am. Did you come to watch? Oops, my phone is ringing." O'Brien let her down, and she pulled her phone out of the back pocket of her jeans and looked at the caller ID, *Shamrock-100.*

"It's Daddy. Hi Daddy. No sir, I'm on my way. Yes sir." Irish closed her phone and ran back to her go-cart. "I have to go now. Daddy's on his way. Let's go, Bear." They jumped into the go-cart and made a U-turn off the road, skidding the tires in the grass and blowing the siren. The ATV, with a guard dressed like O'Shea, followed closely behind.

O'Shea walked over to O'Brien and said, "She is something else."

"One of a kind."

"Smartest little girl I've ever seen. Sir, do you want to just follow Irish, or would you rather me show you the way?" O'Shea asked.

"Thank you, but I know the way. If you would, call the delivery gate and let them know we're coming."

"I'll take care of that, and you know how to get in touch with me if you need anything, today or in the future. Sorry about the misunderstanding."

O'Shea climbed onto his ATV, pulled off the road, and tipped his cap to O'Connor, smiling as she drove by. Watching them drive down the road, he called the delivery gate on his radio and told them to pass through two guests, a male and a female, in a red Porsche convertible. He then radioed the main gate and asked them to check the guest list for an O'Brien. Shortly, there was a call back on the radio that Bishop Thomas O'Brien was on the list as a VIP with one guest, a Chancellor McKenzie O'Connor. O'Shea pulled his cell phone from his belt and speed-dialed a number.

"Director, a Father O'Brien and a Chancellor O'Connor are coming through the delivery gate; he says he knows you."

"*Bishop*, Kevin," Director Maddox said.

"Father, Bishop, what difference does it make?"

"You should know the difference."

"Why? I'm not a Catholic."

"How about the fact there are one billion Catholics, and they care, so you should too, *Lieutenant.*"

"That's Captain, sir . . . Oh I see, Father—Bishop and Captain—Lieutenant."

"You're learning, Kevin, you're learning."

"Yes sir, but . . ."

"This is not the time for this discussion. Was the Bishop's name on the guest list?"

"Yes sir. His and the Chancellor's, both listed as VIPs."

"Good boy. And, Kevin, when you come up to the main house, wear your long-sleeved uniform shirt."

"Sir?"

"Cover the tats, Kevin . . . the tats."

CHAPTER 12

AS MCKENZIE APPROACHED the delivery gate, she saw a white sawhorse with a red stop sign blocking the drive. She slowed to a stop, looked to her right and saw a long line of waiting cars, and realized she was back where she started at the main gate. The delivery gate was a porte-cochere type gate attached to the south side of the main gate. Once through both gates the roads merged into one. McKenzie saw a guard dressed much like Captain O'Shea walked over from the main gate to the convertible.

"What a beauty!" the guard said. "A Speedster?"Don't tell me. Let me guess . . . a '55?"

"Very good, but it's a '54. I'm sorry, but could you let us pass? We don't want to be late."

"Sure, Captain O'Shea just called. Great car."

McKenzie waved as she passed through the delivery gate and stopped to let a car from the main gate ahead of her. She couldn't believe her eyes; oak trees towered over the road, blocking the sunlight, and a huge, twenty-five foot tall stone wall, covered in purple wisteria with an arched opening on each side for the entrance and exit. A large volume of water poured over the top of the wall and down through natural stones, forming a pool at the bottom.

Multi-colored water lilies bloomed in the center of the pool with a border of tall yellow and purple irises. "My goodness, look at this! This place is unbelievable. Did you say it was 170 acres?"

"Yes, outside these walls is the City Park. That's 170 acres, but inside these walls—about 30 acres—is all privately owned."

"By whom?"

"A trust," said O'Brien. "Years ago, I don't remember the exact year, a grand lady by the name of Irish Malloy—well, her real name was Rosa Leigh Montague—she married a fellow named Malloy, and they had a tugboat named the *Irish Mist*. That's where the Horatio Alger story begins." O'Brien looked over at McKenzie. "It's a long story."

"Tell me. I want to hear it, please?" McKenzie said.

"Well, she and her husband, Malloy, were making a good living pushing barges up and down the river. Then one day, tragically, he was killed in a river barge accident, and everything started falling apart—rapidly. The banks immediately started foreclosing on everything they owned, the house and the car, and a repo man was headed for the *Irish Mist*.

"The story goes that, early one morning, way before daylight, Irish woke her teenage brother, Mickey—fresh from Ireland—and took off down river with the *Irish Mist*. They lived on the tugboat for a couple of years, working 24/7, and saved enough money for a down payment for another tugboat for Mickey to operate. Soon they were passing each other up and down the river, and, on the tugboat's radios, she was always called Irish, and the name stuck. She paid off the *Irish Mist*, and, shortly after that, business started booming—before long she had a fleet of tugboats. From there she bought businesses and properties along the river, and soon they were servicing the river traffic with food, fuel, salvage work, marine repairs, etc."

"Smart lady," McKenzie said.

"She never finished high school but had a business acumen second to none. She had a simple financial philosophy—debt free—slave to no bank ever again."

"What in the world does it cost her to maintain this property and the park?"

"Strangely enough, there are no taxes on any of the property. There's a rumor that Irish made $100,000 cash in one day, a lot of money back then. She bought the salvage from some barges that broke loose down near Helena and ran up on some dikes. The barges were loaded with corn, and a little river water got into the corn, spoiling it for human consumption.

She was seen standing on the barges after midnight, negotiating with an insurance adjuster. She bought the corn at a steep discount and, early the next morning, started offloading the corn into other barges, sent them up and down the river, and had it all sold to cattle farmers before nightfall that same day.

"Supposedly, the next day, she flew her own plane up here from Vicksburg with cash in a grocery sack and made a deal with the Mayor for this property. And I might add, it was an election year. All five commissioners voted along with the Mayor, approving the sale of the property with one caveat: that the 170 acres had to be used as a park, and that none of the property could be sold or subdivided. Irish agreed but had some conditions of her own, not the least important was that she negotiated a perpetual tax freeze on all the property—*all* being the keyword here. Shortly after the deed was registered and title insurance was purchased, it was discovered—after Irish had the property surveyed—that the Legal Description of the property was correct, but the amount of acreage stated on the deed was not 170 acres but 200 acres. In a private meeting, the Mayor acknowledged that when the State gave the property to the city, the city failed to have the property surveyed, and, legally, Irish owned the extra 30 acres. To save face and not hold the city's feet to the fire, Irish made a generous offer to purchase the 30 acres outright with two conditions. One, the 30 acres would not be subject to the city's caveat. In other words, it would be privately owned and not a part of the park. And two, the deep creek that was a natural boundary between the two parcels, would be the property and liability of the owner of the 30 acres. The city agreed with Irish's proposal with one exception: the 30 acres could never be zoned as commercial property. Irish argued that if the city barred her from developing the property commercially, there would be no income to pay the taxes. Yes, she was a benefactor of the city, but she couldn't be for long if she made bad deals. The city countered with an offer of the same tax freeze for the 30 acres as they had allowed for the 170-acre park; Irish agreed to the deal."

"As I said, smart lady. Do you think she knew about the 30 acres when she bought the 170 acres?"

O'Brien just smiled.

"Okay . . . are you related? I heard the little girl call you uncle," McKenzie asked.

"No, fictive kinship. Her father and I are close friends. Like you, I baptized her when she was born."

McKenzie drove slowly now, her head turning right and left, mesmerized by the thick forest of trees. The lower limbs had been trimmed so you could see flashes of mixed colors of the wild redbuds, white dogwoods, the blue spruce, and red maples. The golf course-like grass ran right up to the edge of the forest, and, on the left side of the road, large openings framed by weeping willows, magnolias, and crepe myrtles, had been cut at intervals to view the water running in the creek bed. This was no happenstance but a long, thought-out plan, beautifully designed and manicured.

McKenzie slowed the car when she saw another long barricade blocking the road with a sign marked *Parking*. A guard stood in front, pointing to the left, where cars were parked in an open field. McKenzie watched a black limousine pull up behind the barricade and park parallel. The driver's door opened, and a large black man got out and held up his hand for her to stop.

"Now, *what* the hell is going on?" She looked over at O'Brien.

O'Brien opened his door and struggled getting out of the car. "Otis, how are you?"

Otis stepped over the barricade with ease. "I'm fine Doctor, yourself?"

"No complaints. The Lord has blessed us greatly with this weather today."

"Amen to that. Miss Irish just gave me my orders to get down here and pick you up. Of course, I'm no different from anyone else she has wrapped around her little finger," he laughed. "You can park your car over there under that tree—it'll be safe there—and I'll take you up to the house and make sure you get a ride back when you all are ready."

Otis moved the barricade, and McKenzie followed him as he pointed to the tree. The guard stood by the limo, waiting with the back door opened. O'Brien and McKenzie climbed into the back seat and, when Otis started the limo, O'Brien said, "Otis, this is Chancellor O'Connor."

"Yes sir, I *do* know the judge. Excuse me, let me answer my phone." Otis's phone was not ringing, but he opened it, and put it to his ear, and, at the same time, reached over and pushed a button that closed the glass window that separated the front seat from the back. Otis glanced into his rear-view mirror and saw McKenzie shrug her shoulders and shake her head at O'Brien as if to say, "I don't remember him . . . .."

Of course not, you wouldn't remember me, bitch. All us niggers look alike, right? You sent me to jail for 90 days for violating a restraining order for taking my 9-year-old son. Caused me to lose my job at the trucking company, my utilities to be disconnected, and I almost was thrown out of my house. Why? 'Cause you wanted to teach me a lesson. Did you not hear me when I shouted that my son had called me after he found his mother on the kitchen floor, OD'd on crack cocaine? Did you stop for one second—while your two Gestapo goons dragged me from your courtroom—to think what damages you caused my son or me?

Otis turned off the road and up a winding drive that ended on a plateau at the highest point of the property. He eased past a tramcar unloading people from the parking lot and turned into the main entrance of the walled courtyard and down the brick-paved driveway. Bypassing the front entrance, he pulled under the porte-cochere on the left side of the house as a female attendant opened the rear door.

"Welcome to Shamrock," she said, and in a low voice continued, "There are two ladies' rooms outside: one in the pool house and another in the flower garden at the gazebo. The birthday party is about to start down in the Grove," she pointed in the direction of the gardens.

Shamrock? McKenzie thought.

O'Brien and McKenzie walked around to the rear of the house and stopped. "I guess they don't want you going into the house to go to the bathroom. I would die to see the inside." A waiter carrying a tray of glasses filled with champagne stopped in front of them. McKenzie took two glasses and gave one to O'Brien. They touched glasses and took a sip.

"Ah, party water, very good," said O'Brien and drained the glass. "I was as dry as a Sudanese camel."

"A Sudanese camel?" McKenzie smiled and went back to sipping her champagne and studying the exterior of the house. *Very unusual,* she thought; all elevations of the house had a different style, eclectic, yet were compatible. Overall—she would bet—the architecture was Italian Renaissance with some touches of Spanish, Greek, and maybe a little Moorish thrown in, definitely mannish with just the right touch of elegance.

Walking across the terrace, which was enclosed with an imported waist-high Italian marble balustrade, they stopped at the top of the steps leading down to the gardens. Looking out over the surrounding treetops, McKenzie tried to visualize the clearing and design of this large swath of land. Her first thoughts were of the Gardens of Versailles—of course miniature compared to the 2,000 acres at Versailles—but the giant hedges, palisades, pruned yews shaped into balls, the arcades, the marble-rimmed water canal flowing 500 feet down the middle of the garden, and peacocks walking freely throughout the grounds were super impressive—*a European landscape architect, I'd wager.*

"This is just magnificent. I can't believe this place. As my daddy would say, 'These are not rich people, Honey. These are what you call weaaaalthy.' Look at the black swan—I have never seen a real one. How beautiful. Why haven't I read or heard something about this place?"

"Privacy, my dear. He cherishes his *obscurity*," O'Brien said, looking up in the sky.

"Who is he?"

O'Brien pointed out over the treetops at a black ball headed straight for them. The jet helicopter dropped from the tree line, streaking up the water canal at less than 30 feet above, then flared out and turned left at the house, hovering, and then descending, landing onto the concrete helicopter pad.

O'Brien took McKenzie's arm and said, "Come on, let's go down to Beethoven's party, and I'll introduce you to the owner."

They walked with other people along the canal, watching spotted goldfish swimming with their babies. Waiters collected glasses and ushered everyone down to the Grove. At the end of the canal was a high, semicircular waterfall, with fish racing through the splash of the water. At the end of the waterfall, the guests walked into the Grove through an arched entranceway leading to an amphitheater. The seating was tiered rows of grass in a three-quarter circle with an elevated grass area—much like a stage—in the opening of the circle. On the grass staging area, a white cloth covered a piano, as well as the white cushions along each row, and white covers over the chairs, for additional seating, made a beautiful contrast for an intimate setting.

O'Brien was busy talking to a large woman in a dress that was way too tight. McKenzie discreetly pulled on his coat sleeve, pointed to the first row of tiered seating beside them, and whispered, "Is this okay?"

O'Brien nodded and said, "Lucy, I would like for you to meet my friend,

Chancellor McKenzie O'Connor. McKenzie, this is Ms. Lucille Ludwig, long-time President of the Beethoven Club. Lucy is an accomplished concert pianist."

"Lucy Ludwig, that's a nice name. The Beethoven Club and Ludwig Beethoven, any connection?" McKenzie asked.

"No, other than we are both German and I have a passion for his music. Why?" Lucy asked, with a slight German accent, both hands on her large hips, and her breasts bulging out at McKenzie, eye level. "You do not like Beethoven?"

What the hell did I ask that question for? Thankfully, before McKenzie could respond, Lucy turned and waved at some people on the upper level.

"You will excuse me. I must get . . . how do they say? On with the show.'" Lucy walked through the rows of people to the stage area, was handed a wireless microphone, and helped onto the stage.

"Good afternoon. May I have your attention, please? Thank you . . . thank you." The noise quieted down while Lucy waited for a few stragglers to find a seat.

"Today, we are here to celebrate the 125th birthday of the Beethoven Club. First and foremost, I cannot tell you how pleased and truly thankful we are for the generosity of one single person for allowing this auspicious occasion to occur here at Shamrock in these spectacular surroundings."

Hearing the word Shamrock for the second time, McKenzie looked over at O'Brien, but he appeared to be avoiding her stare.

Lucy continued, "I think we can all agree that Shamrock is truly a Shangri-La. Once inside these walls—isolated from the outside world—you begin to experience the tranquility and, in a brief time, understand why God created the Garden of Eden.

"It is my sincere pleasure to introduce the man responsible for all this, a most generous man, not for recognition or ego, but because of his passion for music . . . Mr. Mack Shannon."

McKenzie grabbed O'Brien's arm and whispered between clenched teeth and in measured words, "Oh-my-God! Why-didn't-you-tell-me . . .?" O'Brien lifted a finger to his lips and continued to look straight ahead.

Mack Shannon walked from behind a hedge in a relaxed gait and stopped in front of the grass stage. He helped Lucy step down from the stage, and she handed him the microphone. Mack took the microphone, laid it on the stage, and walked midway down the aisle between the chairs.

"Thank you, Lucy, for your kind words, and I thank all of you for coming. Welcome to Shamrock and to The Grove."

McKenzie was in shock. *Nice voice . . . and pretty teeth.*

"For you who might not know, Ms. Lucile Ludwig is the President of the Beethoven Club and has been as long as I can remember. Lucy is the most tenacious, dedicated, and single-minded person whom I know when it comes to the mission of the club—Grow Beethoven—and that is just what we intend to do today."

Hmm, very poised. This couldn't be the drunk Irishman on the bulldozer at Arthur's?

"Plato once said, 'Music training is more potent than any other, because rhythm and harmony find their way into the inward places of the soul.' To experience that intimacy you need three things: a composer, an instrument, and the artist."

Masculine and sensitive . . . a real hottie.

Mack lifted up a book of sheet music he had placed on one of the chairs. "We have the composer: the Master, whose music was written over 200 years ago, Ludwig van Beethoven.

"We have the instrument: You cannot have a birthday party without a birthday present." Two men stepped up onto the stage. "There are many pianos as there are many composers, but I truly believe this handcrafted masterpiece—six years in its creation—*is* one that follows the intuitions of the great composers. I am pleased to donate this 1892 Imperial Grand Bosendorfer, the largest concert grand in the world, to the Beethoven Club." The two men on the stage folded back the white cover and opened the top of the ebony piano.

About half the people applauded, not knowing the rarity of such a gift, then everyone started standing and applauding. O'Brien leaned over and whispered to McKenzie, "About a half-million dollars."

"What?"

"That gift."

"The *piano*?"

O'Brien nodded his head and continued clapping.

When the crowd settled down, they noticed a young girl standing between Lucy and Mack, holding their hands. She was very tanned with thick dark eyebrows and a mouth full of blue dotted braces. A full slip was under the white Irish lace dress that clung to her slim body.

"That's the little girl in the go-cart?" McKenzie whispered.

O'Brien nodded his head again.

"Thank you. We have the composer—Beethoven. We have the instrument—Bosendorfer. We now have the artist—Miss Irish Shannon." Mack and Lucy sat down.

"She's gorgeous," McKenzie whispered and, at the same time, could have said the same about a beautiful woman sitting by herself, left of the stage. She was dressed like the little girl Irish, an all-white dress and had her long blond hair. *Is that her mother? Maybe . . . no, she has darker skin. My God, look at those huge brown eyes.*

Mimicking her father, Irish walked a few steps up the aisle away from the stage.

"When I was young . . ." There was laughter among the crowd, "well . . . young-*er*, I used to cry a lot, and Daddy would ask me what was wrong. I always said, 'Nothing.'" She smiled, showing all her braces. "You ladies know what I mean . . .. He said since I was *so* emotional I should learn to play Beethoven. *That's* when I first started playing Beethoven."

Irish walked back, stepped up on the stage, and looked down at her father. "This is for my Daddy. You'd think he would get tired of this song, but it's his favorite piece—'Moonlight Sonata.'"

"She *is* spunky," McKenzie whispered.

Irish looked small behind the huge piano. She sat quietly, waiting, her hands in her lap, her back straight, and no sheet music. She had rehearsed all three movements of this complicated piece, over and over every day from memory, for the last two weeks.

For the next fifteen minutes, beginning with the soft touch of the first key, through the rich sustaining tone singing from the strings and timbers of the Bosendorfer, the guests were captivated. After the last note was played, the guests were motionless. Total silence filled the air. Bear crawled out from under the piano, threw his head back with his mouth opened, and pointed to the sky, howling his appreciation. The guests exploded in applause and laughter as Irish jumped from the stage and wrapped her arms around Bear. The guests gathered in close around the piano, shouting *brava* and clapping.

Irish stood next to the woman with the large brown eyes, holding her hand, then ran and leaped into her father's arms, "How did I do, Daddy?"

"You played beautifully, Darling. Not one mistake. I loved it; the best ever."

"Phew, I was so nervous. I'm glad that's over. I need a drink!" Irish said.

"*Whaaat?*"

"Ah, Daddy, you're so easy. I'm starving, can we eat now?"

"*Mack.*"

Mack lowered Irish to the ground and turned into the crowd to see who had called his name. He felt his heart skip a beat. Standing before him—so close he could smell her minted breath—was the most beautiful woman he had seen in a long time. He stared for the longest time into her green eyes. Sure, he had seen big baby blues and those of the doe-eyed Latinos, but for the first time he understood what the songwriter meant when he wrote: *When Irish eyes are smiling, they steal your heart away.* He realized he was holding his breath and slowly exhaled. He saw O'Brien standing behind her.

So, this is the Chancellor. The one Isaac said had a beautiful body with steel balls? Yes, O'Connor, I've heard a lot about you. But beware, Mack. That child-like interest deep in those emerald eyes are like any precious stone. You look long enough you'll find minute spots of black carbon.

"Irish, you played magnificently," O'Brien said.

"Uncle Tom!" Irish ran to him and wrapped her arms around his waist, "Thank you."

O'Brien took Irish's hand. "Mack, Irish, Lea, I want you to meet a close friend of mine, McKenzie O'Connor. McKenzie, this is Miss Irish Shannon, Lea, Irish's governess, and as you have probably devised, her Daddy, Mack Shannon."

McKenzie reached out and shook Irish's hand. "I have never heard the piano played with such perfection."

"Ahhh, thank you. Really?" Irish said as Bear bumped her, "and this is Bear."

"Hello, Bear." McKenzie laughed, "I heard you liked it too." She did not attempt to pet him.

"Mr. Shannon, I also have never seen such a, how would you say . . . *sui generis* setting for a home as yours. I never use that word, but it is such a perfect description, and I'm sure the inside of your home is just as applicable." *Does he know I signed an order to have him arrested?*

Is she being haughty? Naw, just baiting me maybe or like a cat . . . toying. Be cool.

"Chancellor, not being from the academic world but more from the other side of the tracks, as they say, seldom do I have the opportunity to experience such a refined vocabulary. I apologize, I don't know if you just insulted me or praised me. I do believe in the old axiom, there is no such thing as a dumb question. What does *sui generis* mean?"

Got him. "My intent was to praise, Mr. Shannon. Shamrock is truly palatial and unique. *Sui generis* is Latin, meaning 'of his own kind.' Your elegant stamp is wide reaching. I feel honored to be a guest."

Touché, Chancellor, nice rebound.

"Daddy, let's eat!" Irish demanded, pulling her father and Lea by the hand.

CHAPTER 13

A WARM BREEZE PUSHED the clouds through the bottom quarter of the reddish-orange setting sun, causing it to bob up and down on the horizon. Beethoven's party was winding down, and the soft music from the string quartet drifted like a fog over the rooftop, where Mack had invited a select group to join him.

It puzzled Mack why most people never utilized their rooftops; it was private, peaceful, there was almost always a breeze, and in most cases afforded a panoramic vista, day and night. The rooftop patio was on the west end of the house with a matching marble balustrade on top of a parapet wall—same as the terrace below.

Mack had walked over to the corner of the roof, listening to the music and watching the sunset, both elbows resting on the railing, while he sipped on his after-dinner drink.

"What a beautiful closing curtain to a great party," McKenzie said as she walked over to Mack.

"Yes, well put, thank you. I almost hate to see it end. Well, Chancellor, did Bradley give you a complete tour of the house?"

"Yes, *sui generis*, as I expected," she smiled. "Would you please call me McKenzie, and I'll call you Mack?"

Mack sipped his drink; the warm cognac skillfully blended with bitter oranges, worked its way down, revealing a unique palate, delicate and strong. He smiled, "It's a deal," he said and extended his hand. Her hand was on fire—he could feel the heat before they touched, and she knew it too, holding his look eye to eye as the heat radiated slowly up his arm. He took a deep breath and forced himself to slow down, to enjoy this moment, knowing it was the beginning of something powerful. Mack released her hand, and the words describing the 50-year-old cuvee he was sipping came to mind: *A long lingering finish prolongs the pleasure well after the liqueur has been consumed.*

"I'm sorry. Would you like a drink?" Mack asked.

"What are you having?"

"A Grand Marnier, it's a special cuvee they created to celebrate their 150th anniversary. I thought it appropriate for the Beethoven Club's birthday. Would you like a sniff?" Mack handed her his glass.

She tilted the crystal snifter and rolled the liqueur around in the glass. "Is this the way it's done?"

You know how it's done, Chancellor, you don't need to ask.

She lifted the glass to her nose. "Very good," she said, and put her lips to the glass, and took a sip. "Hmm, what did you say *you* were drinking?"

Mack caught the eye of a waiter and asked for two doubles.

"Thank you," McKenzie said. "This Bradley fellow is quite impressive. Is he your butler?"

"No, his official title is Personal Assistant, or PA, and you're right, he is extremely efficient. Irish secretly calls him Mr. Google, because she says there is nothing he doesn't know."

"Just out of curiosity, what *does* a PA do, and how did you find Bradley?"

Mack looked over her shoulder and noticed Bradley, about 20 feet away, staring at him. He had always thought it somewhat pretentious and unnecessary to have a butler or a PA, but Maureen insisted. In retrospect, he had felt the same way about Maureen being his Personal Administrator, and now he could not envision running a company, much less multiple companies without her. The everyday, mundane work that she liberated him from—plus completing the tasks twice as fast and in less time—had freed him to focus more on current and future projects. Now, he was just as addicted to Bradley as he was to Maureen, and still, his toughest challenge was delegating authority.

"Excuse me a minute," nodding his head toward Bradley, "he needs to speak with me."

Bradley was standing perfectly still, wearing his poker face when Mack walked up to him, no frown and no smile, always assuming someone may be watching. He was as tall as Mack and a shade lighter in his complexion, which was rare in an East Indian, and, as always, immaculately dressed with his head freshly shaved.

"Good evening, Mr. Singh," Mack said with a smile.

"Good evening, sir. Sorry to bother you."

"Is there a problem?"

"Yes sir, in the kitchen."

"And . . ."

"The chef—in a fit of rage—has trashed the kitchen. He has locked all the kitchen help in the walk-in freezer and barred anyone from entering the kitchen. He is drinking vodka, or was—the bottle he threw at me was empty—and he's waving a large butcher knife and threatening to kill any-one who walks through the door. Sorry for the bad news, sir. Would you like me to get Captain O'Shea? He's still here."

"No, not yet. Let me check it out first. Please tell the Chancellor some-thing came up that needs my immediate attention, and that I'll be back shortly."

*

Mack eased the kitchen door half-open. "Leo! Mack Shannon here, I'm coming in."

"Stay out of my kitchen!" Leo shouted.

Mack could tell from Leo's voice that he was on the other side of the kitchen from the door. He held the door as he slipped through the open-ing and was pissed at what he saw: shelves were pulled over and the con-tents spilled out over everything, prep tables were upside down, broken glasses and plates were scattered all over the floor, and pots and pans strewn throughout—nothing was where it was supposed to be. But the biggest mess was the dark substances and blood red liquid splattered all over the walls, the refrigerators, the stoves, and even the ceiling, along with dozens of small, white ramekins.

Leo was slumped down against the freezer door, a half-empty bottle of vodka in one hand and a 10" chef's knife in the other. He staggered to his feet when he saw Mack, his tall chef's hat knocked to one side and the dark substance all over his white chef's jacket.

"I told . . . no one in this kitchen . . . get out!" Leo waved his knife.

Mack kept the stainless steel table, which was bolted to the floor, between Leo and himself while he looked for some other form of protection. "Leo, I'm Mack Shannon, remember me? How long have they been locked in the freezer?"

"*Mr. Shannon*!" It finally dawned on Leo who Mack was. "Look at my kitchen. Look what they've done."

Mack picked up a stockpot lid by its handle.

"Who did this, Leo?"

"They caused it," pointing to the freezer. "Mr. Shannon, look at my dessert—dark chocolate soufflé—this is what I got!" He ran his hands over the chocolate and raspberry sauce smeared down the front of his chef's jacket and shouted, *The stupid shits mixed salt instead of sugar in my soufflés!*" Mack raised the pot lid, shielding himself as the vodka bottle came flying across the room. Leo dropped the knife as he slid to the floor, sobbing, with both hands covering his face.

Mack walked over with the pot lid still in his hand and picked up the large knife. He stepped around Leo and opened the freezer door, and six people scampered out as if the house were on fire. Mack turned as the kitchen door swung open and saw Bradley standing there with a baseball bat in his hand.

Mack walked past Bradley, handing him the knife, "Going for a little batting practice, are you? I like his cooking, so don't fire him; he's had a rough 24 hours with this party. I'll be on the roof if you need me."

*

Mack stopped on the landing at the top of the stairs, looking for McKenzie on the rooftop; she was no longer over in the corner. It was crowded now. Had more people invited themselves to the rooftop? He saw her walking toward him, a snifter in each hand, her eyes locked on him as she turned her shoulders and edged her way through the crowd, her smile warm and inviting as she reached out and handed him his drink.

"That didn't take too long. Hope it wasn't anything serious?"

Mack took a sip of his drink, took McKenzie by the elbow, and guided her back to the corner of the rooftop. "Do you know much about chefs?"

She stopped and tilted her head up to him, smiling, her lips full and wet, her dark red hair falling over one eye, "No, why?"

God, what I would give to take her now—to kiss those succulent lips. "Most chefs are temperamental, passionate about their creations, and, when something goes wrong, they explode like a child with a temper tantrum."

"Did something go wrong with your chef?"

"He's not *my* chef—I mean we don't have enough folks here to justify a full-time chef. Bradley hires Leo for parties and small dinners. About once a week he's out here to cook up a specialty and maybe a large turkey or roast that will last us through the week. Plus, all of us like to cook once in a while. Anyway, we will have to drink our desert because Leo's dark chocolate soufflés blew up. Enough of that, how would you like to join me in a walk? There's a nice trail around the property, and it's a beautiful night. What do you say?"

"Daddy, Daddy." Irish came running through the crowd, dragging O'Brien and Lea by the hand with Bear following close behind.

"Slow down, honey, what's the matter?"

"Uncle Tom wants to leave, and I want to show him the baby button quails that hatched yesterday."

Mack turned to McKenzie, "Have you ever seen a button quail? How about we all walk down to the hatchery and see them?"

Irish rushed off down the steps with O'Brien and Lea in tow.

"You game?" Mack asked, taking McKenzie by the hand.

Walking down the steps from the rooftop, McKenzie asked, "Does Irish always get what she wants?"

"Yes."

"Do you think you are spoiling her?"

"No. Do you think she is spoiled?"

"I have no idea; it just seems she has everything a little girl could want."

"What's wrong with that? I have everything I want." He let go of her hand and pointed to an asphalt walkway running downhill away from the house and into a wooded area. "This is the way to the barn."

McKenzie noticed that Mack had become quiet as they were walking. "I hope I didn't offend you by asking about your daughter."

"She *is* a great little girl—had a hard time without her mother and has worked for everything she's got." *Why should I tell her that Irish makes all A's in one of the highest-ranked academic schools in the South? That she is the president of her foreign language club at school and speaks Spanish and French? That she plays number one on her school tennis team and runs cross-country, sings in her church choir, and works as a volunteer reading and playing the piano for the children at St. Jude Children's Hospital? You don't get those accomplishments sitting on your ass playing video game or gossiping on the phone . . . the hell with her; I don't need to sell my daughter to anyone. I don't even know this woman.*

"I'm sorry, I didn't know." *Oh my, dumbass—I've stepped in it now— I should have known better than to cross that line. Where is the mother?* "I know one thing; she plays the piano like no one I have ever heard before."

"Yes, she does do that, too."

"My God, look, a white peacock!"

Strutting up the path was a large male albino peacock, displaying his full-blown tail plumage for inspection by the females traveling with him.

Mack took McKenzie's arm and moved her closer to him. "If you stand still, they'll walk right by you."

Four peahens walked out of the underbrush onto the walkway, pecking the ground and eating the blossoms from the hibiscuses. The white peacock jumped straight up and then danced from one foot to the other, fanning his iridescent tail feathers with 1,000 eyes. When the male peacock walked past McKenzie, she held out her hand and let his tail feathers brush through her fingers.

"He's majestic. Look at him 'strutting like a peacock.' His feathers are so luminescent—what a beauty. Oh, I wish I'd brought my camera," McKenzie said.

Mack pointed up into the trees as two of the peahens took flight and landed on a large limb hanging over the walkway. "At dusk, they go to roost in the trees overnight."

"What keeps them from flying away?"

"This is their home. Why would they want to leave?"

Bear came walking up the path and stopped in front of them. When the peacocks started walking, Bear moved off the walkway to the left side of Mack and walked beside him.

"I notice Bear follows Irish everywhere she goes, what a nice pet." McKenzie said.

"He's not a pet, that's his job."

"He's a guard dog?"

"The Dutch use them as police dogs."

"But, he's seems so gentle."

"Bear is, like most Bouviers. They're a quiet breed, calm, even-tempered, and love children. But, inherently they are fearless, very protective, and naturally aloof with strangers."

He doesn't bother the peacocks?" McKenzie asked.

Bear bumped Mack's leg, hearing his name again, and looked up. Mack grabbed his rough fur and shook him playfully. "Naw, he wouldn't lower himself to that level. It's just a happenstance that Bear inhabits the body of a dog; he's really of royal lineage. In his past lives I'm sure he was probably a great warrior or a ruler of some tribe. There's no doubt he feels he is a member of our immediate family—right up there with Bradley and Lea, Irish's governess," *and surrogate mother,* he started to add. *Was that the truth? Yes—emphatically, and Lea was much more. He never thought of them as Governess, Personal Assistant, or Personal Administrator—he was with them 24/7; they were part of his family, and he gave them whatever they wanted.*

Mack remembered how little time he had had to mourn the death of his wife, the former Katherine Willingham. Everything happened so fast—one blunder after the other—until it seemed she could not escape what was predestined. It was late in Kate's pregnancy when she went for a routine ultrasound and they discovered what the doctor called placenta previa. The placenta was blocking the cervix, some of the blood vessels had ruptured, and there was some blood. She was told her OB/GYN was out of town at a medical seminar, and one of their other doctors, who was on his way back from an emergency delivery at the hospital next door, would examine her. Her nurse hurried off to assist a patient whose water had broken and inadvertently left her file in the waiting room. An hour or so later, a doctor saw Kate Shannon standing in the hall with bright red blood running down the inside of her legs; confused, pale in color, with one hand between her legs and the other clasped over her rapid beating heart. After an examination, he called for a gurney and had her wheeled next door for an emergency C-section. Mack was called, and after waiting outside the operating room for over two hours, the OB/GYN came out and told Mack that during the C-section, she started hemorrhaging again. They had everyone available working on her but couldn't stop her bleeding. The baby was delivered immediately, was stable and healthy, and not the direct cause of her hemorrhaging. She died on the operating table during intubation and could not be resuscitated. Attempts were stopped after 30 minutes. Mack came home with a newborn baby. He hired a nanny but didn't trust her and took Irish everywhere he went with a book, *How Babies Work*, in the diaper bag. Finally, Maureen moved in, and she and Bradley helped with Irish until they got Lea.

From then on, Mack's philosophy on life and death was somewhat different from most. It wasn't as if you didn't have all the facts—you're born and you die—that's the deal. It's a contract. We all come with an expiration date. He didn't understand all this pissing and moaning when someone died, especially with the Catholic doctrine. If you were a believer, and basically a good person when you died, then you go to heaven where the streets are paved with gold. No sickness, no pain, no work, just happiness—all the time. If you were bad, but not too bad, like a murderer, rapist, or child molester, then you could go to purgatory and have your friends pray you into heaven—what a deal.

"Does Irish ever see her mother?" McKenzie asked, as if reading his mind.

"No, she died when Irish was born."

"Ohhh, I'm so sorry. I had no idea. How terrible that must have been for you and Irish."

"Yeah, at first, then everyone stepped up. There was a lot of co-parenthood, *compadrazgo,* as Lea called it. She has been a lifesaver; I couldn't have made it without her. Do you have any children?"

"No. My husband and I agreed we both were too busy with our careers to have children."

"And Mr. O'Connor, does he practice law as well?" Mack asked, knowing her husband was a doctor.

"No, he practices medicine, and I kept my maiden name. His last name is Winchester."

"Oh, you didn't take his name?"

"No, it's less complicated that way, and I think it's a little old-fashioned to have to take someone else's name."

"What did he think?"

"I'm sure it was okay with him. I don't remember if it came up for discussion. Why, you disapprove?" McKenzie asked.

"Let's just say, 'I'm a little old-fashioned.' Here's the barn. Let's join the other animals."

McKenzie pulled him over and locked arms, "Okay, Grandpa, lead the way."

CHAPTER 14

BISHOP O'BRIEN LOOKED at his watch as he waited in line at the walk-through metal detector inside the courthouse at the corner of Third and Adams, and realized he was 30 minutes early. The line was moving fast. At almost nine in the morning, most were lawyers rushing to meet their clients in the corridor outside their assigned courtrooms. O'Brien, dressed in a navy blue suit and carrying a briefcase, emptied his pockets and passed through without any problem.

He stepped off the elevator onto the third floor and, looking to the left, saw the sign with gold letters, Supreme Court of Tennessee. The attorney representing Arthur and his restaurant, Sid Goldman, requested the hearing be held in this courtroom, countering O'Brien's offer of his office at the rectory. O'Brien agreed, realizing that Goldman was probably Jewish, and a neutral location would be less questionable. Abby reserved the courtroom after finding out there were no cases scheduled.

Looking around the inside of the courtroom, O'Brien was glad he was early. It would give him a chance to set up the courtroom the way he wanted.

He stepped up behind the judge's bench, walked behind the five high-backed chairs, and stood looking out over the courtroom. He knew he didn't want to sit up here. He wanted to get this thing settled and needed something more intimate. He opened the door behind the chairs and stepped down into the judge's chambers. *Pretty sparse,* he thought; a chair behind a desk, two chairs in front, and two against the wall.

O'Brien walked back into the courtroom, and inside the railing was the counsel table, with a table lectern in the middle, and six leather chairs on rollers. O'Brien removed the lectern, pushed two chairs on the opposite side of the table, and positioned one at the end of the table for him. He placed a folder to his right, and his briefcase to the left on the table in front, reserving that space for him. He didn't like anyone sitting too close where someone could read his notes. He looked up when he heard a door open, and Isaac Brenner, president of Shamrock International, walked in smiling. O'Brien looked at the clock on the wall; it read 9:15.

"Good morning, Your Honor." He scanned the courtroom, stopping at the paneled ceiling. "Quite impressive."

"Certainly more than what we need—I tried to fix up a table here that would be more workable."

"Just the two of us?" Isaac asked, looking at his watch.

"So far . . ."

"Yeah, never met one that was on time. I understand you were out to Mack's house last week. Sorry I missed the party." Isaac placed his briefcase on the table. "I heard everyone had a good time—lots of people?"

"For a party that started with about 40 invitations and ended up with over a 100 people, I'd say it was remarkable. Mack said you and Anna were out of town?"

"We had to fly to Germany and meet with Karl Mueller on his Volkswagen plant."

"I thought you were finished with that project. The one in Brazil?"

"This is an addition to the . . ."

The double doors swung open as Sid Goldman backed through the doors and into the room with both arms loaded as usual. "Good morning, I'm Sid Goldman," he said, then immediately had a coughing seizure, barely making it to the table to unload his briefcases and folders. Wheezing, he said, "I have to run over to Part Two to make an announcement and will be right back." He picked up one of his briefcases and started for the doors, unwrapping a throat lozenge. "Oh, I almost forgot," he stopped, shaking all over with another coughing spasm and almost dropped his lozenge. "Mr. Fox is on his way. He got held up coming through the scanner." He turned and scurried out the door.

"Busy fellow, sounds as if he needs to be in a hospital," O'Brien said.

"Yes, but typical throughout the law field. Most businesses couldn't keep their doors open operating like that."

O'Brien knew Isaac graduated from Harvard Business School and was a Marine officer in the military. He first thought—like most who knew them both—that Mack would be the tough guy, but soon realized that Shamrock and their subsidiary companies all operated under the daily scrutiny of Isaac Brenner. Mack was the boss but had learned that Isaac was much better than he at running the day-to-day operations; his often-repeated words to Isaac were, "If you need me, call me."

"It's accepted as part of their system now, I'm afraid," O'Brien said. "A friend was telling me the other day that he was at his son's graduation—a graduate school on the east coast—and they were announcing separate schools to stand and be recognized, like the School of Engineering, from which his son was graduating. He said they called the School of Medicine, and the graduating class of medicine stood and everyone applauded. When they got to the School of Law and asked them to stand and be recognized, everyone booed. It was hard for me to believe, so I asked, 'Do you mean *some* booed, mixed with applause?' He said, 'No, everyone booed.'"

"The tragedy of it all is that they won't discipline themselves; they have a board, but it's useless," Brenner said.

"Speaking of lawyers, where's Shamrock's lawyer . . . Bickford?"

"I think they call it *pro se*."

"You're representing yourself?"

"I'm representing the companies and Mack. Why not, you're not a lawyer are you?" Isaac asked smiling.

"No."

"Well then, how much trouble can *we* get into?"

They both turned when they heard a slight tap on the glass insert of the door and saw Arthur Fox's head sticking inside. "Is this the right place?" he asked with a slight accent. At the same time, Goldman walked up and pulled Fox back and asked if it was okay to talk to his client a few minutes—out in the hall—before they came in.

"Please, no more than five minutes. We need to get started." O'Brien said.

Isaac looked at his watch—almost 10 a.m.

Ten minutes later, O'Brien stepped outside to the hall and told Goldman it was time to start.

Goldman reached inside his coat pocket and screwed the top off a small dark bottle, took a swig, made a terrible face, and introduced himself. Everyone was seated around the table but Fox, who continued to stand searching the courtroom. Fox leaned over and whispered something to Goldman, who got up, walked behind the judge's bench and into the judge's chambers, and came out with a straight-back chair, *without* armrests, and placed it next to his chair. All the chairs in the courtroom had armrests, and it was obvious Fox was too big to fit between them.

O'Brien started, "First, let's take care of a little housekeeping." O'Brien pulled out his cell phone and shut it off. "Please, no cell phones."

"In my letter I sent out last week, whereas we all agreed on the time and date for this hearing, I requested a deposit toward the Special Master's fees of $2,000 each. I have received a check from Shamrock. Mr. Goldman, did you bring a check with you today?"

Goldman looked at Fox searching his pockets. After finding the check, he signed it and gave it to Goldman, and Goldman handed it to O'Brien.

"Good. This money will be deposited in the church's escrow account, and, if more is needed as we go along, I will request another deposit. If we settle this dispute before that time, an accounting will be reported and whatever balance is left will be divided equally and checks issued. The money for my services goes to St. Jerome's Orphanage for Boys."

"Is that tax-deductible?" Goldman asked.

"Yes." O'Brien said, and removed a writing pad from his briefcase and laid it on the table. "By consent, you both agreed to forego the services of a court reporter; therefore, there will be no transcript of this hearing, and the record will be the exhibits and my report." O'Brien stopped and made notes on his pad. "I would appreciate it if both parties took notes during the entire hearing so we might compare if later there are any misunderstandings. Are there any questions so far?

"Good. For the record, Mr. Goldman is representing the Plaintiffs, Arthur Fox, Individually, and Arthur's Restaurant. Mr. Brenner, *pro se*, is representing the Defendants: Mack Shannon, Global Construction, Inc., and Shamrock International."

"Your Honor, are you saying that Mack Shannon is *not* going to be here for questioning or to testify? Mr. Shannon, solely the *cause* for this lawsuit, owns Global Construction and Shamrock International. I have filed a subpoena and a motion for contempt to have Mr. Shannon brought before this court. How can we have a hearing without him?" Goldman asked.

"Please, it's not necessary to address me as Your Honor. Mr. Goldman, I did not say anything about Mr. Shannon. In my letter I asked if there was any desire to settle this dispute, and both of you agreed there was, and that's where I'm headed. Also Mr. Goldman, I was appointed Special Master by Chancery Court, and in the Order of Reference—signed by you and Mr. Bickford—I don't remember reading anything about subpoenas or contempt charges. I think that was filed in Part Three; you would have to take that up with the Chancellor over there. Regardless, let me add this: I would appreciate it if you would let me finish *my* opening statement, and then hopefully everyone will understand the procedure I'm suggesting we follow."

"I apologize to the Court, Bishop," Goldman said in between coughs.

"May I say something? It might help clear up some confusion," Brenner said. "For the record, Mr. Shannon does not own Shamrock International or any of the subsidiary companies of Shamrock; they are all corporations or LLC. I am the President of Shamrock International and the Chairman and CEO of Global Construction, and I have power of attorney to settle claims against any entity named in this complaint. Also, it was my understanding that the major reason for meeting this morning was to see if we could settle this dispute. I have been focused and ready to do just that since 9:15 a.m., unlike Mr. Goldman, who has stolen . . .." Brenner looked at his watch, "over 45 minutes of this court's time and my time on incidental matters not related to this hearing, and I might add, without the common courtesy of an apology. If this continues, I will suggest to the court that an equitable credit be forfeited from the Plaintiff and added to the Defendant's deposit."

"Thank you, Mr. Brenner. I would like to . . ."

Goldman stood, "Bishop . . ."

"Mr. Goldman, please sit down and let *me* finish." O'Brien stood up, all six feet, four inches, leaned over the table, and in a strong but low voice, said, "Gentlemen, *we* cannot start off on the wrong foot if we want to settle this case. Please, no adversarial statements." He sat back down, and the tone of his voice changed.

"The good thing about conducting a Special Master hearing is that you have options. I have never understood why—when given the opportunity to settle a lawsuit—parties elect to dump it back into the lap of a judge or, in this case, a chancellor, regardless a total stranger, who in most cases knows nothing about your personal situations. You subject yourselves to be tied up in a bureaucratic quagmire for years; thousands of dollars wasted on discovery, depositions, interrogatories, court costs, and attorney fees. And the remarkable thing is, at the end of the day, the *findings* are about the same as if you settled it yourself.

"Listen to me, gentlemen, you can walk out of here today, and all this can be behind you. Circumvent the quicksand; go forward with your life and about your businesses. You can't make any money sitting in a courtroom. All you can do is lose it."

O'Brien waited. No one said anything. "Okay, my little speech is over. This is your hearing, not mine. I'm going to continue as if you both still have a desire to settle this case—if not, stop me.

"Mr. Goldman, you represent the Plaintiff, so you make the opening statement. Both of you try to keep to the facts and the accusations to a minimum. I have read your briefs, your letters, and motions, and I'm familiar with both your cause-of-action and claims.

"Mr. Brenner, you can make your opening statement after Mr. Goldman, and then you both can make your rebuttals. There are no witnesses testifying . . ."

"Excuse me, Your Honor, Mr. Fox can't testify?" Goldman asked.

"At this juncture, I don't need to hear from Mr. Fox. I have read the complaint, and it is extensive. After your rebuttals, I would like for Mr. Brenner to move to the judge's chambers for caucusing, and Mr. Goldman and Mr. Fox, you can stay here in the courtroom. That way I can go back and forth while meeting with you individually. Please understand that whatever is said in our meeting is strictly confidential and will not be discussed with the opposing party or anyone else without your permission.

"In my letter, I asked for a total amount of your claims, so when you separate I will want an explanation, a breakdown if you will, of how you reached that amount. Mr. Goldman, you can make your opening statement."

*

O'Brien was happy with the end results; although it took longer than he expected to reach a settlement. He did not break for lunch but ordered out for everyone, fearing a loss of focus with the many cases Goldman had on the table in front of him.

Isaac Brenner did a good job, all things considered. In his opening statement, he hit hard on what he knows best—money. He dissected their claim and listed a value figure for each item. O'Brien let Brenner attack Fox, accusing him of being a deadbeat, and when Goldman objected, Brenner countered with "it goes to the character of the Plaintiff. There is a written contract and Mr. Fox violated that contract when he failed to make payments." Brenner stated that it was Mr. Shannon's word against Fox, and that there were no witnesses to any threats made by Mr. Shannon. "Mr. Fox's dog attacked and injured Mr. Shannon. Mr. Fox is not the injured party in this dispute, Mr. Shannon is."

It was Goldman who was tenacious, earnestly and rightly so, to get as much as he could for his client. He argued Mr. Fox's damages, compensatory and nominal. He stated the legal aspect of the case, siting case law and rules of court. "The defendant's wrongful conduct caused his client physical and mental pain and suffering, that triggered bouts of fright, grief, emotional trauma, humiliation, and indignity. The defendant's wrongful actions caused structural damage to the property, and loss of profits." And in his closing argument, he fired his last shot—punitive damages. "We ask this court to rule in favor of the plaintiff, and award the sum of one hundred thousand dollars for punitive damages, to punish the defendant for his wrongdoing, and to act as a deterrent to others who might engage in similar conduct."

But, in the end, Goldman conceded that Mr. Fox had no proof: no doctor's or structural engineer's reports, no medical bills or construction repair invoices.

O'Brien didn't care too much for Goldman at first. He thought Goldman, with all his legal mumbo-jumbo, was trying to talk over his head, but tried not to let that interfere with his judgment. As he went back and forth throughout the day—room-to-room—with suggestions and offers, he gained a lot of respect for Goldman. And at the end of the day, while Goldman wrote out the Consent Order of the settlement, O'Brien realized, in the legal sense, what a wise and deceptive chess player he had spent the day with.

CHAPTER 15

MCKENZIE LOOKED DOWN at her desk phone when it rang, recognized the number and snatched it up. "Tell me you settled it."

"You know my favorite Scotch, don't you?"

"*Yes!* Carroll Thomas O'Brien, you should have been a politician!"

"Am I to take that as a compliment?"

"Where are you?"

"Across the hall."

McKenzie looked at her watch; it was ten minutes 'til six. "In the courtroom?"

"Everyone has left but Goldman; he's in the law library making copies of the signed agreement."

"Can you stop by?"

"Be there as soon as Goldman brings me my copy of the agreement."

A few minutes later O'Brien tapped on the door and stuck his head in the chambers of Chancellor O'Connor; she waved him in. "Let's see the agreement." McKenzie motioned him to have a seat as she perused the handwritten copy of the Consent Order he handed her.

"Excellent," she said, continuing to read. "You did a great job: concise, clear, and a fair settlement . . . and everyone's signature. This calls for a celebration." McKenzie pulled out the bottom drawer of her desk and placed a bottle of fifteen-year-old single-malt Scotch with two glasses in front of her. "You've got *me* drinking Macallan now. Neat or a little water?"

"Wee bit of agua to wake up the fairies."

"Remember how you scared me to death, telling me the stories about all the fairies, especially the Banshee and how she could only cry for the five major Irish families? Let's see, the O'Neill's, the O'Brien's, O'Connor's, O'Grady's, and who was the other one?"

"The Kavanagh's," he raised his glass in a toast. "To the O'Connor's and the O'Brien's. Cheers!"

They both took a good swig and then heard a light knock on the door, "Chancellor?"

"Come in," McKenzie said.

Sid Goldman started coughing and couldn't stop. McKenzie rushed to the door and helped Goldman to a chair, but he refused to sit. He hurried to McKenzie's bathroom and you could hear him coughing up the phlegm. The toilet flushed, and Goldman came out with a dark bottle in his hand.

McKenzie cringed a little, realizing she hadn't heard any running water and knew he had not washed his hands, a freakish whim of hers. "You look terrible. Have you seen a doctor?" McKenzie said.

"I'm sorry, Father, I didn't know you were here. No, I couldn't get an appointment; his nurse called in this prescription," he said as he held up the bottle. "It's helping to break up all this infection in my chest and relieving my cough a little."

"You sound as if you might have pneumonia; you sure you shouldn't go to the emergency room?" O'Brien said.

"Oh no, I just stopped in to give the Chancellor a copy of this agreement, but I see she has one already."

"Sid, would you like a drink," holding up her glass, "if you think it will help?"

"No thanks, I have to get back to my office. I've been gone all day and have a room full of clients waiting for me, and both my cell phones are to the max with messages. I'll have this agreement typed into a Consent Order and over for your signature tomorrow."

"You know you should go home and stay in bed," McKenzie said as Goldman picked up his briefcases and folders.

"I'll be alright. Thanks a lot, Father O'Brien, you did a great job."

McKenzie followed him out into the hall. "Sid, I owe you for getting this thing settled for me. Anything I can do to help, call me, okay?"

Goldman nodded and hurried off. McKenzie walked back into her chambers.

"If he doesn't slow down, he's going to drop dead of a heart attack. Doesn't he know you are a Bishop?" McKenzie said.

"No different from anyone else, they almost had me confused today; I was called Father, Doctor, Bishop, Your Honor, Your Excellency, and I'm sure some other things they didn't want me to hear. I'm just glad we got it settled—he's one sharp cookie though, I'll say that."

"Goldman?"

"You bet. I misjudged him. I thought I was the one who was directing each party and moving this case to a resolution. But at the end of the day, I realized it was all *his* strategy, not mine. He knew all along what the exact number was to settle it, and he got it for his client, but what really chaps my ego is that he did it with such ease, because in reality, he should have been in the hospital; I'm impressed."

"I've got to find some way to help him. Here's someone who graduated at the top of his law class from Harvard, and he's wasting his talents running from courtroom to courtroom with these nickel and dime cases like someone just out of law school."

"You say he graduated from Harvard? So did Brenner."

"Who's Brenner?"

"Isaac Brenner, Mack Shannon's right-hand man. He's the CEO of Shamrock, Global, and some other companies. He represented Mack today in the hearing; they didn't have a lawyer."

"Did I meet him at the party?"

"No, he and Anna Brown, Mack's CFO, were in Europe on a business trip. And I just thought of something; they're both Jewish."

"Who?"

"Brenner and Goldman."

"So?"

"It's nothing." O'Brien had to think about this. *For some reason Bickford must be out of the picture. Bickford, Overton, and Guthrie . . . big time law firm, and McKenzie would know if there were a break up or something. I'll sit tight on this for the time being.*

"Well, *this* is something." McKenzie pushed a green embossed envelope across the desk.

O'Brien picked up the envelope with McKenzie's name on the front, turned it over, and saw *PERSONAL* in bold letters. The enveloped had a broken seal with the imprint of a green shamrock. O'Brien looked up, "You want me to read this?"

McKenzie nodded.

O'Brien removed the single card from the envelope:

I hope this note finds you in great spirits. Thank you for coming to the Beethoven Club's 125th birthday party. I enjoyed meeting you and our tête-à-tête.

I am hosting a party at The Celebration in Shelbyville the end of this month, Friday & Saturday with a Sunday brunch, and would like you to be my guest. Feel free to bring a friend.

Please call Maureen @ 901- 325-5555 for details or regrets.

O'Brien turned the card over and back again and reread the note. He looked up at McKenzie, "And?" He pushed the invitation back across her desk.

"What am I supposed to do? I can't just run off to some place I've never heard of and stay the weekend with a stranger—who's this Maureen?"

"Settle down; don't get your Irish up. Number one, Maureen is my sister."

"Your sister? I thought she was a nun."

"Ex-nun, she's been working at Shamrock for years. Mack is probably trying to help you here; he's like that—doing favors for people. I'm sure JB will be there. You'll meet a lot of influential people."

"What is The Celebration?"

"Do you like horses?"

"I love horse races. Is this a big race?"

"It's big alright, but not a race. They sell about a quarter-million tickets to the judging of the World's Grand Championship of Tennessee Walking Horses. The Grand Champion is crowned Saturday night, and there will be around 40,000 people there. It's 11 days and nights of one barn party after the other. Mack will probably have 20 to 30 guests staying in his house or on the property somewhere. People will be flying in from all over the world."

"Where is Shelbyville?" McKenzie asked.

"It's about 200 miles east of here and south of Nashville. We flew in

Mack's plane the last time, so I don't know exactly where it is. He has a four-year-old in the show this year that is a favorite contender for the Grand Championship."

"A horse?"

"Yes, a horse. Have you ever seen a Tennessee Walker?"

"No, not that I know of."

"They're quite impressive. Mack has a black stallion."

"Why does that not surprise me?"

"I think his name is . . . something like Midnight Explosion."

"You're *kidding* me?"

"No, why? This is very hush-hush . . . esoteric; no outsider has seen this horse in two years. They've kept him locked inside his barn and under constant watch."

"Why?"

"To create a mystique, I guess. The competition is very strong, and there is always home cooking in these small towns. The inside rumor is Mack has bred something exceptional, a unique horse, a *super*horse, nothing like it before."

"Really? Are you going?"

"I have to be in St. Louis that weekend, but make sure you go. You'll have a great time—take Randolph."

Sure, sure, exactly what I'll do. "I'll ask Abby to go with me."

"You know, it wouldn't hurt your image to be seen with Randolph once in a awhile—he is your husband, and a lot of his patients will support your appointment."

"I know. It's not as if you and I haven't talked about this before. There is no disharmony between us. It's just—he has his friends, and I have mine. We've always had different tastes . . . he practices medicine, and I practice law. He tells me he likes being married, and he's certainly generous enough and thoughtful. We both work 24/7. I don't know . . . what can I tell you?"

Confess that we NEVER have sex?

CHAPTER 16

MCKENZIE AND ABBY hurried through the swinging doors and down the steps of the courthouse. A black limo was out front in a no parking zone with the trunk and a rear door open. Otis, Mack's driver, was waiting for them and took their luggage. Shutting the trunk lid and the rear door, he hurried to the driver's seat and headed north on Third Street; they were 25 minutes late. Otis timed the lights to avoid stopping, and ten minutes later eased the limo through the private gates onto the tarmac at the downtown airport.

Otis drove carefully, watching for taxiing aircraft, gas trucks, and other traffic. Passing a row of King Airs, a couple Citations, and one small Lear, he often thought how easy it would be to clip the wings of one of these multi-million dollar babies. Wouldn't that cause a shit storm?

There was no control tower, so everyone took off and landed by visual flight rules after making a general announcement over the airways. Weekend visitors flying in from all over the Mid-South circumvented the air traffic of Memphis International and FedEx to land at the small downtown airport.

Otis eased the limo to a stop alongside the helicopter parked in front of the open hangar doors. He popped the trunk release button from inside and opened the back door for McKenzie and Abby. Carrying their luggage, he nodded to the open door of the helicopter, placed the luggage into the rear baggage compartment, and moved to the front as the rotor blades started turning. The pilot nodded as Otis gave him a thumbs up.

Otis moved to the limo and watched the helicopter rise to about a hundred feet and hover. Rotating its nose north and south, the aircraft then banked to the east and lifted off at a slow rate of speed, its landing gear retracting. Otis headed back to Shamrock's offices to pick up Mack.

Inside the helicopter the voice of the pilot came over the speaker, "On behalf of Shamrock International let me welcome you aboard. I'm Hank Larkin, your Captain for today. Please make sure your seat belts are secure and keep them buckled while in your seat. We are a little behind schedule, but we have good weather, clear and sunny all the way, and wind from the southwest will help us make up a little time. We'll climb to 3,000 feet and basically follow Highway 64 east out of Memphis for about an hour, then turn north for about 30 minutes and land in Shelbyville. Please make yourselves at home. There is a small galley in the rear of the aircraft with drinks, sandwiches, and other goodies, and the lavatory is just behind the galley. Everything is kind of self-service. If you need something and can't find it, just pick up one of the phones. Enjoy your flight."

When McKenzie and Abby entered the aircraft, there were three men seated in the first cabin, all of Asian descent, bent over a computer with papers and blueprints spread over a table. These were the Chinese who represented a group of investors whom Takumi & JB had recommended. They paid little notice to McKenzie and Abby when they walked to the rear cabin where there were the two leather recliners and a matching couch. Abby looked at McKenzie with raised eyebrows, cocking her head toward the woman stretched out on the couch with her back to them. Her long black hair was splayed over a light blanket pulled up over her shoulders. A sleeping mask covered her eyes. Her alligator cowboy boots and travel bag were neatly placed at the end of the couch with a cowboy hat on top. McKenzie scrutinized every detail about the woman: her tight fitting jeans, outlining the muscular curvature of her legs and rear end, the designer sports watch, and even the small L/V initials on her bag. Abby watched McKenzie, and, when she looked over at her, Abby whispered, "Nice package, huh?"

*

The helicopter came in nose first, the red roof of the barn its target, then banked right. At 100 feet it flared and hovered over a large painted red X and descended. A Chevy Suburban waited at the end of the driveway that ran from the main house. The Asians were already in the Suburban, waiting, when McKenzie and Abby stepped off the aircraft. As they walked to the Suburban, they heard a shout, "Hey girls, hold up." Stormy leaped the two steps from the helicopter and rushed over. She had her cowboy boots and hat on, and McKenzie thought to herself, *She is more beautiful than I thought.*

"I'm Stormy Bordeaux," she said, reaching out, smiling, and shaking their hands. "I'm a horse trainer here." Her smile was big—teeth snow white and even and her eyes the color of the sky behind her. "You two are a sight for sore eyes. I'm surrounded by men all the time and look-at-you-two, so beautiful. We girls need to stick together; it's going to be a madhouse here this weekend. Let me show you around and give you a tour of the barn where the next world champion lives. I can't show you the champion though; he's all locked up till tomorrow night. Kinda under protective custody. Here, just put your bags in the back of the Suburban, and Butch will take them up to the main house. Don't worry about your things; thievery is a hanging offense around here. Come on, we can walk to the barn. It's right over there." She pointed to the white brick building with a red metal roof.

*

Mack sat in the back of the limo as Otis drove east on I-40 toward Nashville. A storage box marked *Trinity Town Towers* and *Shamrock-100* sat beside him full of file folders. Each folder contained summaries of bottom-line figures of a comparison between the estimated construction cost and the actual construction cost. Others were stuff with bank and private loan balance sheets, a CPM Construction Scheduling and Project Control and other reports labeled at the top of each folder. Mack's open briefcase sat on the floor at his feet. Papers and blueprints were scattered all over the seat and floor.

He sat the empty bottle of Guinness in a hole on the pull-down tray, well aware that he had ruined a few laptops with coffee or some other spilled liquid. He reached down into his briefcase, removed a small disk, and inserted it into his computer; red letters spelling *Risk Management* filled the screen. Mack perused each bullet as he scrolled down page one:

Cost Overruns, Delays, Disruptions, Construction Claims, and Litigation Support. A red light blinked on the center console; he was grateful for the interruption and pushed the speaker button, when he saw the name Shamrock-200.

"Sonnyman, what's up?" This was a nickname Mack had called Isaac from their childhood.

"Am I on the speaker phone?"

"Hold a minute." Mack lifted the handset and pressed the button that closed the window between the front and back seats. "Go on with yourself."

"You're in high spirits."

"We always have a choice. I was trying to stay positive after reading the balance sheets on Trinity."

"Not to pour fuel on an open fire, but it's one of the reasons I called. The bank is making threatening innuendos."

"Like what?"

"Maureen and Anna have gotten phone calls and a couple of registered letters this morning. Anna called and tried to pacify them, but they got pretty short with her."

"Which bank?"

"All three, and they are demanding to talk to you. I didn't want to talk to them until after we get together. Have you heard from the Chinese?"

"They should be in Shelbyville by now; they flew up in the chopper. Listen, the banks can *kiss* my ass. We're the ones way out on the limb here. I'm not going to do a thing until after this weekend. Are you coming up?"

"No-sir-ree. The last I looked, there were no black cowboys in Shelbyville."

"Strange, I thought you would be looking for cow-*girls?*"

"You are full of it, aren't you?"

"Keep in touch. We'll meet Monday, and, hopefully, I'll have some good news." Mack clicked off and lowered the window to the front seat, "Otis, how far to Nashville?"

"Well, if you look real quick to your left, you will see Bucksnort, Tennessee. Uh oh, we just passed it. Let me see the mile marker coming up . . . we're 51 miles out."

Mack had known Otis from their boxing days. He was a good amateur heavyweight, and Mack used to see him at the gym all the time and sparred with him, with the understanding he didn't go full speed. One night they ran into each other in the men's room at the FedEx Forum, and Otis told him he had retired from the Memphis Police Department with a full disability. He had lost an eye in a freak accident when the air bag in his cruiser accidently exploded in his face, smashing his sunglasses into his eye. Mack had given him his number in case he ever needed some extra work. Soon after that, he was hired as a chauffeur for Shamrock, then later as Mack's personal driver. About a year after Irish was born, Otis was driving them downtown and asked him a strange question, "What is the most important thing in your life?"

Mack didn't hesitate, "My daughter, Irish."

The next question from Otis was, "How much do you spend on her protection?" He went on telling Mack of the hundreds of cases of kidnapping going on in all of South America and Mexico. It was mostly members of wealthy families. Otis suggested a tighter security around the house and property. A short time later, Otis was promoted to head of security at the office, the house, and most importantly, as Irish's personal bodyguard. Otis hired and trained a security staff for the gates, property, the house, and the rotation of three men for 24-hour protection of Irish. After Irish started school, Otis explained to Mack he was bored to death and that he felt he could do both: go back to driving for him and continue to supervise security.

"See if you can get Senator Parnell on the horn. I think he's at the Loews Vanderbilt. If not, try his cell." Mack went back to reading the Risk Management report until Otis told him there was a message at the desk that the Senator would be waiting in the lobby of the Loews.

Mack was sure he had a good grasp of where they were financially with the construction of the Towers. He had checked individual estimates and the Senior Estimator and the Chief Estimator's figures, and everything was pretty close. To cross-check his figures he did a quick cost estimate of the footprint by figuring the square foot price times 33 stories. This would give him an inflated cost because it was cheaper to build up than out, but he used that figure as a safety value to let him know they were not too low with their estimates. On the big dollar items, like Site work, Foundations, Concrete, Steel, Mechanical, and Electrical he had reviewed Global's estimates against the sub-contractor's bids. Mack knew they needed nothing less than $500 million to finish all three buildings. He hadn't finished the computation of the cost of the development of the roads and bridges, train and tram station, shopping mall, marina, parks, and the amphitheater. He realized that the long-term leases on T-1 and other concessions would infuse the kitty, and he could borrow on that to start Tower Two. The banks were not an immediate problem. *They were all alarmists; what are they going to do, take over the project?—I don't think so.* Besides, if JB's influence with the Treasury Secretary can swing this loan with the Chinese, he could pay everybody off, and it would all be downhill.

Mack noticed Otis had turned off I-40 onto West End Avenue. He closed his computer, folded the drawings, and replaced the folders in his briefcase.

Otis watched a lime green motorcycle through his rear view mirror. It looked like one of those European racing bikes as it pulled off the Interstate when he did and tailgated him down West End. Otis turned right into Loews and pulled under the porte-cochere. He watched the two men on the motorcycle roar past him toward the parking lot, both wearing helmets that looked like wasps' heads. *What's a "Ninja" bike doing turning into Loews . . . sometimes this limo draws the wrong kind of attention; a couple of fat cats, easy marks. Maybe they're part of the work force?*

Mack saw JB standing at the entrance talking to a tall young man in a dark, tailored suit. He had his briefcase in his hand and a clothing bag laid over a small piece of luggage at his feet. The doorman opened the back door, and Mack got out and walked across the driveway to JB. Otis popped the trunk lid from inside, removed the trash from the back seat and moved the storage box to the trunk.

"Good morning, JB. Or is it, afternoon?" Mack said.

"Good morning, Mack, good timing. Let me introduce Mark Hilton, the new General Manager here at Loews. Mark, Mack Shannon." Mack shook the hand of the dark-haired, baby faced, young man; *his name is Hilton and he works for Loews?*

The doorman stood next to JB. "Senator, I'll put these in the trunk for you," pointing to his clothing bag and luggage. JB moved forward to follow the doorman as he carried the luggage to the limo. They all turned toward the revved-up *Ninja* motorcycle as it exploded up the driveway, slicing between the doorman and JB. They were dressed in black leather with dark shields hiding their faces. The one in the back leaned over, almost touching the ground, and tore the briefcase from JB's hand, pulling him forward face down onto the brick driveway.

Otis was leaning over into the trunk when he heard the racing of the motorcycle and knew there was going to be trouble. He took a deep breath and removed his .45 caliber Glock-21 holding it slightly behind his right leg and stepped out from behind the limo right in front of the oncoming motorcycle. It was too late to move so he stood his ground while the motorcycle bore down on him. The driver swerved to the left at the last minute, almost laying the bike over, and that's when Otis jumped forward with all of his 255 pounds and kicked the side of the gas tank just as he had kicked doors in while on the police department.

The rear rider catapulted from the motorcycle, skidded down the driveway, the back of his helmet bouncing against the pavers like a bobble-head doll, and stopped against the curb, spread eagle on his back. The motorcycle wobbled down the driveway out of control and crashed into a huge concrete planter, ejecting the driver, up and into the 16-foot magnolia tree growing out of a planter.

Mack ran to JB while Otis walked down the driveway and stood over the rider who was semi-conscious, but still holding tight to JB's briefcase. He took his size 14 shoe and placed it on the man's wrist and leaned forward. Like a mechanical robot the fist opened, and Otis picked up the briefcase. He heard a siren and looked out on West End and saw a Nashville police car pull into the driveway and slid his Glock back into his underarm holster. He walked back to check on JB as hotel security scrambled all over the place.

Mack was holding JB's torn suit coat and a doctor, who was staying at the hotel, was checking his bloody knee where his pants were torn.

"Thank you Doctor, it's very thoughtful of you to help, but I am fine." JB turned and whispered to Mack and Otis, "Let's get out of here now before the press shows up." Mack nodded to Otis, and he walked JB over to the limo.

"Otis, I've got a pair of khaki pants in my garment bag, please get those for me, and I will change in the car." JB said as he climbed into the back seat.

Mark Hilton, the GM, walked with Mack over to the limo. "Mr.

Shannon, my deepest apologies, I'm so embarrassed about this. I want you to know that whatever it takes to right this wrong I will take care of it personally. Here's my card with my home and cell phone number. If I do not hear from you in the next few days I will contact you."

"Mr. Hilton." JB said from the back window. "You have my card, please let the police Lieutenant or whoever is in charge know that this was just an accident. I wasn't looking where I was going and stepped in front of the motorcycle as it was leaving. Make sure those two 'bums' understand, okay?"

"I'll take care of everything, Senator. I know the officer in charge, and I thank you for understanding; and you will be hearing from me."

Otis eased the limo out onto West End and headed for the south loop toward I-24 down to Shelbyville.

"Mack, my good friend, I think we both need a stiff drink." JB said as he leaned back, trying to stretch out his leg. "Damn, I thought a truck ran over me at first. I was tumbling down the driveway, and when I looked up I saw this figure flying over me waving my briefcase."

Mack handed JB a glass with Scotch and ice. "You okay?"

"Hell, yeah," taking a large drink of his Scotch. "This was like the old days. Did you see that son-of-a-bitch flying through the air? You did great, Otis. That's what you call literally kicking the shit out of somebody. I wish I could have seen you drop kick that motorcycle. We're headed for the farm, right?" JB asked.

Mack nodded.

"Cheers." They clinked glasses.

CHAPTER 17

THE DRIVE FROM Nashville to Shelbyville gave JB time to tell Mack about his meeting with John Gettlefinger, Secretary of the Treasury. "I asked Gettlefinger if he could tell me about his upcoming meeting with Lu Hanchen. He said it had to do with the U.S. and China's Strategic and Economic Dialogue. Hanchen is the Chinese banker, Sam's friend, the one Sam told me about."

"Was that all he said?"

"I told him there was a rumor of a scheduled meeting between just the two of them. He smiled but said nothing."

"What did that meeting cost me?" Mack asked.

"Nothing yet."

JB told Mack the Secretary was a straight-up guy, above taking any money or payoffs. His personal net worth was well over $100 million, most of it made running a global investment bank, and he considered political service a duty.

"But," JB added, "like all good politicians, he's not above a little arm-twisting for one of his favorite charities. While he was the U.S. Ambassador to China, he founded the Global Children's Fund, and each year he heads up their big fundraiser. I hinted that you were a large contributor to Saint Jude Children's Research Hospital and would be honored to participate in Global Children's next fundraiser. He seemed quite excited when I suggested you as a possible guest speaker or chairman of the fundraising."

"You didn't!"

"I did."

JB, unlike Gettlefinger, was not a wealthy man. Mack could trade favors with most of his contacts, but with JB, he would have to figure out a substantial, yet untraceable gift. His influence was well worth whatever the cost. Of course, all this was contingent upon the loan from the Chinese going through and, if it did, that's what they made gold for—an Irishman's favorite untraceable asset.

Otis had stopped at a Walgreens and bought an instant cold pack and an Ace bandage for JB's knee. With the 10 milligrams of Valium from Mack and the double shot of Scotch, he was now sleeping like a baby.

Mack wanted to put everything regarding Trinity Town on hold and enjoy the weekend but he had been multi-tasking for so long that it was impossible to avoid the habit of putting out fires when they started or taking advantage of lucrative opportunities as they popped up. With so many irons in the fire, he had to act instantly to minimize his losses or maximize his gains, regardless of his schedule. This drove his friends and employees mad.

He opened his calendar on his phone and read his to-do list for today. He was staring at the name of McKenzie O'Connor when his phone vibrated in his hand. Less than ten people had his private number. Most of his calls came from his office or through Isaac, Anna, or Bradley. Mack's first thought was another fire to put out, until he looked at the display window and smiled; printed on the screen was Shamrock 99. Codes were given out to identify all staff personnel, their emails, memos, etc. Mack's code number was 100; Isaac's was 200, Anna Brown's 300, security 500, legal 600, and so on. Everyone who personally worked for Mack had a code: Maureen O'Brien, his Personal Administrator, was 101; Bradley, his Personal Assistant, was 102, Lea, Irish's Governess, was 103; on and on. Of course, Irish insisted on having her own code, so she was assigned number 99 as her personal code.

"Yaba daba doo—guess who?" Mack said.

"Daddy," Irish said.

"*Daddy?* Is that your name?"

"No, it's *me.*"

"Who me?"

"Irish."

"Is this the most beautiful girl in the world?" Mack said.

"Is this the most *handsomest* Daddy in the world?"

"You betcha. I named you right, Baby Girl, you're full of the Irish. Where are you?"

"I just finished my tennis lesson, and I'm walking to the car."

"Is Coach Tony with you?"

"Yes sir."

"Did he work with you coming to the net?"

"Yes sir."

"Annnd?"

"I didn't back away."

"Good girl. Where's Lea?"

"Waiting for me in the car?"

"Everything's copasetic then, right?"

There was no answer from Irish.

"I don't hear you little girl. What's the matter?"

"Nothing."

"Sure there is. Tell Daddy allll about it. Is it your boyfriend?"

"No! You know I don't have a boyfriend."

"You better not have. Come on, what's up?"

"I want to see Midnight."

"No. I told you this is a grown-up party. There's going to be a lot of drinking and cursing, all-night partying."

"But Daddy, I'll be in bed by that time. I haven't seen Midnight in I don't know when. I want to see him win the championship, and Lea said she wanted to come too. Pleeeease, Daddy."

"Let me talk to Lea."

"Ohhhh, thank you, thank you, you're the best Daddy in the world."

"I didn't say . . ."

"Here's Lea."

"Yes sir?"

"Lea, I've asked you not to sir me, okay?"

"Yes sir."

"Lea." Mack heard them both laughing. "Okay, you two, very funny. Now tell me the truth, do *you* really want to come, or did you just let Irish talk you into coming?"

"You mean, like she talked *you* into her coming?"

"Okay, I give up. You two are going to drive me nuts. I'll call Captain Hank to fly you up here. Remember though, early to bed, no parties."

"Does that go for me too?"

"Lea . . ."

"Sorry. Irish wanted me to ask you if she could bring Bear and could he ride up front with Captain Hank?"

"You bring whomever you want. I have to go now, goodbye." Mack often took Lea for granted, and chastised himself for forgetting how fortunate he was to have her. She was a lifesaver—for him and Irish. A strict disciplinarian with a velvet glove was the perfect combination for such a strong-willed girl. "Lea?" It was too late; she had already disconnected.

"What's the problem?" JB asked as he raised his reclining seat.

"Women," Mack said and went back to his to-do list and entered: *Spend more time with Irish.*

"How's your knee?" Mack asked.

"What knee? That pill, I forget what a miracle drug that is, and the double Scotch didn't hurt; we almost there?"

"Yeah. If you are going to change pants, now's the time."

The small downtown of Shelbyville was packed; the sidewalks were so full of people, some were walking in the street. The American and Tennessee flags flew from every power pole, and banners advertising The Celebration streamed across every corner of Main Street. Otis turned onto State Road 82 toward Flat Creek, away from town and into rolling and bucolic landscapes dotted with signs along the road advertising Jack Daniel's Distillery.

Otis slowed the limo when he saw the beginning of the white, four-rail horse fencing. He turned into the driveway where the green sign above the gate read: SHAMROCK FARMS.

Otis stopped at the top of the hill when he heard a plane very close overhead. They all watched the candy-apple red, single-engine biplane touch down on the grass landing strip parallel to the driveway. Otis followed the plane as it taxied down the strip.

"Nice little plane," JB said.

"Yeah, that's a Pitts Aerobatic. Expensive little toy, probably a couple hundred grand."

"You're kidding. Whose plane?"

"Beats me," Mack said.

People and all kinds of machines—from 4-wheelers to backhoes—were all over the place. Work had been going on for a week getting ready for tonight, The Party of Mimics. Some had hired architects and full construction crews in their desire to win the prestigious First Place prize: ten days at Mack's house in Key West for two, including Mack's private jet transporting the lucky party there and back.

Two weeks ago they pulled names from a feed bucket, and each contestant was presented a plat showing a 100-by-100 foot section of land on the farm on which to create any theme, no matter how avant-garde. It was suggested that contestants use their wildest imagination. Tents, tarpaulins, or fabric fencing covered each structure to prevent anyone knowing what their themes were. At 4:00 pm today a small parade with five judges leading the way would visit each party site, drinking and eating along the way, to determine a winner.

*

McKenzie stood on the second floor balcony outside her room looking out over the landscape and at the fast-setting sun out beyond the tree line. Her room was very comfortable: a 12-foot ceiling and a high canopy bed with an upholstered bench at the end facing a fireplace. She looked to her right when she heard the little red airplane and watched as it taxied out of view behind a black limo headed for the barn. The back door opened, and Mack Shannon stepped out dressed in jeans, cowboy boots, and what looked to be a leather shirt. McKenzie smiled, not quite sure of her feelings but happy to see him again. Why else was she here? She loved horses but knew very little about them, especially Tennessee Walkers. She studied the outline of his body in the tight-fitting jeans as he leaned over, talking to someone in the back seat. She had mixed emotions, and he stoked some repressed embers lying deep in her subconscious. After all, she was a married woman, legally that is, and yet his presence . . .. Unconsciously, she brought the side of her hand up to her mouth and kissed where her finger and thumb met, moving her lips and sucking lightly. How long had it been since she had been kissed on the mouth? Had she forgotten how? She loved to kiss; her lips were one of the most erogenous zones of her body.

The limo turned around and headed toward the house. McKenzie watched Mack walk to the barn, saw the doors swing open, then saw Stormy, running full speed, jump into Mack's arms. She wrapped her legs around his waist and Mack spun her around and around. McKenzie's hand dropped from her lips, she froze in place, and like a raptor stalking its prey, she stared fiercely, watching them kiss, her arms stiff as she leaned forward, her hands like talons clutching the handrail, her supple lips now a tight beak.

"Martini time," Abby shouted, stepping out on the balcony balancing two full martinis. "Don't you know how to knock?"

"I did knock . . . what's the matter?" Abby saw the black limo almost to the house now and followed McKenzie's stare out to the barn. She saw Stormy riding piggyback on Mack as they trotted through the barn doors. "Is that our host, Mr. Shannon?"

"Mr. Midnight Explosion himself."

"Wow, she not only rides his horse, she rides him too."

"Just what I was thinking." *What else, when a young babe like her is sleeping in his helicopter.*

"I'm sorry, Honey . . ."

"Don't be," McKenzie snapped, grabbing one of the martinis, and downing it, scarcely cooling her Irish blood. "We came to party; let's party. If I decide I want it, I'll get it."

Abby said, "No doubt in *my* mind," and followed McKenzie inside. "Just be careful you don't bite off more than you can chew . . ." *With this guy you could choke to death.*

CHAPTER 18

EVERYONE LOOKED TO the sky when they heard the thumping of the whirling blades approaching and hurriedly covered their eyes from the dirt and grass created by the whirlwind. The flaps of the camouflaged tent thrashed like a chained bird as the helicopter, with a red cross painted on each side, descended. Two loud speakers blasted the announcement,

ATTENTION! Now hear this! We have incoming wounded. All personnel from MASH 4077th report to the surgical tent immediately!

Organized chaos was everywhere; heavy artillery exploded in the background with smoke bombs going off around the tent. Nurses and orderlies scrambled to the helicopter removing the stretchers with bandaged-wrapped soldiers to the tent. A military jeep skidded to a stop and "Hawkeye" and "Trapper" ran inside as the music from M*A*S*H, a 1970s American satirical black comedy TV show, blared over the loud speakers.

The closing scene ended when all the cast—dressed in surgical gowns, masks, and caps—gathered over Hawkeye's operating table to watch a delicate and complicated surgical procedure. In an explosion of laughter, Hawkeye lifted a crying baby doll by its heels out from under the sheet and the mother, Corporal Klinger, sprang upright wearing a long blonde wig, waving his discharge papers. The full cast of characters, already in a celebratory mood, handed out martinis and moved with the crowd to the next contestants.

"How authentic was that? Wow, I thought we were watching a real filming. I love to watch those reruns; they'll win first place for sure," Abby said, finishing her martini.

"Some of them looked just like the actors in the TV series, especially the blonde with the big tits, Hotlips. What was her name?" McKenzie asked.

"Major Houlihan."

"No, I mean her real name. It's Loretta . . . Swift, or something like that."

"Swit."

"Really, Swit?" They toasted their empty plastic martini glasses. "Come on, let's follow the crowd."

"First things first; we need to find a filling station."

A woman behind them, dressed in a nurse's uniform and pushing a soldier in a wheelchair said, "Did I hear someone say refill?"

The "soldier," with a fake cast on his foot, lifted the coiled IV tubing that ran from a large bag filled with pink liquid, hanging from the IV pole on the back of his wheelchair. He released the clamp on the tubing and filled McKenzie and Abby's glasses as others gathered and stuck out their glasses and cups, shouting, "Refills."

*

The center island in the kitchen was loaded with food, and Mack had almost emptied the double door refrigerator.

"No mayo, Daddy, I'm on a diet," Irish said. "I'm eating mustard now; it's less fattening."

"A diet? You're a growing child, for God's sake. There's not an ounce of fat on your skinny butt."

"You don't think I've gained weight?"

Mack shook his head as he sliced the chicken breast for her sandwich. Bear, sitting on his haunches, watched every move. "Listen Baby, you're growing, and you're supposed to be gaining weight. Plus, if you don't put fuel in your tank, you'll run out of gas; you don't want that to happen in the middle of a tennis tournament, do you?"

"Ooo-kay, put a little mayo with my honey mustard. Is that on Wheat Berry?"

The kitchen door opened, and JB walked in. "This is where you two have been hiding."

"Hi, Uncle JB, you want a Dagwood sandwich?"

"Hi nothing, you better get over here and give me a big hug."

Irish ran over and jumped into JB's arms, giving him a big hug, Bear right behind her. JB kissed her on both cheeks and carried her back to her bar stool. "What do you know about a Dagwood sandwich, little lady? That's way before your time."

"There is Dagwood Bumstead, his wife Blondie, and their two children, Alexander and Cookie, and their dog, Daisy. Dagwood always got hungry late at night and . . ."

"Okay, Irish, he knows all about the Bumsteads." Mack sat Irish's sandwich in front of her.

"Is it still a comic strip? She knows a lot more than I remember. Irish, how in the world are you going to get your mouth around that sandwich?" Picking up the chef's knife, JB said, "Here, let me cut that for you."

Irish covered her sandwich with both hands. "No, Uncle JB, Dagwood never cuts his sandwich. Did you know Dagwood was a billionaire and in construction just like Daddy?"

"That's enough, Irish." Looking at JB, Mack asked, "You want a sandwich, or I've got fried chicken, potato salad . . .?"

"I'm stuffed, but a cold beer would be good?"

"Sure. Did you get to see any of the contests?" Mack said.

"I did. You remember Danny Sled, don't you? His group did this *Out of Africa* skit from the movie. The food was great. They had stuffed pheasant, antelope tenderloins, and a huge African fish on a grill with shaved almonds, *lar-ru-pin*. They were all dressed in safari gear with big game rifles and had this long formal table setting with candelabras and a Mombasa mosquito net hanging over it all. I sampled everything except the monkey and some other things I wasn't sure of. Did you and Irish see the hot air balloons from the *Around-the-World-in-80-Days* theme?"

"Daddy wouldn't let me ride in the balloons. What's *larrupin?*"

Mack handed JB his beer. "We watched as they floated low over the crowds and threw grapes and poured wine on everyone; it was getting pretty rowdy. One of the balloons got caught in a cross wind and bounced across a field, knocking down a fence and dumped out a couple of people. They were having a great time, and, fortunately, no one was hurt."

Mack and JB stopped talking when they heard a door slam and loud voices.

"Come on, this way; I'm hungry. Where's the chef? I bet he's hiding in here."

"Abby, don't go in there, please," McKenzie said.

Abby banged the kitchen door open and staggered in. "Well, well, here's the party and Prince Charming himself." Abby turned back to McKenzie who was following and whispered loud enough for all to hear, "Or should I say, Mr. Midnight Explosion himself, heh, heh, heh."

"I'm *so* sorry, Mr. Shannon," McKenzie said, putting both arms around Abby, "She's had way too much to drink and nothing to eat."

"Would you like me to fix her a sandwich?" Mack said.

"Oh-my-God!" McKenzie squealed as Abby broke away from her, and a geyser of vomit spewed out over the kitchen floor and down the side of the island. Dropping to her knees, Abby upchucked again.

Irish jumped off her bar stool and grabbed a dishtowel, went to the sink, and soaked the towel in cold water, and gave it to Abby.

"Thank you, Sweetie . . . how thoughtful," McKenzie said. "This is embarrassing." She lifted Abby and wiped her face and folded the towel and tried to clean up the side of the island.

There was a knock on the kitchen door, "Irish, are you in there?" The door opened, and Lea stood in her pajamas with a puzzled look on her face. "I was going to put Irish to bed . . . can I help?"

Mack waved Lea in, and JB said, "Come on, let's get her in bed, and she will feel a lot better," helping McKenzie guide Abby out of the kitchen. "She's had a little accident," JB said to Lea.

Mack kissed Irish on the head, "You did good, Baby Girl. I'm proud of you." He took the towel to the sink, ran hot water over it, and rung it out. "Most little girls would have taken off running when . . ."

"This happens at school all the time, Daddy."

"You mean . . . *you* girls are drinking at school?" Mack teased.

"*No*, Daddy. They get sick. I know what you're going to say, 'I-told-you-so.' That's why you didn't want me here, seeing things like this, right?"

He started washing off the cabinets. "It's not something I like you being around."

Lea had a mop from the closet and was cleaning up the floor.

"Lea, stop that. It's not your job. I'll get somebody to do that."

"There is no one awake, and you can't leave this overnight. It won't take but a minute."

Lea made some hot soapy water and Pine Sol in a mop bucket, and in a few minutes everything was clean. "That cleared up the smell," Mack said.

"Daddy, I don't want this sandwich. I'm sorry."

"I think we've all lost our appetites. Let's get you to bed," he said, looking at Lea.

"Carry me, Daddy?"

"Not tonight, Baby—I'm beat."

"Pleeeease, Daddy."

"All right, hop aboard," Mack said, lifting her to the counter top and turning his back.

"No, no. Princess style."

"You're pushing your luck, young lady." Mack picked her up and carried her up the steps like a bride over a threshold. "You're getting way too big, or I'm getting too old for this."

Lea followed them up the steps. "Mr. Shannon, do you want me to put the food up?"

"No, you've done enough, and please, Lea, can't you call me Mack like everyone else?"

"No, I can't, Mr. Shannon."

"Then what *are* you comfortable calling me?" Mack said.

"How about, Big Daddy?"

Irish's giggle prompted all three of them to laugh. Bear barked and raced up the stairs, pushing everyone out of his way, letting them all know he was going to be first in Irish's bed.

After Mack had put up the food and wiped everything down with Clorox wipes, he sat on the bar stool thinking; his chin rested on his fist, going over today's events. He was not sleepy or hungry or thirsty—just restless. He had heard a lot of compliments about the competition and the hot air balloon rides. His part-time chef, Leo, had assured him everything was in place for the Barn Party tomorrow night. Earlier he had called down to the barn and talked to Stormy, who was sleeping in the barn with "Midnight" to ensure he had no late night visitors and to keep him calm so that he would peak at the right time tomorrow. She said he was locked up tight in his stall biting at the bit to strut his stuff, and they had placed barricades and yellow *No Trespassing* tape about twenty feet out from the barn for security. She had suggested that if Mack was too excited and couldn't sleep that she would be up late in case *he* needed calming down. Mack had crossed that line before and regretted it each time; it was bad business. She was one of the wildest women he had ever been with, but it was strictly recreational copulation—no more than Midnight mounting a mare in season.

He was not a negative person, but sometimes he felt wasted. The same thing, over and over, like a treadmill he couldn't get off. There had to be more to life than just working, making money, buying meaningless toys, and propagating.

Then he laughed, thinking about Lea calling him Big Daddy. She's a feisty little thing, not intimidated by anyone—great for Irish to be around. And did she ever look sexy in those pajamas? *I know . . . I know . . . hands off—way too close to home.*

The kitchen door eased open, and McKenzie stuck her head in.

"The Thinker!" she said.

"What?"

"Rodin, his statue." She posed with her fist under her chin, *"The Thinker?"*

"Oh yeah, the French sculpture."

"You okay? You look in deep thought. I came down to clean up Abby's mess."

"I'm fine, just going over my to-do list in my head to see what all I forgot."

"You do that too? I bet you're an ESTJ!"

"Am I that obvious? Are you a Jungian?"

"Sort of. I do like a lot of his theories, especially his Individuation, the central concept of analytical psychology. We use his, or I should say Myers and Briggs' personality test in the courts."

"How's that?"

"In a lot of cases we order psychological evaluations to determine if one of the parties, or both, is unstable or dysfunctional. For example, in child support cases or inheritance . . ."

"You're a very interesting woman . . ." Mack interrupted.

"You're a very interesting man."

" . . . and fine-looking and charming too."

"Thank you. I am very sorry for Abby's mishap; it's uncharacteristic of her."

"What's wrong, you don't think I'm fine-looking and charming too?"

"I think you know you are and have been told many times."

"Ouch. Was that a spear or a dagger?"

"Neither. You asked."

"Am I that transparent?"

"Not transparent, but apparent."

"How so?"

"You have a certain magnetism about you. Any woman, young or old, beautiful or ugly, rich or poor, would be susceptible to your charm, your money, and your looks."

"Not you though?"

"No . . . not me. I'm a married woman."

"Ouch, another coup de grâce. Would you like a nightcap with that fatal thrust?"

"No thank you. I've had enough to drink tonight, and I'm headed to bed. I understand tomorrow is the big day for your *stallion* and then your barn party?"

Mack nodded.

She headed for the door and stopped. "The kitchen looks spic and span; did you do this?"

Mack nodded again, "The finishing touches . . ."

"I'm impressed. Good night."

"No good night hug or a kiss on the cheek?"

"Mr. Shannon, I'm surprised. A man of your conviction, I would've expected him to *take* a kiss, not *ask* for one. Besides, you need to save those kisses for that fine young filly that was riding you at the barn this afternoon."

"Ohhh . . . now I understand. That's why Abby referred to me as Midnight Explosion?"

"Could be, is it midnight yet?" McKenzie said over her shoulder as the swinging door closed behind her.

"Okay, enough already, I'm dead. Why do you keep stabbing me?" He moaned, loud enough for her to hear as she climbed the stairs, and he heard the door close. He shook his head, thought a minute, and looked over at the kitchen clock.

It's not midnight yet. I wonder if Stormy is still awake?

CHAPTER 19

MACK STOOD IN front of the horse barn reading the sign posted on the door.

HORSES

They are intelligent, courageous, strong, fast, agile, loyal, and yet independent. Never in history has an animal played such a huge part in revolutionizing the world in war, work, travel, or sport. With love and patience the horse will be a respected partner for life.

Sure, the dog is "man's best friend," but that was because of all the natural working and hunting instincts and as a protector. But now dogs were bred down to spineless, yipping pets—like a lot of men now. He'd seen them scooping dog poop and wiping the dog's ass. Bear would bite your hand off if you tried to wipe his ass. Tennessee Walkers and Bouviers, they're working animals, not pets.

There is something vibrant about walking into an indoor arena at a horse show with the earthy smells of dirt, sawdust, grain, and hay, and the mass of horse people. One is caught up in the festivities and the high energy level of competition between horses and people. This last event of the Celebration was the Super Bowl for Walking Horses.

Mack had a reserved box in the west grand stands on the "fifty-yard line" for his guests, but he was too anxious to sit still for long, moving from seat to seat and talking to friends and finally, ending in the center ring of the arena just before the judging of the World's Grand Champion.

He stepped up on the platform and saw JB politicking with some owners and judges. They all watched the drawing of three colored balls from the judge's box to determine the three judges for the World's Grand Champion. Mack looked out over the crowd, saw someone waving, and noticed it was McKenzie with Abby. He wondered how they got through security to the center ring without a pass. He nodded and started toward them when he realized she was waving at someone else who was now walking up to them. He was tall with blond hair, had a gold pass hanging from his neck, and carried three drinks in his hands—dressed with a European slant, definitely not from around here. Mack stopped and watched them as they toasted their drinks, laughing; he turned away and walked over to JB.

A few minutes later Mack heard someone call his name and turned to find McKenzie at the foot of the steps. He walked over and stepped down from the platform.

"Mack, this is Carlos Hinnermann, from Argentina. You remember Abby?"

"Yes, of course."

Abby stood silent, embarrassed, and speechless.

"Herr Hinnermann, willkommen to The Celebration," Mack said.

"Please, call me Carlos. Do you speak German?"

"No, unfortunately. I have a client I do a lot of work for from Germany, and I've spent some time there. Were you born there?"

"No, I was born in Argentina but went to a German school in Buenos Aires. But to answer your question, this is my first time at The Celebration. I have never seen such a, how do you say . . . a *sammlung*, a gathering of the most magnificent horses in the world."

"Argentina is known for their horses and skilled vaqueros. Are you a horse person, Carlos?"

"Yes, Señor, but I would trade a hundred of my horses for your Midnight."

"You have seen Midnight?" Mack said.

"No, but the mystery behind him is enough to wager 100 horses," he laughed. "And, if the mystery is half-true . . . maybe two hundred of my horses?"

The Ringmaster started his announcement, "Ladies and gentlemen, this is the event we all have been waiting for . . ."

"Let's cross over quickly to the box seats. You'll have a closer look," Mack said, looking back for JB who was in deep conversation with the judges.

There was never any doubt in Mack's mind which horse the judges would select as the world champion. It wasn't arrogance; it was a fact. Judging a Walking Horse was not unlike judging a Mr. Universe or a Mr. Olympia contest. Arnold Schwarzenegger won both seven times. His outstanding advantage was that he was a head taller and carried fifty pounds more muscle than other contestants. Ten horses were vying for the World Grand Champion, and Midnight was like Arnold, a foot taller than the other horses: 17 hands tall and weighing 1,260 pounds. Midnight was a once-in-a-lifetime phenomenon—all the stars had lined up in sequence. The bloodlines of 70 years of breeding Grand Champions had boiled to the top and blossomed in this one horse.

That's the way Mack first saw him as a colt: feral, bigger, stronger, and faster than all the other colts. Old man Galina must have known he had a diamond in the rough, because he charged Mack four times what any of his colts had sold for previously.

McKenzie stood next to Mack, leaning over the short railing on the edge of the dirt track as the crowd pushed for a closer look. Midnight and the other nine horses had finished their required three distinct gaits: the flat walk, running walk, and canter. The judges were huddled, and everyone waited impatiently for their decision. The Ringmaster left the judges' table, walked to the center of the ring, and announced that all three judges requested a workout of one of the horses, number 99, "Midnight Explosion."

"Is something wrong?" McKenzie asked.

"The judges want another look at Midnight, by himself. Stay close. This is when he *explodes.*"

Mack knew why the judges had called for a workout. Midnight, with his size alone, overshadowed the other horses when trying to judge them together. The judges needed to back up their first impression: a combination of awe, shock, and admiration. With a workout by himself, they could judge him on all aspects of his conformation, his uniquely inherited running walk, his true color, his temperament, and of course the symmetry and balance of the complete animal.

"You don't seem too concerned?" Carlos said.

"No, not at all. For the last two years, I've had retired judges using the same grading forms as they're using now. He has no flaws."

The lights flickered on and off in the arena, then dimmed, and a long reaching spotlight searched for the tunnel-like entrance to the track. Stormy pulled Midnight back, just out of the range of the spotlight, then dropped the reins and kicked him to go, then pulled him back again, teasing him for his grand entrance. The spotlight settled on the shadow of Midnight, standing back from the entrance, and then the voice of Johnny Cash blared out over the loudspeaker, "I hear that train a comin' . . . ."

It was as if a stick of dynamite had blown the barn door down when Midnight exploded onto the track out of a whirling mass of dirt and dust, attacking the arena. His rear end was low and un-swaying, his huge head nodding up and down, like a metronome in perfect rhythm with his running walk. His eyes were clear and excited, his nostrils flaring in and out while his small ears pointed forward.

This night was all about Midnight, and Stormy let him have his way but blended in perfectly: black leather pants, cowboy boots, and a long black leather coat. Her raven tresses streamed, matching Midnight's mane and tail. She sat still in the saddle, her hands in mid-air gripping the reins, her strong legs locked around half-a-ton of volatile explosives.

Mack and McKenzie leaned over the railing watching Midnight *coming* down the track. His long stride covered twenty miles every hour. Each front hoof reached up and out as if he were climbing a steep hill. McKenzie felt him coming, the ground shaking with the thunderous cadence of hoof beats, hypnotizing her and pulling her in closer to the rail until dirt and sweat flew everywhere and the sound of his racing heartbeat, his snorting, and hot breath blowing over the top of her . . . She screamed, "Oh my God!" and grabbed Mack, throwing both arms around him, burying her face.

"Now *that's* what you call a *Big Lick*," Mack said, brushing the dirt off him and McKenzie as Midnight roared by with booming applause.

*

They all walked back across the track to the center ring, jubilant. Mack held Irish's hand while McKenzie, Lea, Abby, and Carlos followed. Stormy rode Midnight up beside them and jumped to the ground, grabbing and hugging Mack wildly, turning him around and around, shouting, "I told you. I told you. I told you." A rowdy crowd of Stormy's friends gathered around her, pulling her away, while three grooms wiped Midnight down with towels and brushed his mane and tail. Mack held his bridle, whispering in his ear, praising him over and over, his massive chest heaving in and out, while they all waited for the judges' decision.

McKenzie walked over to Mack. Midnight's flecks of white foam still in her hair. "I don't understand. Everyone here talks about how calm and docile the walking horse's temperament . . . I didn't see that in Midnight. I don't see how Stormy stayed on."

"These are show horses, and, like great athletes, they're trained to perfection to peak at this very moment. And like any performer—actor, singer, athlete—they love an audience and let it all hang out. Any other time, they're as gentle as a baby." Mack watched Irish as she gave Midnight his favorite treat, lemon drops. He bent over and whispered something in her ear then lifted her onto the saddle of Midnight.

"Ladies and gentlemen, by a unanimous decision of all three judges, it is my pleasure to present to you, the World's Grand Champion Tennessee Walking Horse . . . Midnight Explosion."

"Walk *only*, no other gaits," Mack said while adjusting the stirrups for Irish. "Don't hold him too tight; just let him go his way. Sit up straight now, one time around. *NO* running, *comprende?*"

Irish pulled lightly on the left rein and touched Midnight with her heels. The big stallion turned immediately, his head high, looking out into the crowd, hearing the exultation. "Daddy, this is not my *first rodeo*," Irish said, riding off toward the track, kicking her shoes off behind her and taking the slack out of the reins.

The song, "The Tennessee Waltz," started playing over the loud speakers. Irish sat in contrast to Midnight, long blonde hair and a white dress, as the World's Champion glided down the track to the Waltz in an over-striding Flat Walk. Flash bulbs went off with every step around the ring, the crowd applauding and some shouting "big lick, big lick." Irish took a deep breath and kept repeating to herself to relax, enjoy the ride, and Midnight loves her. She sat upright in the saddle, looking straight ahead, her legs tight against Midnight, feeling his heat and every muscle moving under her. When they made the last turn on to the straightaway to the judge's box, the music had stopped, and the audience started a slow, hand-clapping cadence to Midnight's Flat Walk. Irish felt the reins pulling slightly as the nodding of Midnight's head got faster and his stride got longer. The cadence of the clapping increased and got louder. Irish leaned forward over Midnight, grabbing two fists full of mane and shouted, "Big Lick."

Irish slapped both heels into Midnight and held on as the big stallion switched gears, firing off instantly, covering four times the distance from Flat Walk to Running Walk, and the crowd clapped faster and faster, with wild satisfaction.

Irish pulled back on the reins, the bit signaling Midnight to stop, but like a big Morgan in a pulling contest, he didn't want to stop. He loved the center stage and the roar of the crowd. They were halfway around the ring again before Irish got him turned and walked him back up the track to the grassy area in the center ring. Mack helped her off the horse while the grooms and photographers were all over Midnight again.

"Are you hard-headed or what? You're in for a lot of trouble little girl, when you get older."

"Ohhhh, Daddy, I was sooo scared. I almost wet myself." She hugged his waist. "All I could do was hold on. Did I look alright?"

"You did great, Baby," Mack said.

Lea hurried over and hugged Irish.

Mack looked around the crowd for McKenzie. "Have you seen Chancellor O'Connor?" Mack asked Lea.

"She was standing right here a few minutes ago . . . .." Lea had seen McKenzie walk off with Carlos but didn't feel it was any of her business.

"How about Otis?"

"He's right behind you," Lea said.

Mack turned and saw Otis standing over at the judge's platform and walked over to him, leaving Lea to watch Irish.

"Everyone is talking about Irish riding Midnight," Otis said.

"Keep a close watch on her. Have you seen the Chancellor?" Mack looked out over the crowd.

"I saw her walk off with the blond-headed guy. They were leading a horse out to the trailers in the parking lot. Did he have a horse in the show?"

Stormy hurried over with an open bottle of champagne and pulled Mack by the arm, "Come on, the photographers from the paper and the TV people are waiting for us."

Mack downed the glass of champagne Stormy handed him. *If she would rather be with him, so be it.* Champagne ran over the top of his glass as Stormy poured him a refill while they walked over to the press section.

Mack searched one more time over the crowd—*The hell with her.* He shoved his glass out to Stormy for a second refill.

CHAPTER 20

OTIS STOPPED AT the house, and a couple of the security guards ran to open the limo's doors. JB kissed Irish good night and told Lea he was beat and headed up to bed. It was a beautiful night with clear skies and a full moon. The barn was lit up with multi-colored lights, and one could hear the music and smell the barbecue cooking on the grills. Irish wanted to go down to the barn with Otis and Abby to practice her dancing, but Mack had set strict rules, and Irish knew that it was useless to persist. Lea agreed they could practice a few steps out on the balcony as soon as Irish changed to her PJs.

Mack and Stormy had been making the rounds of the other barn parties celebrating Midnight's win. Champagne bottles rolled around in the bed of the pickup when Stormy turned into the drive of Shamrock Farms and slammed on her brakes just as a huge white light filled the truck. Mack shaded his eyes from the light to see what had happened. Then he heard the powerful engine and saw the tail section overhead of a red airplane as it dropped from the treetops onto the threshold.

"Landing lights," Mack shouted over the noise.

"Damn! Am I that drunk? I thought it was a train behind us," Stormy said.

They watched the plane skim the full length of the darkened runway, twenty feet above the ground, and at the end of the runway the plane turned straight up, toward the full moon, made a slow roll and then a full loop. Making its second approach over the treetops, the plane dropped onto the grass landing strip and taxied toward the parking area.

"That's the same plane we saw yesterday. Follow him over to the parking area, but stop and check before you cross the strip." *There could be another dumb-ass landing on an unlit field.*

They both sat in the truck and watched as Carlos helped McKenzie out of the cockpit, her long hair blowing in the wind.

Stormy blinked the headlights from low to high and drove over to the plane. "You all want a lift to the barn? Jump in the back."

The music was loud at the barn with all the doors opened and a paneled wood floor, level with the dirt, had been installed in the center ring. Mack helped McKenzie down from the back of the truck. She held on to Mack's hand and led him toward the music.

"That was so much fun. It felt like you could reach out and touch the stars. Wow, listen to that music." She backed into the barn pulling Mack with both hands. "I love to dance . . ."

Mack hesitated a moment, "I'm . . .."

"I wanna dance." She dropped Mack's hands and ran back, grabbing Carlos and leading him to the dance floor, passing Mack. "I'll save the next dance for you, Mack."

"And they say I'm wild," Stormy said, as she was pulled past Mack to the dance floor by one of the judges from The Celebration.

Mack watched Carlos leading McKenzie around the crowded dance floor with ease; he was a smooth dancer, moving effortlessly, floating in and around the other dancers. It was late but she was going full speed and having a good time; he was glad. He moved to the side, away from the main door where people were still coming in from other parties—this could go on all night. He was thirsty and walked over to one of the six-foot long galvanized horse trouths filled with iced beer, wine, and champagne. He popped the top on a cold Bud, downed half of it, and stepped up on a bale of hay against the wall to get out of the way while two guards broke up a fight between two drunken cowboys. A slight breeze pulled the smoky, sweet smell of the blackstrap molasses barbeque sauce, cooking outside, through the entire length of the barn. Mack thought if you could take that smell, mixed with the smells of horse feed and hay, someone could come up with a good aftershave for cowboys. The last time he was at such a wild and freewheeling party was Bella's tango *milonga*. Big Bella, he thought, as a huge smile spread across his face while thinking back to the night she was waiting for him, standing in the middle of her bed dressed as a Norse Goddess: stoned, almost naked, with a riding crop in one hand, a gold sword in the other; he didn't know if he was going to be raped, stabbed, whipped, or all three . . . he needed to call her.

"What are you so happy about?" McKenzie shouted above all the noise. She reached up and took his beer, emptied it in one gulp, and handed it back to him.

"You're welcome." Mack said.

"I was dying of thirst." She grabbed Mack's hand, "Come on, let's dance."

Mack loved to dance, but this music was some hillbilly shuffle that he would feel foolish trying to dance to. "Let's wait till the next song, I'm not sure of this music, I'd make a fool of myself."

"Who cares? Loosen up, you own the place." She pulled Mack out onto the dance floor, locked arms and started swinging him around and around, then reversed, stomping her foot on each turn, laughing. She had tied her hair back with a scarf that now had pulled loose and her thick red hair flew freely, framing her glowing happiness.

The big smile was still on Mack's face . . . he was mesmerized.

The music stopped. Mack and McKenzie stood looking at each other, holding hands, and both breathing heavily. A female singer started singing a slow bluesy song; Mack eased his hand around to the middle of her back, felt dampness, and pulled her in close. "You want to rest this one?"

She slid both arms around his neck, dropped her head into his shoulder, her lips close, her warm breath on his neck. "This is nice," she whispered as she followed him in perfect rhythm with the music. She struggled to keep her heartbeat normal as their tightly wrapped bodies swayed from side to side. "You're a good dancer," she said.

"It's been awhile, but a good partner makes it easy."

"Is that what I am, a good partner?"

"I hope so." Mack said.

"Why?"

Because you're hot, breathtaking, and probably dangerous for me, but I would eat you up right now if I could. That's what Mack wanted to say but instead, "You're a beautiful woman, quite intriguing, and someone I'm going to pursue." He swirled her around as the song ended.

"A true Irishman, never without the right words," she said. "You know what I would love? A large cup of ice water."

"Your wish is my command, Lady O."

With two cups of ice water, Mack weaved back through the crowd to the edge of the dance floor and searched for McKenzie. He spotted her red hair on the other side in a close embrace dancing with Carlos, the Argentine. He waited, trying to catch her eye, but not once did she look toward him. His vibrating phone saved him from feeling like a fool standing alone, like some wait-staff serving drinks. He walked over to a trash barrel and dumped the two cups of water, then read the text on his phone, *ASAP. JB.* He walked out of the barn dialing JB. "Hey, what's going on?"

"I got a call from my office. We need to be in Nashville for a meeting. I'm at the house. Where are you?"

"At the barn. I'll be right up."

JB was sitting on one of the bar stools at the kitchen island when Mack walked in. "Who we meeting in Nashville?"

"Lu Hanchen, Chairman of the Bank of China in Beijing. The man who has the final say on your loan."

"He's flying all the way from Beijing?"

"No, remember, he was in Washington, meeting with the Secretary of the Treasury, Gettlefinger, but tonight he's in Nashville at the Grand Ole Opry to hear Hank Williams, Jr." JB shrugged his shoulders. "He's some kind of country western fan and plays the guitar. A lobbyist got him box seats for tonight's show. He's leaving to go back to Washington after he meets with us."

"What time is our meeting?"

"Ten in the morning; is that good for you?"

"Hey, the man with the gold makes the rules, and we *need* the gold. You got the lobbyist's name and number? I'd like to talk with him before I meet Han . . . *chen*?"

"His number is on my cell," JB scrolled down his list, "name's Mike Woo. He's in Washington."

"Ring him up on your phone; I'm sure he'll answer when he sees *U. S. Senate*."

JB hit the call button and handed Mack the phone, "I've got a call in to an old friend of mine from law school, a professor over at Vanderbilt, to find us a Chinese translator for in the morning, just in case."

"Good. Where's the meeting?"

"They're staying at the Loews, so I had my office call that Hilton kid to reserve the penthouse because of the extra rooms. I figured a big brunch buffet for our meeting. Is that good with you?"

Mack held one finger to his lips, "Mr. Woo, I'm Mack Shannon, a friend of Senator Parnell . . . thank you, that's kind of you to say. Good, then hopefully you won't mind if I ask some questions about Mr. Lu Hanchen. Did I pronounce his name correctly?" Mack nodded his head again at JB. "Mr. Woo . . . okay, Mike, what kind of guitar does Mr. Hanchen play? A Gibson electric . . . I thought he liked country music? Oh, he's a jazz guitarist, I see. One last question, well, two. Would you know his date of birth and where he was born? Sure." Mack covered the phone with his hand.

"He's checking his phone. A buffet sounds good, more selection. Give me your pen." Mack held up a finger again. "I'm still here, Mike," and wrote on his pad, "March 12, 1955." "How do you spell that? Zhan-ji-ang, China. Thank you, Mike. We'll be in touch." Mack closed the phone and handed it back to JB.

"What's that all about?" JB asked as his phone started vibrating.

Mack whispered as JB opened his phone. "We'll talk later. I'm going to run upstairs and tell Irish I have to leave early in the morning."

Holding his hand over the phone, JB said, "I called Otis and told him we would be leaving early, around seven, but to check with you."

"Good," Mack said, running up the stairs.

*

It was 5 a.m. the next morning, and Mack couldn't sleep. He stood over the stove making coffee for a thermos when he heard the kitchen door open. Thinking it was JB, he said over his shoulder, "You want some coffee?"

"No, thank you," McKenzie said. "I found your note under the door when I came in last night and wanted to catch you before you left. I didn't want you to get away before I could tell you how much I enjoyed myself.

I don't get away much from work, and this was an enjoyable break for me. Thank you. I'm sorry we didn't get to dance the last dance of the night."

"You didn't miss much. Besides, it's a wee bit daunting to follow the Red Baron. He dances like a professional."

"I got a feeling you could hold your own with the best."

"To be honest, I love to dance, especially the tango."

"Then it's settled. The next time we are together you can teach me the tango." She heard a door shut upstairs. "That must be JB. You all have a safe trip." She moved to Mack and gave him a quick kiss on his cheek. He stopped her when she turned to leave, felt her shiver, but she didn't resist and turned easily. He wrapped both arms around her and pulled her to him. He heard a short gasp, felt her breasts against his chest, and waited until she looked him in the eyes, then kissed her on the lips passionately.

She responded wildly, both her arms flying around his neck, pulling him down, and kissing his face and neck.

He lifted her, sat her on the island counter top, and wedged his hips between her open knees.

She heard footsteps coming down the staircase, and a red caution light flashed behind her closed eyes. She grabbed his hair with both hands and moved his head away from her breast.

He heard the footsteps and said, "Can I see you back in Memphis?"

With rapid breathing she pulled his head down, and after a long fervent kiss, she whispered, *"Tá súil agam sin."* Hurrying out the kitchen door, she bumped into JB on the stair landing. She hugged him quickly and rushed up the stairs to her room; hopefully he was unaware of the flower blooming on her lips.

CHAPTER 21

HEADED NORTH ON I-24, about thirty minutes outside of Nashville, Mack poured a cup of coffee from the thermos and handed it to JB.

"You wouldn't happen to have an apple fritter to go with this, would you?" They both smiled knowing they had sworn off all pastries. "I passed McKenzie this morning coming down the stairs, and she seemed a little . . . say, upset?" JB said

"Really? She seemed okay to me. She came down to thank me for inviting her and to say good-bye."

"Maybe the word is not upset. Let's say . . . flustered?"

"Well, maybe because she had been out partying all night. By the way, how's your Irish translation?"

"A hundred words, maybe. Why?"

"Tá *súil agam sin*? Is that pronounced right?"

"Beats me, only my da insisted on speaking it when he came over here. I think *agam* means *you* or *I* . . . I forgot." JB pointed to Mack's cell phone, "You have a translator in there don't you? Google it."

Mack entered the Irish words and read the translation to himself: *I hope,* is what McKenzie whispered to him.

"What's the translation?"

"As usual, with these translator apps it's . . . mismatched words."

They rode along quietly for a while, sipping their coffee, and JB said,

"You were going to tell me why you wanted Hanchen's birth date and where he was born . . . are you running a background check on him?"

Mack turned and stared over the top of his coffee cup at JB.

"Never mind," JB said, shaking his head, "forget I asked. I don't need to know."

"I thought a gift would be a nice gesture. Sort of seal the deal for the loan."

"A gift," JB shook his head, "what kind of gift?"

"You'll see."

"So, Mike Woo tells Hanchen you asked for his birth date and his place of birth, and Hanchen figures you're investigating him. You realize he will know you ran a check on him, and it could jeopardize your loan?"

"I don't think so."

"Why not? 'Cause of the gift, right?"

"You remember the old story about the inquisitive cat, don't you?" Mack said.

"Come on, you can tell me."

"Wait a couple of hours; I want your first impression when you see what I bought." Mack hesitated, "I meant to tell you that Anna is flying up with Hank this morning. I want her here in case there are any questions about the financing."

*

Mack sipped his coffee as he gazed out the bedroom window of the penthouse at the Loews Hotel. Students and faculty members across the street scurried past each other on the campus of Vanderbilt University. He picked up his phone and checked the time; everything was on schedule for his meeting with Lu Hanchen. He was asking to borrow a billion dollars with an immediate injection of half that to clear everybody out: pay off the past due bridge loans, a reimbursement to Shamrock for 32 weeks of making payroll out of his pocket, topping out Tower One, the continuation of the construction of the 12 stories so far on Tower Two, and the start of the foundation work on Tower Three. Anna Brown had been working around the clock to ensure The Bank of China's CFO had all the necessary paperwork and that Mack was briefed continuously on her exchange of documents.

There was a knock at the door, and JB walked in. "Did you want to talk with the interpreter before Hanchen gets here? She's outside."

"Thanks, JB. Ask her to come in here."

Wei Ling walked into Mack's bedroom, stopping just inside the door, looking at the bed.

"I'm Mack Shannon, Ms. Ling. Please, if you don't mind, come in and have a seat." Mack smiled and pointed to two chairs and a desk against the window. "We need to talk in privacy before we meet with Mr. Hanchen."

Wei Ling waited till Mack walked over and sat in one of the chairs. Mack watched as she moved across the room to the other chair. She was tall for an Asian, dressed in a tailored suit: very young, but very business-like, with her dark, straight-line framed eyeglasses.

"Would you like some coffee?"

"No, thank you."

"I assume Senator Parnell brought you up to date on our meeting with Mr. Hanchen this morning?"

"Yes. Your company, Shamrock International, is seeking funding for a large construction project, located on the Mississippi River in Memphis, from Mr. Lu Hanchen's Bank of China."

"Did the Senator tell you the amount of money we are trying to borrow?"

"No."

"One billion dollars." Mack stared, watching for a reaction. "Are you impressed?"

"That's a lot of money."

"But you're not impressed?"

"Old Chinese Master says: 'He who has the greatest possessions is he who will lose most heavily.'"

"What would your Old Chinese Master say about that stainless and gold Rolex peeking out of your sleeve, or for that matter, the suit jacket you're wearing; isn't that a Prada?"

"Now, I am impressed," Wei said, as she removed her glasses and smiled.

"I've shopped with my daughter in New York."

JB knocked on the door and stuck his head in, "The desk just called and said Mr. Hanchen is on his way up."

"Thanks, JB. Can you entertain him? We'll be right out." JB nodded and closed the door.

"Mr. Shannon, before we meet with Mr. Hanchen, I would like to discuss my fee."

"Okay, how much are you charging me?"

"My fee for this type of personal service is three hundred dollars an hour. Is that acceptable to you?"

"What other types of services do you provide?"

Wei Ling stared at Mack, searching for a double entendre. "I do a lot of translating of documents, review manuscripts, research, some teaching, and of course in my position now, it's publish or perish. I charge more for outside work—that is, when I'm required to leave my office to meet with a client—unless I have a contract."

"For some reason I thought you were a student. Are you a Teacher Assistant?"

"No. I'm Chair of the Department of Language across the street at Vanderbilt. I specialize in Asia, covering about 48 countries."

"You certainly look young enough to be a student."

"I am thirty-six years old. I do look younger than some of my students, and sometimes that is not an advantage—your reaction is a case in point. I confess that when Dr. Smith called me last night he did ask for a student, who would be much cheaper, but I didn't have anyone on this short notice, so he asked me if I could help him out, and I agreed."

"I appreciate that and will be glad to compensate you for your troubles with an advance or something like a sign-on bonus?"

"Thank you, but three hundred is my rate."

"Agreed. You're hired." Mack reached across the table and shook her hand. "You have to be the youngest chairperson of a department at a major university, ever."

"It was a rare opportunity—I was in the right place at the right time—plus, I'm very qualified."

"I have no doubts. Let's talk about Mr. Hanchen. Do you think he speaks English?"

"Yes. When Dr. Smith gave me Mr. Lu Hanchen's name. I did some research, at no charge, of course." She opened her purse and pulled out her phone and referred to her notes. "Would you like to know what I found?"

"Please."

"Mr. Hanchen not only speaks English but Japanese and Korean and, of course, Mandarin and Cantonese. And being that he was born in the city of Zhanjiang, he more than likely speaks Min, Southern Min, and . . ."

"Do you read and write Chinese? Legal contracts?"

Wei Ling looked up from her notes somewhat puzzled at the interruption but quickly recovered. *Remember, show no facial reactions. He is paying the bill and, unlike academia, independent business leaders operate by their own set of rules.*

"Yes sir, and other languages as well. I have translated and transcribed legal documents, but I would never release such documents without a final verification, an affidavit by a certified *legal* interpreter."

"Very good, please continue."

"Mr. Hanchen is a fifty-four-year-old widower with one child, a son, in his second year of law school at Stanford. He loves country western music, karaoke, and gambling—Mr. Hanchen that is, not his son. His two favorite singers are Johnny Cash and Dolly Parton. He is a good musician with a real passion for the jazz guitar and drops in late at night in many jazz clubs around the globe and sits in with the group that's playing. One of his favorites is the Asian American Jazz Club out in the Bay area, and he played in the Asian American Jazz festival in Chicago. Also he's an avid bridge and chess player."

Mack's cell phone vibrated on the table. He glanced at the caller, saw the number 99, and tapped the ignore key. She looked up to see if he wanted her to stop. "It's my daughter. I'll call her back." He nodded his head to continue.

"He is currently in the United States esoterically negotiating the purchasing and/or partnering of American banks that are on the blocks. It is rumored that the Federal Reserve has reached a tentative approval for his applications due to his limited ties with the Chinese government and the CCP, Communist Party of China. In addition, the Feds are looking for a door into China's booming economy. He is a very wealthy man with diverse business interests. One is The Dynasty, a 240,000 sq. ft. casino in Macau and a couple of other gambling places, a horse track and greyhound racing, as well as a variety of banks. He is known as a big spender and somewhat eccentric in his dress and behavior. One of his banks was fined twenty million dollars by both the Chinese and U.S. governments for some questionable high-yield loans a few years back."

"I'm impressed. My people had very little of this information."

"They probably didn't have Chinese apps."

"I'm sure of that."

"Mr. Shannon, now that you know Mr. Hanchen speaks English, do you still need my services?"

"Yes, more now than before. We shook hands, didn't we?"

Wei was glad, and for the first time in a long time, she felt . . . a little flushed.

Mack stood up. "Let's go meet Mr. Hanchen. One other thing before we go in," Mack's phone started vibrated again. "It's her again. She won't stop until I answer, excuse me," he said nodding for her to stay seated.

"Yes, Miss Shannon, I got your calls. Once is enough. I'm very busy. Can I call you back?"

"No, no, Daddy, you are always busy. Puh-leeze, one quick question? Can I go to the mall after school with my friends?"

"What friends?"

"Daddy? From school, where else?"

"Don't you have a tennis lesson today after school?"

"It's raining."

"They have indoors . . ."

"Puh-leeze, Daddy."

"I want the home and cell phone numbers of the parents and make sure Lea and one of Otis' men are with you at all times. You hear me?"

"Bye, Daddy, sorry I bothered you."

"How old is she?" Wei asked when Mack placed his phone back on the table.

"I really don't know. Sometimes five, sometimes fifteen, and every now and then I think she's more mature than I am. I know I'm supposed to be teaching her, but I think I've learned more from her than she has from me."

"Is that the daughter you buy Prada for?"

"No, I didn't mean for my daughter. I used to shop for her mother . . . a long time ago. Do you have children?"

"No," she said, lowering her head. "I've never been married."

"Well, she's a handful. Okay, where were we? Oh yeah, if at any time during the meeting, you feel a need to warn me or talk to me in private, just remove your glasses and start cleaning them, or if you feel confident enough, you can text me." Mack handed his phone to Wei, "I noticed we have the same phone, and here's my number. Text me now." Mack opened the door for Wei and they walked into the adjoining conference room.

A white linen tablecloth covered the buffet table at the far end of the conference room, and deluxe, gold-accented, lift-top chafing dishes lined the tabletop side by side. Mack's sense of smell was like Bear, and his stomach growled while he tried to remember when he had last eaten. A round table with six chairs was in the center of the room, and extra chairs were against the wall. The two Chinese men carrying briefcases walked through the hall door with JB and stopped to watch the tall, willowy Wei walk across the room to the buffet table. The chef bowed and spoke Chinese in a soft voice to Wei while removing the top of one of the chafers. "Ahhh . . . Mazu, Mazu, blessings from the sea, my mother's dumplings. I would know that smell anywhere." Lu Hanchen shouted in Southern Min dialect as he hurried to the buffet table next to Wei. A head shorter than Wei, Hanchen hovered over each chafer pan as the chef removed the tops and offered tidbits with chopsticks, exclaiming the joy of each dish in his home town dialect.

So this little man was Hanchen. Mack marveled at the brassiness in the way Hanchen was dressed: a black frock coat, black jeans, and shirt, with his gelled black hair piled above his head in a large pompadour; obviously, the Man in Black.

Wei turned toward Mack and in Min said, "Mr. Hanchen, Mr. Youguang, let me introduce you to Mr. Mack Shannon."

Hanchen looked up at Mack, sucked up a long noodle, stuck out his hand, and with a deep Southern accent said,

"Hello, I'm Johnny Cash."

Mack broke up and couldn't choke down his laughing. *Is he for real? Am I being punked?*

Hanchen was not laughing, and neither was anyone else. He stood there, still holding his hand out in total silence.

Mack looked down at the little man, stifled another outburst, and stoically shook his hand, "Nice to meet you Johnny . . . I'm Elvis from Memphis."

Hanchen, with a quizzical look, shook his head and laughed, slapping Mack on the shoulder, and in perfect English said, "I like that . . . I like that, good sense of humor. Let's eat, I'm starving."

Hanchen raved with glowing praise about the dumplings cooked in oyster sauce, the noodles and shrimp balls—all were just like his mother's cooking—and how for the first time, outside of China, four people in the same room spoke his dialect. "Very impressive," he told Wei. Only Wei knew that the Loews chef was her brother-in-law and was from Hainan Island, a tropical paradise across the peninsula from Hanchen's hometown of Zhanjiang. She had called him the night before about the scheduled brunch, and her brother-in-law had suggested all the local dishes from Hanchen's area.

Wei sat between Mack and Hanchen and, recognizing the value of Hanchen's strong sense of humor, she kept the conversation going in English with short, amusing, self-deprecating stories about her cultural experiences when she first came to the United States. Mack smiled as he listened and congratulated himself on his $300-an-hour bargain.

Everyone had finished eating, the table was cleared, and waiters had left the room, when Mack's cell phone vibrated. He looked over at Wei, who was saying goodbye to the chef, and saw the slight nod in his direction. He dropped his table napkin and, while picking it up, discreetly read the message:

Just in: Lu H's Dynasty Casino sold. H, holding beaucoup cash.

Mack thought, *Knowledge is power and great ammo for me going into negotiations.* His phone starting vibrating again, and he sneaked another quick look with the phone in the napkin.

Thank U. Thank U. Best Da n the world. I Love U. ☺

All the questions and answers regarding the construction and financing of The Towers had been addressed. After the construction drawings, specifications, and other documents had been cleared from the table, Hanchen requested that he and Mack talk in private.

The two sat with their chairs turned facing each other, with a large plate of sliced fruit between them and two cups of steaming green tea.

Mack sipped his tea as his wheels spun around and around—*Power vs. power, vis-à-vis. Now—right here on the front end—is where a lot of the profit will be made or lost.*

This wasn't just about money. They both had an unquenchable thirst for power—money was no more than casino chips. Negotiating the terms of the financing and the cost of construction were Mack's forte that he had learned over the years from trial and error. He had made plenty of mistakes but never the same mistake twice, and he *never* underestimated his opponent, especially Asian, and particularly Chinese. Hanchen may have that *joie de vivre* about him, but you can bet under that Johnny Cash façade was a sagacious bantam warrior. He had always envied people who never got excited and could stay unruffled in the heat of battle. He had tried to emulate that trait, but unfortunately, after a period of time his patience waned, especially if he was personally being attacked. He remembered how Sgt. Buck had warned him about trying to suppress his hot temper, how most combat medal winners, in a fit of rage and against unbelievable odds, had performed heroic actions, saving many lives. There is a time to talk and be cool, and there's a time to fight. *Always follow your instincts in the heat of battle. Under pressure, even serene leaders have a seething cauldron just below the boiling point, and at some point in time you have to piss or get off the pot and punch somebody in the face.* While training his young neophytes, Buck had preached an old Klingon proverb: *Act and you shall have dinner; wait and you shall be dinner.*

"Elvis, is it okay if I call you Mack?" Hanchen smiled.

Here we go. The first move of the chess master. "Of course, Johnny," Mack smiled back.

It's his money. Let him pitch, and I'll catch . . . for a short time.

"Then please call me Lu, like Lew Rawls, okay?" Hanchen got up from his chair, found the remote, and turned on the television across the room. Moving his chair closer, he said, "Very thin walls in these hotels. Senator Parnell, he is very close friend of yours?"

Aggressive: A Bobby Fisher opening move. "We've known each other for a long time."

"He is an important man, right . . . influential in Washington?"

Mack leaned over and whispered, "He's the Senate Majority Leader. I'm sure you knew that."

"Yes, yes, my point is . . . I might need some help with the Federal Reserve?"

"What kind of help?"

"The acquisition of American banks," Hanchen said.

"Senators represent *all* the people."

"I understand, but I'm a foreigner, not a U.S. citizen."

"Certainly you are aware that JB is also the Chairman of the Senate *Foreign* Relations Committee. They review and consider all diplomatic nominations and international treaties, as well as legislation relating to U.S. foreign policy."

"I would think Senator Parnell would be an excellent friend to cultivate. Could you facilitate that?"

Remember Kasparov's middle game: Attack now. "That's possible, but he's an extremely busy man."

"I would expect him to be generously compensated for his time away from his busy schedule."

"I might make a suggestion, since we are talking about an international relationship."

"Please do," Hanchen said.

"Sometimes when dealing with high-profile people and politicians, it's best to have an intermediary, for arm's length transactions. A very inexpensive insurance policy, so there's no question of a conflict of *interest* or favoritism."

"And you would be the go-between for all the business and personal transactions?"

"Lu, I would make myself available whenever needed."

"Thank you, Mack. You are being most helpful. How can I repay you for such generosity?"

Now—capture his queen. "Approve my loan."

"What is the saying over here in America, fish or cut bait? I've read the reports from my finance and real estate directors, the documents prepared by your Dr. Brown, and what I have seen this morning—it all looks positive and like something I would be interested in. How about if I have some preliminary papers drawn up itemizing the major details? Better yet, why don't you have your people draw up the terms and conditions of what you need to make this happen? Once I have that I could have you an answer within a few days; is that fast enough?" Hanchen asked.

"That's the way I like to do business. But there are a couple of items we need to discuss before we turn this over to our number crunchers, to make sure we're in the same ball park. One is the interest rate, points, if any, and the maturity of the loan?"

"Do you have some numbers in mind?" Hanchen asked.

Do not give him any numbers, Mack. Sit tight. "No, I thought you would be competitive and fair."

"What would it take to please you? Give me some numbers."

No, Mack. His numbers may be smaller. "Lu, you're the banker, I don't want to embarrass myself."

"Okay, how about a floating rate using the Libor index? Today's rate is 0.761 percent. I figured a three year construction loan, no points, and a one year grace period after completion to find a permanent lender."

Number one axiom to remember when negotiating: two ears and one mouth. Seal the deal. "That's fair; how soon?"

"The other banks are pressing you, right? Well, according to our figures, your schedule of work completed, and the short-term bridge loans . . . I would say that about half the loan, five hundred million, would clear everyone out with enough to finish Tower 1, the Casino, the Tram, the Marina, and most of the site work. If that's right, I could deposit the money when we sign the papers and start your monthly draws after that."

"Mister Johnny Cash, you have a deal. When would you like a tour of the site and Tower One?"

"That won't be necessary. Maybe later on when you start Tower Three."

Mack had no idea Hanchen had already inspected the construction site while he was in Brazil on the VW Plant. It was an unexpected opportunity for Hanchen to follow along unnoticed with a group bidding for the operations of Mack's casino.

"With all the reports and drawings, I feel very familiar with the project, plus our mutual friend, Takumi Sama. He talked about nothing else when we met."

Hanchen stood up, "Oh, one last thing." He reached into his briefcase and pulled out a manila envelope, then hesitated. "Please forgive me for being a little paranoid; I'm sure you'll understand . . . let's call it an irritating itch that I have to scratch? I couldn't help noticing Ms. Ling—discreet, as she was—texting during our discussions and shortly afterwards you checking your phone. Can I ask if it had something to do with our negotiations?"

Caution—Dragon counterattack. "I didn't notice her texting. I did check my phone," Mack removed his phone from his pocket. "Let see, my last text was . . . here it is." He handed his phone to Hanchen and he read, *Thank u. Thank u. Best Da n the world. I Love U. 99* ☺

"99 is a code for my young daughter. Earlier she had called and asked to go shopping with her friends."

Hanchen stood up and, with a slight bow, "I am so sorry; I humbly apologize for my lack of trust. I will make it up to you, my friend." He handed Mack the envelope he was holding. "Please, a list of banks in the order of my interest. The Federal Reserve has the same list but arranged in a different order. Do we have a deal?" Hanchen reached over to shake Mack's hand.

Now, the end game. "Oh, one last thing," Mack picked up an envelope from under his chair and put it in Hanchen's outreached hand. "I took the liberty of drawing up the major details of the terms and conditions of our loan agreement with blank lines to be filled in with our agreed numbers." *Checkmate.*

Hanchen looked at the envelope, "Are you a chess player, Mack?"

"Just a wee bit, Lu. But hardly in your class."

"This is going to be an interesting relationship."

There was a knock at the door, and Anna Brown stuck her head in.

"Come on in, Anna." Mack walked over and punched the off button on the TV. "We were just finishing up."

Anna carried a large package wrapped in brown paper and twine. "This package just came in and they asked me to bring it to you right away." She sat the package on the floor next to Mack. "Captain Hank is outside, and if you don't need him, he's on his way to pick up Irish and Lea in Shelbyville."

"No, just remind him to take special care with the cargo," Mack said. "Anna, this is Mr. Lu Hanchen. You all have been exchanging documents with his people, and it looks as if we have our loan."

Hanchen bowed slightly, "Dr. Brown, I congratulate you. Your financial records were flawless, and your presentation was straightforward and uncomplicated, which expedited this whole procedure."

"Now look what you've done, Lu. I'll have to give her another raise. But I agree one hundred per cent. You did a *superb* job, Anna." Mack walked over and opened the door, "If you'll tell Captain Hank he can take off now, we'll finish up here."

Anna shut the door behind her, and Mack turned to Hanchen, "Are we finished?"

"Yes, I think so."

"Just one last thing," Mack reached over and picked up the package Anna had brought in. "When I close a successful business deal and make a friend at the same time, I like to seal the deal with a personal gift." Mack handed Lu the package.

As Hanchen fumbled with unraveling the string, he was childlike with excitement, as if he had never received a gift. Once the paper was off, he stared at the vintage guitar case, a CaliGirl, brown on the outside and pink on the inside. He ran his hands over it like a palmist searching the past for what might lie inside. He waited for Mack to say something, but then quickly placed it on the table and opened the latches. Inside, like an ancient piece of Egyptian artifact discovered in a sarcophagus, embedded in pink faux-fur for over a half-century, rested a 1957 Gibson Les Paul Goldtop electric guitar. Stuck between the strings was a small envelope that Hanchen opened and he read the enclosed card, *Happy Birthday Lu Hanchen*. At the bottom of the card was an embossed green shamrock and just below that were the initials, *MS*.

Hanchen wiped both hands on his pants and reverently lifted the guitar from the case. You could barely hear him whisper, "A fifty-seven LP, the year I was born . . . and it looks new." Under the guitar was another envelope with the name Gruhn Guitars printed on the front. He opened the envelope and removed a Certificate of Authenticity:

We have performed an in-depth examination on this 1957 Gibson Les Paul "Goldtop" and found everything to be original, including the case. We rate this instrument, Near Mint condition, or, if using the numeric grading system, a 9.8.

Our highest rating is Mint condition or 10 points.

It was easy to see the emotion well up inside of Hanchen. He looked at Mack and slowly shook his head, "You don't know what this means to me—it's better than having a Stradivarius. I am stunned . . . and most grateful." Hanchen placed the guitar back in the case, walked over to Mack, and wrapped his arms around him, his head resting against Mack's chest. "Thank you. Thank you, my dear friend."

Mack could hear Hanchen's cell phone vibrating. Hanchen stepped back and removed his phone. "It's from my pilot," he said reading the text to

Mack. "The latest weather briefing from flight services. There's a major storm brewing in the Pacific, and to get out in front of it, we will need to leave immediately."

"I can have Captain Hank fly you direct to Nashville International; he's on the roof." Mack picked up his phone.

"We have checked out of our rooms, and our luggage is at the desk in the lobby."

"I'll have them bring everything to the roof." Mack called Capt. Hank to see if he had left. He told Mack he was in the adjoining room eating dumplings and shrimp balls, leftovers from the brunch buffet. Mack walked over, opened the bedroom door, and motioned for everyone to come in, and announced they had reached an agreement. As they all walked in, Hanchen looked up and saw Wei and Mr. Youguang, and, like a small child again, he held his Les Paul in the air and started extolling—in rapid Chinese—the virtues of his birthday present from Mack. Mack walked out of the bedroom and over to Capt. Hank, who was still eating, and told him the hotel was taking Hanchen's luggage to the roof, and he had two passengers to drop off immediately at the Nashville airport.

*

Mack felt good about the outcome of his one-on-one negotiation with Hanchen; they both got what they wanted. A good deal for both of them, as Mr. Goodman the jeweler would say. With the loan finalized—all but the signatures on the bottom line—Mack could relax a little. Anna and Isaac could tell the banks that the bridge loans would be bought out within thirty days. He emphasized, under no circumstances was the source of their permanent financing to be revealed.

With that monkey off his back, he could get to what had now moved to the top of his list, McKenzie O'Connor. He had called her cell phone, got her voice mail, and left a message. Mack felt great and wanted to celebrate, and one of the wildest parties in the world, Fantasy Fest, was climaxing this weekend in Key West. The storm looked like it would be here for a couple of days, and now was a good time to get away. She had given him her direct line to her chambers, so he tried that and got her recording. He didn't leave a message this time. He called information, got the number of Chancery Court, and was told she was on the bench. He asked if Abby was available and was told she was in the courtroom with the Chancellor. He said he would call back later. Mack's cell phone started vibrating. He looked at the screen, saw Shamrock 99, and thought, *Well, somebody loves me.* Mack hit the connect button and, with a deep Irish brogue, said, "Buffalo Fish Market."

Irish, caught off guard for a minute, paused, but quickly recovered, "Do you have fresh fish today?" She asked with the same Irish accent.

"Caught this morning."

"Is your refrigerator running?"

"Hold, and I'll check . . . yes, it's running. Why do you ask?"

"Well, if I see it running by here, I'll try and stop it!"

"*Who* is this?" Mack barked. He could hear giggling in the background. "Is this 'the most beautiful girl in the world?'"

"No, Daddy, there are lots of girls at school who are more beautiful, smarter, and . . ."

"Not to me they're not. What's your trouble, double-bubble? You know you're not suppose to use your cell phone at school."

"I'm not, silly. I'm at the orthodontist. Did you forget?"

"Oh, sorry. Did Lea take you?" Mack's phone started vibrating, and he looked at the screen and read, *Unknown.*

"Duh, Otis is with you. Who else would be taking me?"

"Watch your mouth little girl . . ."

"Oops. Sorry, Daddy."

"I've got to go, Irish, someone is calling on the other line. Did you call me for something specific or were you just thinking of me?"

"When are you coming home?"

"I'll let you know. I have to catch this other call."

"I love you."

"I love you too." Mack switched over but missed the call. He never answered unknown, blocked, or withheld calls, but he thought it might have been McKenzie. He waited a minute to see if the caller left a message. His phone started vibrating in his hand, but when he read the screen it didn't say *voicemail* it read *Vanderbilt University.*

"Hello," Mack said.

"Hello, Mr. Shannon?"

"Yes."

"This is Wei Ling . . . from the University? Am I imposing?"

"What a nice surprise."

"Thank you for the beautiful flowers. Your generous check was more than enough and much more than we agreed on."

"You earned every penny: class, intellect, and beauty are rare combinations these days."

"Thank you, you're very kind for saying that."

"Only the truth."

"I was hoping you would let me reciprocate your kindness by joining me tonight for a rare performance of the famous cellist, Yo-Yo Ma. He has invited some personal friends to a closed rehearsal with the Nashville Symphony and afterwards to join him for a late dinner. He is a very interesting fellow, world-traveled, with wonderful stories. It will all be quite informal with casual dress."

He thought about his call to McKenzie. "Thank you, I'd love to but . . ."

"I know this is at the last minute, but I just got the invite myself."

"Can I get back to you? I have a tentative appointment and was waiting for a phone call to confirm. I could let you know in about an hour?"

"Of course, let me give you my cell phone number."

"I have it, remember?"

"Oh, that's right. Then you will call me?"

"Under one condition."

"What's that?"

"That you call me Mack, and I'll call you Wee."

"It's W-a-y, like, way too much."

"I thought I heard someone call you Wee?"

"You did, and I've been called worse."

"Okay *Wei,* we have a deal. I'll call you back shortly."

JB walked into the room. "Whatever that *get-tar* cost, you sure got your money's worth. You made a friend for life; great idea."

"They got off okay?"

"Yeah, he couldn't stop jabbering about that guitar. Wouldn't let anyone carry it. Climbed in the helicopter with both arms wrapped around the case. What did you have to pay for that bad boy, thirty, forty grand?"

Mack shook his head and looked up at the ceiling.

"More? Fifty?"

Mack shook his head and looked up at the ceiling again

"Seventy-five?"

Mack said, "Hundred and ten."

"Wow, that much?"

"It's an original, and the only 9.8 around; I wanted the best. Besides, that's a small token; a trifling premium for such a high return."

"That's for sure. How'd you do on the loan?"

"The terms couldn't have been better if I had written them myself."

"Anything in there for me?"

"Oh yeah. I'm your *liaison* partner."

"Alll right, *partner,*" JB said as he walked over to the mini-bar. "Any single malt in this thing?"

CHAPTER 22

MACK OPENED HIS eyes to complete darkness. He tried to roll over, but something held his legs down. He pushed up on his elbow, the room was spinning, and he fell back onto the pillow. He waited, staring at the ceiling, his brain feeling like the gyroscope in his plane during a thunderstorm. He surveyed his surroundings: the blackout curtains, the luminous dial on the clock radio, and then tried to remember how many bottles of champagne they had drunk last night. The clock blinked 6:20. He hoped that was not p.m. but knew alcohol would not let him sleep over three or four hours at one time.

He felt something move at his feet and raised his head to find Boo staring at him. The big standard poodle dropped his head back onto Mack and closed his eyes. Mack heard soft breathing next to him. He lifted the covers, pulled his legs free of Boo, and eased off his side of the bed, picking up his underwear and socks. Downstairs he found the rest of his clothes scattered about, and, after dressing, he sat down at the kitchen bar and wrote out a quick note—*I had a great time. Have important meeting. Must run. Will call later. Mack.*

He walked out of the condos overlooking the Cumberland River along First Avenue. He tried to think of the name of the all-night diner that was downtown and served a great breakfast; he was dying for a cup of coffee. It was on Third or Fourth Avenue, always busy with people going to work, and a lot of docs, nurses, and late night musicians. He turned up Broadway; the walk would do him good.

As he walked, he thought about last night: *How many times had this scene been played out? Is this it—is this all there is—this empty feeling? There must be more than this merry-go-round of repeating the same act over and over. Seducing one woman after another? Then back to work, work, work, 24/7. WHY? What for? Another house, a bigger, faster airplane, another car, more toys, and more women?* He thought of Solomon, his seven hundred wives and three hundred concubines—*how did that work out . . .? Meaningless. And GOD commanded him.*

He was at Fourth Avenue now and saw the neon sign one block over, on the corner of Opry; "Skeeter's Diner." He continued walking in that direction.

It wasn't that he didn't enjoy Wei. She was sweet and had a lovely body, and it was great sex. But why the empty feeling? I mean, it wasn't love, so what was it? Just self-gratification, instinct, like a dog or a bull . . . you smell it, jump it, bip bam thank you ma'am? Regardless, what was he supposed to do? She undressed him. Wasn't he obligated?

Who knows? Who cares? It happened. I'll ask Freud the next time I see him.

The diner was packed. Mack saw a policeman at the end of the counter get up and a big-hair blonde waitress motioned him to the empty stool.

"Have a seat, handsome," she said, pouring him a cup of coffee without asking.

He smiled at her and ordered a glass of ice water and the breakfast special.

Before he could fix his coffee, she had a glass of ice water in front of him. "Anything else you need? Dolly's the name."

"Thank you, Dolly." He removed his phone to call Otis to pick him up and saw there was a new message. He hit view and read, *Where are you? I called twice. MO.*

His first thought, *MO*, who is *MO?* Then it hit him, McKenzie O'Connor. Hot damn! He checked the time of her text, 1:20 a.m. It was too early for him to call, so he hit reply and texted,

In Nashville. Be in Memphis by noon. Dinner and/or drinks tonight? MS.

He caught Dolly's eye, held up his empty cup smiling, then gulped down the glass of ice water before sitting it down.

"Thirsty, huh? I like a man with a *big* thirst," Dolly said, placing an oversized plate of food in front of him and leaning way over the counter to fill his coffee cup. Mack moved back instinctively, trying to escape the attack of her huge breasts fighting each other to break out of the under-sized bra.

"Dolll'ly, order up," shouted the short order cook.

"Hold your horses," she shouted back, winking at Mack as she hurried off.

"Thank you, Lord," he mumbled.

On the drive back to Memphis, Mack received a text from McKenzie: *Have plans tonight. Can meet for one drink only, 5:30 at Arthur's. U do know where Arthur's is, right?;)*

*

It was still twilight with unlimited visibility and not a cloud in the sky. Captain Hank checked his airspeed, altimeter, and turn coordinator as Mack slid into the right seat.

"You want to set her down?"

"Yeah, I need the time." Mack took the controls, "I got it." He had flown the plane a couple of times but needed to log some pilot-in-com-mand flight time. He had left McKenzie in the cabin stretched out asleep in one of the executive recliners with her shoes off. It was his first oppor-tunity to really study all her features, from her thick red hair down to her manicured toes—his evaluating was more chaste than sexual. Yet he won-dered if the hair on her head was the same color on other parts of her body. He didn't care for the latest fad of shaving and thought it bordered on something psychosexual: damn, leave some things to the imagination.

Mack lowered the flaps twenty degrees. He was low over the end of the island and could see they had closed off Duval Street downtown, and thousands of people covered the street and sidewalks celebrating Fantasy Feast. He had the runway in sight now and eased the yoke left to a head-ing of 270 on final approach. He made a visual check of the area for birds and any other air traffic. Captain Hank reminded him of the FAA rule of extreme noise sensitivity.

The tower was closed, so he switched his radio frequency to UNICOM: 122.95 for a general announcement to anyone in the area. "This is Citation

November-two-five-niner-Echo-Whisky on final approach, runway two-seven, at Key West International Airport."

The 53-foot long jet touched down with plenty of runway, rolled to the end, and taxied back up close to the terminal building. Captain Hank locked the brakes and checked the instrument panel. Outside temperature was 73 degrees, wind out of the west at 12 miles, and the time was 22:20 EST—not bad, less than two hours from lift-off to touch-down; he cut both engines.

Mack moved to the cabin to check on McKenzie and open the door.

"I've never been to Key West," McKenzie said. She set her empty champagne glass on the tabletop and unbuckled her safety belt. Looking out the window, she saw an old sign on a rooftop, The Conch Flyer Bar. In the window of the bar was a hand-painted sign in tropical colors, *Free Beer Tomorrow.*

The airport was across from the beach, and between the beckoning palm trees a full moon greeted Mack and McKenzie. They stood on the steps while a warm breeze washed over them, carrying the smell of the sea.

"Welcome to Paradise," Mack said, looking around for Sergio, his care-taker. He helped McKenzie down the steps. The deserted airport had been remodeled, yes, but it was still the Conch Republic Airport. How many international airports could you fly into, and no one was there—not many. Yet that was the charm, the spell that lured dreamers to the end of the road; to fish, to dive, to kick back in a hammock for a siesta. No one came here to work, but they all had one thing in common: They all caught the same sickness—island fever.

Mack opened the nose cone baggage compartment and set the luggage on the ground while Captain Hank tied down the aircraft.

"Hank, you're staying at the Casa Marina, right?"

"Yes sir, I called for a cab to meet me out front. I don't see Captain Sergio. Wasn't he meeting you here?"

"Hey, we're on Conch time now, remember?"

"I'll carry your luggage out front."

"No, you go ahead. I'll get the luggage and lock up after I get some other things out of the plane." Mack climbed back in and removed a couple of small bags from the back of the plane. When he came back to the door, he saw Captain Sergio loading the doorless electric car. McKenzie had a large red hibiscus flower stuck behind her ear.

"See what Captain Sergio brought me?"

"You know what they say about those Cuban lovers," Mack said. Sergio was about as tall as he was round; too much yellow rice, black beans, and plantains. Mack wasn't sure how old he was, maybe sixty, but his skin was wrinkle-free and the color of dark coffee. He was a fourth generation Conch.

"Welcome home, Señor Mack. I'll take those for you." He took the two bags and put them with the others on a wooden bed built on the rear of the car.

Mack knew better than to say anything to Sergio about being late picking them up. He had learned the hard way that most Conchs were in Key West for the *joie de vivre* and not the pressure of work and worry; if pushed, it could be adios time. Mack paid for Sergio to keep his commercial fishing licenses current, and over the years they had recorded the coordinates of all the honey holes. Mack always tried to get on Conch time, to kick back and relax, but it was not an easy task. Usually by the time he was acclimated, it was time to leave.

*

When Mack met McKenzie for the one-drink-only at Arthur's, it turned out to be more than one drink. He told her about JB and him being in Nashville, and his success at negotiating a loan for his Trinity Town Towers' project. He was surprised at how quickly she accepted his invitation to fly down to Fantasy Feast to celebrate his success. She said her husband was leaving town Thursday for a medical convention in Los Angeles and would not be back until Monday.

Mack had mixed emotions about breaking one of his strict rules against being with a married woman. Every time the situation came up, Mack was reminded of Ronny Rodriquez, one of his closest buddies in the Marine Corps. He was a handsome devil whom women chased, even with the jagged scar from his ear lobe to the corner of his mouth—inflicted by an ex-girlfriend slamming a beer mug to the side of his head while he was talking to another woman.

Ronny had called and left a message, and when Mack returned his call three or four days later, he got a recording saying the phone was no longer in service. He called Ronny's sister and she told him what had happened.

He was drinking at his neighborhood sports bar when a young woman came on to him, told him she was divorced, and after drinking all night, they ended up in a motel. All during this time the husband was waiting outside in his truck and followed them to the motel. He drove his pickup through the front door of the motel room, got out of his truck, and casually walked over and shot Ronny five times.

At the trial, the husband's attorney agreed to a charge of "murder with extenuating circumstances." The charges carried a mandatory sentencing of two to ten years. The young woman broke down in the courtroom and shouted she still loved her husband and would wait for him no matter how long. The husband smiled, holding up two fingers as he swaggered out of the courtroom.

That story was imbedded in Mack's brain—*how many times could this have been him?* But when McKenzie told him that she and her husband did not share the same bed, and that their relationship had been strictly platonic for years—Ronny Rodriquez was lost in a euphoric fog.

*

On this side of the island, behind the Key West Airport, you would think you were in a different city compared to downtown. It was very quiet and peaceful as Captain Sergio drove the electric car down a sandy service road lined with tightly woven mangroves on each side of the salt ponds. Mack and McKenzie rode in the back seat holding hands, enjoying the serenity of the noiseless ride. The road ended at a deep-water canal that had been dredged years ago by the La Fayette Salt Company. One of Mack's favorite water toys was tied off to an old wooden dock. Captain Sergio loaded the luggage into the vintage, 16-foot Chris Craft Custom Runabout, with its rich mahogany and black walnut completely refurbished.

"What time in the morning, Señor Mack?" Sergio asked, standing by with the dock line while Mack started the engine.

Mack looked over at McKenzie, "You up for *early* fishing and diving for lobster? Sunrises on the water down here are magical."

"What's that old saying, 'In for a penny, in for a pound?'"

Mack smiled, "What time is sunrise, Sergio?"

"Around 7:30, Señor Mack. I could do a little bait fishing early in the morning and be at the house . . . say 6:30?"

"6:30's good. Call me when you're on the way—hasta mañana." Mack eased the throttle forward and pulled away from the dock with McKenzie next to him. She leaned back on the soft leather seats looking up at the stars. The canal was straight and narrow and ran out into a larger canal where Mack turned east, moving quietly past small million-dollar-plus houses on Sunrise Lane. Startled, she grabbed Mack's arm as a large bird took flight from her side of the boat.

"What was that?"

"A great blue heron. We probably scared her off her nest."

"Well, we're even; she scared me off mine."

*

Once under the Roosevelt Bridge, Mack turned north at Cow Key Channel, then passed under the Overseas Highway and was in open water.

"Ohhh, this is so beautiful . . . and this boat is like something out of *The Great Gatsby.*"

"Actually, my love affair with this boat started with an old movie starring Elizabeth Taylor and Montgomery Cliff. She was racing across the lake of their country club house in this same model boat, and I fell in love with the boat and her too, both ageless classics."

"Is that what you are?"

"Wow, I'm not that old. Hold on." He shoved the throttles all the way forward, and, like a rocket, the new OMC 350 V-8 engine blasted the boat out of the water. Mack stood when the boat planed and searched through the saltwater spray until he saw the lights of his house. It was the only house on the man-made coral rock peninsula that jutted out 300 feet with a third of the house cantilevered out over the water. The design provided a 270 degree unobstructed view of the Gulf of Mexico.

Mack slowed the boat and turned parallel to the peninsula, moving past a concrete dock. He pressed a number on his phone as he turned into a dugout entrance into the side of the peninsula. Exterior lights came on, and a continuous bell started ringing as a large overhead door rose above the water; and Mack motored forward. Security cameras recorded as he maneuvered the Chris Craft carefully around the rear of a much larger boat. He thought of Bear, his dog, wagging his bobbed tail as he watched the 52-foot Hatteras Motor Yacht rock side to side in his wake, as if welcoming him home. Mack shifted into reverse and coasted against the rubber dock bumpers inside the boathouse. The bell stopped ringing as the overhead door closed automatically behind them.

Mack picked up their luggage and walked up the steps to a door that opened into the main hallway, leading to the living area. Sergio's wife had cleaned the house spotless, opened all the doors and windows, and stocked the fridge. Pygmy Date Palms filled numerous five-foot jardinières, and planters with bougainvillea, hibiscus, and heliconia were everywhere. The Gulf breeze moved through the house, carrying the scent of the potted jasmine and gardenia. Tropical flowers floated in an elongated bowl of water, recessed into the kitchen bar.

"Mack, this *is* paradise; look at this place!" McKenzie said, as she walked through the house, touching and smelling everything. She stopped in front of a life-sized painting of Mack holding Irish in his arms, both with deep tans and dressed in all white. They stood at the stern of the Hatteras with the name *IRISH* written across the back of the boat.

"What year was this?" McKenzie asked.

Mack removed a bottle of champagne from an ice bucket and walked over with two glasses. "Irish was about three years old."

"Your hair was all black."

"Yeah . . . lots of changes since then." Mack handed her a glass of champagne.

"I think you're more handsome now," she said, running her fingers through the gray strands in his hair, "more distinguished." With a quick kiss on the lips she touched their glasses in a toast and knocked back the champagne. "Now, show me where my bed is. I'm beat," handing him the empty glass.

*

Mack let the rope slide through his hands watching the anchor until it settled on the bottom at a depth of 30 feet. The water was so clear he could see the minnow-size, multicolored fish circling the anchor at the bottom. The boat floated until the anchor dug into the sandy bottom and settled over a coral reef the size of the Key West Custom House on Front Street.

It was dead calm, and the water was a comfortable 81 degrees. Two yellow air hoses, each 150 feet long, floated on the surface, one on each side of the boat. Sergio gave McKenzie a brief lesson on diving with a Hookah system. Once underwater, he had her remove her regulator and use her snorkel, while he adjusted her BC and the weights on her belt. He had Mack remove his regulator and hold it in McKenzie's mouth while she breathed from his regulator. They practiced this back and forth while underwater.

Sergio floated face-down in the water like a dead man. In one hand he had an underwater video camera and in the other a Hawaiian Sling for shooting a good sized fish for supper, like a grouper or a mango snapper. He had started filming McKenzie while still in the boat as Mack helped her put on her dive gear. Sergio continued shooting as they descended to the bottom.

Mack motioned for McKenzie to follow him to the bottom. Each of them had a drawstring net hooked on their weight belt, gloves, a tickle stick, and a handheld net. Mack pointed to himself, then to a lobster's two antennas sticking out from under a coral heads on the bottom. He moved his tickle stick behind the lobster's tail and tickled the lobster out from its hiding place, placed his handheld net behind the lobster, and tapped the lobster on its head. The lobster backed into the net and he removed it with his gloved hand and stuffed it in her lobster bag. He pointed to a couple of large antennas off to the right for her to pursue and moved off to the left, disappearing under a large overhanging coral ledge.

Sergio continued filming McKenzie, watching her losing battle with two lobsters while trying to stuff them in her lobster bag. Finally, after overcoming her initial nervousness, she now had three lobsters secured in her bag drifting behind her on a drawstring attached to her weight belt. Sergio told McKenzie that if she got turned around or lost to look up and follow her bubbles, and he would be there, floating on the surface.

He smiled as he filmed her upside down, her legs floating above her as she stuck her head under a coral boulder. Then he noticed movement out of the corner of his eye and turned the camera on a loggerhead turtle and a nurse shark. The shark bumped his head into the turtle, rolling it over, and then, as if bored, moved off effortlessly, weaving in and out of the reef hunting for an easier meal. Sergio then filmed Mack pulling himself up the anchor line with a full bag of lobsters and saw him stop about half way as he watched the 9-foot nurse shark swim over the top of McKenzie and then abruptly make a U-turn, and started circling about three feet above her.

Mack unsnapped his bag of lobsters and followed them as the net dropped to the bottom. McKenzie wrestled with what looked like at least an eight-pound lobster with both hands, its wide tail flapping wildly as she kicked her feet trying to stand upright. Her flippers roiled the sand and sediment like a dust storm. She was unaware of the shark until she felt a strong pull on her lobster bag, then a violent shake, pulling her upright. Through the cloudy water all she saw was the shape of the head of what looked like a large catfish trying to steal her lobsters. With both hands holding a death grip on her trophy lobster, she pounded the shark on the head with the lobster.

Mack had removed his diving knife from the sheath strapped to his calf and was pulling on the shark's tail, waiting for McKenzie to stop her attack so he could cut the bag loose. Sergio had raced down at the same time without air and was sticking the shark with the point of his spear, trying to get his attention.

Mack thought: *The poor nurse shark didn't know what was going on with three people attacking him.* Finally the mesh bag ripped, and the lobsters scampered across the sandy bottom, leaving a cloudy trail behind them. Mack watched as the sluggish shark flipped his tail and ambled off, the mesh bag trailing behind him, caught in his teeth. He removed his regulator and held the mouthpiece while Sergio sucked in a couple of shots of air, and they all kicked back up to the surface.

Once in the boat, drinking cold beers, Sergio rewound the video footage on the camera that was attached to a 15-foot pole and was motion-activated. Sergio showed Mack the part where McKenzie pounded the shark's head, and they both started laughing.

McKenzie stood up in the boat with a beer in one hand, shaking her dead *trophy* lobster in the other; its legs were smashed and both antennas broken off.

"Hell no, I wasn't going to let that big fish steal my lobsters," she shouted. This set off another round of uproarious laughter. Mack admired her fighting-Irish spirit but could hardly wait till she found out the "big fish" was a nine-foot shark.

*

Prior to getting dressed, Mack explained to McKenzie what their plans were for the night. First, the Pretenders-in-Paradise costume competition and afterward to the all night Royal-Masquerade-Ball where the Conch King and Queen were crowned. This was the last big party in October and the culmination of Fantasy Fest: ten days of the wildest, raunchiest, Sodom-and-Gomorrah-like festivities with as many as 55,000 visitors and 25,000 locals—conchs and bubbas.

With Duval Street open to only foot traffic, people packed the street and sidewalks so close one could hardly move. Finding a parking place, whether for a car, bike, or boat at the marinas was impossible, but Mack had tied his Chris Craft up to a friend's yacht that had yearly dockage one block from Duval. Mack and McKenzie stopped in an alley shop called Foreplay or Roleplay Costumes and Masks, and she picked out a feathered Venetian mask while Mack chose a black leather Phantom of the Opera mask.

They arrived late at the Masquerade Ball feeling no pain. Carrying plastic cups with champagne from the Pretenders-in-Paradise party, they entered an old vacant warehouse someone had started renovating before running out of money. The live Latin music was thunderous, and the place was packed as they tangoed across the dance floor to the bar. The female bartenders wore eye masks and were all topless with their names painted on their chest. Mack ordered their drinks and watched McKenzie wiggle her butt backward, mimicking the lobsters, out onto the floor, motioning with both hands for him to come catch her. Everyone was in costume, from the elaborate to the all-nude airbrushed painted bodies. Most came to see how far they would go to live out their private fantasies in public. Others came to watch, and many were just drunk exhibitionists.

Mack was no ballroom dancer. He had rhythm and loved to dance, but he knew not to try to follow McKenzie's wild, uninhibited, sexual gyrations. He stood squashed between other dancers and moved to a simple three-quarter beat, watching her with great excitement and anticipation. When the band switched to a slow dance, McKenzie wrapped both arms around his neck. She was breathing hard, her blouse was sticking to her, and sweat glistened off her bare shoulders. Mack held her tight as they danced across the floor until she stopped suddenly and pushed him away.

"What's wrong?" Mack said.

"That's my dress she's got on," McKenzie said, staring at a woman on the dance floor.

"Where?"

"There, behind the couple in the Batman and Robin costume, in the red dress."

"The woman with the long blonde hair?"

"Yes."

"How do you know it's your dress?"

"It's an original, only one shoulder strap, and the gold pendant hanging from the back zipper . . . that dress is mine." McKenzie guided Mack closer to the dancing couple.

The man was lean and tall wearing an Elvis, gold sequined jumpsuit and cape with oversized sunglasses. He moved with ease as he waltzed across the floor, leading the blonde with quick short steps and then turning her with great fanfare. People around them had stopped dancing to watch. McKenzie pulled Mack inside the crowded circle as the couple came out of a double spin, then watched as he dipped her low, swaying from side to side to the music, her blonde hair sweeping the floor. He held her like that as the music ended and jerked her up in a close embrace, kissing her. There was a loud applause from the crowd. The blonde removed her Marilyn Monroe mask and bowed, her back to Mack and McKenzie, and the applause tripled. Mack thought she must be some famous dancer or actress, but McKenzie couldn't care less. She seethed with rage and feeling no pain, leaped out and grabbed the blonde by her long hair screaming, "What are you doing wearing my dress?"

Mack was stunned, as was McKenzie, who stood holding the long blonde wig in her hand. Her mouth was wide open staring at a bald headed man with a black mustache wearing her red dress, "What the . . .?" but before she could finish her sentence, the tall "Elvis" removed his mask and shouted, "Are you crazy, woman?"

Mack saw the blonde wig fall from McKenzie's hand and tried to catch her before she hit the floor, but only partly checked her fall. The crowd closed in around them, and Mack heard people asking, "Is it her heart? Is she drunk?" A woman in a Cleopatra costume pushed through the crowd, "Let's take her to the ladies room. She probably just fainted."

Mack picked McKenzie up and followed the woman through the crowd; Elvis and Marilyn trailed close behind.

Mack heard McKenzie mumble something as he carried her through the door and set her in a chair. "What happened? Where am I?" she asked.

"In the ladies' room. How do you feel?"

"I'm okay, just too much to drink. Could I have some water?"

The woman, dressed in a Cleopatra costume, handed her a plastic cup with water when the door opened.

"Can I help? I'm a doctor." Elvis stood over McKenzie, and put his fingers on her neck, and checked her pulse. He removed his sunglasses, "Let's check your pupils now," he said removing her mask.

"Ahhhh!" he screamed, jumping back. "Ooooh my GOD! McKenzie! What are you doing here?" he said.

McKenzie stood up, "I *knew* that was you! You're supposed to be in LA . . . you *kissed* that *man*! My God, Randolph . . . and . . . and *he's* wearing *my* dress!" The door swung open again.

"Where's that bitch who yanked off my wig?" The man staggered through the door with his Marilyn Monroe mask back on, but it was somewhat lopsided. The blonde wig sat on his head too far back and off-center.

"Take my dress off," McKenzie shouted.

He saw the expression on Randolph's face, tried to stand up straight, and with slurred words demanded, "Who's she?"

In a low dissonant voice, Randolph said, "She's-my-wife," and collapsed into a chair beside McKenzie. "Take off that silly looking mask and please shut up."

Marilyn stumbled backward into the countertop sink, righted himself, removed the mask and wig, and tried a reverent bow toward McKenzie, but fell to his knees upchucking and spewing a gusher of vomit.

McKenzie looked down at her new sandals covered in puke.

"Crazy Ray!" Mack shouted. *He's supposed to be dead.*

"You know him?" Randolph and McKenzie asked simultaneously.

When Ray Flynn heard someone call him Crazy Ray, he jumped up quickly, slipped on his vomit, and fell. Looking up with a shocked expression, he slurred, "Mack Shannon?" and threw up again, falling back against the base cabinet, passing out.

Mack stood over him, wiping the vomit off his shoes onto McKenzie's dress. "I don't think you'll ever wear that dress again." He noticed a prescription vial roll from Crazy Ray's open hand and disappear under the base cabinet. "I've known him since grammar school, where everyone called him Crazy Ray and for a reason. The last I heard he was transported by helicopter in a coma to Baptist Hospital dying from AIDS."

"Excuse me, folks, but I'm out of here," The woman in the Cleopatra costume said, tiptoeing around Crazy Ray.

"AIDS?" McKenzie jumped up. "You're sleeping with someone who has AIDS?" she shouted at Randolph.

Mack bent over, picked up the vial, but couldn't read the name and tossed it in the toilet.

"Okay girls, let's don't hog the toilet!" A couple of men dressed as Jack & Jill busted through the door, giggling and holding their crotches. "Eeeww, nasty, nasty," the first one said, looking at all the vomit. "Hurry, let's go pee-pee in the ocean," the other one squealed as they backed out the door.

CHAPTER 23

FANTASY FEST WAS a fiasco, a tainted episode that no one enjoyed and left a lingering, bitter taste in Mack's mouth. McKenzie had asked Mack if Randolph could fly back to Memphis with them, and, if not, they would take a commercial flight back together. Mack didn't like ultimatums, but he wanted to talk to McKenzie alone. Uncharacteristically he capitulated, and they all three took off in Mack's plane at daylight the next morning. McKenzie mentioned that Randolph had left Crazy Ray a note with some money and his plane ticket back to Memphis before leaving their hotel that morning. Mack told her he couldn't care less, and if they had brought him along, he would have thrown him off the plane . . . as soon as they reached a thousand feet. As far as he was concerned, Crazy Ray's worth was no more than dog shit you scrape off the bottom of your shoe. He was a parasite spreading his deadly disease, just what the world needed.

On the flight home, McKenzie avoided Mack, just sitting next to her husband, hiding behind dark sunglasses the whole time. He would *never* understand women. Hours ago, she was carefree, fun to be around, even affectionate and sexual, hugging and kissing on him. Now, she was cold and withdrawn, a completely different person, treating him like a stranger. *What was he supposed to say? After all, he was the one with another man's wife . . . the hell with it all.* He stormed off to the cockpit and took over flying the plane, letting Captain Hank catch up on his sleep.

*

Otis watched the plane as it taxied up to the FBO at Memphis International and drove out on the wet tarmac when it stopped. It was a steady rain, and he held the umbrella for McKenzie and walked her over to the limo. He loaded their luggage in the trunk after Mack convinced McKenzie it was no problem dropping them off on his way home. He sat up front with Otis, leaving McKenzie and Randolph alone in the back.

On the way, Mack changed his mind and told Otis to drop him off at the Towers construction site and then take them home.

Mack watched, standing in the rain, as the limo pulled away from the construction gate. She didn't look back, wave, or say anything when he got out of the limo. No thank you, or even kiss my butt, as if it were entirely his fault.

*

Randolph assured McKenzie that he had recently been tested for HIV, that the test had come back negative, and that he had always used protection when intimate with Ray. Regardless, she demanded they both be tested immediately. Randolph agreed, and the first thing Monday morning they drove to Randolph's pain clinic where he drew blood and labeled them with the names of old patients of his who had died. He walked to the lab in the rear of the building with the two specimens and ordered an immediate rapid HIV test from one of his technicians. McKenzie was extremely nervous, actually terrified, trying not to throw up. Randolph had offered her a shot of Valium, but she didn't want anything to do with a needle or blood. It was all she could do to let him stick her finger. She tried to remember the last time she had had sex with Randolph . . . six months or even longer she supposed. If rumors got out that she had been tested for HIV, it could destroy her career. She waited in Randolph's office, her head down, praying, her fingers moving over each bead of her rosary, "*Hail Mary, full of grace. Our Lord is with thee. Blessed art thou among women, and blessed is the fruit of thy womb, Jesus. Holy Mary, Mother of God, pray for us sinners, now and at the hour of our death.*"

She stopped praying when the door opened. Randolph walked over and placed a folder on his desk in front of her and moved to the window, staring out blindly, his back to her. She knew the lab report was in the folder but refused to touch it. After a few minutes, Randolph said, "Your test was negative." He continued to look out the window.

"Ohh, Holy Mother of God . . . thank you, thank you," McKenzie whispered, making the sign of the cross.

Randolph reached across the desk and picked up the folder. "I'm sorry I caused you this much trouble. I have not been a very good husband for you. You are my dearest friend, and I would never do anything to hurt you; you know that don't you?" He sat down and opened the folder.

"Yes, I know that."

"I have done a very stupid thing and it appears I will pay a heavy price for my mistake." He slid a sheet of paper across to her from the opened folder. She looked at the report.

Patient's Name: Henry Johnson
Test: Rapid HIV
Test Results: <u>POSITIVE</u>

"Who is Henry Johnson?" she asked.

"Me. I used fictitious names for the tests." He slid another sheet across to her.

She picked up the paper; her hand was shaking. She saw the name Alice Johnson, the same test and the results: NEGATIVE. "This is me?"

He nodded. "I'll do whatever you need . . . even a divorce, or if you want me to move out of the house immediately, I will. I'm afraid this will hurt your chances for your Federal Judgeship if this ever got out."

"I'm *so* sorry. I thought you said you had tested negative before. Are you sure there's not some mistake?"

"I sent it back to the lab with a new sample of my blood before I came in here. It came back positive again. I tested negative six weeks ago when I was in Miami, but there is a window before the virus shows up."

"But *why*? Why in the world would you take a chance with someone infected with AIDS and ruin your whole life? Where did you meet this . . . this *Crazy* Ray?"

"I've never heard anyone call him that before; his name is Ray Flynn, and he is a patient of mine. I saved his life. You know my passion for research—the primary reason I built the addition onto the clinic—it doesn't pay anything, but I make more than enough money with the pain management. Anyway, I was called in for an emergency at Baptist Hospital one night, and Ray was in a coma. He was in terrible shape: skin and bones, hepatitis, kidney infection, skin lesions all over his face and body . . . .."

"Sounds like that mangy dog you brought home one time. Why did they call you in?"

"I *saved* that dog and got him a good home. I wondered why they had called me too, but if you remember, we were one of the first clinics to treat HIV/AIDS patients for pain, and once the word got out, we had more patients than the medicine to help them. It was a shame; they were outcast, like lepers, everyone afraid to help. There was a fellow called Dago, a close friend who came to the emergency room with Ray. He told the doctor in charge that Ray was HIV positive, and the EMT on the helicopter said he was in a coma. The ER doc admitted him into ICU hooked up to an IV. Come to find out he was not in a coma but a drug-induced stupor. He was taking so many different narcotics, plus drugs for his OIs infections—fungal, viral, bacterial, PCP, and a malignancy, KS, Kaposi's sarcoma. The poor man was a mess. Once all his drugs wore off, he was dying from pain, and I was called for a consult."

"My God, how terrible," McKenzie said. "I remember you telling me before, but I forgot. What's the difference between HIV and AIDS?"

"When someone is HIV positive, you're infected with the virus, and if antiretroviral (ARV) therapy is started early enough, the average life expectancy is pretty good, around 70.

"AIDS, Acquired Immune Deficiency Syndrome, is the final stage of HIV. AIDS is when the CD4 cells fall below 200 cells per millimeter of blood, overwhelming your immune system. It is a way of describing a whole group of symptoms and diseases associated with the damage HIV does to the immune system. As an HIV infection progresses, there is ongoing damage to immune defense cells, and the body becomes increasingly less able to fight off infection."

"What was Ray Flynn's CD4 count?"

"At that time . . . below 100."

"What is yours?"

"I don't know yet. I have no symptoms, and I won't start any treatment until my CD4 count starts to fall."

"How did your relationship with Ray start as a patient and progress to your . . . is calling him your lover too cruel? Should I say partner?" McKenzie asked.

"No, that's okay. He was my lover, and I still love him. Once he got better, he was the happiest man in the world, and I was too. He made me laugh, and he loved to dance. It was a new experience for both of us . . . being totally open, free. We'd take long walks in the park, feed the ducks, and go to the museum. He was so spontaneous, never called. Just showed up at the office and made me stop whatever I was doing. We'd take an hour or two off for lunch. He knew his time was limited, and he wanted to squeeze every minute out of every hour." Randolph saw the hurt look on McKenzie's face.

"*You* were always so busy, and so was I. Unfortunately, it takes something like this to make you appreciate each day we live." He took both her hands, "You know I love you, always have, ever since I first saw you in grammar school. I wanted to be just like you." They both giggled.

"Are you sleeping with this construction guy? I ask only professionally."

"God NO! Oh, I didn't mean it that way. I mean, thank God, no we haven't had sex. Why, would he need to be tested? You said my test *is* negative, right?"

"Yes, you are negative. The window sometimes can be as much as three to four months after contact, and it has been almost a year, New Year's Eve, since you and I got drunk on that champagne and ah . . . were together."

"No one knows about this, right?" she asked.

"Only Ray Flynn. I won't be seeing him again, except to find him another doctor and a job; I promised him that. At one time he was very well off, money wise, owned numerous businesses, but lost everything when he got sick. Some clinic out in San Francisco took all his money experimenting with different drugs that did more harm than good. Now, he doesn't have a job or a place to live. I talked to Eli, and he has an opening for a night watchman's job at the church."

"Is he in good enough condition to work?"

"Yes, as long as he takes his medication. It's not a labor intensive job, mostly riding around in a golf cart all night. It'll give me time to find him a hospice when the time comes."

"He won't know about today's test, only the one in Miami that tested negative, right? So only the two of us know you are HIV positive?"

"What about your construction friend? He knows Ray is infected with AIDS, and I've been with Ray, and you and I live together."

"Mack Shannon is a very private person, somewhat clandestine even. I'll write to him."

*

Mack couldn't stop thinking about the AIDS virus and the chain of infection from Crazy Ray to Randolph and from Randolph to McKenzie. Is he bisexual . . . he'd have to be. He's married. She may not even know *if* she's infected. She *did* say they slept in separate bedrooms, but does that mean they don't have sex, *ever*? Surely, Randolph had used protection when he and Crazy Ray were intimate, and being a doctor he would have been tested . . . right?

Mack wasn't worried about being infected because he hadn't had sex with McKenzie. But he asked himself *if* he had, would he have used protection? Beautiful woman, healthy, married, fastidiously clean—he shook his head, probably not.

When he had called his doctor at home the night before, Mack had been told some shocking statics: worldwide, over 35 million are HIV positive, and 25% don't even know they have the virus. Half are women, and the most common way of acquiring the virus is through vaginal intercourse. Knowing Mack's single status and his reputation with women, Dr. Osteen told Mack to come in early, before his rounds at the hospital, and he would draw some blood and run a few tests.

He was in his car when the doctor's nurse called. He closed the window between Otis and the back seat. "Mr. Smith, Dr. Osteen had an emergency at the hospital but wanted me to tell you that he called the lab, everything looks good with your blood work, and he would call you tonight."

Mack appreciated the confidentiality of the test being in a Mr. Smith's name and tried to remember if he had ever been tested for a sexual disease. Maybe years ago when he joined the Marines? Regardless, he felt a tremendous relief. He hated wearing a rubber, but knew nowadays it was like playing Russian roulette without one.

There were some local statistics gathered from the mid-South and printed in a brochure his doctor had given him. Mack removed the brochure from his pocket and started reading:

Memphis is ranked #7 out of the top 25 cities in USA with the HIV virus; Miami is #1. Of the one million in the USA who are infected with HIV, half are black; every year 18,000 die of the virus, and 56,300 are infected.

In Memphis the ratio of those infected with HIV is over 78% Black & 19% White. Lifetime risk of HIV for Black Males is 1 in 16, for Black Females it is 1 in 30, for White Males it is 1 in 104, and for White Females it is 1 in 588.

HIV is a life sentence—incurable.

Mack sent up one of those bullet prayers his aunt Irish always talked about, a quick thank you to God for protecting him. He had often thought about a monastic life, a new beginning, a one-on-one with God. Maybe find a Walden Pond like Thoreau or a monastery and try it for a year?

Who was he kidding? With his overactive libido, he wouldn't last a month, much less a year. He felt like Apostle Paul, one of Christ's most devout followers:

"I don't understand myself at all,
for I really want to do what's right,
but I can't.
I do what I don't want to—what I hate.
I know perfectly well that what I'm doing is wrong,
but I can't help myself.
It is sin inside me that is stronger than I am
that makes me do those evil things."

*

Mack thought he would have heard from McKenzie by now. He missed her, thought about her all the time, but had made a decision not to call her, not yet. He needed time and distraction.

He was sweating as he approached the end of his run, turned onto the bridge, and then sprinted full speed to the peak. He took deep breaths as he walked down the other side of the bridge. A feeling of pride and accomplishment came over him when he stopped and studied the construction site of Tower-One rising 33 stories out of a garden setting. The sun sparkled against the green-tinted glass curtain walls, with the river and the tree-lined riverbanks reflecting the harmony with nature that Mack endeavored to accomplish. It was beautiful, and like the sun, he soaked in the rays of success as he walked down to his job site.

While he was walking through the security gate, a guard ran over and gave him a white envelope. Mack recognized McKenzie's stationery and decided to wait until he got to his office before opening the note. A chain link fence surrounded the construction site with two gates in the front: one for workers and the other for visitors. All visitors were required to obtain a photo ID issued from Shamrock Construction before entering the jobsite.

He stepped inside one of the high-speed elevators in T-1 (Tower One) and pressed a button for the 33rd floor. The walls and floor inside the elevator were covered with CDX grade plywood to protect the interior from construction workers. Construction workers on the elevator stared at him, but none asked any questions.

The 33rd floor was empty, no workers, just an open, dried-in space, with dull gray concrete. He walked up the dark stairwell and opened the door onto the roof garden; his spirit lifted. A huge Leyland cypress carved in the shape of a shamrock greeted him. *It was a good idea, Shannon.* He had remembered the topiary at Shamrock Farms, and, with the landscape architect, they had worked long hours to design a unique garden with mature trees, plants, and a thick Bermuda lawn. Dwarf yaupon hollies, carved in the shape of leprechauns and planted under overhanging bushes, looked as if they were hiding. Lighted Fairies blew in the wind, hanging in the trees from undetectable monofilament fishing lines.

He walked across a stone pathway and leaned against the parapet wall, looking down on the construction of Tower Two and the panoramic view of the mighty Mississippi River, an unappreciated commodity for most Memphians. He would soon reverse that trend and the white flight of businesses, and people would start moving back downtown.

He unlocked the double brass gates to the wall-enclosed penthouse, disarmed the alarm, opened the door, walked over to his desk, and sat down. He looked at the note in his hand and tossed it onto the desk, wondering what she wrote. Should he open it or tear it up unopened? McKenzie—the one woman who had been in his thoughts every day, and the only one in years with the greatest potential for him to fall in love with . . . he tore open the note:

Dear Mack,

You are MY sunshine.

I know you are unaware of how often you hum and whistle that song. I now find myself doing the same. You did make me happy when my skies were gray. Your magnetism, generosity, and masculinity took my breath away. Frightening sometimes, but an adventure that allowed me to bathe in dreams and fantasies rarely encountered in a woman's lifetime. I cannot imagine how much more of my heart you would have stolen if we would have had our Sunday, our love-day. I will always have your image to escape the gray skies, and the sorrow of knowing I missed waking up wrapped in your protective arms. I am so sorry for the disaster at the dance.

Please be discreet about Randolph's aberration. He is my husband, "for better or for worse, in sickness and in health," as they say.

And you will always be MY sunshine. MO

He had wanted to hear from her, and now he had, albeit with a bittersweet message. He read it again, slowly, choked up a bit, took a deep breath, and swallowed. He remembered their very first meeting and how the pheromones were flying all over the place. Her smell, her touch, and later her taste, all triggered a steady stream of sexual attractants. Even their telephone conversations—especially late at night—got around to sexuality with questions like what excited them the most, and where each one's erogenous zones were; just thinking about it now aroused him.

She had teasingly planned what she called her love-day—Sunday—their last day in Key West. Their first time to make love would be in bed, when they woke up Sunday morning, then again after lunch, on the private beach with the hot sun matching the passion of their nude bodies. She said she saved the last for the best, after a lobster dinner with champagne, out by the pool under the stars.

He picked up the note, cringed, his gut tightening. It had been exciting, a prolonged sexual foreplay, but there would be no climax. The note was the closing chapter, and whatever relationship they had was over. He crumbled the note in his hand and threw it across the room, *woulda—coulda—shoulda.*

CHAPTER 24

MACK LOOKED UP from a set of drawings he was working on. He heard the old ship's bell ring outside the penthouse gates, which was unusual. The rooftop was locked off from the other floors and except for building maintenance personnel, he had the only other keys. The bell was from the *Irish Mist*, and Mack had it installed because it reminded him of his time on the towboat when he was growing up. He looked over at the security monitor and saw something moving back and forth to block the camera lens outside. He opened his desk drawer, placed his Colt 45 automatic on the top, and flipped on the intercom, "Who's there?"

"Gooood-after-*noon*!"

Mack heard a low, barely audible, voice.

"Dis-is-Counnnt *Drac-u-la*! Do *not* be a'fraid . . . I just want to *suck* your *blooood*!"

Mack smiled, "Go away, you bloodsucker."

"The Wicked Witch of the West is with me. We have come to sweep you away." Irish whispered to Lea, "Don't let him see us; keep holding your broom over the camera."

Mack could hear them giggling as he sneaked out the back door and around to the front gate, dragging a water hose. He opened the nozzle in a straight stream and arched it over the wall.

"Noooo, Daddy! That's not fair. You're going to get our costumes wet."

Mack shut off the nozzle and opened the gate. Irish was dressed in all black with a cape dragging the ground, a wig with long black hair, fake canine teeth dripping blood, and her eyes painted dark.

Lea looked like a hunchback dressed in black with a green witch's mask, a long pointed nose with hairy warts, a big floppy pointed hat, and a tall black broom.

"Trick or treat, Daddy?" Irish shouted, running with her plastic pumpkin full of candy.

"Halloween's over, baby girl." Mack picked her up and swung her around and around.

"I know that, but you weren't there. Lea and I won the best dressed at the church party, and we wanted you to see our costumes, and I brought you candy."

"And the witch brought the potage," Lea said, holding up a wicker basket. "Your favorite seafood gumbo with jalapeño cheese muffins, for a picnic on the rooftop."

"If you two weren't so ugly, I would kiss you."

Lea removed her mask and stuck out her cheek, tapping on it with her finger. Mack leaned over to kiss her on her cheek, and she turned quickly and kissed him on the lips. "Trick or treat," she said.

Mack shocked, backed away, searched if there was some meaning behind the kiss, and quickly recovered. "Now, all we need with that gumbo is a nice bottle of vino."

"Voila!" Lea removed a bottle of wine from the basket and held it up for Mack. "I robbed the wine cellar."

"I picked that out Daddy. Lea is teaching me all about wines. That's a Bordeaux, from France."

Mack whispered, "Thank you, Sweetie, but remember *all* Bordeaux's are from France."

Irish looked over at Lea, and Lea nodded her head.

"Oh," Irish said.

Mack held Lea's hand a little too long while looking at the name on the bottle. She removed her hand slowly and reluctantly, leaving Mack holding the bottle. "White Bordeaux, very good choice, Irish. Let's eat out on the patio."

*

Later, after their picnic on the roof, Mack walked Irish and Lea to the car when a guard raced up in a golf cart, slamming on the brakes. Highly nervous, he tried to explain in jumbled words to Mack there was an emergency at the casino site. Mack picked up Irish, hugged and kissed her, hesitated, then hugged and kissed Lea on the cheek, and jumped into the golf cart, speeding away.

"The casino is not on fire, is it?" Mack asked.

"No sir," the guard said.

"Then relax and slow this cart down so we both get there in one piece."

Years back, Mack had read a special issue of *Architectural Digest* where they featured what they called the jewel of New York City—the original Penn Station—and referred to it as an outstanding masterpiece of the Beaux-Arts style of architecture. Ever since reading that article Mack had researched, collected photos and drawings, visited sites, and made sketches of features he wanted to add to his working drawings of the Trinityee Towers. He favored the Beaux-Arts style because it allowed and complemented the mixture of other designs without clashing. And finally his dream was coming true, a one billion dollar monument, designed and built by Mack Shannon.

The guard stopped the golf cart a good distance from the entrance of the Towers along the side of the Amtrak rails where it began its underground travel to the subway station under the main concourse.

"What are you doing?" Mack said.

"I'm not allowed to drive into the construction area, sir."

"Hop out. I'm going to drive. Find someone to take you back," Mack said, easing the golf cart over a curb and headed across the construction site, dodging stock piles of dirt, sand, rebar, and pallets of building materials.

Mack watched the Grand Entrance to the concourse grow taller and wider as he got closer. He saw the entrance taking shape of the old Penn Station and the Roman Baths of Caracalla, exactly like the drawings and the scale model he had worked so long and fought so hard for. His engineers and architects insisted it was too dangerous, too expensive (a million dollars every time Mack moved it one foot higher on paper), or it was too big and overpowering and wasted space. Mack was adamant, and demanded that the Grand Entrance be the front door of Trinity Towers and the focal point of the whole project; it had to be dramatic. Now, they were all receiving national and international awards and praise for such a groundbreaking design. His phoned buzzed again; he stopped under the huge semicircular arch and read a text from his office. *You're needed ASAP at the casino job site.* Mack looked up at the highest point under the arch, 100 feet from the ground. He felt small, insignificant, just what he wanted to accomplish, something overwhelming, celestial.

"Mister Mack!" he heard someone shout his name and saw a man in a slow jog coming toward him, waving. A crown of tightly woven cotton circled his head. He stopped in front of Mack, taking deep breaths. "Mr. Mack, Mr. Sonny sent me to find you. The casino is flooded, almost knee deep."

"You had better slow down, Zeke, or you'll have a heart attack. You want to ride back with me?" Ezekiel Edwards was one of the first men Mack had hired when he started Global Construction.

"No sir, Mr. Sonny told me to find some more men and another pump as soon as I found you." Zeke took off in a fast walk.

Mack drove inside the concourse over a temporary road of crushed limestone. He passed towering columns lined on each side of the concourse that supported the umbrella-shaped stained glass ceiling; a design stolen from one of Louis Comfort Tiffany's lampshades. Twisted steel cables, like the web of the Sierra Dome Spider, held the multi-colored glass panels secure in its webbing. Workers installing the high-speed moving sidewalks on each side of the concourse stared at Mack as he drove across restricted areas to reach the center of the concourse and turned south at the pathway that led to the entrance of the casino. He parked the golf cart inside on the marble floor and hurried down the steps, crossing the main floor. He slowed his walk and fell in behind three men in rubber boots pushing a compressor with air hoses and jackhammers. Water was over his ankles as he followed the three men into an open area where a line of men were carrying slot machines out of harm's way. He stepped over a large black suction hose and heard his Project Manager, Sonny Newman, barking out orders.

Pushing through the crowded room, he saw Sonny standing knee-deep in water and waited behind him until he finished talking.

"You called for me, *Mr.* Newman?" They were longtime friends and had worked and partied together for years until Mack got so busy running Shamrock. Sonny had been in Brazil the last two years running a job for Mack, and before that was a year and a half in Panama. He had worked for Mack's Global Construction since he was eighteen and could handle just about anything tossed his way.

"Yeah, I did." Sonny turned around, "Thought maybe you might want to know we sprung a leak." Sonny leaned over and cupped his hands full of water. "It's potable; not river water, but I can't stop the flow. I cut the water supply off to the casino, but it's still rising faster than I can pump."

"You called Light Gas & Water?"

"Yeah, they're standing by at the end of the street. I told them not to cut the main water supply till I call them. We're pouring concrete on Tower Two and I need water there so I've got some men filling up the water truck. If I can't get this stopped soon, I'll have to cut it all off." Sonny pointed to the corner of the room, "The waters a lot deeper over there."

Mack looked to where Sonny was pointing and saw two men, waist deep, grappling with a large suction hose as it sucked water from the rear corner. The water was above his knees now and, as he reached to move his cell phone from his pants pocket to his shirt pocket, he felt the floor move. He reached out to steady himself and dropped his cell phone as the whole building shook, a powerful swooshing sound of air engulfed the room, and the floor gave way. Like a flushed toilet, they were all sucked under by the cave-in. Mack locked both arms around the large suction hose that dangled twenty-feet in the air from what was left of the floor above. He fought to keep his head above the fast-moving underground river as heads started popping up. He reached out, grabbed a flailing survivor, and pulled him over to the suction hose. As he bobbled up and down, he saw Sonny holding on to some rebar sticking out from a large chunk of concrete, the left side of his face covered in blood.

The force of the water had Mack's legs pinned against an underground wall of dirt and gravel that was washing away fast. He heard a shout and felt a thud when a yellow extension cord hit him on the head. He looked up and saw the white dome of Ezekiel Edwards pulling the slack out of the cord. Mack stuck his head into the looped end of the cord, tightened the slipknot around his chests, and pulled his legs free of the current. An emergency horn had gone off, and every trade had rushed to the cave-in. Yellow and orange extension cords were raining down into the hole now.

Mack felt the water rising, grabbed the man he had pulled from the current, and they both floated to the top as the water climbed back to floor level. Construction workers jumped in immediately to help remove a worker who had floated to the surface face down.

*

What a disaster. After the cave-in, Memphis Light, Gas, and Water Division had shut off all water to the island, and that set off a chain of events that caused a major investigation. The next day all departments of the city government had to get involved and then Shelby County, which precipitated the snooping around by the engineers and architects of the State of Tennessee.

Mack had been running on empty, having been up all night with the clean up crew, and he had overslept this morning—rare for him. When he checked his messages there was a "911" text from Sonny, and he hurried to the jobsite dressed in jeans, a tee shirt, and his running shoes. The first thing he noticed was there were no sounds of construction equipment; no one was working. A long line of men waited outside Global Construction's doublewide office trailer with a "Stop Work Order" attached to the door. Instantly, Mack was wide awake as he stomped into the trailer unshaven, with bed hair, and blood boiling, "Everyone out of this trailer and back to work . . . NOW!" he shouted.

Global Construction's payroll, just for *their* hourly workers, was over $250,000 a month. This included form carpenters, concrete finishers, equipment operators, labors, etc. With all these men standing around, Mack figured he was losing about $13,000 dollars every hour.

Inside the trailer, men had been waiting outside Mack's closed office door but now were scrambling to get out of the trailer. A large red poster had been taped to Mack's door:

EMPLOYEE RIGHTS UNDER THE
DAVIS-BACON ACT
U.S. DEPARTMENT OF LABOR

What the hell, this is not a Fed project! Private money is building this job.

Mack took two steps and, with a powerful kick, the hollow-core door disintegrated, the top half dangling by a single hinge. A woman in a gray suit sat in Mack's chair behind his desk. Her horn-rimmed glasses magnified her huge blue eyes, now dilated from fear. Her white construction hard hat with bold red letters, DOL, sat on top of Mack's computer. She stood up, uncertain, searching for the right words.

Mack's face was beet red. He held up one finger, stopping her. He took a deep breath.

The woman quickly spouted out, "Sir, you will have to wait outside like everyone . . ."

"OUT!" Mack shouted, loud enough to rattle the windows. Two other people were in the room: Sonny Newman, the Project Manager, with a bandage covering the stitches over his cheekbone and a middle age, gray-haired man in a navy suit. His hard hat had the letters, OSHA, printed on both sides.

Mack picked up the woman's hardhat and threw it out the kicked-in door. She started to protest, and Mack shouted again, "OUT!"

The OSHA man was already out the door when Mack said, "Sonny, I want both of them off *my* island immediately. In five minutes I'm going to walk out this trailer, and I don't want to see anything but assholes and elbows hard at work. You understand me?"

"Yes sir," Sonny said as he escorted the DOL lady out of the trailer.

*

Mack called Senator JB Parnell, and the Stop Work Order was lifted, but that only fueled the fire of the Federal Government, who sent a team demanding all kinds of documents. Still, no one could say definitively what caused the water main to break; it was a sinkhole—it was not a sinkhole. With such dubious information, Mack ordered Sonny to stop pumping concrete grout into the hole and move all the men over to Tower Two. This gave Mack a little breathing room until he got a call from Maureen, his Administrator. She had received a call from a friend of hers, not to be revealed, who worked for the Tennessee Engineer's Club. Maureen's source told her that the government investigators reported the cause of the cave in was what the seismologist calls a "slow slip."

"What the hell is that?" Mack asked?

"You're not going to like this . . . an earthquake."

"*Whaaaat?*" Mack shouted.

Maureen, accustomed to Mack's outbursts, explained, "It's called a 'silent quake.' I'm supposed to receive a copy of the full report after work tonight. It'll cost us. She could lose her job."

"Maureen, there is over ten grand in the *cash can*. That *should* cover it, don't you think?"

"Just letting you know. I'll call you first thing in the morning."

"No. Call me tonight."

CHAPTER 25

MACK KNEW HE'D pissed off a lot of people with his outburst and expected a backlash, but not to this extent. The government was always like that, bringing an elephant gun to a knife fight. The Stop Work Order was back in effect and posted on the gates, chained and locked. A federal prosecutor had made wild, unsubstantiated claims and got a federal judge to sign a temporary restraining order until a motion for a preliminary injunction could be heard in federal court.

Mack had made some powerful friends on his climb up the business ladder. He had used the Godfather approach: never refusing someone needing a reasonable favor, but always hoarding their return favor, sometimes for years. Now was the time for one of those return favors. He called JB to do his bidding. A courier the next morning delivered a petition requesting an emergency hearing before the Tennessee Court of Appeals in Nashville that day. Late that afternoon, Mack received a text from JB that he was faxing a court order overruling the TRO on grounds of irreparable harm—over a hundred thousand dollars a day could be lost to the economy of Memphis and Tennessee for every day the project was shut down.

*

Sonny was drilling and pouring 20-foot pilings with rebar at the casino floor cave-in, and so far they were holding. Mack had jump-started construction with extra manpower, and everyone was working overtime. With all the small fires breaking out around him, he was behind schedule:

commercial tenants with signed leases were ready to move in, the Casino was late for the grand opening, office condos had been sold with promises of immediate occupancy, and Amtrak was threatening to pull off the job if Global didn't get everybody back on schedule.

This sinkhole problem was the last thing he needed, especially with the government watching his every move. Adding fuel to the fire, Mack had found out from JB that the Stop Work Order was *not* because of the sink-hole but because the U.S. Government may own King's Island. Someone had written a letter, attaching a copy of an alleged map by the Spanish explorer, Hernando de Soto, dated 1540, showing de Soto meeting with the Chickasaw Indians on King's Island. The letter claimed that, in 1832, the U.S. authorities forced the Chickasaw Indians to sell King's Island, and then they were moved to Indian Territory in Oklahoma. Mack sent JB a copy of Irish's Land Deed Transfer with the title in his name and a copy of her will, highlighting the page where King's Island was gifted to him. He made a note to call Zira to track down *who* had sent the letter and map to the government. Breaking some bones would make him feel a lot better.

Maureen had brought Mack the report of the seismologist, but after reading the report, it didn't answer his most private question; *Was it safe to continue building The Towers?* He needed some experts and told Maureen to find them.

Later, Mack and Maureen narrowed down a list of experts to Mack's specs. He talked to them on the phone and reached an agreement on cost, including flying them to Memphis and back. He sent his plane to California to pick up a Rosemary Jackson, a world renowned seismolo-gist, with an earned moniker, The Earthquake Lady. After his stop in San Francisco, Captain Hank stopped in Boulder, Colorado, to pick up Dr. Stanford Shaw, President of The Geological Society of America and a lead-ing expert in scientific research specializing in geophysical hazards.

Otis had the limo waiting when the plane landed, and Maureen greeted the guests and got them checked in downtown at the Peabody Hotel. Mack had paid $5,000 each, plus all expenses, for them to drop what they were doing, fly the next day to Memphis, and return home the following day. Once the scientists had agreed to Mack's proposal over the phone, Maureen gave Sonny agreements to be signed, a brief history of the Trinity Town Towers project with photos of the sinkhole, different proposed solutions, the report Maureen had received from The Engineer's Club with certain sensitive information redacted, and the results of the core drilling samples. On the flight back to Memphis, Sonny went over all the details of the cave-in under the casino, so they could hit the ground running. Mack didn't need a long drawn-out written technical report, and told the two experts that in two days, he would meet with them in his office for a brief verbal report in layman's terms, with a Q&A session.

*

On Monday at noon, after hearing and discussing all options with the two scientists, Mack concluded their reports were of no value to him, a waste of time and money. It all boiled down to someone having the balls to make a difficult decision—continue building or shut down the project. The two scientists reported that after examining the site, the results of the deep core drillings, and the in-depth research of the history of the area, that King's Island was located on one of the most hazardous fault lines in the United States: the New Madrid Fault Zone, a fault line that ran from Memphis to St. Louis, 120 miles long, and referred to by The Earthquake Lady as the Sleeping Giant.

It had been sleeping quietly, until the morning of February 7, 1812, when it awoke, shaking the earth's core with a magnitude of level 9. The center of this massive earthquake, with 2,000 aftershocks over a five month period, occurred where the city of Memphis was now located. It blew out windows over 1,000 miles away in 23 states, affecting 15 million people. The energy force was so powerful, some say it reversed the flow of the Mississippi River, the fourth longest river in the world. But in fact the records of eyewitnesses verify that it was a *thrust fault*, sometimes called *reverse fault uplift*. So, instead of a *hole*, you now have a *wall* in the middle of the river, somewhere between 20 to 30 feet high, that dammed up the river, causing it to run backward, which created waterfalls in the upper part of the Mississippi River.

There was no way Mack's experts could determine when and if there would be another quake. The major problem was that these "silent quakes" gave no warning and registered no seismic waves. They were *tiny quakes*, a slow slipping of the planet's shell of tectonic plates. What they did tell

Mack was that earthquakes ran in cycles of 200 plus years; in other words, Memphis, at the present, was in that time cycle.

Rosemary Jackson, The Earthquake Lady, did allow that there was a recent research study by Northwestern and Purdue Universities, reporting that the New Madrid System may be shutting down and dying out, but hastened to add that she disagreed with those findings.

Again, another decision had to be made and quickly. As they say in the Marines, shit or get off the pot. He couldn't just walk off, quit. He knew that all kinds of rumors were rapidly spreading, and that a lot of people would love to see the man on top come tumbling down. Not that Lu Hanchen would, but he had already left a couple of messages to call him.

Mack stood up, stretched the tight muscles in his back and neck, and walked out of his penthouse office for some fresh air. *What if,* he thought . . . *if I completed the construction of the Towers and sometime in the near future there was an earthquake in the middle of a work week?* How many lives would be lost because all three Towers tumbled? Would he be blamed? Would the Shannon name be a black mark in history, synonymous with avarice and mass murder? What kind of legacy would that be for Irish?

Still, *if* an earthquake did hit, what about the One Hundred North Main Building with its 37 stories, or the 403-foot tall Morgan Keegan Tower, or say, the 83-year old Sterick Building, with its 29 floors? Would the public blame the builder of those buildings if destroyed?

It was *his* decision to make; no one could make it for him. *That's why you get paid the big bucks, right?* But everything he owned was on the line, all his assets, including the ten million he borrowed from his Clearwater investment accounts. His whole life could disappear, flushed down a bottomless hole in the earth.

To hell with the money. It didn't look like he was going to make a profit anyway. He'd be satisfied just to get his ten-million-dollar investment back. It was too late to bring the buildings up to the latest earthquake-proof design, but he could incorporate some of the latest changes.

All right, enough's enough, I'm wasting time. A decision needs to be made . . . now.

"Everyone back to work," Mack said out loud. He felt a huge weight lifted as he walked inside to call Sonny and tell him to get everybody back on the job. The phone rang as he reached to pick it up, "This is Mack."

"I told you I would drop a dime on your ass if you tried to screw me over."

Crazy Ray? "You're the one who sent the letter?"

"You're the one who kidnapped my mother! You think I would forget that?"

"Are you ever going to die, you scum bag?"

"Never. If I have to dig my way up from the depths of hell, I'll get my revenge. NO one messes with *my mother*! I swear to God," Crazy Ray shouted and then started coughing uncontrollably for almost a full minute before he was back on the phone. His shouting had ceased, and Mack strained to hear what he was saying.

"No more waiting. The price has gone up to three million, *plus* the weed. I'm talking about now. I want my money *now!*"

He's desperate, dead broke. "I don't have a *thousand* dollars much less three million, and I don't know what you're talking about, what *weed?*"

"I'll kill yo . . ."

"Shut up, and you listen!" Mack shouted. "Can't you understand, you dummy? Every penny I have is tied up in the Towers."

"If I don't get my three million dollars in twenty-four hours, the DEA will get a letter from me."

"Saying what? While you're sending, send one to the IRS and the FBI too. You're still not listening, you dumb-ass. *There-is-no-money! There-are-no-drugs!*"

"I swear on my mother's life I will get you. I will get . . ." Mack heard the phone drop and the beginning of another coughing attack, then a loud collision that ended with a hard thud.

Mack slammed his phone down. Maybe the bastard keeled over dead this time. His nine lives should be over by now. He picked the phone back up and called Zira's private number. She owned one of the largest PI agencies in the state now, and Mack had used her many times over the years. Now that Crazy Ray had resurfaced, Mack needed to keep an eye on him.

*

Men and a few women stood from one parapet wall across the roof to the other outside Mack's penthouse. Everyone involved with the construction of The Towers was told to be there: the subcontractors of every trade, their superintendents, materialsmen, architects, engineers, insurance representatives, bondsmen, and of course, always, lawyers.

Mack called the meeting to squelch all rumors and to make sure everyone was back on schedule. A tent covered a long table filled with barbeque and beer and a projection screen that Sonny had tied into his computer. On screen was the summary page of the Critical Path Method, a scheduling technique that showed every trade—from start to finish—their dates, their actual time and proposed time, on all three towers.

When one of the cranes was down, or material had to be backordered, or an accident like the cave-in happened, these delays caused a domino effect throughout the project. Sonny could then make changes on his computer, and everyone could see where they were or should be currently. These changes were made daily on a large screen TV in the office construction trailer. Having Tower One and Tower Two under construction at the same time, and starting Tower Three, helped Sonny keep from having any downtime by moving men and materials from one tower to the other.

Mack owed JB big time for getting the Feds off his back and keeping them away from his project. Everything was running smoothly, and the CPM showed they were soon to be back on schedule.

Mack was exhausted, mentally and physically. Between the troubles at The Towers and his constant depressed feelings over McKenzie, he needed a break. Everything was pretty much under control now, and he thought JB might want to fly down to Key West with him and do a little fishing. They could anchor out near one of the reefs and kick back, soak up some rays and drink some beer. *Maybe ask McKenzie . . . although her letter sounded pretty definite. Who the hell knows? I'll find someone, leave Thursday night and come back Monday, have me a relaxing weekend. What was that Buffett song he had been humming . . . "Changes in latitudes, changes in attitudes."*

*

For some reason or another, being at Memphis International on the taxiways late at night reminded Mack of Las Vegas Blvd, the strip, with all its colored lights. Captain Hank followed the green lights on the yellow centerline of the taxiway passing a fleet of FedEx planes, *global overnight deliverers*, stacked and waiting to take off on a parallel runway. He pushed his left brake, turning the plane west, and stopped at the red bar lights in a holding position for runway 18C. Cleared for takeoff, he taxied onto the runway and pointed the plane south. The Citation Ten lifted off at a steep angle, the two quiet but powerful Rolls-Royce engines rocketed them into a starry sky with a brilliant yellow-gold crescent moon. Mack, in the right seat, looked out at the mass of stars and thought of Van Gogh's much copied painting, *Starry Nights. The poor bastard, and I think I've got problems; he only sold one painting before he died in a mental asylum at 37.*

Mack searched the sky until he saw Dog Star, the brightest star in the sky, almost like a sparkler, with a large orb around it. Then he picked out Canopus and Alpha Centauri, both competing for the second brightest. It was good to fly in the right seat, surrendering all the responsibilities to Hank, as he drifted off into space, free of all his problems. He checked the altimeter and noticed they had just entered the stratosphere, six miles above the earth: less fuel consumption, better weather, and less traffic— just the stars and the moon.

Mack had called JB to go with him, but he was in Washington and couldn't leave. He finally capitulated and called McKenzie, but she didn't answer her cell phone, and he didn't leave a message. He wasn't that sure he really wanted any company. At the moment, surrounded by the vastness of the celestial sky, the countless stars, and the singular moon—all his worries had quickly vanished. He felt minuscule, a microdot . . . a wee thing in this tiny capsule.

Captain Hank leveled off at 40,000 feet, the autopilot turning to a southeast heading of 144 degrees. It was smooth, no turbulence, as he engaged the auto throttle setting the cruise speed at 675 miles per hour.

*

Mack had dozed off over the Gulf of Mexico, about 100 miles west of the coast of Florida.

"Citation Ten, November two five niner Delta Whiskey?"

"Citation Ten, November two five niner Delta Whiskey, over," Captain Hank said.

"Niner delta whiskey, this is Miami Center, go to frequency one two one point eight for an important message."

Mack was awake immediately and switched radio frequencies.

"Miami Center, niner delta whiskey on one two one point eight?"

"Citation Ten we have an important message for Mack Shannon. Is he aboard your aircraft?"

"This is Mack Shannon. What's the message?" *Please God, not Irish.*

"Niner delta whisky, the message reads, 'Call Sonny immediately, 911.'"

"Thanks, Miami. Niner delta whisky back to frequency one two three." Mack moved to the back of the plane quickly, opened his briefcase, and removed his Iridium satellite phone. He turned the antenna till his got a signal and called Sonny; he answered on the first ring.

"What's up?"

"Bad news, Boss."

Mack waited.

"We had another quake; no one was injured, thank God. I'm at the job-site now, and our office is patching all emergency calls to my cell phone."

"How much damage?"

"Not good. It got Tower Two as well as Tower One again. I've got a crew here, and we've got emergency lighting up everywhere. No damages along the river front or downtown Memphis. The quake was confined to King's Island, a crack right down the middle. I didn't know the Center for Earthquake Research was here at the University of Memphis. The Center is reporting over all the news station, their global positioning satellites revealed that the tremors were preceded by a silent, magnitude 6.0 quake. It takes a magnitude of 7 or more to be a major quake."

"Then the Towers are okay, repairable?"

Sonny went silent and knew he had said too much.

"Sonny! Are you there?"

"Can't we wait . . . you're almost here? We can walk the site together."

"NOW! Sonny! Right this minute. NO bullshit."

"I'm sorry, Mack. The towers look like two Leaning Towers of Pisa."

CHAPTER 26

DRIVING NORTH ON the NAFTA Superhighway I-69 through downtown Memphis, Randolph Winchester thought about how his little brother, Eli Sunday, could have qualified for a leading character in one of Horatio Alger's rags-to-riches stories.

Their father, Johnny Sunday, was a Pentecostal holiness evangelist and never had a church or owned a home. They traveled year around in an old 28-foot Airstream Ambassador, preaching fire and brimstone at tent revivals and churches whose pastors had left, were sick, or wanted a vacation. Johnny never made much money, but they always had plenty to eat and wore nice hand-me-down church clothes. He had many offers to pastor a church but his calling was evangelizing; he lived like a gypsy and loved it. When their mother divorced Johnny, Randolph left with his mother, who moved to Memphis, married a doctor named Winchester, and Randolph took his name. Eli stayed with his father, but felt abandoned, as his older brother was his only friend, and it took him years to overcome his sadness.

Randolph reduced his speed when the Interstate narrowed to three lanes as he approached the new, Tri-State Cloverleaf with eight ramps. The top level, I-69 and I-55, four lanes north and four south, were high-speed lanes, and passing motorists blew their horns at Randolph and gave him the middle finger for slowing down. This was the largest cloverleaf interchange in the south, with the world's busiest cargo airport, the home to five Class One railroads, the nation's fourth largest inland port, and interstate routes that carried some of the highest truck volumes in the nation.

Like a giant octopus with its eight tentacles, the cloverleaf's ramps served the huge Intermodal Railroad and Highway Facility (rail, barge, truck) located on the riverfront. This interchange streamlined and expedited rapid access to I-69, I-40, I-55, I-269, I-240, and I-22. From this cloverleaf, you could travel to the Atlantic or the Pacific coast, or to Canada or Mexico and never change highways.

Randolph sped up, back to 70 mph, and moved to the right lane for the next exit as cars whizzed by. Coming over the top of the cloverleaf, he looked toward the river and saw Eli's church and the new stainless steel lighted cross, 100 feet in the air, coming out of the top of the old Pyramid Arena. He had no problem reading the LED banner-type sign, halfway up each side of the pyramid—CHURCH ON THE RIVER—because the church was lit up like a casino. Their father, a staunch conservative Apostolic Pentecostal preacher, was probably in a rage, shouting from his grave.

He pulled into the massive, almost empty, parking lot, parked up close to the front, and walked across the lot. Having to make an appointment to see his own brother was something he never imagined would happen; more like the other way around. But in all fairness, *he* was the one who needed the favor.

As he walked inside the glass doors, an elevator-like bell rang, and he noticed a video camera high in the lobby corner. A guard told him to wait and someone would take him to Pastor Eli's office. He felt somewhat intimidated by the massiveness of this place, yet impressed with all the security. This was his first time inside the Pyramid; *how long had the building been here, 15 years?* He remembered reading about a lot of construction problems throughout its history: the river rising and flooding their lower floors, electrical and acoustic problems, and that it stood vacant for a long time. He looked around some more, then walked back over to the guard and asked if it was okay to look inside the arena.

"You mean the sanctuary, don't you?" The guard said, nodding his approval but still following him with his eyes.

Randolph stood at the end of one of the portals, looking down and out over the vastness of the bowl-shaped pit. He estimated he was on the second floor or mezzanine level. He was not a religious person, but not an atheist, maybe agnostic. But there was spirituality here, an ethereal feeling of warmth and peacefulness. The guard was right; this *is* a sanctuary. Whoever redesigned this place knew what they were doing. Unquestionably, a first-class job.

"Randolph, what brings you to my humble abode?" Eli stood behind him, dressed in khaki pants and a polo shirt, promoting the church's policy of come-as-you-are. He reached out to shake Randolph's hand, something he thought he would never do again. But God had removed the ill will he had for his brother. It had been over ten years since they last spoke, when Eli had informed him of their father's death and invited him to be part of the services. He had failed to show up for his own father's funeral, no flowers, not even a card.

"Eli," Randolph said, shaking his hand, "surely you jest. There's nothing humble about this place; it's overpowering."

"Would you like a short tour?"

"No, no, I've got to get back, I have an office full of patients." Randolph looked out over the sanctuary. "But, I am curious, how many seats are in here?"

"Originally there were 20,000, now we have a little less than half of that, 9,300 permanent seats. We lowered the ceiling by building three floors from the top down, high above the sanctuary. We needed extra rooms for our other ministries and, at the same time, it created some of the intimacy of our old church."

"Well, you certainly accomplished that. I've seen you on TV a couple of times, but it's much different being here. The stage area is . . . huge."

"That was necessary to accommodate the choir, the orchestra pit in front, and the viewing screen across the stage. We boxed everything in behind the stage for a backdrop and to hide the elevator shaft."

"How big is that screen?"

"100 feet wide and 20 feet tall with seven projectors sweeping across the length of the stage."

"Brother Eli?" They both turned when they heard the deep whisper behind them. "You wanted me to let you know, lunch is being served in ten minutes."

"Thank you, John." Eli turned to Randolph, "Would you like to join us?"

"No thanks. I don't want you to miss your lunch, but can I steal a few more minutes?"

"The lunch is not for me. We serve free lunches two days a week and supper every Wednesday night. When I'm not traveling, I welcome the visitors and members with a short talk." He nodded to John, "One of the associate pastors can handle that today." Eli pointed to some seats on the back row. "Let's talk here."

"Sure." Randolph watched the guard hurry off, then moved down to the middle of the back row and took a seat. "I know how you've always helped the downtrodden, and I have a patient who needs your help. He's an intelligent fellow and was a successful businessman at one time, but like a lot of people, he lost everything due to bad investments and to his illness."

"How can I help?"

Randolph removed a folded paper from his coat. "Someone gave him one of your Sunday programs with this small article about the church needing a night watchman. Somehow, he knew we were related and asked me to intervene. Of course, I would continue to provide medical treatment for him, so the church wouldn't have to furnish any insurance."

"He wants the night watchman's job?"

"Yes. It would be perfect for him."

This is strange . . . unlike Randolph to put himself out like this. He could have handled this over the phone. "What's his illness?"

Randolph hesitated. "If I tell you, surely it will jeopardize his chances of being hired."

Eli said nothing; he waited, staring at Randolph.

"His name is Ray Flynn; he's HIV positive."

"How sick is he?"

"Stage 4, AIDS. I know this is a lot to ask, but he's responding to the medication and strong enough to do the job of a night watchman. Plus, he has a close friend, a part-time handyman, carpenter mostly, who could sub for him if ever he's too sick to work. I will be totally responsible for him if anything should happen."

"He's more than just your patient, right?"

Randolph hesitated, "Yes."

"Randolph, I do not pick and choose whom God sends me. Matthew said, in 8:2.3, a man with leprosy, an infectious disease like AIDS today, stopped Jesus on the road and, kneeling before him, said, 'Lord, if you are willing, you can make me clean.' Jesus reached out his hand and touched the man even though his skin was covered with the dreaded disease and said, 'I am willing.' Can I do any less?"

Randolph felt as if someone was watching them and looked down at the end of the row and saw John, the guard, just standing there.

"Excuse me," Eli said, and walked down the row to John.

After a few minutes Eli came over and said to Randolph, "Is your patients name Ray Flynn?"

"Why yes," he said, standing, somewhat shocked.

"He's waiting in the lobby, asking to see you."

"Please Eli, I had no idea. Could you wait?"

"I'll wait right here."

Randolph followed John to the lobby and when he saw Ray standing there, his heart skipped a beat. He was dressed in dark slacks with a starched white shirt, clean-shaven and his hair was trimmed. His normal pallid face had a healthy glow as if he had been in the sun. He wasn't a handsome man, by a long shot, but to Randolph he was everything he was not: a free spirit—open, funny, and unpredictable.

"I hope I'm not embarrassing you." Ray said with a "happy face" smile.

Randolph took Ray by the elbow and led him to the glass doors.

"What's wrong?" Ray asked.

"Wait." Randolph whispered. Once outside in the parking lot, Randolph said, "I didn't want us talking in front of the guards. How did you know I was here?"

"Are you upset with me?"

"Noooo, no . . . I'm *so* glad to see you." He hooked his arm through Ray's arm as they walked around the back of the lot.

Ray stopped walking and turned facing Randolph. "I want to tell you something. I've been thinking about this so long it's making me sick." He looked around the parking lot and didn't see anyone. He took both of Randolph's hands in his, "I'm an ungrateful son-of-a-bitch. You are the kindest person I have ever known. You took care of me when I was dying, treated my body and my mind. You bath me, fed me, and bought my clothes . . . saved my life . . . and never asked for a thing in return. What did I do? I've used you . . . I'm sorry!" Ray opened his arms, "I need you."

Randolph was shocked. Tears streamed down his face.

Ray dropped his arms and hung his head.

Randolph wrapped both arms around Ray, squeezed him as close to him as possible, lifting him off the ground. "You love me . . . you love me!" he said.

Later, inside Eli's office, Randolph, Ray, and Eli talked. Eli got up from his desk and handed Ray a folder, as his secretary, Ellen, came into the office. "Mr. Flynn, if you will follow Ellen, she will help you with the information needed, introduce you to the maintenance people and the head of security. Once that's all taking care of you can start to work immediately.

Ray followed Ellen out the office, but looked back at Randolph and thanked them both.

"He doesn't look sick, not what I was expecting from someone with AIDS." Eli said.

"No he doesn't. Every day they're coming out with newer medicines to treat this infection. Patients are living longer and longer and if we can keep them alive long enough, we'll soon have a cure," Randolph said as he stood up. "I've taken up too much of your time. I can't tell you how much I appreciate what you're doing for me. I don't want to embarrass you or cheapen your kindness, but can I make a donation to the church?"

"No, Randolph, you're my brother, my big brother, remember? Just don't wait another ten years to come see me, okay?" Eli walked over and they embraced, both a little teary-eyed.

As Randolph walked across the parking lot to his car to wait on Ray, he removed his handkerchief and wiped his eyes. *My God! What an emotional couple of hours. I feel exhausted . . . but happy.*

*

"Go around one more time, low and slow," Mack ordered Captain Hank as they flew over King's Island. It was sickening, and he couldn't believe his eyes. He wanted to believe it wasn't that bad, but with all the emergency lighting, you could see the zigzag fissure snaking its way across the island, plowing right between the two towers. As the plane flew low over the top, Mack craned his neck to see more and wanted to throw up when he saw Tower One and Tower Two almost touching at the top, like two drunks holding each other up.

He choked down the swill that roiled up from his stomach and backed up into his esophagus. Slumping back in the co-pilot's seat, he closed his eyes, took a couple of deep breaths, and tried to hold off the sickening migraine building in his head.

He felt the wheels touchdown on the runway and was afraid to open his eyes. The pain was so intense, and the vibration of the airplane was giving him vertigo.

"Mack, you okay? You don't look too good. Are you sick?"

Mack waited till he felt the plane turn onto the taxiway and then make another right turn into the FBO. He opened his eyes, looked out, and saw a blur of Otis standing by the limo. When the plane stopped, he staggered to the door, made it to the bottom step. Holding onto the handrail, the blood vessels pounding inside his head, he threw up all over the tarmac. With each wrenching spasm, his head felt like it was going to explode.

Otis ran to him with a bottle of water and paper towels he kept in the limo. Mack gargled the water, rinsing the bile from his throat and mouth, poured some over his head and face, and dried off with the paper towels. He brushed Otis' arm aside when he tried to help him and stumbled into the car.

In the backseat of the limo, he opened a black bag filled with everything he had in his medicine cabinet at home, and removed a syringe. He leaned back against the seat, arching his body, pushed his pants down to his knees, and injected his thigh with 6 mg of Imitrex. He pulled up his pants and closed his eyes. Instantly, he felt his blood vessels constricting in his legs, tightening in his chest and throat. *Voila! No more migraine.* He reached back into his black bag and removed two purple capsules of 40 mg Nexium, a blue Xanax pill, two anti-vertigo tabs, and washed them down with a mouthful of double strength Maalox.

Otis watched from his rearview mirror. "You okay, Boss?"

"Take me to the Towers."

*

Crazy Ray opened the door of the commercial refrigerator and removed a glazed spiral ham, a large stainless steel bowl of potato salad, and half of an apple pie that was left over from the Wednesday night church fellowship supper. After making a sandwich, he poured himself a glass of iced tea and looked at the kitchen clock to see if it was time to take his packet of meds. Randy was emphatic about Crazy Ray adhering to the dosing regimen he had prescribed, and it was making a difference. He felt a lot better, and his appetite was back. It was almost 2 a.m., time for him to make his outside rounds and take his meds—after he ate his sandwich.

He could only eat half his sandwich, a few bites of potato salad, and none of the pie. If he forced it down, the sores in his mouth and throat would start bleeding, and the raw blood would bring on an attack of uncontrollable diarrhea. He put the food back in the refrigerator and left the kitchen to start his two o'clock patrol around the outside of the church. He climbed into the John Deere Gator with a power dump bed in the back, and his cell phone alarm beeped to remind him to take his meds. With all the drugs in his body, it was a miracle he even had a memory. He walked back into the kitchen and opened his nylon travel pack with seven boxes of pills. He would be lost without his pill organizer and pill identifier. Trying to remember the names of all the drugs he was taking, especially the antiretroviral drugs: Sustiva, Cenicriviroc, Truvada, plus all the vitamins and antibiotics, was impossible. As he swallowed his last pill, his phone rang. He looked at the number; it was Dago.

"You outside?" Crazy Ray asked.

"Yeah."

"I'm on my way." Crazy Ray followed the headlights as he drove the utility vehicle along the dimly lit corridors until he reached the maintenance shop. He turned down a short corridor and stopped at a 12 x 16 steel roll up door. With his remote, he opened the overhead door and drove the Gator outside, lowering the door behind him.

Dago shut the door on the pickup truck and walked over to the Gator. "What's up?"

"Get in. I got to make my rounds. Whose truck you driving?"

"My mother's boyfriend's. Got to have it back by daybreak."

"Where's your truck?"

"In the shop, needed new brakes."

"I thought you did all the work on your truck, you paying someone else?"

"Naw, we traded out. I'm re-tiling his bathroom floor." Dago stood looking up at the top of the pyramid. "Damn, look at the size of this mother. It doesn't look that big from a distance."

"32 stories, let's go."

"What do you mean, making your rounds?"

"What do you think, dummy? Every hour, I have to drive around the building and turn a key into a watchman clock."

"That's a bummer. No sleeping on the job, huh?"

"Just like the old days, except the time is registered to a computer instead of on paper."

"How many clocks are there?"

"Four. One in the front of the church, one in the back along the river, and one on the north and south side." Crazy Ray put it in gear and headed for the first checkpoint.

"What are you looking for?" Dago asked.

"Anything out of the ordinary."

"Man, you got it made, riding around in this new four-wheeler, free eats, and no boss. You sure you can't get me a job here?"

"Yeah, I'm sure."

"You ever find anything out of the ordinary?"

"Not really. A couple screwing in the parking lot, a bum passed out now and then, a car on fire, stuff like that."

"Really? You carrying your pistol?"

"In a *church*?"

"Well, you always carried one before."

"I hide it upstairs."

"What did you want me to help you with?"

They were back from checking the outside, and Crazy Ray opened the overhead door with his remote and drove the Gator inside. "I'll tell you as soon as we get loaded up." He lowered the door and drove around to the maintenance shop, got out, and opened the double doors.

Dago moved over behind the steering wheel. "I can back it up."

"You sure?"

"I drove the pickup over here, didn't I?"

"Okay, but be careful . . ."

"Where's the clutch?"

"There *is* no clutch . . ."

"How do I put it in reverse?"

"The floor shift, it only has two gears, forward and backward. Pull it back."

Dago backed the Gator up, and Crazy Ray pointed out the construction material that needed to be loaded into the dump bed: sheetrock, wood studs, tools, and a short ladder.

Crazy Ray drove to the elevator on the west side of the church, behind the stage. They loaded the equipment and materials in the elevator and pushed the button for the third floor.

"How many floors are there?" Dago asked.

"Three floors above the mezzanine, counting the Observation Deck."

"What the hell's a magazine?"

"Not magazine, mezz . . . mezz-a-neen, a balcony, the second level. Don't ask so many stupid questions."

Inside the elevator, Crazy Ray pointed to each button on the panel as the elevator climbed. "This is the ground floor, marked with the G, then the next floor is marked with the M, for mezzanine. Three hundred feet up is the start of the third floor, then the fourth floor, and at the top is the fifth, the Observation Deck."

The elevator stopped at the third floor, directly under the sanctuary. Dago carried the material down an unfinished hallway with empty rooms on each side. All the sheetrock in the rooms and hallway had been hung and finished, ready for paint. Vinyl floor tile had been installed. The doors hung with their hardware, but not painted. Some of the acoustical ceiling tiles were missing, probably removed by the heating and air contractor and the electricians working above the ceiling grid. There were extra doors, rolls of insulation, filing cabinets, desks and chairs, and boxes stored in every room. "These rooms have never been occupied. It's a catch-all floor, storage rooms, etc." Crazy Ray said.

"Take all the material down to the end of the hall at that closet door," Crazy Ray said as he followed, carrying the stepladder and a tool belt. He opened the closet door and they both stood looking at the unfinished closet: wooden studs, electric wire for the light and switch, and metal bands holding up the heating and air ductwork.

"I want you to build me a ten-by-ten foot room behind those studs with a secret door in the back of this closet. I've got more studs and sheet-rock stored in the back room."

"What for?"

"I'm going to live here."

"*Live!* In there?" Dago pointed behind the closet.

"Not live, just a pad, a place to sleep. They have bathrooms, show-ers, and a huge kitchen downstairs. I'm paying $600 for that one-bed-room dump I'm living in now, and with all the noise and music blaring, I haven't had a good night's sleep since I've been there. Here I pay nothing. Free food, TV, computer with Wi-Fi, and even the church's handicap van or their pickup when I need it."

Dago squeezed between the studs and behind the closet into the attic space. "This is a lot of work. I thought the doc was getting you a new place to live."

"Not yet, and I don't want to push it. Besides, I've got another idea."

"This will take a lot more time than I figured."

"What? It's just studs and sheetrock. You had no idea what I wanted, so how did you *figure* the amount of time?"

"I just thought you needed a couple hours, not a couple of days."

"Bullshit! You going to help or not?"

"I said I would, didn't I?"

CHAPTER 27

AT THE APEX of the BTN Bridge, Mack said to Otis, "Pull over into the right lane and stop." Mack opened the door and stepped out from the back seat. "Put your emergency blinker on and get out if you want." There was more traffic on the bridge than usual for this time of night. Some blew their horns and flashed their lights as they passed, heading to the earthquake site. Mack walked to the front of the limo and leaned back against the grille, his foot on the bumper. He and Otis stood side-by-side perusing the Trinity Town Towers with all the emergency lighting: red lights of the fire department, blue lights of the police cars blocking sightseers, and five media trucks that he could count.

Mack had no pain. The migraine was gone, his stomach caustic but settled, and the Xanax had thwarted the main attack to his central nervous system. He grunted while staring at the two towers, T-1 and T-2. Silhouetted against the river skyline, they looked like two cyclopean drunks holding each other up. "Well, Otis, you think this is a first . . . a billion dollars flushed through a large crack in the earth?"

"You got insurance, don't you?"

"Not for an earthquake. We talked about it. Isaac even checked with Lloyd's of London. We found out it had been 200 years since the last earthquake in Memphis. Someone figured the odds were 73,000 to 1."

"Some expert on TV said it was a tiny quake . . . no, he said, a *silent* quake. It didn't even register on some kind of meter they use."

"If a silent quake does a billion dollars' worth of damages, I'd hate to see what a noisy one would do." Mack stared a long time at the silhouette of the towers, then turned and walked to the back of the limo. "Take me home, Otis. This is not a good time to talk to the press. I'm sure to say something that I'll regret tomorrow. God is pissed off at me about something."

*

"It's all over the world news, across the front page of the major newspapers." Isaac showed Mack a couple of out-of-town newspapers and a copy of *The Commercial Appeal*, Memphis' morning paper. Across the front page in bold letters was printed, TWIN TOWERS OF PISA, with a half-page photo of the Towers almost touching at the top.

Mack sat between Anna and Isaac in the back seat of the limo on their way to the construction site. It was early morning with a dark, overcast sky that looked like rain.

Anna reviewed her notes. "The phones have been ringing constantly— news media, nationally and locally, demanding interviews with you. A lot of the construction workers and subcontractors are outside our office wanting to get paid."

"Yeah, I've been getting a lot of anonymous calls, making all kinds of threats, then hanging up," Isaac said.

"I don't mean to load you up, I can fend off all these calls. Just tell me what you want me to handle," Anna said.

"I'll know more about what to do and say after we inspect the damages," Mack said.

Sonny stood by the opened double gates to the construction site with a pair of bolt cutters dangling from his hand. Threatening government signs hung from the fence and gates. A few photographers snapped photos as Otis drove through, and Mack checked out the doublewide construction office to make sure it was in one piece. Sonny had one of his construction laborers shut the gates and stand guard. He waited in the four-seater golf cart until they were loaded in. "Good morning, everyone."

"Is it?" Mack said

"It is if you don't have cancer," Sonny said.

"Always the optimist."

"They can only kill you once, boss."

"Are you saying it's my time to go?"

"Nope, I know better. I've seen you *resurrected* too many times. Where do you want to start?"

"You've been here all night; lead the way."

Sonny drove to the south end of the island where they all got out of the golf cart. Mack looked back at Anna and Isaac and shook his head. It was dangerously steep and muddy as he followed Sonny down to the river's edge. The earthquake had cut a deep inlet into the island, about ten feet wide, now filled with water. As the cut climbed up the riverbank, it narrowed down to no more than two feet wide. Mack and Sonny followed the crack north through uprooted trees and shrubs that hadn't been cleared for construction. There were rumors of mini tremors still going on deep underground, so Isaac and Anna followed in the cart at what they hoped was a safe distance.

When Mack and Sonny broke out of the wooded area onto flat-graded ground, a black jagged scar, as straight as if one popped a chalk line, opened up the earth all the way to the leaning towers.

Mack looked up from the fissure when he heard the siren and saw the flashing light of a police car racing toward them. Two cops jumped out of the car, but they stopped immediately when they saw Mack. "Sorry, Mr. Shannon, the federal government has taken possession of this island, and no one is allowed on this property. I have strict orders to arrest any trespassers."

Mack stared at the two cops, his hands on his hips.

"If you see any trespassers, please let us know. Have a good day, sir."

Like his Uncle Mickey, Mack had continued the tradition of the marine service centers feeding the fire and police personnel 24/7. In the last year he started something new, feeding the homeless coffee and biscuits every morning.

Mack turned and walked toward the Towers. Sonny hurried beside him. "I know this is devastating, boss, but we've been through a lot together and we'll get through this."

They kept walking, side-by-side, following the fissure until they got to a yellow caution tape and fabric fence, about a football field's length from the Towers. Mack looked at the tops of the Towers and judged the distance from the top to the fence. *If the Towers fell, would they crumble or fall over like an uprooted tree?* With all the rebar, Mack figured it would fall like a tree. They may need to move the fence back some more. He took his foot and pushed one of the metal U posts to the ground and kept on walking.

He noticed the east side of the fissure had pushed up from the west side, and by the time they were standing under the Grand Entrance, the east side of the fissure was waist-high above the west side. Mack jumped up on the east side of the fissure to get a better view. He could see the plowed up imported Italian marble that covered the floors of the Grand Hall and the three atria of the towers. The tunnel for the Amtrak train had caved in, having fallen into the crevice, and now was nothing but a huge sinkhole.

Mack walked along the top of the raised fissure to the highest point, stopping at the sinkhole, then traced it as it sliced through the concrete foundations of Tower 3, out the other side and back down to the river— one long cut. It was like a bad sci-fi movie, in which a pissed off Megalodon shark, at a sonic rate of speed, went through the island instead of around it, his dorsal fin making a surgical incision from one end of the island to the other, a long deadly cut that destroyed his dream of a landmark monument stamped with the Shannon name.

He stared at the uprooted foundation piers and grade beams that now exposed the bent rebar, the dark sinkhole, and the zigzag crack from the bottom to the top of the 100-foot arch of the Grand Entrance.

He felt the drops of acid pooling in the bottom of his stomach and the muscles tightening in the back of his neck. He tried to force his brain to think positive thoughts: *It happened—it wasn't your fault. There's nothing to salvage here.*

It was all over. Every asset he owned was used to collateralize the billion-dollar loan to build Trinity Town, including his ten million dollar credit line from Clearwater. He had always wondered why successful men jumped off the tops of buildings or blew their brains out with a gun. He had always said he would just walk away, go to Key West, sit in the sunshine, hang his feet off the pier, and fish all day. He started with nothing, so it wasn't like the end of his world. He had been at the bottom before. Yet the degradation, the failure, the worthlessness all closed in on him as he stood looking down into the bottomless sinkhole: *One more step and there would be no more problems.* He took a deep breath and looked over at

Sonny, "The hell with it. They couldn't save Penn Station or the Baths of Caracalla either. Let's go back to the office. I've seen enough."

*

"For the time being, here's what we're going to do about Trinity Town . . . *nothing,*" Mack said. "We're out of it. It's over. The government: the city, county, state, and feds have seized the island, posted it hazardous and unsafe, and barred all unauthorized personnel. There's nothing we can salvage; let them fight over the ruins." Isaac, Anna, Sonny, and Maureen sat at the round conference table in Mack's office.

"I've been knocked down a couple of times but never knocked out. Remember what Napoleon Hill said, 'With every adversity, there's an equal or greater benefit.' Maureen, get Sid on the phone for me."

"He's outside my office, waiting."

"Really?"

"He called, and I told him to come on up. You want to see him now?"

"In a few minutes. Isaac, I want you to hold a press conference tomorrow at noon. Draft a one-page speech, and then let's go over it. Keep it short: 'We're still in business. We're evaluating the damages. We're thankful the earthquake was limited to King's Island, and that no one was injured, etc, etc.'"

"Anna, get your crew and find out where we are money-wise. Everybody will be coming after the money. Be creative; let's move it around. Global Construction will take the hit on this, but see how much exposure our other companies have. You can meet with Sid after he and I finish.

"Sonny, first thing, I need all the construction time-lapse cameras, photos, and everything out of the construction office trailers. Clean them out now. Keep the gates locked while you're going in and out and try to be as inconspicuous as possible. Later tonight I want you to move the storage trailers, all of our tools, equipment, and any materials we've paid for.

"We are going to have to do some deep-cutting layoffs in *all* departments. Maureen, get us a list of employees and each of you mark who to let go and the amount of severance pay, if any. Give a list to Sonny. Keep me informed. Now, let me talk with Sid."

Maureen was transcribing, and after editing out any incriminating statements, she would bring Mack a hard copy of the meeting.

Mack saw Sid talking to Anna outside his door.

"Do you need me?" Maureen asked.

Mack shook his head, as Sid Goldman hurried in and stood before his desk.

What a transformation!

When Mack fired the law firm of Bickford, Overton, and Guthrie, Isaac suggested it was time to have their own legal department and recommended hiring Sid Goldman as General Counsel for Shamrock and their sister companies. Isaac's endorsement was based on Sid's masterful representation of his client at the Special Master's hearing, when Arthur sued Global Construction, Shamrock, and Mack Shannon. After hearing the same praise from Father O'Brien, Mack agreed to interview Sid.

It was a memorable interview: Sid came rushing into Mack's office late, obviously working in the appointment between court appearances, looking like a homeless person. His suit appeared to have been picked from a box donated to the Salvation Army. Mack, Anna, and Maureen stared at Isaac, who was smiling. Was this some kind of joke?

After the interview, Mack asked the others to give him a minute alone with Sid. He opened a folder and was looking over Sid's one-page resume, "You graduated from Vanderbilt Law School, first in your class?"

Sid nodded.

"What's this 'Order of the Coif?'"

"It's a scholastic honor society membership."

Mack closed the folder. "So, Sid. Can we be candid?" Mack asked.

"Sure, works for me."

"Good, I have a couple of questions. Do you *want* to work for Shamrock, and seeing that I don't know a lot about building a legal department, do you have any experience as an in-house lawyer?

"Being candid, I don't know if I want to work for someone else or not. I'm not quite house broken, and I know nothing about building a legal department or being an in-house lawyer."

"Mr. Shannon, I'm what they call a *street lawyer*. I work a lot of hours, under a lot of pressure, and sometimes I'm paid and sometimes I'm not. I practice law every day, in every court from General Session, Criminal, Chancery, and Federal. I turn away very few clients. A respectable comparison to what I envision being an in-house counsel would be like my primary physician, an Internist. Today, everything is specialized: medicine, law, even auto mechanics. You ever try to work on a car nowadays? As far as a legal department or in-house counsel . . . there's no part of the law that I would run from. Lawyering is research, networking, and gambling—like when to hold'em, when to show'em, and when to fold'em. As I told Isaac, I'm looking to make a complete change in my lifestyle. So, what kind of money are you offering, Mack?"

Mack smiled, "What kind of money are you making now?"

"No, you go first."

"We've never had a legal department. I have no idea what lawyers make."

"Okay. Straight away, cards on the table. I need $200,000 guaranteed for the first year. Win, lose, or draw.

Weather or not you decide to fire me, I get paid the $200 thou. If that's agreeable, then I'll need to hire one other lawyer, two law students, a legal secretary, and I will only answer to you or Isaac."

*

Mack congratulated himself. Now, with the help of Isaac's tailor, Sid stood before him in a bespoke suit, looking like a model in *GQ*—a complete metamorphosis, even hair and teeth implants.

"Nice suit," Mack said.

"You want me to get you one?"

"No thanks. Have you been by the job site?"

"I drove by there, but couldn't get in . . . really didn't need to. It's all over the TV."

"What's your thinking? Isaac's holding a press conference tomorrow at noon."

"It depends. That's what I wanted to talk about. A billion dollar loss is hard to overcome. Let's review the options. We've got insurance but no earthquake coverage. There was no negligence, so you have no personal responsibility, although you did personally indemnify the loan with your assets. The investors can take everything you own but not your house. So, it would be like starting over again. You do have your good health."

"Yeah, easy for you to say."

"No, it's not. But it's the truth. Our second option is bankruptcy—we list everything you own and everything you owe and give it to a judge."

"I'm not going to declare bankruptcy. That would ruin my credit. I've had triple-A credit since I first went into business."

"Not now you don't." Sid opened a folder he had with him and handed Mack a handful of papers. "I've been receiving faxes all morning: Notice of Nonpayment, Notice of Intent to File Lien, and Notice of Lien. My phone hasn't stopped ringing with demands of payment and threats of lawsuits. A friend of mine at the register's office called and said there was a line outside her office waiting to file liens. Financially, bankruptcy is not going to make a bit of difference from where you are now. What it will do is keep the mass of people from harassing you . . . and me."

"I'm not going to roll over and play dead, Sid. I've got some other jobs, and we can start bidding and negotiating some more work. We can incorporate, form a couple of LLC's under new names, and keep on working, right?"

"I know how you are. You want to fight back immediately. But let's wait a couple of days—let the chips fall where they may—we don't want to jump the gun." Sid got up from his chair and headed for the door, "Meanwhile, let me put out some of the small fires first."

CHAPTER 28

CRAZY RAY SAT on the edge of his twin-sized wall bed, a crude copy of a Murphy bed that Dago had built. Carpet remnants covered the floor, shelves were recessed into the walls, and he had a wooden rod for hanging clothes, a foldout table with a chair, a microwave, and a motel-type refrigerator. It had been over a month since they had finished Crazy Ray's attic room. He got the idea about the attic from an old paperback he found in the church library one night. The story was from the diary of a young Jewish girl, who hid in an attic for two years from the Nazis. He had no plans for staying in the attic that long.

The construction work on the attic had taken a toll on his body, eating up any reserve strength he might have had. But for the last two weeks, with no noise and his new medication, he was sleeping six hours straight through each day, which had strengthened his body. Also, it had refueled the embers of revenge that had been smoldering in the recesses of his mind. It was payback time—time to execute the second phase of his plan.

Most of what he needed was ordered over the Internet, shipped to Dago's mother's house, and now stored in the open duffel bag at his feet. He unfolded a list and checked off each item: Two *burkas*, one small, one large, with matching black veils; one extra-large, man's black *thawb*, with *ghutra* and *agal*; the rope to hold the headdress on the man's head; two magnetic signs to cover the names on the door of the church van; two pepper spray guns; a stolen Tennessee license plate; and a roll of duct tape. Crazy Ray unzipped a pocket on the end of the bag and removed a round toothbrush holder. He removed a syringe from inside, held it upright to make sure the level of fluid was at 100 mgs, and placed the syringe back inside the toothbrush holder. His phone vibrated, and he saw the number of Dago's mother on the screen.

"Are you downstairs?" he asked.

"Yeah, waiting on you," Dago said.

"I'm on my way down." They had rehearsed Crazy Ray's plan over and over. They tried on the clothes, checked the handicap van, and loaded the wheelchair, and now it was *opening* night.

Dago drove the van east on Walnut Grove Road. The streetlights sent a glare off the wet asphalt pavement, making it hard to read the street signs. It had been raining hard all day but now had slowed to a steady light drizzle.

"Slow down. You need to turn right at the light, at Mendenhall," Crazy Ray said.

"I can't see a thing."

"Then slow down. Get in the right lane and turn on the defroster."

"Where's the defroster . . . shit, I'm driving; you do it."

Crazy Ray reached over and turned a knob. "This is the street, turn here."

Dago turned on Mendenhall, drove a couple miles, and slowed down.

"Turn left here, on Sanderlin," Crazy Ray pointed.

"I know, I know, we've been here two times already."

"Go down to the second drive, turn into the Fox and Hound, and park around back, next to the dumpster." Crazy Ray unbuckled his safety belt and moved to the back of the van. He opened the duffel bag and removed one of the black burkas and the two magnetic signs. Dago parked the van, and Crazy Ray handed him the two signs and the pepper spray gun. "Put these on the doors and make sure they cover the church's name while I put this *sheet* on—I feel like a Klansman."

Crazy Ray opened the side door, stepped out next to the dumpster, looked in all directions, and changed the license plate on the back of the van. He slipped the lightweight burka over his head and adjusted the netted face-veil, but his peripheral vision was limited. Dago laughed, and Crazy Ray threw the extra-large *thawb*, an ankle-length robe with long sleeves, at Dago. While Dago dressed, Crazy Ray checked both signs on the doors. "Islamic Center of Memphis" was printed in Lucida Calligraphy font; they looked great.

Back in the truck and on Sanderlin Avenue again, Dago turned into the first drive past the Fox and Hound Bar and Grill. They stopped at the guard shack of the Memphis Racket Club. A barrier arm blocked the entrance. Crazy Ray quickly leaned over and adjusted the *agal*, the black cord on Dago's *ghutrah*, his headdress. "I've never seen a Muslim with peroxide hair," he said.

The guard walked over to the truck. Dago lowered his window and said, "Tennis tournament."

The guard looked at the sign on the door and moved closer to see inside. "Is your daughter playing?"

"Her granddaughter," Dago said, nodding his head towards Crazy Ray, who was hunched over like an old woman.

"Name please?" The guard was looking on his clipboard.

Crazy Ray had printed off the player's draw sheet three days ago and highlighted the first foreign name he saw, Haifa Kahn.

"Kahn," Dago said. He forgot how to pronounce her first name.

"Is that with a C?" The guard said, dragging his finger down the list.

The car behind them started blowing their horn. "With a K," Dago said.

Holding his breath, Crazy Ray let out a lungful of air through the netted veil when he saw the barrier arm rising.

Dago rolled up the window as he pulled through the gate, drove along the east side of the club, and parked next to the curb at the service entrance.

*

Otis looked at all four corners before turning the black limo north off Poplar Avenue onto White Station Road. It was still drizzling rain, and Memphis drivers were notoriously reckless under these conditions.

"I'm going to let you two off at the club, and I'll be back in time for your match," Mack said to Irish, who sat between Lea and Mack in the backseat.

"You're going to miss my match, Daddy."

"No I won't. Your match is not until 8 o'clock, and I will be back before you and Lea finish your warm up. I've got to sign some papers downtown for Sid Goldman, maybe an hour at the most, there and back."

"We'll call him when we finish our warm up," Lea said to Irish.

"Daddy, are we going to have to move?"

"Move? Move where? What are you talking about?"

"It's all on television, and everyone at school is talking about your buildings falling over."

"I had nothing to do with the Towers *falling over*. That was an act of God, baby—an earthquake. Don't you worry about what other people say."

"Why would God do that?" Irish asked. She then turned and tapped on the glass for Otis. He lowered the inside window, and Irish held out an opened tin of cookies, "You want one before I give these to Mr. Charlie?"

Otis took one and stopped at the gate of the Racket Club. Lea lowered the window on her side, and Irish handed the guard the tin of cookies, "I made these for you, Mr. Charlie."

"Good evening, Mr. Shannon, Miss Lea. Thank you, Irish. Good luck tonight." Charlie reached inside Otis's window and punched him on the arm, "You eating one of my cookies, *boy*?"

Otis waved his cookie at Charlie as he pulled through the gate and double-parked next to a white van at the service entrance.

"Give me a kiss," Mack said as Otis stood, holding the back door open for Lea and Irish. Irish leaned back in and kissed her father on the cheek. "Kick butt, right?" he said as Irish followed Lea out the door.

Irish gave Otis a high-five outside the limo. "Sic'm girl," Otis said while handing her the tennis bag.

Lea and Irish both dressed in Nike warm-ups, hurried under the awning that covered the walkway to the service entrance. Inside they walked down a long narrow corridor with a low ceiling that led to the indoor tennis courts. On the walls were photos of the past winners of the U.S. National Indoor Championship. Irish called out each champion's name as she passed them: Connors, McEnroe, Agassi, Sampras, Roddick, Evert, Navratilova, Capriati, Davenport, and Sharapova. The newer champions' photos hung on the walls of the main entrance.

Lea grabbed Irish by her shoulder and stopped her, "Shhhh, listen." They both heard a loud moan. Up ahead, on the left, was a short hallway off the main corridor where the men and women's restrooms were located.

Lea hurried to the hallway with Irish behind her. At the end of the hallway, they saw a wheelchair turned on its side, and a woman in a burka crawling toward the wheelchair, moaning.

Irish dropped her tennis bag and ran to help the woman. Lea shouted at Irish and ran to catch her. "Be careful, she may be injured. Pick up the wheelchair, honey, while I check the lady.

"Are you hurt?" she asked the woman. "Are you by yourself?"

The lady moaned and pointed to the door of the men's room. Lea stepped over to the door, knocked twice, and pushed the door open. Standing in front of her was a large man dressed in an Arabic robe and an Arafat-like headscarf, pointing a black gun in her face. She heard Irish scream and dropped her head and ran forward, kicking and clawing, as hard and fast as she could.

Dago was startled at Lea's reaction, fired the first shot of the pepper gun wildly, and missed. The red gel splattered on the wall behind Lea. He felt Lea trying to kick him between his legs, while he tried to stop her from clawing his eyes. Grabbing Lea in a bear hug, Dago slung her hard into the wall-mounted sink. Lea screamed and bounced back, immediately attacking Dago. This time Dago threw a right hand, hitting her in the face, knocking her down. Lea rolled over, blood gushing from her nose, and tried to get up, but couldn't. Dago stood over her, his foot on her shoulder, pulled the trigger a second time on the pepper gun, shooting her in the face.

Crazy Ray dragged Irish into the men's room, his hand clamped over her mouth. "What the hell?" He looked down at Lea. "Get that wheelchair, roll it in here, and shut the door." He leaned over, with his mouth to Irish's ear, "Listen, little girl, you see your friend? We will kill her if I hear another sound from you . . . you understand?" Crazy Ray said, pushing her to the floor.

Dago rolled the wheelchair in and shut the door.

"Get the duct tape and tape her up," Crazy Ray said, nodding his head toward Irish.

Dago wrapped the tape around Irish's head to cover her mouth, taped her hands in front, and bound her ankles. Moving over to Lea, he did the same.

Crazy Ray kneeled, removed the syringe from the toothbrush holder, and injected Irish in the thigh through her warm-ups. In less than a minute, the 100 milligrams of Ketamine, street name Special K, rendered her semi-conscious. Dago grabbed her ankles while Crazy Ray lifted her under the arms, setting her in the wheelchair. Crazy Ray took the tape from Dago and wrapped Irish across the chest and around the back of the wheelchair twice. They both took ends of the small burka and covered Irish's head and body, stuffing in the sides.

Crazy Ray pushed the wheelchair as Dago held the bathroom door open, then followed Dago as he led them outside, and down the covered walkway to the van. Instead of using the van's wheelchair lift, they hurriedly picked up the wheelchair with Irish in it, and locked the wheelchair onto the floor of the van.

The barrier arm at the exit gate was up, and they drove through without stopping. Charlie watched the rear of the van as it turned west on Sanderlin and made a note on his clipboard of the time. With a furrowed brow, he noticed they had been there a little less than 10 minutes. *Why are they leaving? They just got here. Maybe they forgot something,* he thought.

*

Sid had been talking for 20 minutes straight without stopping and looked over at Mack. "Mack, are you listening?"

Mack was not listening. He was sitting on a leather loveseat in Sid's office, thinking about Cuba, McKenzie, and Lea's suggestion that he needed to get away for a month or two. She said she needed to visit her father in Cuba, and maybe they could all fly down to Nassau then over to Cuba together. Her father had a beach house just outside the old colonial city of Trinidad, on the south side of the island.

"Mack, I was threatened twice today. Your dirt contractor practically forced his way past my secretary and demanded to be paid. He said you owed him last month's draw, over $100,000 . . . Mack!"

Mack hadn't felt this low, ever. He had heard of depression, but always thought it was a weakness, a sissy excuse. *What the hell was going on?* He couldn't focus on any one thing for 5 minutes. Lethargic, yet his mind was jumping all over the place.

"Mack! You okay?"

"Yeah. Sonny didn't approve the dirt contractor's draw, because he hadn't delivered the amount of truckloads of dirt that he listed on his draw."

"There are a lot of angry people stopping by making serious threats."

"Where's the guard? I didn't see him when we came in."

"They let him go with the cutbacks. Isaac said they were going to install an automatic gate opener, and all of us would have remotes."

Mack shook his head.

"Mack, I don't think it would be a good idea for us to start any new businesses right now. It would send the wrong message. We need to wait until this settles down."

Mack got up from the sofa. "I got to get out of here. Irish is in a tournament at the Racquet Club, and I don't want to be late. Anything else you need?" He felt his phone in his pocket vibrate, removed the phone, and saw the text code 103. It was Lea, and the message was all caps, "EMERGENCY 99!"

*

All his life, from his tragic childhood experience of his mother and siblings dying in a house fire, up to now, Mack had been tempered, hardened to face any adversities. Do or die, swim or drown, he always accepted the challenge and press on—this was part of his DNA. There were no developed molecules encoded in him for quit or run away; just charge, full speed ahead. But like any precision machinery when overloaded, there's a built-in circuit breaker, a fail-safe switch that kicks in and shuts down all power—Mack's lights went out.

Mack opened his eyes and tried to focus on the oversized face leaning over him. He heard a far-away voice calling, "Mack? Mack, what's wrong. You just blacked out," Sid asked, helping Mack up from the floor.

Mack struggled to stand, "How long was I out?"

"Less than a minute. Easy, don't get up too fast."

Mack was trying to remember the last thing that happened . . . *he got up to leave . . . his phone vibrated . . . there was a message*—"IRISH!" Mack said out loud, hurrying and staggering out of Sid's office.

"Wait!" Sid shouted.

When Otis saw Mack, he rushed to him.

"Otis, he's not well . . . he just passed out," Sid shouted.

"I've got him, Mister Sid," Otis said, his arm around him, as Mack pushed to the elevator. "Take a couple of deep breathes, boss. Talk to me. You having any chest pain?" Otis could see that Mack was having symptoms of a heart attack: sweating and shortness of breath.

Mack didn't know what was wrong. He was afraid of not having control and being unable to reach Irish. "No, there's no pain. It's Irish. There's an emergency. Get to the Racquet Club fast!"

Mack fell into the back of the limo, fumbled with his phone and finally speed-dialed Lea. A man answered her phone. "Who is this?" Mack demanded.

"Dr. Shea, I'm the emergency room physician at Baptist Hospital. Are you Mr. Shannon?"

"Yes!"

"Ms. Perez texted you."

"I know that! Where is she? What's happened? Where's my daughter?"

"Ms. Perez was injured and treated. She was hysterical when they brought her in, and I gave her a shot. She's with the police now. You can call her back later. "

"Listen closely, *doctor*. I don't give a damn if she's with the Pope. You get her on this phone *now!*" Mack waited and could hear conversation in the background. "Otis, quickly, cut over to the interstate. They're at the emergency room at Baptist."

"Mister Shannon, this is Sergeant Butler with the MPD, I . . . "

"*Sergeant!* Do you know me?"

"Yes sir, but not personally. When I patrolled downtown, I ate at your . . ."

"*Sergeant!* Then you know that I know Jimmy Maddox personally, right?"

"I don't know a Jimmy Maddox."

"*James Maddox,* Director of Police."

"Oh, yes sir."

"Then I don't need to call him . . . you *will* do me this big favor, right, Sergeant Butler? Take Ms. Perez's phone and give it to her *now*, please."

"Yes sir."

While waiting, Mack searched through his medicine bag till he found the vial of blue Xanax. He popped two in his mouth, cracked them with his teeth, and worked them under his tongue for rapid assimilation. He heard someone over the phone gasping for breath, almost moaning. "Lea, is that you?"

"Oh, my God, Mr. Shannon!" Lea cried out hysterically, "They took Irish!"

The vial of Xanax fell from Mack's hand. He watched, almost in slow motion, as the blue pills splayed out over the burgundy sheepskin floor mats. He felt like someone was holding him underwater.

They took Irish?

There was a shock to his body, as if he was hit with a heart defibrillator. He took a deep breath, tried to count to ten, but couldn't, and exploded, "Lea! WHO took Irish?" Mack heard the phone crash. "Hello? Hello?" he shouted.

"Mr. Shannon, Dr. Shea, again. Ms. Perez dropped her phone and is incapable of talking to anyone. She's had a traumatic experience. I suggest you . . ."

Mack punched the face of his phone with his fist as hard as he could until the phone went dead.

When Achilles was a baby, it was foretold that he would die young. To prevent his death, his mother, Thetis, took Achilles to the River Styx, which was supposed to offer powers of invulnerability, and dipped his body into the water. But as Thetis held Achilles by the heel, his heel was not washed over by the water of the magical river. Achilles grew up to be a man of war who survived many great battles. But one day, a poisonous arrow shot at him was lodged in his heel, killing him shortly thereafter.

Someone had just found Mack's Achilles heel.

CHAPTER 29

THE CHOIR STOPPED singing, the musical director walked off the stage, and Brother Eli Sunday walked past the lectern to center stage, close to the kneeler steps. He was dressed in white cotton pants and a white, open-collared shirt, casual and comfortable. He looked out at the 8,000 guests and members of River Church. Intense emotions tested his resolve every time he stood before his congregation, like the first time his high school football coach shouted his name, "Eli, get your butt out there and receive the kickoff . . . and don't drop the damn ball."

He ticked off in his mind the descriptive adjectives of his emotions, like the second hand on a clock: unworthy, deliriously happy, yet terrified . . . until he heard his own words over the speaker system.

"I was watching the news yesterday morning, and this popular television host was outside their studio at Rockefeller Center, in downtown Manhattan. He was conducting man-on-the-street interviews, asking each passerby the same question: 'If you could ask one question to anyone in the world, living or dead, who would you choose, and what would be your question?' Most of the ones interviewed picked movie stars, sport stars, or the President. The host, ambitiously pushing for something more exciting, impulsively stuck the microphone in front of a young girl holding the hand of an older girl, likely her sister or nanny.

'What is your name, sweetie?'

'Jennifer.'

'Okay, Jennifer, who would you pic . . .'

'Jesus Christ,' Jennifer said.

The host struggled to gather his composure. He was expecting to hear the names of someone like Justine Bieber or Miley Cyrus. He looked at his cameraman, who made a motion with his hand that he was still rolling.

'Well, Jennifer, what would you ask Jesus Christ?'

'What is the real truth?'

'About what?'

'The Bible. My girlfriends that are not Christian, are they going to hell? Hannah is Jewish, Asha is Hindu, Shu is . . . I forgot, oh, she's Chinese, and Zumzum is a Muslim. Do you know what Zumzum means?'

'No.'

'Sweet water of paradise. Isn't that pretty? I have to go. Bye.'

"A lot of us have questions like Jennifer, and my sermon for next week will be world religions—who's right, who's wrong?" Eli said, as he looked at a card in his hand. "I want to remind everyone this morning to get your tickets for the Passion Play, Easter Sunday night. Don't forget now. They are going fast."

"One last thing, I want to close with a special prayer request. Will Ms. . . .," Eli looked at the name on the card, "Lea Perez, come down to the stage please?"

"I'm sure all of you are aware of the tragic kidnapping here in Memphis of the young girl, Irish Shannon, over a week ago. Ms. Perez is a new member of our church, and a close friend of the child. In fact, she was with her when the kidnapping occurred. Ms. Perez has requested our special prayers for the child's safe return to her family." Eli asked Lea to kneel on the steps and placed his hand on her head. "If everyone will please stand and follow me in prayer."

I shouldn't have written my name on the prayer request card, Lea thought as she walked across the church's parking lot to her car. *That was embarrassing, him with his hand on my head, and in front of all those people.* She saw Bear sitting upright in the driver's seat, scouting the area while waiting for her. This was the second Sunday she had brought him to church with her. Both times when she left the house, he stood in front of the car howling, blocking her from leaving, and would not move until she let him into the car. She thought he was still in mourning for Irish, and she didn't want to leave him alone. On his first trip, right after church, she let him out to go to the bathroom along the river, and he did something he had never done before: he wouldn't get back into the car. Every time she got close, he would move away, closer to the church, and sat on his haunches, howling while staring at the cross on top of the church. She had to put him on his leash to get him back into the car.

*

"Are you asleep?" Irish whispered. It was very dark in the attic space, but she had her penlight pointed at the floor and thought she saw him stir. They were on the third floor, the first level above the vast sanctuary, and loudspeakers were mounted just below them, up in the nosebleed section. She hoped he was still asleep and didn't hear the special prayer request. She knew Lea had stopped going to the Catholic Church but was shocked to hear the preacher call Lea Perez's name.

Crazy Ray gasped for a deep breath, turned in his bed, and faced Irish. She waited, thinking he had stopped breathing, then after a long period of time, he exhaled. He would wake her up many times doing this while she was sleeping.

Irish rolled over, lifted the corner of her mattress, and removed a black plastic garbage bag. She pulled the slack out of the lightweight chain connected to her ankle with a leather restraint and sat up on the side of her mattress, her back to Crazy Ray. She opened the bag, shined her penlight inside, removed a felt-tip pen, and a handful of *Welcome Visitor* index-sized cards she had squirreled away since being kidnapped. She printed across the face of the card, in large letters, DADDY I AM IN THE ATTIC and signed her name, *Irish Shannon.* She folded each card two times into a square and dropped them into the bag with all the others. When she had the opportunity, she left the folded cards inside songbooks and Bibles on the pew seats, in the library, the women's restroom, and the janitor's closet. She was very careful not to leave them anywhere Crazy Ray would find them. Not that she was afraid of him; he had never threatened or even touched her.

Crazy Ray coughed and gasped for air again. He had a terrible cold, and, with all the drugs he was taking, it was almost impossible to tell if the cold medicine was helping.

"What?" he said, barely lifting his head while coughing up mucus and spitting it into a coffee can at the side of his bed. He struggled to pull himself up by the bathroom handicap bar Dago had installed on the wall and sat on the side of his bed. "Did you say something?"

Irish dropped the pen and cards into the garbage bag and rolled over facing him. "Did you hear the sermon this morning?" she asked.

"I don't think so. Was it a good one?" He started sneezing and blowing his nose on toilet paper stolen from the bathrooms.

"I like the preacher."

"I do too. I think he's a teacher more than preacher, though. Can you turn that lamp on for me?"

To reach the floor lamp, Irish stretched as far as her chain would reach and pulled the string on the lamp. "*Oh my gosh*," she said, her hand covering her mouth.

"What? What's wrong?"

"Your face. It's all swollen and red . . . like, with lots of little blisters."

What now? He grabbed the small mirror on a wooden shelf nailed between two studs. He rubbed his hand over his face while looking in the mirror. It was the reaction from taking the two AIDS drugs, Prezista and Ritonavir; Doc Randy told him it might happen. With his finger, he pushed one large lesion that had come back, Kaposi's sarcoma, Randy had called it. He noticed his eyes were red, enflamed, and he stood up, removed his shirt, and checked his torso and arms. He stepped over to Irish, "Would you pull that lamp over and check my back, please?" He would have to call Randy this morning for some meds; he couldn't chance being seen looking like this.

"No, your back looks okay. Do you want me to get that tube of cream for your face?"

"No, I'm going to call my doctor and see what he says."

"What's wrong?"

"Like we talked about, I've been sick, and my immune system was damaged. Now my body is at war, fighting the attacking bad guys, like the flu, fever blisters, viruses, things like that."

"I'm sorry. Does it hurt?"

"A little. I would feel much better if I could shake this cold," Crazy Ray said as he sneezed.

"Let me go with you tonight when you make your rounds. I can drive the Gator and even turn the watch-clock for you. You won't even have to get out of the Gator."

Crazy Ray thought about it . . . *he had let her drive it before and there was heavy rain forecasted for tonight . . . just what he needed with this cold.* "Okay," he said.

*

Otis stood at the gatehouse, checking everyone coming in for the 10 o'clock meeting that Sid Goldman had arranged. He had strict orders from the main house, 'no news media allowed through the gates.' News reporters, cameramen, and TV trucks, local and out of town, parked along the road outside the gate. Most were in their vehicle, some standing outside under their umbrellas; it had been raining, off and on, for the last three days. Captain Kevin O'Shea and his men patrolled Mack's house and property.

Standing in a huddle, in front of the stone fireplace in Mack's den, were Sid Goldman, Senator J.B. Parnell, Isaac Brenner, and Angus McGregor. "Has anyone talked to Mack this morning?" Parnell asked. They all stood looking at each other, each one shaking his head.

A door opened, and Bradley, Mack's personal assistant, walked in with Captain O'Shea, Zira LeBlanc, and Bishop O'Brien.

"There's hot coffee, orange juice, fruit, and pastries, and if you need anything else, let me know . . . I'll be in the kitchen," Bradley said.

Sid walked over to Bradley and whispered, "Bradley, does Mr. Shannon know we are all here?"

"I'll let him know, sir."

There was a four-cushion leather couch facing the burning fireplace with a club chair on each side.

"If everyone will grab a seat, we'll get started," Sid said.

Kevin, JB, Sonnyman, and Angus sat on the couch; O'Brien and Zira sat in the chairs.

Sid stood with his back to the fireplace. "It has been 10 days since Irish was kidnapped. I've asked Captain O'Shea, whom all of you know, who has organized and is the leader of a special abduction squad that has been working 24/7 in search of Irish. Kevin."

Kevin stood next to Sid in civilian clothes. "First, let me add, it is not only my squad that is working, but many policemen and firemen are working on their days off. We have tracked down every lead, no matter how insignificant." Kevin looked at his notes. "There is no need for me to go over the kidnapping statistics of the FBI's National Crime Information Center. The newspapers and TV have covered all that. We have been focusing on one *positive* statistic. Only 1 child out of every 10,000 reported missing is found not alive."

"What about the statistics on early apprehension?" Sid asked.

"Acting quickly is critical."

"Is 10 days acting quickly?" Angus asked.

"No, it is not. But I swear by all the saints in heaven, I've never stopped looking for Irish, from the day she went missing."

"Kevin, we all know your personal feelings for Irish, and no one from this side has anything but praise for what you've done," O'Brien said.

"I had no control over those important first few days when the city, state, and the FBI were arguing over jurisdiction. I almost lost my job at that meeting for shouting over and over how critical it was to act quickly that first day. I kept repeating the FBI's own statistic: *Seventy-four percent of abducted children who are ultimately murdered are dead within three hours of the abduction.*"

"There has been talk of a ransom note. Has there been any contact with the kidnappers?" JB asked.

"No. We have received hundreds of prank calls, emails, and letters demanding money for information. There were many reported sightings. She was seen in a boat headed down river, locked in a vacant school, a warehouse, at church, in a bus station, and at the airport. We checked them all out . . . nothing."

"What about the River Church downtown, where notes were found saying that she was in the attic?" O'Brien asked.

"The maintenance people at the church reported they had searched every inch of that church and the attic and found nothing. They found other notes in different handwritings and interviewed some of the kids at the church. They admitted it was a big joke, and that all the kids were writing them. When that news got out, we had over 100 calls about different churches in Memphis finding notes, plus food missing, lights left on, and water running: a lot of copycats. Because she's Catholic, we got a call that a retired priest had her locked in his attic, and another call that she was being held at the Sisters of Mercy's convent."

"What about the two Muslim kidnappers?" Isaac asked.

"Only the investigators were supposed to know there were two kidnappers, and that they were Muslims, or dressed like Muslims. Someone leaked that important information to the news media, which caused a firestorm of calls and accusations that the Muslims were dealing in human trafficking. We checked every lead. I am afraid Mr. Shannon's million-dollar reward brought out every cockroach in the walls of this city."

Everyone turned when the door opened and watched Bradley walk over to Zira. "Pardon me, gentlemen, I need to talk to Ms. LeBlanc."

Zira stood up behind her chair, and Bradley leaned over and whispered, "Mr. Shannon would like to see you now."

*

Mack stood in Irish's room, in front of her window, his face buried in her worn baby blanket, sobbing. He knew she needed her *blanky* wherever she was. Bear, at the foot of Irish's bed, rose up on his haunches moaning, threw his head back, and emitted a long, eerie howl. Mack shook his head at Bear. "I can't help you, my friend," he whispered, and looked back out the window and watched the raindrops splatter on the flooded tennis court. *How many times have we hit balls together, played silly games, me letting her win. She was so happy when she beat me. Oh my God! What am I going to do without her? Please God, I know you're testing me, as Lea said you did with Abraham, but don't make her suffer for the things I've done. Let me find her alive and unharmed, and I will do anything you want for the rest of my life, I swear. If she's dead, Lord, don't let her have suffered, or been raped, or tortured.*

Bear walked over and leaned his body against Mack's leg.

Bradley tapped on Irish's door, walked in, and said, "Ms. LeBlanc is waiting in your bedroom study, sir."

Mack wiped his eyes and walked across the room and down the hallway, with Bradley following.

"Mr. Shannon, sir, let me bring you something to eat . . . or one of your favorite protein shakes. You have to eat something."

Mack shook his head as he walked into his bedroom study.

Zira stood in front of the double French doors that overlooked the canal, watching the water flowing the length of the gardens. She turned when she heard Mack enter and gasped, in shock at his appearance. He hadn't shaved in days, needed a haircut, and wore grungy sweats. His face was swollen, his eyes bloodshot and his body odor permeated the room, but she didn't hesitate, just hurried across the room, wrapping her arms around him. "I'm *so* sorry, Mack. I swear to you. I swear to God. We will find who did this. I'm not just saying this. I have a good feeling we will find her soon."

"What have you found?" Mack asked, motioning for her to follow him to his desk.

She pulled up a chair next to him and placed a folder on his desk. "You haven't received any ransom demands, right?"

Mack shook his head.

She opened the folder. "I know you are hurting, and the last thing I want to do is to cause you more pain, but I need to speak candidly or . . . "

"Get on with it."

Zira cringed, gritting her teeth.

"I'm sorry. I didn't mean to snap at you," Mack said.

"I know, I know. We're talking about your baby girl, and I can barely stand it myself."

Mack put his hand on hers, as he watched the tears roll down her cheeks

"But I do have some *good* news," she said, wiping the tears away.

"Tell me. God knows I need it."

"I believe this to be true. I talked extensively with Lea and Charlie, the guard at the Racquet Club; they're our only known witnesses. We know it was two men, one big and one small, and not a man and a woman. From my research of cases like this one, and we went back the last 30 years, serial killers and sex offenders almost always operate alone, 95% of the time. So what's left? Kidnappers. But there's no demand for ransom, so why take her? What's the motive? I think the reason is for revenge."

"Who? Who would do something like this?"

"What about the Towers? A lot of people lost big time financially from that disaster."

"I'm well aware. I lost every penny I had."

"Have you received any threats?"

"Sure, all kinds. But nothing so extreme that would justify taking my daughter. They would have to be *crazy* not to know I was broke after the loss of the Towers."

"Exactly. Lea gave us a great description of the attackers, and Charlie confirmed it. We talked to every employee, member, player, and guest of the Racket Club, but no one saw anyone dressed as Muslims. I got the license number and the name on the truck from the video cameras at the gate. The plates were stolen, and there is no such name as the Islamic Center of Memphis. We're still checking the truck registration: make, model, year, and color, with the state. I'll come up with something, I promise. Meanwhile, you try to think of someone seeking revenge or who might want to punish you."

Mack stood up, "I know you're trying your best." He walked her to the door, and when opened, Bear raced out and down the stairs, stopping at the front door.

Zira stood on the stair's landing, watching Lea open the front door to let Bear out. *There is something Lea told me when I questioned her about the attack, and it's stuck in the back of my mind. What was it?*

Lea picked up the food tray, started up the stairs, and stopped in front of Zira.

"Will he eat all of that?" Zira asked.

"I'll be happy if he eats any of it. Bradley has been leaving trays outside his door for a week and picks them up the next day untouched. He won't let anyone in his room. Today is the first time outside his room."

"He looks and smells terrible."

"He's going to eat today, *and* take a bath, even if I have to force him," Lea said, starting up the steps.

"Lea?" Zira said. "When we first spoke about the kidnapping, I asked you about the big guy you fought with, and you said something about his head scarf?"

"When I clawed his face?"

"Something else."

"His yellow hair?"

"Yes! That's it, thank you."

Lea watched Zira rush down the stairs and out the door.

Outside, Zira sat in her new Suburban parked in Mack's driveway. She hurriedly typed on her mobile keypad—*yellow hair* and watched the word pop up on the built-in computer screen under her radio. Next, she typed the word *crazy*, remembering what Mack had just said when they were talking about ransom money, "They would have to be *crazy* not to know I was broke after the loss of the Towers." The last word she typed was *kidnapped*.

She studied the 3 keywords, hoping this word association would solve the jumbled puzzle racking her brain. *Yellow hair—Crazy—Kidnapped.*

Kidnapped. Kidnapped who, she asked. *Irish? No.* Then, out of nowhere, she heard her own past words questioning Mack, "*You kidnapped his mother?*"

The puzzle started coming together. She heard her own words again. *I see this red Cadillac convertible go by with this big yellow-headed goon driving. Yellow hair*—Dago!

Whose mother was kidnapped? *Crazy* Ray's! Why? Revenge! One of them was big, and one was small—Dago and Crazy Ray—*payback* for kidnapping Crazy Ray's mother.

Zira shifted into low gear, turned on the windshield wipers, stomped the gas pedal, and the truck raced down Mack's driveway. *Find either one of them, and I'll find Irish.*

*

Lea, carrying a medley of Mack's favorite foods on a tray, tapped on his bedroom door with her foot. She waited, sat the tray on the floor, and knocked harder with her knuckles, then turned the doorknob. She was surprised when it opened; it had been locked for days. Picking up the tray, she called out, "Mack" as she stepped inside. After all this time, she was still not comfortable calling her boss by his first name, but he insisted. Yet with such feelings about him, she was also uncomfortable calling him Mr. Shannon, which she always did in the presence of others. Bradley and Maureen never referred to him as Mack, even in private.

Placing the tray on his desktop, she looked out the window and saw Bear racing across the gardens in the rain toward the front gates. *Now where is he going?* She watched until he was out of sight, then headed for the master bathroom, one of her favorite rooms. Sometimes, when Mack was out of town, she would luxuriate in the long copper claw-foot tub, filled to the brim, and soak for over an hour. She turned the hot water on full force and—drip by drip—poured from a bottle of her favorite mixture of therapeutic oils: eucalyptus, cedarwood, and peppermint. The steam rose from the tub, saturating the room with the smells of aromatherapy. Lea was determined to lift Mack out of his depth of despair and had planned her tactics methodically, writing down each step.

She was bent over the tub, checking the temperature of the water, when she felt the presence of someone else in the room. She turned quickly and saw Mack standing in the doorway of the bathroom, like a zombie. He wasn't even looking at her, just staring off into space. He looked lost, like a homeless person with Alzheimer's. She hurried to him, putting her arms around him, and led him over to a copper bathroom bench. She pulled up a vanity chair and sat face to face with him. "Mack, I know Irish is alive." She held his face in her hands. "God did not do this to punish you. You must believe this; he loves you no matter what you have done. But you can't give up. You must stay strong and have faith. You are a warrior, you must fight, and you can't let this destroy you."

He blinked the tears from his eyes, "Do you *truly* believe she's alive?"

She held both his hands. "Mack, I know my God. He created Irish as a special soul, to reflect his glory, love, kindness, and faithfulness. He would never let any harm come to her. Every morning when I pray, I feel Irish next to me. She is so alive—I can reach out and touch her. Please let me help you." She lifted his hands, guided him up from the bench, and removed his sweatshirt. "I want you to take a long hot bath." She reached for the drawstring on his sweatpants, but he stopped her with his hand.

"Remember, I was a nurse," she said.

Mack untied the drawstring, turned his back to her, and the sweatpants fell to the floor. He stepped over into the tub and slowly eased down into the steaming water.

Lea picked up his clothes, holding them out and away from her, "Can I burn these?" she said, jokingly.

Mack paid little notice to what she said. He was submerged to his chin—the aromatherapy doing its job.

CHAPTER 30

BEAR LAY STRETCHED out in the woods, about 20 feet from the front gate, taking a short nap. He was in no hurry; the darker it was, the better. With his ears able to register a much higher frequency than humans, about 80,000 cycles per second compared to 18,000, he was up and ready to go when he heard a car approaching the gates. As the gates opened, Bear ambled through as if they were being opened for him, and then turned into the woods again. At North Parkway, he stopped, looked for traffic, then crossed over, and entered Overton Park to avoid being seen. It was pitch dark now and still raining, but with excellent night vision he had no trouble finding the old abandoned L&N railroad as he exited the park. The rails and ties had been removed, the gravel bed smoothed, packed, and ready for paving to extend the west bound Greater Memphis Greenline, a bike and walk trail. He could smell the river now and knew this track bed would take him to his destination.

*

Crazy Ray was in the church kitchen drinking coffee and thinking about Irish; it was time for him to let her go. But he knew that when Mack found out it was he who kidnapped her, he would be hunted to the four corners of the earth. He needed money, a lot of it.

Earlier, he and Irish had a good time watching a Disney movie and eating popcorn. She had fallen asleep, and, when he picked her up, both her arms wrapped around his neck. He stood, holding her in his arms and staring down at her face. Her long blond hair fell over his shoulder and down his arm. He felt loathsome, a degenerate, for having to lock her in the attic and chain her to the wall like a wild animal. He had committed many criminal acts and never felt remorseful, not even for a second, but kidnapping a child was like a permanent black stain on his soul. He was too weak to carry her, so he had eased her down into one of the wheelchairs, pushed her to the elevator, up to their secret attic space, and shackled her to the wall.

He emptied the cold coffee into the sink and looked up at the wall clock—it was time to check the outside and punch the clocks for his 4 a.m. patrol.

*

Dago drove his pickup down a narrow alley, parked in the rear of Shorty's Bar and Grill, and checked his hair in the rearview mirror before getting out of the truck. He had spent the night with one of his tattooed hipster girlfriends who liked to change the color of his hair. It was dyed platinum, a pure white, instead of his usual peroxide yellow color. Dago flipped the bird to the beer truck driver, a regular at Shorty's, who was loading cases of beer on his two-wheeler, and had wolf-whistled at Dago's new hair color.

Dago entered the back door of his favorite watering hole and stopped at the end of the bar. The bartender handed Dago a Budweiser and pointed to the corner table. Dago took a long swig from the bottle and walked over to the corner table, "What's up, Shorty?"

Shorty pushed a chair out from the table with his foot, "Have a seat." Shorty looked around, making sure no one was listening, and leaned in close, "Someone's looking for you, asking a lot of questions."

"Yeah, who?"

"A chick, a real fox. Said she was looking for someone to remodel her kitchen. She left her number." Shorty pushed a bar napkin across to him. "She wasn't a cop, but . . ."

"What?"

"She was packing, I could tell, and she sure ain't no housewife."

Dago read her name and number. "You see what she was driving?"

"Black Suburban."

"Anybody with her?"

Shorty shook his head, "Don't know, man, all the windows were tinted, and it was raining."

Dago stood up, removed his truck keys, and dropped them on the table. "Let me borrow your wheels for a little drive-by of my house, okay?"

Shorty handed his keys to Dago, "Be careful, man."

Dago stopped about halfway across the floor and looked back, "You told her nada, right?"

Shorty nodded his head, "Right . . . nothing."

Out in the parking lot, Dago walked over to the beer truck driver, "Bo, you got another one of those Bud caps?"

"Sure, look in the front seat up there."

Dago found a cap and was adjusting the band while walking to Shorty's car.

"Hey, Dago, who you hiding from?" Bo shouted, as Dago drove off with the Bud cap pulled low on his head and wearing his sunglasses.

Dago's mother's house was on the corner of Berclair Road and Zelda Lane, in an older mixed neighborhood of Mexicans, Blacks, and some Whites sprinkled in. He drove north on Berclair, slowed as he passed Zelda, and saw the black Suburban parked on the street, two houses down. He turned left at the next street, then left again at the first street, and backtracked south. He stopped at the corner of an alley, looked down at the other end, and saw a second black Suburban parked in the rear of his mother's house. He felt a cold chill of fear shiver up the back of his neck. Shorty was right: this was not the cops . . . or the Feds. The little Shannon girl hadn't been taken across the state line, thank God.

It's Mack Shannon, you dummy! That's who it is. I warned Crazy Ray there would be all kinds of hell to pay if he kidnapped his daughter. Shannon would kill them a slow death, regardless if Crazy Ray let her go unharmed.

Dago drove back to Shorty's, exchanged vehicles, and drove to the YMCA where he had a private locker. He was so rattled it took him three times to open the combination lock before he got into his locker. He had a lockbox screwed from the inside to the back of the locker, from which he removed an envelope stuffed with money, his passport, and other sundry items. He dumped everything else from his locker into his gym bag and hurried outside. He stood in the shadow of the building, checking the parking lot before rushing to his truck.

He drove west on the I-240 loop, staying in the left lane and planning to take I-40 across the river into Arkansas. He removed his phone and called Crazy Ray, got his recording, hesitated, and then hung up: *the hell with him.* He swerved across three lanes to the outside lane and took the ramp onto I-55. He would go south instead of west, and mapped out the route in his head: I-55 south to I-10, west to Houston, TX, then take Highway-59 S/W to Laredo. If his calculations were right, he should cross the border into Mexico around daylight.

*

Zira checked her watch; they had been waiting for a little over 2 hours, and still no sign of Dago. Earlier, she had one of her men, dressed in a black raincoat and a FedEx hat, go to the door with a package that required his signature. His mother said he wasn't home, and they would have to come back if she couldn't sign for him.

Zira's phone buzzed, and she saw the number 100 on her computer screen. She pushed the speaker icon on her keypad, "Mack?"

"You left a message to call ASAP? Have you found something?"

When she first learned Mack's code number at Shamrock, she had deleted his name on her phone and entered the number 100. "I think I've found who kidnapped Irish."

"WHO, for God's sake?"

"Crazy Ray. Remember Lea saying the men who attacked her, one was small and the other bigger and taller, and she saw blonde hair when she scratched his face? That was *Dago,* and the other was Crazy Ray. You kidnapped Crazy Ray's mother, and he has kidnapped Irish as payback, *revenge.*"

Mack shook his head as he listen to Zira. *How stupid, he should have been the first one I thought of, but I thought he was dead. He's always been a snake, slithering in and out of my life; I should have cut his head off years ago.* "Where are you?"

"We're sitting on Dago's mother's house."

"I'm on my way. What's the address?"

"No, Mack. We've got it covered here. Any more people and we'll just spook him."

"What the hell are you talking about? This is *my daughter!*"

"Please Mack, do this for me. I need you to find Crazy Ray; he's the one who has Irish. Think back, everything you've known about him, all his contacts. I've got to go. I'll be in touch."

*

Like the couchant Great Sphinx, Bear had been waiting for hours on the bluff, just inside the tall shrubs on the edge of the church's property. He could smell and hear the rapid current of the flooding river below. He stood, arched his back, stretching, and walked through the tall grass over to the edge of the bluff. There was a dark overcast of storm clouds as he stood, almost invisible, his black double coat shedding the rain while he watched the fast-moving river washing away some parts of the embankment. He turned back, stopped at a puddle, and took long slurps of the cold rainwater. A clanging noise stopped his drinking. He lifted his head and waited while his nose searched the air currents. Water dripped from his heavy beard as he crept back to his post, all his senses on alert as his muzzle pushed through the tall grass. He stopped, his eyes focused on where the sound was coming from.

Crazy Ray had opened the overhead steel door and moved the John Deere Gator outside, closing the door behind him. It was time for his 4 a.m. rounds.

Bear crouched in the tall grass, watching Crazy Ray drive off in the four-wheeler. A strong scent of Irish emanated from Crazy Ray as Bear followed, staying in the dark shadow of the building while he gleaned and stored the distinctive decaying smell of Crazy Ray's disease.

Crazy Ray parked at the last watchman's clock, leaving the motor running. The clock was mounted on a pole in the rear of the church, on the far west side of the property line. He inserted the key that marked the time into a wireless router to the church's computer system. He turned up the collar of his raincoat and took a couple of steps into the tall grass to listen to the sound of the rushing river. Red images covered all the local TV screens, broadcasting weather warnings of flash flooding, and pictures of the fast rising Mississippi River. Crazy Ray decided to have a look for himself and walked through the waist-high grass when a bolt of lightning lit up the sky followed by an explosive crash of thunder. "Whoa, that was way too close," he said aloud, and quickly turned back, heading for the four-wheeler.

As he stepped from the tall grass, he saw a dark figure standing between him and the four-wheeler . . . *was it a black bear? No, there are no bears in West Tennessee . . . are there?"* Crazy Ray looked around for a weapon of any kind. *What does it want? It's just crouching there in the rain.* Crazy Ray remembered there was a shovel in the back of the Gator and worked his way around to the back of the four-wheeler.

Bear rose up from his haunches.

It's a dog, a damn big one too. Crazy Ray eased the shovel from the bed of the Gator and held it out in front of him as he walked to the driver's side of the four-wheeler. He froze when he heard a long, low growl.

"Go! Get outta here!" he shouted, poking the shovel toward Bear.

Bear barked and stepped closer, growling.

Crazy Ray threw the shovel like a spear at Bear and jumped into the four-wheeler.

The shovel bounced off Bear's back as he leaped into the air, his white canine teeth flashing in the dark as his powerful jaws clamped down on Crazy Ray's arm.

In a panic, Crazy Ray stomped the gas pedal, jerked the gearshift back instead of pushing it forward, and the Gator leaped backward, bouncing through the tall grass, dragging Bear over the rough terrain down toward the river.

Crazy Ray was almost standing on the brake pedal now but couldn't stop the downhill momentum of the Gator from sliding over the slippery grass and mud. The four-wheeler came to an abrupt stop, the front axle snagged on a stump of an uprooted tree, while the rear end dangled over the edge of the bluff. The top of the uprooted tree lay on the surface of the rushing water thirty feet below, swaying back and forth against the riverbank.

Crazy Ray's right hand held a death grip on the steering wheel, but in his weakened condition, and with Bear hanging from his left arm out over the river, he couldn't hold on much longer. Then he felt the meat tearing from his forearm, and without thought, tried to jerk his arm free, but now Bear's canine teeth were caught in the sleeve of his raincoat. He felt the sleeve rip, and Bear dropped a few inches, but one of his canines had punctured the double-sewed seam in the sleeve, anchoring him in midair. Crazy Ray was spent; he had no strength left. He was sure the bone in his left arm was crushed, and he was barely holding himself inside the Gator with his right hand. In desperation, he leaned down and started chewing on the seam, trying to tear it loose from Bear's jaws. It didn't matter . . . his effort was in vain. The powerful current pulled the bushy top of the uprooted tree away from the riverbank, dragging the stump with it, and a portion of the river bluff.

Like the closing ceremony of the annual Sunset Symphony fireworks, the sky exploded with multiple lightning strikes—jumping from cloud to cloud—with thousands of white spidery fingers falling from the sky, lighting the surface of the river. But at four o'clock in the morning, while under the hood of this lightning storm, no one saw the strange caravan below: a 30-foot tree trailering an odd looking green vehicle, and a large black dog dragging a screaming man wearing a raincoat.

The curtain closed on the dramatic lightning performance, the ink black overcast returned, and again, no one saw the silent, treacherous whirlpool of current suck the caravan deep into the muddy water of the Mississippi River.

CHAPTER 31

I T WAS EASTER Sunday. Mack was exhausted, lying across his bed with his arm covering his eyes. He had promised Lea he would go with her to the Passion Play tonight at her church to pray for Irish.

Dago had failed to show, escaping from Zira's dragnet, and causing her to call for another meeting at Mack's house with the same group that was organized by Sid Goldman. She had convinced Mack, for the time being, to keep the names of the kidnappers from the group, only referring to them as the two suspects. The last thing she wanted was a Crazy Ray and Dago's photo televised all over the country. She was afraid once Crazy Ray knew they had been identified, it would spook them, forcing them to run, *without* Irish—the only true witness to their identity.

During the meeting, Captain Kevin O'Shea argued that they needed the publicity, and told Zira that the police department, the news media, and almost everyone else believed that Irish was already dead. Zira had agreed that in three days, if Irish had not been found, she would give the names to O'Shea and the newspapers, television, and radio could go public. Tomorrow, Monday, was the fourth day.

There was a light tap on Mack's door. "Come in," he said.

"Did I wake you?" Lea asked.

"No."

"Bradley has some food laid out for us before we leave."

"Lea, I'm sorry, I know you mean well, but I'm not going. God is sure as hell no friend of mine, and he certainly wouldn't want to hear what I have to tell him."

"Don't do it for God then, do it for me, *please.* You've trusted me all these years with your most precious possession. Why not trust me this *one* time when I tell you that *God* is protecting Irish, and she's alive?"

Mack sat upright, with his back against the headboard. "She's dead, Lea. Everyone knows that and we are going to have to accept this. All the odds are against us." He handed her an article he had printed from the Internet.

Lea read the underlined area of the article: *The Washington State Attorney General's Office conducted a research on child abduction murders, and the primary conclusion of the study was that child abductions perpetrated by strangers rarely occur. However, when they do occur, the results can be tragic: in 76 percent of the murders of an abducted child, the child was murdered within 3 hours of the abduction and in 89 percent of the cases, the missing child died within 24 hours of disappearing.*

"That's humanism. We're talking about God *Almighty.* He doesn't play *odds!* Irish is in *His* hands, and you must open your heart to God. He's knocking on your door, and you won't open it. But if you want to play the secular game, here are the best odds you will ever get—I bet my life that Irish is alive." Lea raised her hand above her head. "I swear before God, he can strike me dead in my tracks if we don't find her alive."

"This Passion Play is just a spectacle; you should realize that. All those actors in costumes, live animals, and this famous Broadway guy they hired to play Jesus. It's *The Greatest Show on Earth* all over again."

"I'm not preaching to you, Mack. But let me ask you one more thing, what have you got to lose by trusting in God? It's *all* good."

With those last words, Mack surrendered. He rolled out of bed and started getting dressed.

*

Irish was bundled up in the fetal position on her bed, scared and crying. It had been pouring down rain on the metal roof of the church, and the strikes of thunder had awakened her. It had been three days of complete isolation. Never in her young life had she been so alone. She worried about

Mr. Ray; he had never been gone for this long. *Maybe the doctor put him in the hospital,* she thought. *Oh, I hope he's okay.*

She sat up and stretched out, as far as her chained ankle would let her, and grabbed a roll of toilet paper. She tore off a couple of sheet, dried her eyes, and turned on the lamp. She thought about what her daddy told her to do every time she started feeling sorry for herself. She picked up her pad and pen and started writing down all the positive things about her situation.

1. I'm not dead. *Of course not.* She giggled.
2. I'm not sick or hurt . . . just chained to the wall. *No. No negative stuff, just positive.*
3. I have a half a box of raisins, an apple, a bottle of water, and a candy bar.
4. I'm in a church. *I know God is with me and is not going to let me die.*
5. My Daddy will . . .

Irish flinched when she heard the loud bugles from the orchestra downstairs; it must be Sunday morning. She knew it was the beginning of another rehearsal for the Passion Play. She counted the days off to make sure . . . yes, it was Sunday. The Passion Play would start tonight, Easter Sunday. She could hear the preacher all week, rushing all over the sanctuary, barking orders over his wireless microphone while directing the building of different stage sets, rehearsing the music, and overseeing the installation of the various types of lighting required. The scene they were rehearsing now, with the buglers, was the Romans announcing the presence of the King of Jews, as they marched Jesus through Jerusalem to be crucified. *Poor Jesus, I bet he was scared, too,* Irish thought.

*

Otis was parked in the limo under the porte-cochere waiting for Mack. Lea was in the back seat and was beginning to worry that Mack was backing out.

Otis, looking at Lea through the rearview mirror, said, "Are you going to stay or leave?"

"Why would I leave? Who would take care of Irish?"

She can't face the truth; Irish is not coming back. "There's no money. Mr. Mack's busted."

Lea stared at the mirror, "I have a place to live, food to eat, and I have my own money; what more do I need? Are you leaving?"

"I've got a job offer, but don't say anything to Mr. Mack. I want to talk to him first. I didn't get a check this week, I don't have any money, and *I* won't have a place to live if I don't pay my rent."

They both turned when Mack opened the rear door and hurried inside, out of the rain that was blowing under the canopy. "Is this damn rain ever going to stop? It's flooding everywhere." He was dressed in khaki pants, a white dress shirt, and his Barbour wax cotton jacket. Lea had told him that he would be out of place in a coat and tie. "Okay, let get this farce over with."

Lea stared at him, then looked away, and whispered under her breath, "Please, no blasphemy."

When Otis eased the limo into the large parking lot of the pyramid church, he pulled behind a waiting line of cars letting out guests and church members. Ushers with umbrellas walked them from the cars to the front door of the church.

One of the ushers opened the rear door, stuck his head in, and said, "Happy Easter, sir, and welcome to the Church on the River Passion Play."

Mack stepped out of the car, helped Lea out, and said to the usher, "I don't need the umbrella, just the lady." As they walked off, Mack said to Otis, "If you want to watch this show, park the car, and come on in." He handed Otis an extra ticket Lea had given him.

Lea waited at one of the portals, then handed two tickets to a lady usher as Mack walked up, and they both followed the lady to their seats, about halfway down on the first floor. There were very few vacant seats, and a lot of people were standing along the back wall.

"This place looks a lot different since it was a basketball arena. They did a good job." Mack said.

"Why it's a *miracle*! It must be God's presence. The *man* said something nice for a change."

Mack stared at Lea, shaking his head. Lea continued to look center stage.

"Sir?" A tall usher was holding up a white envelope, leaned over, and whispered to Mack, "You have two reserved seats down front. If you will follow me, please."

"You must be mistaken. These seats are fine," Mack said.

"Brother Eli insisted, sir."

Lea poked Mack with her elbow.

Mack shrugged his shoulders, got up, and they followed the man down the aisle. The usher played his flashlight on two empty seats in the front row, about 8 feet from the steps leading to the stage, and handed Mack the envelope. Mack removed his coat, sat down, opened the envelope, and read a handwritten note:

Dear Mr. Shannon,

I have followed your tragic and frightening experience on TV, in the newspapers, and have read Ms. Perez's personal account. I cannot imagine your pain and suffering.

On the night of Good Friday, all the men at our church held a special prayer service for Irish and will continue to pray every night until she is returned.

Please accept my humble request for a short meeting, just between the two of us, in my private office after the services tonight. An usher will be available to escort you.

God bless you,

Eli Sunday

Mack looked around and handed the note to Lea, as the lights in the sanctuary dimmed to darkness. It was quiet, except for the thunder and rain pounding on the outside of the building. The blackness of the ceiling changed to a midnight blue, and everyone looked up to the highest point of the ceiling at a single brilliant twinkling star. *This must be Jacob's Star,* Mack thought. Then slowly, the sky-like ceiling opened up with a cluster of stars, like the Pleiades. He felt relaxed in the quiet and darkness, and continued to stare, watching Jacob's Star begin to fade and blend in with the other stars. Mack thought of van Gogh's famous painting, *Starry Night,* and van Gogh's lifetime spiritual search. Many suggested his inspiration for the painting came from reading the Bible. And in his biography it was mentioned that where he wrote to his brother, Theo, who was in Paris, about Starry Night: *"That doesn't stop me having a tremendous need for, shall I say the word—for religion—so I go outside at night to paint the stars."*

As the ceiling lights dimmed, one could hear the faint voices of men talking, and the lights came up on the right side of the stage. It was a scene of The Last Supper, with Jesus and his 12 disciples. It was in a large, elevated room, and ceremonial food covered the table: Passover lamb, unleavened bread, sauces, dates stuffed with almonds, and pitchers of wine.

'I tell you the truth,' Jesus said, all the disciples leaning toward him, *'one of you will betray me—one who is eating with me.'*

Then Judas, the one who would betray him, said, *'Surely not I, Rabbi?'*

There were many other scenes that followed: the largest being on the 100-foot long center stage. This scene was along the crowded Via Dolorosa, a main street in Jerusalem, with a live camel, donkeys, sheep, and many merchants and shoppers. The noise was loud, with shouts of insults from the crowd hurled toward Jesus, and Roman soldiers led the procession announcing, *'Make way for the King of the Jews.'* A beaten and bloodied Jesus struggled behind, dragging his cross over the cobblestone pavement while soldiers followed, lashing out with their *flagrum*, a lead-tipped whip designed to tear the flesh away from the body.

The lights dimmed, and the next sequence followed as the lights came up stage right, on one of the most recognized scenes in the world, the crucifixion of Jesus Christ. You could hear Jesus crying out in excruciating agony, his bloodied body quivering as it hung from a wooden cross by spikes driven through his hands and feet.

Mack heard gasps of shock, then sniffles all around him. He looked over at Lea and saw tears running down her cheeks. The actor playing Jesus was exceptionally skilled, and sitting this close, with all the blood, sweat, and the pain and suffering, you couldn't help from being caught up in the passion.

If this was true, and Mack believed the crucifixion was (there was too much recorded history to deny it), then why in the world would God send His only son down to earth to go through the most painful and humiliating torture one could bear?

'My God, my God, why have you forsaken me?' Jesus shouted mournfully throughout the church.

Yeah, God, why? Mack wanted to shout. He had heard many opinions and read extensively about *why,* but he didn't believe any of it. *I mean, He's God. He can do anything he wants to do. He built the earth, the skies, and the seas. Yet He does nothing when His son screams for His help?*

Three more scenes followed: Joseph and Nicodemus buried Jesus in the tomb, sealing it with a huge rolling stone. The next scene was when Mary Magdalene found the stone rolled away from the entrance, and Jesus was no longer in the tomb. But the last scene was the most deeply poignant, the climax of the play.

The church went completely dark. The rumbling sounds of thunder started as if from a distance, and the dimmer lights and colored filters changed the ceiling to a midnight blue sky again. But now the sky was filled with roiling dark gray clouds and the sounds of howling winds. Everyone was jolted with loud thunder as lightning raced across the ceiling, the clouds parted, and a shaft of golden light shone down as if from heaven. Jesus appeared on stage, his body clean and dressed in a pure white gown with the golden light encircling him.

Mack was almost blinded by the light. He hung his head, and tears welled up in his eyes as the light moved over him. Mack felt as if God put his hand on his shoulder.

A few people moved from their seats to the front of the stage and kneeled on the carpeted steps, their heads bowed, and their arms rose in praise.

Lea stood, moved in front of Mack, and stopped. She reached down, clasped his hand, and led him to the steps, and they kneeled, side by side.

Mack looked up into the bright light and saw Jesus with his arms held out. He thought of his childhood, kneeling in Mass every morning before class, saying his prayers by rote, without comprehension. But now there was hope. God had opened Mack's heart by showing him that His son was not dead. Mack no longer felt lost. There was hope that Irish was still alive. He raised his hands into the golden light and prayed: "I pray to you, O Lord, because you are my God Almighty, and without you there would only be darkness. Please forgive me my sins and bless me one more time by sending me my daughter, Irish, unharmed. I ask this in the name of your son, Jesus Christ."

The shaft of golden light opened to cover the complete sanctuary as Jesus ascended into heaven. As the cables lifted Jesus into the sky, the lights dimmed as black clouds enveloped Jesus, and the sanctuary went dark again.

Everyone waited for the lights to come up, but suddenly there was a tremendous explosion that shook the church. At first, Mack, like everyone else, thought it was part of the play, until he saw pieces of acoustical ceiling tile, insulation, and other debris falling from the ceiling onto the stage. But when everyone saw the gaping hole in the roof and part of the wooden stage destroyed where Jesus had been standing, they started to panic. Some crying out, *earthquake*!

The lights came up immediately over the entire sanctuary, and Brother Eli ran up on the stage and announced over a hand-held microphone, "Attention! Attention please, everyone keep your seats. There is no danger . . . *no* earthquake!"

Ushers hurried down each aisle, assuring the thousands that there was no danger, and asked them to keep their seats. The Musical Director started the orchestra playing, and the choir started singing Handel's "Hallelujah." Soon, with the ushers singing and waving their arms, the congregation joined in and the whole church was filled with, *Hallelujah! Hallelujah!*

When the building first shook, Mack thought of The Towers and the aftershock that was predicted. Now that the lights were on, he perused the damages with a critical eye, starting with the hole in the wooden stage floor in front of him, large enough for a Volkswagen Beetle to fit in. At the bottom of the hole was a pile of splintered wood, what was left of the cross Jesus had been hanging from. He followed where the path of the light from the ceiling was and focused on the steel framing of the Observation Deck. There was another hole the same size as the one in the stage floor that traveled through the ceiling and floors above, and through the rooftop outside. The glass apex of the Pyramid, with its 100-foot steel cross, was gone. Mack knew it wasn't an earthquake, or a shooting star of some kind. It was a thunderbolt. Some can carry up to 1 billion volts, and it was obvious this one didn't like crosses. What were the chances of that happening? Strange.

"What are you looking at?" Lea asked.

"Look," Mack pointed to the hole in the ceiling, "it's stopped raining, and the stars are out."

"It's about time," Lea said. While both were looking, white flakes started floating down out of the hole. "Is that snow?"

"Not in April," Mack said, cupping his hands and catching one of the floating white squares. He opened it and saw *Church on the River* printed in bold letters, turned it over, and read, DADDY I'M IN THE ATTIC, in all caps. He felt as if another thunderbolt had struck him.

Lea saw the shock on Mack's face, "What the matter?" She took the card from his hand and read what Irish had written. She grabbed Mack's hand, "Quick! Hurry," she said, pulling him up onto the stage in front of Brother Eli, shouting, "Mr. Shannon's daughter is in your attic! How do we get there? We have to hurry!" She shoved the note in front of him to read.

"Follow me," Eli said, "the elevator is around the back of the stage."

Inside the elevator, Mack said, "We'll have to be careful, there's a lot of damage up there. I hope to God she's okay."

"Amen," Eli said. "There are three floors. We'll stop at the first one."

When the elevator doors opened, Mack was the first off, and halfway down the corridor he saw Irish for the first time in . . . he couldn't remember and didn't try to.

"DADDY! Daddy, did you see that bolt of lightning?"

Tears poured down Mack's face. His heart was in his throat. "I know baby." He made the sign of the cross. "Are you okay?"

"I dumped all my notes down the hole, and this chain saved me from falling in."

"Don't move while I figure this out." Mack held both arms out blocking the corridor, stopping Lea and Eli from coming forward. He wasn't sure the floor would hold him. Eli turned back and started searching in the other rooms.

"Lea!" Irish shouted when she saw her, then started crying.

"Irish, listen to your father, he's going to get you out of here."

Mack studied the room damages. At the end of the corridor, where the closet door had been, was now a gaping hole with a dangling floor joist. It was about six feet across the hole to reach Irish on the other side. One end of the chain was wrapped around a wall stud, secured by a padlock. The other end was fastened to a leather ankle-bracelet that encircled Irish's ankle.

"Daddy," Irish said through teary eyes, pointing to the wall on the other side of the hole, next to where the door was, "The key to the lock is hanging there."

Eli remembered that one of the other rooms was used for storage of leftover materials. He came down the corridor carrying a 10-foot long 2x8, "We can use this as a walk-board, should be plenty long enough to reach across the hole."

Mack took one end, fed it across the hole, and let it rest on the sole plate, between two studs of the far wall.

"Eli, stand on this end while I walk across and get her. Irish, you'll have to walk across the board by yourself, baby—okay? I'll be right behind you. Just don't look down." Mack took a couple of steps out on the board, stopped to test it, and reached over and removed the key that was attached to an elastic band. He wrapped the band around his wrist and walked across to Irish. "No Irish, don't move, stay were you are, and let me come to you."

Mack sat next to her on the floor, hugging and kissing her, both crying. "Okay, big girl, let's do this. You ready?"

Irish shook her head. Then smiled and nodded with tears running down her face.

Mack removed the lock, pulled the chain from around the stud, locked the lock onto the end of the chain, and threw it across the hole to Eli with the key wrapped around it. "Lock the chain to that stud beside you, just in case," Mack told Eli.

He looked at Irish, "You nervous? Remember, it ain't squat, you could do this blindfolded. Take a couple of deep breaths and then what?"

"Start counting," she said.

"That's right. Take baby steps, and before you can count to ten, you'll be in Lea's arms. Remember, keep-your-eyes-on-the-tennis-ball, right? In this case, the ball is your tennis shoes. You have to focus, Irish, nothing else. One foot in front of the other till ten." They both stood up. "Pick up and hold the chain as you walk. Lea and Brother Eli will take up the slack on the other side. Remember—do not rush. Baby steps only." Mack held onto her until the first step, then she stopped. "Stare at your shoestrings and start counting, now, out loud if you want."

"*One*," she shouted, took a step, and then whispered the rest of the numbers until Lea reached out and grabbed her.

CHAPTER 32

MACK INHALED THE sweet-smelling jasmine, its vines weaving through the latticework of the arches, and marveled at the continuous and unlimited songs of the mockingbirds. From years of experience, he knew, for him at least, that the sun had medicinal powers, physically and mentally. Everything seemed to be in bloom: white, red, and pink azaleas, purple wisteria, and white dogwoods. Lounging poolside at his house, he sipped on a tall glass of café con leche after dropping Irish off at school. He insisted on walking her to her classroom, which she argued was embarrassing, but he was reluctant to leave her side. The doctor had signed off on her going back to school so soon. Leave it up to her, she will tell you when she ready, he said.

Mack had kept Irish at home for two weeks, just the two of them, and never left the house. They had their groceries delivered, played tennis, swam, worked out in the gym, and stayed up late at night. And then, right out of the blue, she told him she wanted to go back to school and graduate next month with her class.

Mack didn't ask her any questions about her time with Crazy Ray. He just let her talk. Eventually, she got around to talking about *Mr. Ray* and how sick he was. She said he went out one day, never came back, and she was afraid he was dead. She was emphatic, contending he never would have run off without unchaining her first.

Many things had changed in Mack's life. He planned very little, taking one day at a time. Only a few people had his new cell phone number.

Shamrock's main number had been forwarded to Sid Goldman's office, and all other phones had been disconnected. Everything he owned was on the block: his office building, Shamrock Farms, Malloy Marine Services Centers, and the walking horse barn up in Shelbyville, along with the house. All of it was being sold for whatever it would bring at auction. Every checking, savings, and investment account he had was locked up and being scrutinized by the bankruptcy court. The bankruptcy trustee took possession of his cars, airplanes, boats, and anything they could sell, but not the house in Memphis— it was in a trust with a *pur autre vie* type life estate in Irish's name, and they didn't get the house in Key West, the only house he owned and was listed as his permanent resident. Florida has a homestead exemption law that provides a "no limit" value exemption from forced sale of real property, and is protected from all creditors.

Uncle Mickey's old Fleetwood Cadillac was the only set of wheels Mack had to drive. Sure, it was a letdown, a big change, but he thought back to when they first started: Buck, Li, hell, all of them together didn't have enough money to buy Angus a *sweatsuit*. He started with nothing, so it wasn't as if he hadn't been here before. Besides, the only thing that really mattered was getting Irish back, and he owed God big time for that.

On the positive side, Mack no longer had a payroll to worry about, the first time in years, and that included Otis and Bradley. Zira came to him and asked about hiring Otis, but only if it was okay with him. Otis had worked out fine and was now one of her investigators. Senator Parnell found Bradley a job in Washington as a PA to the Ambassador from India and traveled back and forth to his native city, Mumbai.

Angus decided to move back to Colorado. An amendment was passed and Colorado legalized the sale of marijuana for medicinal and recreational use. One of his old classmates from Ole Miss had moved to Denver and opened a marijuana dispensary. His friend offered Angus a buy-in on a second store he was opening in Aspen. The governor of Colorado expects the combined sales from legal medical and recreational marijuana in the state to reach nearly one billion dollars in the next fiscal year. The state stands to collect at least $134 million in taxes and fees.

Isaac Brenner, Anna Brown, and Sonny Newman, his Project Manager, met with Mack, and with his blessings they had Sid Goldman form a LLC called Triangle Construction. Using Mack's contacts and whatever else they could salvage from Shamrock and Global Construction, they felt they would have a good chance of success. Mack assured them he wanted no part of the construction business or any other business. As a parting gift, and a fortuitous one, they all agreed that Mack should keep the cash money in the contingency account lockbox, the one he had set up to pay legal fees. He had taken the biggest hit and needed it the most. Mack made sure Shamrock paid Sid to end of the year, about a $100,000, before the bankruptcy lawyers closed in. Most of Mack's legal problems were over and Sid handled the bankruptcy of Shamrock and Global and some other subsidiary companies and investments Mack had an interest in. Sid enjoyed practicing construction law and agreed to stay on as Triangle Construction's in-house council with a cut in pay until they got on their feet.

His most unexpected loss was Lea. On the second day after Irish was home, Lea got a call from a nurse in Havana, telling her that her father had had a heart attack, and needed an operation ASAP. Mack gave her five thousand in cash; she refused to take it, reminding him that all medical health care in Cuba was free. He reminded her that *free* would not get her a choice of surgeons, or hospitals, or place her father at the top of the list for an immediate operation, but the US dollar, in cash, opened many doors over there. Mack put her on a Delta flight from Memphis to the Bahamas; there she could buy a ticket from Nassau direct to Havana on Cuba's airline, Cubana.

After a couple of days, Lea had called and left a message on Mack's cell phone that she wasn't sure when or if she would be able to return. He tried to return her call but got no answer, and there was no longer a recording on her phone, so he couldn't leave a message, which he wasn't happy about.

Mack missed Lea. He thought about her every day since she had left. He never realized what an important part of his life she was. He had never thought about *not* having her in their lives.

His cell phone rang. He was sure it was Lea. "Hola!" he said, without looking to see who was calling.

"Hola to you too, mi amigo."

"Oh, hi Buck. I thought it was . . . someone else."

"You got a minute?"

"Sure."

"You doing okay? How's my little girl?"

"All's well. She's at school; you'd never know anything had happened. I'm sitting outside by the pool, soaking up some rays. What's up?"

"Good, she's tough like her daddy. I know you said you didn't want any money from us, but you know I have more than I can spend, and if you need any, at any time, you will call me, right?"

"Right. Thanks, Buck."

"One other thing. I'm here at the airport in Natchez, ready to take off for Memphis, and want to take you to lunch. Can you meet me at the Downtown Airport? I've got something I need to give you ASAP. I know you have to pick Irish up from school, but it won't take long."

"Are *you* flying the plane?"

"Yeah."

"I thought you weren't flying anymore."

"I'm not; this is probably my last solo. I can hardly read the instruments anymore even with this coke bottle monocle I'm wearing now."

"I'll see you at noon then. Be careful."

*

Mack sat in the big Cadillac, the sun shining through the windshield, warming up the car, and watched different planes come and go. He didn't know what Buck was flying, since he had sold all the planes down at Shamrock, and here at the airport too, he imagined. He got out of the car and walked around, peeking into different hangars. He wasn't sure if they had gotten a new FBO manager since Buck retired, but the place still looked clean and busy.

He heard the plane, off in the distance, like a racecar, fast, low, coming in over the taxiway, watched it turn on final, and land smoothly on runway 35. It was a beautiful single-engine V-tail Bonanza 35, white and black with red stripes, and it looked brand new, but Mack knew that Beechcraft had stopped making the V-tail in the early '80s. Mack stood on the tarmac in front of the office, watching as Buck taxied the plane up to him, park, and shut down the engine. He saw Buck wave at him and walked over as he stepped down off the wing.

"Nice ride," Mack shouted.

"Look inside."

Mack stepped up on the wing, opened the door, and stuck his head in.

"Wow!" The headliner, door panels, carpet, and the two-tone leather seats were all new. "Looks like the inside of a mini-Gulfstream. What year is this?"

"A '79. V35B, 300 horsepower, cruising speed 173 knots. It was a hidden jewel—always hangared. One owner, a doctor in Natchez who retired to treat the poor and traveled three days a week to small towns all over Mississippi. He has a grass airstrip and a hangar on his farm, gave up flying, but didn't want to sell the plane. Total time is 1200, fresh annual, and all the latest avionics." He handed the flight logs to Mack, "Clean history."

Mack looked through the logbook and handed it back, but Buck threw his hands up, "I don't want it. It's yours."

"*What?*" Mack was stunned.

"Mack, you wouldn't let me give you any money. You don't have a plane. I saw this one-of-a-kind classic . . . it's you, Mack; fast, classy, low maintenance, fits you to a tee. A corvette in the sky."

"I don't know what to say . . .."

"Say thank you." Buck took his arm and walked him toward the car. "Let's go pick up Irish. I need to get back before dark. I can visit with her while you fly me back, and I can check you out on the V-tail at the same time. There's only one thing you have to remember with this plane, *never push the envelope!*"

*

Irish was out of school for the summer and had talked Mack into flying down to Cuba for a surprise visit to see Lea. He didn't need much convincing. He had been thinking of ways to get her back, even if it meant maybe proposing to her. Why not? He had been single a long time and he did have strong feelings for her—plus, she and Irish were inseparable. Did he love her? Hell, it's like Tina Turner sings, *What's love got to do with it?* She met his prerequisites: young, beautiful, great body, intelligent, and no children.

"Daddy, I'm tired of flying. Can you take the wheel?"

"You mean the yoke. You did great, a straight and level flight the whole time." Mack put his feet on the pedals and hands on the yoke. "I have the controls, *Amelia.* Now you can say you flew a plane across the Atlantic Ocean."

"You helped . . .."

"No, I never touched the controls after you took over as co-pilot. You flew the plane by yourself, kept the heading, airspeed, and altitude constant. Only two critiques: you gripped the controls too tight. Relax." He put his hand on the small wheel on the floor between them. "Use the trim tab, and you won't get tired. Second thing is scanning. You *have to* always be on the lookout for other airplanes."

"I know, VFR, right?"

"Right. See if you can *scan* out there and find a small island, should be right off the nose of the plane."

"I see it, right there."

"Now see if you can find it on the sectional."

Irish looked at the map. "There's too many lines . . . wait. Bim-i-ni, is that it?"

"Right. Now look out to your left, that's the Grand Bahamas. Over on your right is Andros, and straight ahead, that watermelon-shaped island, that's Nassau. We're going to spend the night in the home of Captain Graysmith, a famous pirate of the Caribbean. He was the captain of the notorious ship, *Graywolf,* and plundered treasure ships along the Spanish Main."

"Where's the Spanish Main?"

"Here, right in this area of the Caribbean, and all of Florida. Back then Spain owned the state of Florida, the Gulf of Mexico, and the northern coast of South America.

"Graysmith built this house on a hillside in Nassau, and called it Graycliff. It's now a boutique hotel and a five-star restaurant with a cellar stuffed with over 250,000 bottles of wine. We'll eat a fabulous meal there tonight; have a great bottle of wine and one of their signature desserts with a café con leche. How's that sound?"

"Can I wear my new sundress?"

"You bet, and we'll go down to their cellar and see the oldest bottle of wine in the world, a German wine. Guess what the price of that one bottle of wine is?"

"One thousand dollars!"

"Nope. Multiply that by 200."

"*$200,000* for one bottle of wine? No way, Jose! Will they let me have a sip?"

*

The next morning, Mack and Irish, having already bought their Cuban tourist cards and plane tickets for Havana, walked through the airport, admiring the bright colors of the new international B terminal where Cubana was located. There was only one flight a day from Havana to Nassau, leaving at 9:30 a.m. and arriving at Nassau at 11:00 a.m., returning to Havana at 12:40 p.m. and arriving at 1:30 p.m.

Mack and Irish watched from the large window as the flight from Havana, two hours late, taxied up to the gate and parked. He recognized the ATR 42, French-made, twin-engine turboprop, and was relieved to know they were not going to fly in one of Cuba's older Russian planes. FedEx and American Eagle flew the ATR 42 regularly for short flights, and it had a good record. They walked over to the seating area and watched as the anxious passengers rushed to see if they had missed their connecting flights. Irish showed Mack a text from one of her classmates when he heard an announcement from Cubana, looked up, and was flabbergasted. Hurrying from the loading bridge was Lea Perez. She looked like a teenager on a summer vacation in her yellow sleeveless sundress, her dark tan, and free-flowing hair. His first instinct was to shout out her name, but he waited when he saw her stop, and she started waving to someone running down the corridor toward her. It was . . . *Angus McGregor! What?* A hundred questions locked up his brain. *What the hell is going on?* He moved behind a column and watched as they kissed and hugged, then Angus picked up her bag, and they rushed off as if to catch another flight.

"Who you hiding from, Daddy?" Irish said.

"No one. I thought I saw a couple of friends. I was wrong. Wait here, I'm going to step over and check on our flight." He felt cuckolded. He didn't know why. He just did. Standing at the Cubana counter, he inquired about a refund. Cubana did not give refunds.

*

Irish was asleep, stretched out across the backseats of the Bonanza, her head on her blanky. Mack had told Irish there was a law that required a special visa for all U.S. citizens to enter Cuba. It wasn't a lie. He wouldn't lie to Irish, but it wasn't a Cuban law; it was a U. S. law. He would tell her about Lea when he figured it out himself. He needed time to think; meanwhile, they were on their way back to Memphis.

What was he thinking anyway? He would just fly into Cuba and sweep Lea off her feet? *How stupid! You're almost twice her age, no job, and flat broke.*

Well, not flat broke, but his net worth was severely diminished. *How could you blame her?* Angus still had his millions.

Aww, suck it up, crybaby! You're not the first one to lose your ass. Remember King Solomon, over 3,000 years ago? He had it all—immeasurable wealth, superior intellect, and indisputable power, plus 700 wives and 300 concubines. What was his summation on HIS life's work? It was all meaningless: A chasing after the wind.

Mack heard Irish stirring in the back seat; he looked back, and saw her sitting up. "You couldn't sleep?"

"No sir. Where are we?"

"In the middle of the Caribbean. Come on up here and keep me company." Mack patted the seat next to him. Irish stepped over onto the co-pilot seat and buckled up. Without looking at her, he said, "I was thinking, Nassau gave me a little island fever, and I thought maybe we'd fly down to Key West and hang out for a couple of weeks, maybe a month. What do you think, Baby Girl?"

"Do we still have the house?"

"Yep, good ole Florida law. We're on the good side this time for a change."

"Yeeeeah, we can ride our bikes!"

"I'll have to sell the house after everything cools down, too much overhead."

"What do you mean?"

"Operating cost: taxes, insurance, utilities, pool and yard services, maintenance, stuff like that."

"Oh," Irish said, and started humming a Buffett song.

Mack started singing the words along with her:

> *I blew out my flip-flop*
> *Stepped on a pop-top*
> *Cut my heel had to cruise on back home*

Mack adjusted the compass heading to 240 degrees; Key West bound. They both started singing, louder and laughing, and when they reached the last verse they were both screaming:

> *Some people claim that there's a woman to blame*
> *But I know it's my own damn fault.*

"A Man's Hungry Heart"
You have just read the second book of Jim Carson's trilogy.
In his third book, *A Woman's Choice*, Mack Shannon is living
in Key West struggling with the humiliation of having to
bankrupt all that he owned.
Will he continue to waste away in Margaritaville?
Or will he repeat history and fight his way back up the ladder
to power and riches?
Or maybe it is all about the love of a woman—*A Woman's*
***Choice*—a woman like McKenzie O'Connor?**

The first book of his trilogy, *A Chasing After The Wind,* and the sequel, *A Man's Hungry Heart* are available in hardcover, paperback and e-book at Amazon.com or his website: www.jamesacarson.com. His third novel, *A Woman's Choice* is under construction and should be available for purchase in the spring of 2016.

ABOUT THE AUTHOR

JIM CARSON, A former Marine, studied Theatre Arts at various California universities where he won numerous awards in acting, directing, and speech. His pursuit of a vocation that would satisfy his dreams led him to many occupations: firefighter, soybean farmer, director of Underwater Rescue, night school teacher, and the job that always paid the bills, a commercial general contractor. Ask him to tell you about the time he was flying to his house in Key West and walked away after totaling his V-tail Bonanza on takeoff from the Destin Airport or the time when he was hired as a sparring partner, unaware it was Davy Moore, the Featherweight Champion of the World—he was paid $10 a round.

Jim was born and raised in Memphis, Tennessee. He has two adult children, one in Nashville, Tennessee and the other in Richmond, Virginia. He lives on 3 acres in a 1920 Italian Renaissance house with a small leak in the tile roof that nobody can find.

From the Author: "*Out of millions of writers, only 2% make enough money to live on, so reviews are important and good ones fuel our egos which motivates us to write better books. If you like my books, I would appreciate you telling your friends and if you write me a review on Amazon.com, I will send you a free e-book. Please email me at my website:* www.jamesacarson.com."

JIM CARSON

A CHASING AFTER THE WIND

CPSIA information can be obtained at www.ICGtesting.com
Printed in the USA
LVOW11*2352030916

503070LV00001B/2/P

9 780692 378359